Medusa's Child

· · · · · · · · · ·

Also by John J. Nance

PANDORA'S CLOCK
PHOENIX RISING
SCORPION STRIKE
FINAL APPROACH
WHAT GOES UP
ON SHAKY GROUND
BLIND TRUST
SPLASH OF COLORS

Medusa's Child

· · · · · · · · · · ·

John J. Nance

DOUBLEDAY

New York London Toronto Sydney Auckland

PUBLISHED BY DOUBLEDAY

A division of Bantam Doubleday Dell Publishing Group, Inc.
1540 Broadway, New York, New York 10036

DOUBLEDAY and the portrayal of an anchor with a dolphin are trademarks of
Doubleday, a division of Bantam Doubleday Dell Publishing Group, Inc.

Library of Congress Cataloging-in-Publication Data
Nance, John J.
    Medusa's child/ John Nance. — 1st ed.
        p.   cm.
    I. Title.
    PS3564.A546M43   1997
    813'.54—dc20   96-27656
                                                        CIP

ISBN 0-385-48343-0
10 9 8 7 6 5 4 3 2

To my Daughters and Son, of whom I'm infinitely proud!

Dawn Michelle Nance

Bridgitte Cathleen Nance

Christopher Sean Nance

Acknowledgments

High-energy fiction requires a very large, very accomplished team of professionals hand-carrying the author's words into print, and I'm privileged to have the best.

First, I'm very fortunate to have as my literary agents and dear friends the indomitable George Wieser and the indefatigable Olga Wieser (of the Wieser and Wieser Agency in New York). Quite simply, they make my books possible.

Medusa's Child took shape at home in Tacoma with the creative assistance of my wife, Bunny Nance, who also provided editorial scrutiny as the chapters moved out of my laptop (yes, I do live with a computer; and no, I don't write in the cockpit). *Medusa* reached literary maturity under the accomplished care of my samurai editor and business partner, Patricia Davenport (for some reason I keep buying her red pens with which to slash my copy to shreds).

Finally, in New York—in the offices of my publisher, Doubleday—*Medusa's Child* received the expert developmental and editorial skills of my editors Lori Lipsky and Rob Robertson, and the attention and enthusiasm of my publisher Arlene Friedman and editor-in-chief Pat Mulcahy, as well as the extraordinary efforts of our promotion guru, Jane Schorn.

And to all these world-class pros, my heartfelt thanks.

Thank you as well to the folks who helped with fact-checking and technical suggestions, such as Dr. Alan Diehl and Air Force F-15 pilot Captain Gary Rhoades, who was last thanked with his name misspelled (this time, Gary, we're getting it right!). To all those nuclear experts who helped on the Internet and by phone, my specific appreciation, and a note of thanks to Greg and Sue Coe of Seattle, whose early insights into the vulnerability of our computer systems helped spark this work.

Special thanks also to Navy Lt. Commander Elmer Nagma for his above-and-beyond assistance with technical details of Navy life accomplished through E-mail from the middle of some distant ocean (we Air Force guys simply don't know a lot about carrier life—we prefer our airfields to remain precisely where we left them!).

Medusa's
Child

· · · · · · · · · ·

THE WHITE HOUSE

MEMO

TO: The President

FROM: National Security Advisor

SUBJ: <u>Urgent Recommendation</u> to establish an emergency program to develop the ability to detect smuggled Weapons-Grade Nuclear Materials at U.S. airports.

Mr. President:

You asked that I review both the Portland, Oregon, FBI seizure of 265 grams of highly-enriched Plutonium 239 last month and the 1994 German seizures of similar materials alleged to have come from Russia.[1]

First, the Germans seriously overstated the threat when they alleged that Russia had lost control of a huge stockpile of weapons-grade material. What was found in Tengen and Munich were a long way from weapons-ready. If this was all we had to contend with, there would be little threat.

What was found by accident in Portland, however, is an entirely different matter. Not only was this highly-enriched weapons-grade material, it was also freshly processed - not recycled from some scrapped or stolen warhead. There was no characteristic "fingerprint" in the mix of the materials with the plutonium that could lead us to the source, or even a suspected country. Therefore, we must consider the very real possibility that someone off our shores has gathered the equipment and the ability to process such bomb-making isotopes by themselves without detection, and sell or distribute it to the highest bidder. The threat, in other words, is suddenly very real and immediate, and we stand exposed, with virtually no direct means of detecting such isotopes directly. Obviously, when the possibility of a nuclear detonation inside our borders is considered, hoping for an intelligence leak or a lucky break is not enough.

RECOMMENDED ACTION: Issue a Presidential Finding that the need for direct detection of so-called fissile materials passing into the United States is a prime intelligence priority, and order the immediate development of such a program to cover all major U.S. ports-of-entry using existing technology (neutron "sniffers").

---

[1] a) Munich, August 10, 1994 - 350 grams of Plutonium seized.
b) Tengen, May 10, 1994 - 5.6 grams Plutonium seized.

1
• • • •

MIAMI, FLORIDA

"Vivian, it's your ex-husband."

The owner of the small florist shop held the telephone receiver to her chest as she delivered the message, startled by the look of shock that swept across the face of her assistant—a tall, elegant woman in her early sixties who seemed frozen in place, a dozen uncut roses clutched in her hand.

"Are you all right, dear?" the shop owner asked.

Vivian Henry's eyes were riveted on the phone as she stepped back in obvious confusion, knocking an empty bud vase off a work table. It crashed to the floor and shattered, but her eyes remained on the receiver.

The diminutive silver-haired owner looked down at the shattered vase, then back at Vivian.

"I take it you don't want to talk to him, then?"

Vivian shook her head vigorously, her eyes wide, as she whispered, "Why is he calling? What does he want?"

"I don't know. Should I ask?"

Vivian nodded, then changed her mind and shook her head no. Slowly she moved forward and held out her hand to take the phone, putting it to her ear as she closed her eyes.

"What do you want, Rogers?" she asked at last.

After three years of blessed silence, the mere sound of her ex-husband's voice triggered the old familiar feelings of panic—the horror of being cornered and unable to run.

"How are you, Vivian?" he asked evenly, the question sending chills down her back.

His voice was different somehow—calm and eerily friendly—just as he'd always sounded before unleashing some withering verbal attack. But there was no hint of the old fury, and no echo of the constant telephone threats he'd hurled at her for months after she'd left him. In their place was the calculating, manipulative Dr. Rogers Henry, a man who clearly wanted something. The strange tone and calm demeanor of his voice made her skin crawl with apprehension.

"You didn't call here to check on my health, Rogers. What do you want?"

I should end this! she cautioned herself, even as she surrendered to the idea that talking might appease him—as if she hadn't made the same mistake for most of the thirty years of captivity—a marriage spent in the yoke of his iron-willed control and abuse.

"Why do you assume I want something?" he asked.

"Then . . ." she began, her voice faltering. The wrong response would bring forth a predictable tirade. "What in the world could you possibly want to say to me after all this time? What . . . could you possibly say after threatening me so many times—so many ways?"

His reply was as calm as before.

"Has it occurred to you I might want to say I'm sorry? Look, I need a couple of minutes to explain. Will you give me a couple of minutes, Vivian?"

His voice, though calm, sounded weak—devoid of the usual menace. She wondered what was wrong. She'd promised herself she would never care again—never play nurturer to her abuser—but she couldn't help it. She could still remember the thrill of being asked out by him, she a young nuclear engineer on her first important job; he, the young genius pushing the frontiers of theoretical physics. Somewhere within his dark and angry soul were the loving remnants of the handsome young scientist she'd married so long ago, or so she'd always told herself. That vain, endless hope had always been her downfall, and she was horrified to find it was still alive, still whispering stupid promises in her ear that this time it would be different.

"Vivian? Are you still there?"

She nodded before realizing she had to speak to be heard.

"Yes."

"Good. I've got something very valuable to give you, and I really want to see you. I . . . want to make amends before it's too late."

Too late? she thought. Somewhere in her head a voice of caution was screaming at her not to listen, not be taken in.

"Are you ill, Rogers?"

There was a pause on the other end.

"I'm dying, Vivian. Pancreatic cancer. No more than a few weeks left at best."

"I'm sorry," she said without emotion.

"Please come. Just for a few minutes. I'm leaving this house to you. No strings. But more than that, I want to see you once more. I've had time to think about a lot of things."

Vivian closed her eyes and rubbed her head. The only sensible response was no, and good-bye. After years of trying to put those decades behind her—years of counseling and learning to function on her own again—there was no way she should walk back into his presence. What if he hadn't changed?

But he was obviously weakened by illness and she found herself wanting to know if the impossible had happened. Maybe he *had* changed.

She had to know.

Vivian heard herself answering, "Very well, Rogers, will this afternoon do?"

The gaunt scarecrow of a man who answered the door of their South Miami home—her former home—bore little resemblance to the world-class nuclear scientist who had followed in the footsteps of nuclear pioneers like Oppenheimer and Teller at Los Alamos. The cadaverous pall, the sunken eyes, and the stooped shoulders startled Vivian deeply as she stood in confusion for a few moments on the front porch, fighting the knowledge that the frail little man before her was only sixty-two.

He looked ninety.

"I'm glad you came, Vivian," he said in the same subdued voice as he held the door for her.

The interior was darker and more foreboding than she remembered, the gloom of closed curtains and the anemic light from a single lamp making the den feel like a funeral parlor. It smelled of mildew and stale smoke. She sat carefully on the tattered couch, her mind still reeling with conflicting emotions as he shuffled to an armchair near the door and sat down heavily, facing her.

"You said something about making amends, Rogers," she began.

"I'll let my deeds speak for me," he said. "I told you you'd never get this house, and that was wrong. I've changed my will." He gestured to an envelope on the end table by the couch, and she retrieved it and read the new provision he had circled, leaving her the house the divorce court had awarded to him.

"There's more," he said when she looked up without finishing. "Provided you carry out one final task for me, the policy is yours, too."

"Policy?" Vivian asked.

"The whole-life policy. The paid-up life insurance. Three hundred thousand."

She nodded. "You swore that money would go to some religious cult. Anyone but me, you said."

Vivian braced for a fiery retort, but Rogers Henry suppressed an impatient scowl and got to his feet to shuffle toward the bookcase on one side of the den.

"The money will be yours, if you complete the task," he repeated.

"And what am I to do for you, Rogers?" she asked evenly.

For several moments there was no answer, but when he turned to face her, there was a spark in his eyes.

"I did it, Vivian! I completed Medusa. The Medusa Wave is achievable, and I've perfected the design!"

She looked stunned and he watched her expression with satisfaction as she groped for words.

"By *yourself*? How? You had a team of forty scientists working for, what was it, a decade?"

"Took me eighteen years after my forced retirement, but I did it, and you're going to take the prototype to Washington after I'm gone."

"I . . . don't understand . . ."

"I've built a mockup. A dummy, of course, but it's a complete working model, without the plutonium. That's what I was doing all those years in my lab. New trigger design, new concept, new everything." He began shuffling back toward the easy chair, his eyebrows animated, his eyes darting toward the far door to the converted garage.

"Why Washington, Rogers? Why not Los Alamos?"

His voice became an angry growl.

"Because the slimy bastards who terminated my program and said it couldn't be done are in the Pentagon now. I want the mockup right there where they can see it and feel it and understand it before they ship it west to study it, as they inevitably will."

He sat down again, breathing heavily.

"But will it work?" she asked.

"It's amazing, Vivian. Turns out, you don't need a hundred miles of altitude to create a devastating electromagnetic pulse. One single Medusa exploding at ground level can bring an industrial society to a halt by triggering a secondary electromagnetic wave covering a radius of two thousand miles. It's everything I promised in the early seventies!"

"And . . . you want me to . . ."

"To take it in a cargo aircraft to Washington and supervise its delivery to the Pentagon."

"For the insurance money, is that correct?"

He nodded and paused, as if trying to decide how far to push. "I guess it's too late to ask you to do it for love."

She stared at him for a long time, expecting to see a sarcastic smirk, but his face was expressionless.

"Love, Rogers? You killed the love I had for you the first time you laid your hands on me in anger."

He snorted and got to his feet as her voice chased after him.

"I thought you wanted to make amends?"

He moved slowly toward the far wall shaking his head, his eyes on his shoes.

"Here's the deal, Vivian. There's a packet of instructions next to you there on the table. There's a key inside that opens the lab." He looked up at her slowly. "Follow the instructions to the letter and the administrator of the small trust I've set up to receive the insurance money will pay it to you. Refuse to do it or screw up the job, you don't get a damn cent. You still get the house—and the mortgage payments—but the three hundred thousand to pay for them goes away."

She got to her feet. "I'm sorry you're dying, Rogers." She moved a step toward the door and hesitated before looking at him. "I don't need your money. Get someone else to do it."

"SIT DOWN!" he roared as he turned, his eyes flaring in the maniacal manner she knew so well. "I should have expected a brainless, stupid response like that!"

Vivian felt her legs go limp. She sank back to the couch as he stopped in midsentence, chewing his lip, then shook his head.

"I'm . . . sorry, Vivian. I'm sorry for the outburst."

She nodded wordlessly, her eyes searching the carpet as he shuffled back toward her.

"I know I was a failure as your husband. I know I made your life horrible and I'm a bastard, and I'm probably going to roast in hell, but I've done one thing right, and I want my country to have the benefit of it, and I want you to have the honor of presenting it. This will change history, Vivian!"

He was moving closer and she felt adrenaline flowing through her bloodstream as she calculated the distance to the front door.

"Vivian? What do you say? Will you do it?" His voice had dropped in tone again. He was almost pleading when she looked up.

"You'd trust your life's work to a brainless, stupid woman?" she asked quietly.

He shook his head again. "I didn't mean that. I talk too much, Vivian. I always have. Big threats, big talk, big put-downs. I didn't mean them." He could see the outburst had shattered the frail bridge he'd built. Suddenly he was sinking to his knees, his right hand reaching for the end table to steady himself, his emaciated body racked with sobs.

"Vivian . . . I never meant to hurt you. I'm sorry I'm such a bastard!"

His words were muffled as he buried his face in his hands and she felt conflicting emotions overwhelm her.

"If you deliver it," he continued, "they'll take note. If you don't, they'll ignore it. This was my life, Vivian. The only part that was ever worth anything. Please . . . !"

For a moment she hesitated, part of her mind screaming for her to get out, run, get away from this house and the shell of a man begging her to do what he couldn't. But if it was real, the significance of his accomplishment was staggering. She had enough years as a nuclear engineer to know that for certain.

But pity was overwhelming her self-protective nature. After all, he was hurting—dying—and that reality somehow eclipsed the memories of his past abuse.

She moved to enfold him as if by habit, holding his head against her breast for several minutes as tears streamed down her face.

"It's all right, Rogers. I'll do it for you. It's not the money."

• • •

He saw her to the door and squeezed her hand before she turned to go.

She left without another word, and he watched through the window until her car disappeared down the street. He straightened up then and smiled a tight little smile of triumph and satisfaction as he walked with some difficulty back to the converted two-car garage that served as his lab, closing the hallway door behind him.

There was a damp chill in the air of the windowless room and he shivered as he clicked on several lights to examine his creation. He moved slowly to an open panel on the side of the large rectangular metal object sitting on the bottom slab of a massive wooden packing crate and occupying nearly half the lab's floor space. The visible sides of a vaultlike container were smooth and unbroken except for a single opening, an inspection hatch two feet square, which had been left open. Within, the lead shielding of the internal chamber was visible, and Rogers Henry moved to it, peered inside, and checked it carefully before closing the compartment and locking it. He activated a small internal computer, set the clock, then lit a welding torch and carefully sealed the case.

The upper portion of the heavy wooden shipping crate hung suspended from a block and tackle attached to a metal beam in the ceiling. Slowly, painfully, he moved the crate into position along the beam, and, satisfied it was aligned, began playing out the heavy rope to lower the box into place. The effort exhausted him and he sat on a nearby crate for nearly ten minutes before taking the rope and guiding the crate once again toward the floor. When it was down, he rested once more before securing it to the bottom slab all around with a series of heavy bolts.

One more item, he reminded himself. A section of the garage roof had been fitted with solar panels to generate enough electricity to charge the battery inside the casing, keeping it fresh indefinitely. He connected the tiny cord to a plug on the back side of the casing, and made sure a small indicator light came on before stepping back for one final look. The cord was designed to disconnect and snap out of sight into the wall as soon as the device was moved, and he checked the tension before getting to his feet.

It was ready. At long last, it was ready.

• • •

A small split of champagne had been purchased and placed in the back of the refrigerator years before, when the plan had first taken shape in his blind fury over Vivian's desertion. He retrieved it now and popped the cork into a hand towel, then filled one of the gold-encrusted goblets from the two-hundred-year-old crystal set Vivian's mother had left her—a set he had gleefully crushed with a hammer and returned to her in a shoe box, leaving only one piece intact for his own use.

He took the goblet to the den and once again sat in his easy chair, turning the goblet around and around in his hand as he reviewed the details of what he had set in motion. A cold smile covered his face as he drained the last of the champagne, then hurled the glass against the bricks of the fireplace, taking pleasure in the finality of its destruction.

The smile broadened when he thought of how she had put her arms around him an hour before. Just as he'd planned it.

It was time, he decided.

Dr. Rogers Henry reached in the drawer of the end table and removed a polished wooden box before pulling the phone to his ear and dialing 911.

"Are you reporting an emergency?" a no-nonsense female voice asked.

"Do you have my address on your computer screen?" he asked.

"Of course," the woman snapped. "Are you reporting an emergency at that address?"

"No."

He opened the box and removed a loaded .44 Magnum from its velvet nest.

"I'm reporting a suicide."

MIAMI—ONE MONTH LATER

The phone had startled Vivian from another fitful dream, a surrealistic rerun of the funeral in which Rogers had climbed out of the coffin during the eulogy and chased her with a carving knife.

She shook off the confusion of the receding nightmare and answered the phone, surprised to hear the voice of the attorney who had been appointed executor of the will. When, he asked, was she going to make the trip to Washington so he could close out the accounts and transfer the house?

"Never," she replied.

"I don't understand," the lawyer replied.

She hadn't really been surprised to discover the part of the will that Rogers had hidden, the provision that kept the executor from transferring the house until the Medusa device had been delivered.

"Mrs. Henry, I can't transfer the house for three years unless you comply with his request."

"I understand."

"I can't let you occupy it, either. I'll have to keep paying to maintain it and cut the grass and pay the taxes and the mortgage payments out of his estate."

"I said I understand. You do what you have to do."

"But you'll lose the three hundred thousand!"

She rubbed her forehead and closed her eyes. "Mr. Wallace, transfer the house when you're ready, or not at all. I don't care. I have a job. I have my ex-husband's survivor annuity awarded in the divorce. I don't need anything else."

She hung up the phone and rubbed her eyes, buoyed by the decision she'd made in the days following the funeral: She would be manipulated no longer. When the house reverted to her, she would sell it. The thought of living in a house that had contained such hatred and death was too chilling to contemplate.

And there was the mockup itself, of course. She would have it destroyed.

After all, the last thing the world needed was another weapon.

2

• • • •

Scott McKay replaced the telephone and sat in silence for a few seconds, a spontaneous smile spreading across his broad, almost squarish face. The call had been a godsend, and he felt overwhelming relief pour over him like a sparkling waterfall, dissolving the monstrous tensions that had been building for weeks as his tiny company careened toward bankruptcy.

But now, armed with a new government contract, the one-airplane cargo airline he'd named ScotAir could stay afloat.

Scott jumped to his feet and grabbed his windbreaker. It was time to celebrate, and exactly where didn't matter. There were more than enough bars in the mountain town, and he was tired of sitting alone and feeling depressed.

The sun had come out, reflecting his rapidly recovering optimism. He paused by the door to the second-story deck of the century-old house, vaguely remembering that the sunlight had come bursting through a shroud of thunderclouds precisely as he got the good news. He let his eyes focus on the main street of Central City, Colorado, the late-season tourists flowing like colorful leaves from shop to shop in an endless stream through the commercial trough of the almost treeless valley—a visage he'd always found dreary.

Suddenly it didn't seem so bad. Suddenly he almost understood why his father had loved the old house—and the town—so much.

A familiar wave of sadness rolled over him at the thought of his dad and the massive unheralded heart attack that had taken the veteran corporate executive two years before. Scott had been at sea flying F-14 fighters, two weeks away from leaving the Navy and returning to Colorado. He'd had to delay the funeral nearly a week in order to get back from the Mediterranean.

But it still felt like last week. The pain of an only child losing his mother to a car crash ten years before, when they lived near Wichita, Kansas, had been devastating, but his father's death had been even worse. Suddenly he was truly alone in the world.

Scott glanced at the painting of his father hanging over the stone fireplace. The senior McKay had saved up hundreds of thousands of dollars in hopes of joining his Annapolis graduate son in business and starting a new company when he left the Navy. It had been fun, keeping up a blizzard of correspondence with his dad, niggling over a thousand ideas for all sorts of enterprises, always hiding his true desire to be an airline pilot instead of an empire builder.

Scott left the second-story den and descended the stairs two at a time to open the front door, pausing for a second to let the cool air slap him gently in the face and ruffle his sandy hair. The pleasant fragrance of an old ponderosa in the front yard reached his nose, actively competing with the aroma of garlic-laden Italian fare from a restaurant a block away.

He was forgetting something, and the struggle to recall what it was held him in the doorway in thought. There were overdue tax forms and reports to the Department of Transportation to complete, and maybe he should just close the door and get back to work. All the previous week he'd been too depressed to get anything done.

A little girl passed on the sidewalk, skipping happily, a bright metallic balloon festooned with happy birthday wishes following her. It made him think of his own birthday rapidly approaching, his thirty-first.

And what, he thought, *have I accomplished?*

He didn't like to admit to himself that he'd established ScotAir because the airline hiring boom had ended just as he'd left the Navy. Suddenly the only way to get an airline job had been to create his own airline, and he'd done exactly that.

He could have waited, of course. He could have held out, flying for smaller commuter and regional lines, until the Uniteds and Americans started hiring again.

But instead he invested the bulk of his father's estate to start the tiny cargo carrier without even one contract, an act which in the glaring light of hindsight seemed less than smart—especially since there were two loyal employees dependent on him . . .

Oh jeez, Jerry and Doc are both waiting by the phone!

Scott flew back into the house and grabbed the telephone on the entryway table to relay the good news to his copilot and flight engineer. He triggered the automatic dialer for Doc Hazzard's number in Colorado Springs, and then toggled on a second line and dialed Jerry Christian's number in Dallas. One more push of a button connected the two lines together, and within seconds both voices were in his ear.

"We got the contract, guys. We're gonna make it!"

"Wonderful!" Doc exclaimed from his end. Scott could hear the sound of a jetliner passing over the former Pan Am captain's apartment south of the Colorado Springs airport, almost drowning out the classical music in the background, a violin concerto that could easily be one of Doc's own recordings with the local symphony. Doc had long been a world-class violinist. It was his passion, but never his profession.

"Thank God, Scott!" Jerry said from Dallas with obvious relief. "When do we start this new contract?"

"Thursday," Scott told them. "We leave for Miami on Thursday, empty. We fly the first load out Friday morning. It's high-priority scientific cargo coming to Miami from somewhere in the south of . . . southern South America."

"That's redundant," Doc needled, still chuckling from the relief of knowing that a year of hard work for a boss thirty years his junior still had a chance to pay off.

"Okay, Southern Chile," Scott replied, aware that the sound of a single cello had replaced the concerto in the background, leaving him to wonder if Doc was alone. "Anyway, it's stuff coming back from an Antarctic expedition that was canceled early. We fly the loads to Denver over the next two months, and in November . . ."

"In November we go to work for Nissan, right?" Jerry asked. "That contract is still intact, isn't it?"

"You bet," Scott replied. For weeks the struggle had been to pay the bills until November, when the new three-year contract hauling high-value, just-in-time auto assembly components would start. By December, they'd have enough money to lease a second plane and hire a second crew.

Jerry's voice came through the receiver with a subdued, almost traumatized timbre. "How close did we come, Scott?"

"What do you mean?"

"To oblivion. To running out of cash."

There was silence as Scott considered what to say to a man whose finances were as perilous as his employer's. Having three children and a diffident wife who demanded an expensive house in North Dallas, good times or bad, had taken its toll on the flight engineer. Jerry couldn't spare a penny, and, financially, he couldn't survive another job loss.

"It was far too close, Jere. We have a lease payment due in ten days for thirty thousand, and I didn't have it."

"You didn't tell me," Jerry said quietly.

"Because I fully expected to get this contract, and now we have. It's gonna work, guys. By January, you'll be the senior of two crews."

When the call ended, John T. "Doc" Hazzard replaced the handset with a broad smile and absently scratched his barrel chest as he stood by the window facing the Colorado Springs airport, where ScotAir's 727 was based.

Life is good, he concluded, *maybe even better since Pan Am collapsed.* At sixty-three he wouldn't be able to fly captain for a passenger airline now anyway.

"You always parade around buck naked in front of the window, Doc?" The feminine voice reached his ears from the vicinity of the couch, and Doc turned to flash an even broader smile at the beautiful blonde, herself clothed only in a small pearl necklace. She had leaned her cello against the wall, and he glanced at the desk to make sure his violin was in no danger of falling. Sheet music spilled off a stand as he brushed it while moving toward her, but Doc ignored it.

"Always." He aped a weight lifter's pose. "This body's too great to keep hidden. You said so yourself!"

She shook her head as he came back to her. "I'll ignore the raging ego. Besides, those fingers are far more enticing than your body, buster."

He smiled. "You mean, what I can do with a fiddle?"

She nodded slowly. "That too." A sultry smile spread across her face. "The phone call was good news, I take it?"

He told her of the reprieve.

"So when are you going to quit, Doc?"

"Quit what? Teaching eager young women about lovemaking?"

"When are you going to quit flying? When are you going to quit being in constant motion? Among your other talents"—she winked at him—"and physical attributes, you're a great violinist, far beyond amateur."

"And you're a great cellist. That's how we met, if I recall. Passion in the orchestra pit."

"No, seriously." She pushed away slightly. "When are you going to settle down and work on your music? Maybe join the symphony full-time? Maybe spend more time with me?"

He kissed her and caressed her blonde hair. "I can't afford to settle down, Karen. I'm still happily divorced to three wives, and they need their money."

"You're the strangest divorcé I've ever encountered, you know. You seem to enjoy it!"

"I still love them all."

"But someday, Doc, you're going to have to slow down."

He gently took her shoulders and rocked her back to look her in the eye. "Honey, I plan to die in motion. I always have. Right now, I'm really enjoying flying with a fine young man who desperately wants to succeed, but who really doesn't have enough background flying big jets. He needs my experience more than he realizes. It's not just the money, it's the challenge—and, I'll admit, it's also the rush of getting on my horse and riding off in all directions, as the old saying goes."

"You're an encyclopedia of old sayings, Hazzard."

"Well, here's a new one." He smiled and cocked his head, his eyes still locked on hers. "When I drop in my tracks, I want the body to skid for a week."

MIAMI—SEPTEMBER 12

The plain white envelope was waiting under a stack of overdue bills as Vivian Henry emptied her apartment mailbox, the words UNITED STATES COURT OF APPEALS instantly twisting her stomach into a knot.

It had to be the verdict—the last chance to restore the annuity the government had refused to pay after Rogers Henry's suicide— the monthly payments she had depended on to support her the rest of her life.

If the piece of paper in the envelope reversed the earlier denials, the bills could be paid, and perhaps she could find a nicer place to live.

But if she lost . . .

Feeling weak—her legs wobbly, her head spinning—Vivian climbed the stairs to her tiny second-floor apartment with gloomy memories of the Washington, D.C., hearing filling her mind.

It had been a nightmare, sitting in silence in the courtroom as her young lawyer fell apart, unable to answer the questions of three stern federal judges who wanted to know why the government should repair the mistake made by her divorce attorney years before. One poorly worded sentence stood between her and poverty—one botched sentence which clearly awarded half the retirement payments while Rogers Henry lived, but failed to clearly order the government to pay the same amount after he died.

One month after the funeral, her checks had stopped coming, and two years of rejected appeals and dwindling accounts had followed. There was one small savings account left, and a monthly check from Social Security for three hundred dollars, and that was it.

Vivian entered her joyless apartment, turned on the light, and sat down at the kitchen table. She arranged the bills on one side and the U.S. Court of Appeals envelope on the other, not daring to hope.

What do I do if I've lost? she wondered. In another two years she would gain title to the house, but she'd never last that long financially. And the thought of caving in and doing Rogers' bidding in order to get the three hundred thousand dollars was more repugnant than moving to a smaller apartment and using her savings. Even when a heart attack had felled her friend and part-time employer, closing the florist shop, Vivian had told herself she was just bridging a tough time until the pension was restored.

The words of the idiot lawyer she'd hired were still echoing in her mind: "There's no appeal this time, Vivian. Whatever the U.S. Court of Appeals decides is the end of the line."

The envelope lay before her like stairs to a gallows, but since there was no point in delaying it further, she pulled it to her suddenly and ripped it open, unfolding the pages inside and dropping her eyes to the word she had hoped against hope she would not see: AFFIRMED.

Vivian slowly placed the papers back on the table. Twenty-five hundred dollars per month for life was now gone forever, and there were other truths she had no choice but to face: She had no job. She had no savings.

She had no choice.

Vivian stood up and moved to the small kitchen counter and flipped through her small address book to a particular listing. She dialed the number and sat back down at the table, holding her forehead in one hand, the receiver in the other, as the voice of her ex-husband's attorney came on the line.

3

••••

Are you Captain McKay?" a female voice asked with a sharpness that belied sultry undertones.

Scott McKay had been studying the left nosewheel tire, his right knee resting on the concrete beneath the nose section of the 727. He turned and shielded his eyes against the sun as he tried to see the face of the young woman standing behind him with her hands on her hips. She was wearing a one-piece khaki jumpsuit and an irritated expression.

"Yep, that's me," Scott said, getting to his feet. He took time to lean over and dust off his pants before straightening up and letting his eyes meet hers, pleased at what he saw.

"Your loadmaster is being an ass, Captain," she said without a smile.

Scott turned to follow her gaze. Jerry Christian, his flight engineer, had been standing in the distance talking to a forklift driver. He saw Scott with the woman and began moving toward the airplane.

"The tall guy over there?" Scott asked.

"That's the one," she replied. "He's refusing to load my cargo. I mean, I know my stuff is not the cargo you're here to transport, but it was NOAA that chartered you, and I'm also from NOAA, and you've got room."

Scott smiled and shook his head. "That's no ass, ma'am. That's my second officer, and he's a really friendly fellow."

"I said he's *acting* like an ass!" she shot back without humor.

Scott chuckled as he examined his shoes for a second, then looked up and extended his hand.

"Maybe we can start over, if you don't mind. Hi, my name is Scott McKay. And you are?"

Dr. Linda McCoy ran her left hand through her shoulder-length raven hair and let her expression change from a scowl to a slight smile as she shrugged and took Scott's hand and shook it.

"Okay . . . all right, look, I'm sorry."

"That's all right."

"I'm Dr. Linda McCoy of the National Oceanic and Atmospheric Administration. I'm on a tight schedule and I've been traveling for days from Antarctica and I really don't have the time or the patience for arguments. I got in from Chile at four this morning, and I've got to get my pallets back to Boulder by this evening. I've got time-critical instruments aboard, and I know there's a hurricane about to batter the upper East Coast and screw up air traffic everywhere, so I'd really like to get out of here."

Jerry moved in beside Scott as he gestured to the engineer. "You say my engineer here doesn't want to take your cargo?"

She nodded. "That's right. He's telling me if they're not listed on his manifest, you can't take them. That's stupid! You're going to Denver, you're chartered by NOAA, and I've got NOAA pallets headed to Denver, as well. The solution is simple."

Scott glanced up at Jerry. "What can we do, Jere?"

Jerry looked embarrassed as he sighed and shrugged. "Scott, the contract says we take only the listed cargo, and that has nothing to do with hers. The cargo we're here to get is the pallet they're about to load back there."

"To hell with the contract," McCoy interjected. "I'll take the responsibility as a NOAA officer and . . ."

Scott held his hand up in a wait gesture to Linda McCoy. "Doctor, you may not understand. These government air cargo contracts are monitored by incredibly rigid bureaucrats. We make one mistake, we'll lose the contract, and I'm not prepared to take that risk."

The scientist moved almost imperceptibly closer to Scott, her eyes boring into his.

"Have you considered, Captain, that the act of leaving my stuff behind might be that very mistake you're trying to avoid? I guarantee if you leave me behind, that rigid contract officer is going to hear all about it from a tired, infuriated senior member of the Boulder facility!"

Scott cocked his head and let himself frown at her. "Lady, threatening me isn't going to get your cargo on board." He saw her eyes flare as the words left his mouth.

"Who are you calling 'lady'?" she snapped, maneuvering even closer.

"I . . . was just trying to be polite to a lovely young woman. I consider 'lady' a compliment."

"The way you were using it is insulting."

Jerry was easing backward, trying to put some judicious distance between himself and the escalating exchange, as Scott stuffed his hands in his pockets, pursed his lips, and looked away for a few seconds before meeting her eyes again with a shrug.

"Look, Doctor, I'm sorry I offended you. I wasn't trying to be sexist. I just can't take your cargo without authorization."

She stood for a few seconds with her hands on her hips, glaring at him, then looked back at the small cargo office before locking her eyes on Scott again.

"So what are we going to do about this?"

Scott took a deep breath and checked his watch. They had little more than a half hour before departure time. "If you'll give me a few minutes, Doctor, I'll get on the phone with Washington and see what we can do."

"Okay. Meanwhile, tell your engineer to load my pallets aboard so we won't lose any time."

"Ah, Dr. McCoy," Scott began, as several potential retorts crossed his mind.

"You have a problem with that?" she asked in a combative tone.

Scott struggled with his natural instinct to counterattack and won. She was, after all, the client. It was counterproductive to make her even angrier.

He looked up and smiled at her, noticing how large her brown eyes seemed to be in anger.

"No. No problem. We'll get them loaded."

She nodded as Scott turned to Jerry to give the order.

MIAMI INTERNATIONAL AIRPORT—11:45 A.M. EDT—
SEPTEMBER 19

The technician felt his blood run cold as he examined the graph for
the third time.

There was no mistake.

The silent, probing beam of neutrons fired by his scanner was
designed to trigger a tiny release of gamma rays if it came in contact with the type of nuclear material used to make bombs, and it
had done precisely that. For several hours during the morning
something within the boundaries of Miami International Airport
had given back gamma rays with each sweep of the neutron beam.

Then, one hour ago—while he and his commander had been off
munching tacos before the scheduled afternoon demonstration—
the level of gamma rays had dropped to zero.

Oh my God, we blew it! he thought, dying inside. Some inspector—maybe military, maybe from the Nuclear Regulatory Commission—had been assigned to waltz by with a suitcase full of
shielded plutonium to test the machine he'd helped design, and he'd
essentially been asleep at the switch. Obviously the demonstration
came at the wrong time. They should have been monitoring during
the morning hours as well.

In the distance his boss—a Navy commander—was proudly explaining the Navy's fast-response nuclear detection capabilities to
three worried officials from the Federal Aviation Administration in
charge of protecting the nation's airports against terrorists. A presidential directive to harden the nation's ports against nuclear terrorism had sparked a frenzy of activity and the flight of the gray
portable trailer to Miami as the first working demonstrator.

"The moment even a capsule of fissionable material enters the
boundaries of an airport like this, inside a terrorist's briefcase or
otherwise," he was saying, "we'd see it."

Yeah, if we're watching, the technician thought to himself as he
motioned his boss over to where the strip of graph paper lay like a
poisonous snake on the table, serpentine evidence of their negligence at the worst possible moment.

The commander took the news with unexpected calm, then
turned immediately to the FAA team with the strip in hand. "We
weren't told we should be on-line this morning, but we did have the
recorders going, and it looks like we caught your test anyway," he

said with a forced smile, noting the puzzled expressions as each of the three men in turn examined the tracings.

The FAA's associate administrator for security spoke first, gesturing to the strip. "So we would see something like this if real bomb material reached an airport?"

The commander nodded. "You'd see exactly this. In fact, we *did* see exactly this." His finger traced the line where it reached its apex. "This was real bomb material spitting gamma rays at us, fellows, as I'm sure you know. By the way, who brought the stuff to Miami for you?"

An exchange of concerned expressions flickered among the three faces as the Navy commander continued, slightly insulted at their feigned act of innocence.

"Look, we're all cleared for Top Secret-Crypto here, and we're also well aware that the only thing that could spike a reading like this is the genuine article: some scary isotope of weapons-grade uranium or plutonium. So I don't see the point in not telling me who was testing us."

There was still no response from the FAA men, and the commander felt his anger rising.

"Look, obviously up until about an hour ago, Miami International had enough plutonium around to build one helluva nuclear . . . bomb . . ." His voice trailed off as he realized something was very wrong. The senior FAA official was shaking his head, his face twisting in alarm as he grabbed the naval officer's forearm with his right hand, his left gesturing in the general direction of the passenger terminal, his voice taut with urgency.

"Commander, you're telling me these readings are real?"

"Yes. Why?"

"Because we didn't arrange a test! You understand what I'm saying? If there was fissionable material on this airport, we didn't bring it!"

SCOTAIR 50, IN FLIGHT, 35,000 FEET, 125 MILES SOUTHEAST OF NEW ORLEANS—12:15 P.M. EDT— SEPTEMBER 19

Scott McKay, the captain of ScotAir Flight 50, glanced toward the cockpit door just as his flight engineer burst in with a deeply worried expression. Jerry Christian moved forward quickly without acknowledging the passenger in the observer's seat behind the captain and leaned toward McKay's ear.

"Problem?" the captain asked, already dreading the answer. Christian always looked sad, but seldom worried.

Jerry Christian gestured to the cargo compartment with his right thumb. A short, nervous stab. For twenty-five years the interior of their leased, aging Boeing 727 had carried passengers for various airlines. Now the converted passenger cabin carried cargo for them. There were three pallets loaded with scientific gear, two of them in the care of the senior atmospheric scientist sitting just behind the captain.

"*What,* Jerry?" Scott McKay prompted again.

"The number three pallet. I was doing a routine check. The numbers don't match our cargo manifest or the contract. In fact, *nothing* matches. Scott, I'm sorry, but I think we loaded the wrong pallet."

McKay looked stunned. "My God, that's our *contract*! That's high-priority cargo. You've got to be wrong!"

Christian could see a shadow of fear cross the young captain's face, replaced just as quickly by a familiar look of determination.

Doc Hazzard, the copilot, had been fiddling with the navigation radios in the right seat. Now he, too, looked up.

"Jerry, we checked all the numbers before loading," Hazzard said. "The numbers matched. Can't be the wrong one."

Jerry Christian shook his head slowly. At six-foot-six, he was too tall to stand upright in the Boeing cockpit. He leaned over the center console even farther and chewed on his lip before answering, his eyes fixing momentarily on the towering cumulus clouds a hundred miles ahead over the Louisiana coastline.

"The forklift driver must've gotten the wrong pallet *after* we inspected everything and signed the papers," Jerry said. "I parked him in front of the right pallet. I can't believe he lifted something else—but however it happened, it's happened. The number three pallet isn't ours. It's off by one digit on the manifest and the tag. I . . . guess I didn't check the numbers well enough once it was aboard. I'm sorry, Scott."

Scott McKay was already unlatching his safety belt as he looked over his right shoulder at the attractive woman in the observer's seat.

"Doctor, could you swing your legs out to the right, please? I need to move this seat back."

"You two aren't talking about my pallets, are you?" Dr. Linda McCoy asked. "I checked after loading. Those first two are definitely mine." She shot a worried look to her right at Jerry Christian, who was shaking his head as he backed toward the door of the cramped cockpit to give them room to maneuver around each other.

"No," Christian said, "it's the other one. The pallet at the rear. Not yours, Doctor."

McKay glanced at Doc Hazzard as he launched himself out of the left-hand seat. The beefy copilot, thirty-two years older than the captain, nodded.

"I'll monitor the radios, Scott." Hazzard pulled on his oxygen mask, the normal precaution when one pilot was out of the seat, as Christian and McKay headed for the cargo compartment.

The captain led the way, his mind racing through a maze of possibilities which all led to the same chilling conclusion: If the high-value, high-priority cargo pallet they were supposed to be hauling to Denver was still sitting on the ramp some seventy minutes behind them, his little upstart airline was in deep trouble, and the contract that was their lifeline would be in danger of cancellation.

The cargo pallets, each approximately eight feet square and piled high with equipment held together by heavy plastic and cargo nets, spanned the Boeing's cabin from fifteen feet aft of the cockpit door to some forty feet back. The remaining seventy feet of the cavernous interior was empty. A small, cramped passageway on the left side—between the pallets and the molded fiberglass sidewall of the old jetliner—permitted access to the back, and the two men squeezed into the passageway and moved rapidly toward the rear until they were standing next to the third pallet, oblivious to the sound of the slipstream passing on the other side of the aluminum fuselage at eighty percent of the speed of sound.

"One damn pallet, Jerry! That's all we had to do was haul one goddamn pallet from Florida to Colorado to collect our money so we could pay our bills. How in hell could we screw it up on the first trip?"

Jerry Christian shook his head in shared frustration, well aware of what was at stake. He pulled the shipper's information from a small plastic pocket on the side of the third pallet and handed it quickly to Scott.

Scott compared the numbers with a sinking feeling, knowing instinctively there would be no reprieve, no sudden discovery that everything was okay. Jerry Christian was too reliable to sound such an alarm prematurely. He was an amazingly good mechanic and flight engineer with a passion for precision, but his skills as a pilot were marginal, and the major airline he'd flown with for nine years had fired him when they couldn't get him through the mandatory checkout as copilot. Northwest may not have wanted Jerry Christian, but Scott McKay knew he'd been lucky to find him.

Scott handed the papers back, not wanting to meet Jerry's eyes. He knew how much this job meant to the lanky engineer who had answered his ad a year ago and become his friend as well as his employee. Rejected by the majors, Christian had been thrown to the nonscheduled world, a slightly seedy fraternity of underpaid mavericks and aging airplanes hauling unpredictable loads to unlikely places.

It was also, Scott reminded himself, a world of demanding clients—clients occasionally as nasty as government contract officers when someone failed to perform.

Scott looked away with a cold ball of apprehension suddenly gaining mass in the pit of his stomach, like the first time he'd missed a nighttime carrier landing as an F-14 pilot. The *Eisenhower* had been too far out at sea for him to fly anywhere else. He could land on the carrier and live, or punch out and probably die, so another approach was the only option. With adrenaline coursing through his body and his feet chattering on the rudder pedals, his sloppy, barely controlled second approach failed as well, leaving barely enough fuel for one last try.

He remembered yelling at himself that he had to remain in control. Navy fighter jocks were never supposed to be scared, but he was more than that—he was terrified. Somehow he had hung on and worked the problem, calming himself down and damping out his control inputs as the lights of the carrier loomed larger in his windscreen. At last the meatball—the visual landing system—had miraculously centered, and he felt his wheels hit the deck as his tailhook caught the number three wire.

Now, too, he was fighting to keep the situation under control and think. If the contract officer in Washington discovered their screw-up before he could smooth it over, the situation could easily spin out of control. He tried not to think of what hung in the balance. The contract, the money, the one chance they had to stay in business, all of it suddenly endangered.

Scott waved the cargo papers in the direction of the cockpit. "We'd better get the agent on the Flitephone. We're probably going to have to go back."

Christian's hand reached out to stop his employer.

"Uh, Scott. Dr. McCoy isn't going to be happy about this. Her cargo is high-priority, too."

"She's not the prime customer," Scott snapped, regretting his tone. "We only took her stuff because she was such a pain in the butt back there, and she was right, the contract did allow additions."

There was a moment of awkward silence between them before Jerry spoke.

"You're always a sucker for pretty females," he offered, hoping to trigger a smile.

There was none. Scott's distraction was total. The perception that the previous year of struggle had been nothing but a house of cards now in collapse filled his mind. Why had he ever had the stupid idea he could start an airline, for God's sake? All his inheritance was about to go down the drain, and he might be powerless to stop it.

Scott looked up suddenly. "What?"

"Nothing," Jerry replied quickly. "I just wanted to, ah, point out, you know, that going back isn't going to sit well with the doctor."

Scott nodded curtly and turned, surprised to see Linda McCoy herself standing at the forward part of the narrow walkway between the left side of the 727's cabin wall and the two cargo pallets that she'd been so desperate to get aboard. She couldn't have heard him over the noise of the slipstream, Scott concluded, but he felt embarrassed nonetheless—especially so as he turned sideways to squeeze past her, a maneuver which put their bodies in contact long enough for Scott to be acutely aware of how well endowed she was. Normally he would have been amused and secretly pleased. Now all he could think of was the missing cargo, and the impending consequences.

"Sorry, Doctor," he explained, diverting his eyes from hers, "I've got to get to the phone."

"Anything I can help with?" McCoy asked, molding herself to the sidewall to keep the encounter from being any more intimate than it already was.

Scott shook his head and moved rapidly toward the flight deck door as Jerry Christian appeared from behind, his tall frame hunched over, his eyes following the captain's rapid return to the cockpit, knowing his friend was sick with worry.

Linda McCoy stayed next to her cargo pallets, blocking the way. She turned to the flight engineer and met his eyes for a few seconds, trying to read the depth of his distress.

"How big a problem is this?" she asked.

Jerry hesitated, unsure how much to say. She'd been iron-willed and assertive in forcing her way on board, and it had taken a half hour to locate the contracting officer by phone in Washington for approval. Dr. McCoy, he'd told Scott, was absolutely right.

"The contract clearly permits NOAA additions to the cargo load," he'd said. "Read the damn contract. Professionals do."

Scott had been deeply embarrassed. Jerry noticed that same steely-eyed look now in Linda McCoy's eyes and had to fight the urge to glance away.

"Well . . ." he began.

She looked toward the cockpit. "I haven't heard of your company. Is he the owner?"

Jerry nodded, noting her gaze had snapped back to him, her expression unreadable.

"Kind of young, isn't he?"

Jerry shrugged. "Scott is thirty-one, but he's an ex-Navy carrier pilot, a lieutenant commander. He flew Tomcats. He's a great pilot."

"How many airplanes do you have?"

"Uh, this is the only one. It's leased. We're real small."

She nodded. "Obviously, which is why he was so concerned about carrying my pallets."

"He didn't want to take a chance with this contract. It's . . . really important to us."

Jerry Christian felt very awkward all of a sudden. He ran his right hand through the unruly mop which passed for hair and glanced at one of her cargo pallets.

"What kind of research do you do, Doctor?"

She steadied herself against the sidewall of the cabin and studied him without responding, her right hand absently working the zipper of a breast pocket on her jumpsuit back and forth.

Jerry tried again. "I mean, I heard you say something about Antarctica."

Again she glanced forward, then turned back to Jerry and drilled her gaze into the engineer's eyes once more.

"He's not thinking of going back, is he?" she asked.

"Well . . ." Jerry began, wondering how she'd figured it out so fast.

"I realize you fellows are worried about leaving that other cargo, but you can't go back before you drop me in Denver. I've got time-critical, battery-powered equipment ticking away in these pallets."

Jerry shrugged. "I'm not the captain. That's . . . I mean, I don't make those decisions."

She nodded and smiled thinly. "Okay, then once more we'd better go talk to the man who does."

4

• • • •

The Navy chief warrant officer who had found the telltale spike in the record of gamma ray activity sat at his station in a corner of the trailer feeling increasingly frightened as the level of noise and confusion escalated. It wasn't the possibility of weapons-grade nuclear isotopes on the loose that scared him, it was the distinct feeling that he'd set off a cherry bomb in a buffalo herd, stampeding weighty bodies in all directions. One way or the other, he was going to get trampled.

Five cellular telephones were built into a command desk in the Navy trailer, and all were in use—along with three other handheld versions brought by the FAA men and a newly arrived FBI agent. The Navy technician had lost count of the number of times he'd explained the tracing to everyone in the trailer plus a dozen back in Washington, as well as faxed it on a secure channel to Navy headquarters in the Pentagon. Besides his own service, the Air Force and Army had somehow become involved, too, as had the National Security Council, the Nuclear Regulatory Commission, the Secret Service, and the Customs Service. No one had questioned his conclusion. All efforts had been focused on finding where the source of the readings had gone, and no fewer than twenty-two outbound passenger flights had been identified as departing during the time frame the readings had dropped to zero.

"What's going on?" he had asked the commander. "Are they going to send all the flights back here?"

His boss had shaken his head and spoken quietly. "They're trying to get them back, but many have landed at their destinations, and even those they can intercept elsewhere"—he shrugged—"no one else has one of these detectors in place. A Geiger counter's probably useless, because the nuclear core material is undoubtedly shielded. So how would anyone know where to look?"

"It could be in a truck, a bus, or even a van," one of the FAA men had warned earlier.

An expert on nuclear terrorism at the NRC had made it even worse. "It could be," he had told them all by secure telephone, "in any garden-variety car as well."

No one had dared voice the question that worried them the most: If the nuclear material couldn't be found, where was it headed? And for what purpose? As the minutes ticked by, the image of the gutted Federal Building in Oklahoma City haunted them all—a single building leveled by nothing more exotic than fertilizer and fuel oil, a tiny fraction of the power of a nuclear explosion.

NOAA HEADQUARTERS, WASHINGTON, D.C.—
12:30 P.M. EDT

With wild weather whipping the nation's capital and a powerful hurricane already battering the mid-Atlantic coast, the logistics officer for the National Oceanic and Atmospheric Administration had been hoping all morning for an early shutdown of federal offices. His small vacation cottage on Chesapeake Bay sixty miles east of the city was in danger and worrying him silly. If the winds got too high before he could get there to board up the windows, it was going to be a disaster, and the winds were already being reported over forty knots. Each phone call interrupted his monitoring of the latest weather reports, and he'd been thinking of leaving the receiver off the hook when an aggravated courier called from Florida to add one more irritant to the list.

Why, the voice demanded to know, had the aircraft chartered to fly high-priority cargo to NOAA's Colorado facility left without taking the cargo?

The logistics officer turned to his computer with a disgusted sigh and let loose a flurry of keystrokes. That would be the ScotAir flight.

"The guy called me several hours ago," he began, "and I gave him permission to take a couple of extra NOAA pallets along."

"Yeah, but he left the main event, the weekly courier pallet from Punta Arenas, Chile, which is what we hired him for. I'm already an hour late. I've got to get this stuff in the air. Get that sumbitch back here! And by the way, when you get him? Tell him the air freight forwarder here wants to talk to him, too. Seems he took off with somebody else's cargo, and they're madder than hell and want it back."

The logistics officer pulled out another stick of gum and tried to ignore his aching for a forbidden cigarette as he toggled the appropriate computer keys to bring up ScotAir's Flitephone number and reached for the receiver.

ABOARD SCOTAIR 50—12:33 P.M. EDT

Scott McKay quietly replaced the receiver of the Flitephone and stared out the windscreen in deep despair, oblivious to the municipal grid of New Orleans passing under the Boeing 727's nose some seven miles below, but acutely aware of the eyes in the cockpit watching his every breath.

He would miss flying the 727.

Stop it! he told himself. *He didn't fire us. He just yelled at us.*

"Captain, we need to talk." The feminine voice inches behind his ear startled him. The presence of Linda McCoy had slipped his mind.

Scott forced himself to respond. He loosened his seat belt and swiveled around to sit sideways, looking at his copilot before glancing around at the scientist.

"Just a second." He turned back toward the right seat. "Doc, call the controller, please, and get us an immediate clearance back to Miami."

Doc immediately reached for the transmit button.

"No!" Linda McCoy barked the word practically in Scott's ear as Doc looked around with a raised eyebrow and hesitated.

Scott looked over his shoulder at her and gestured for time. "Dr. McCoy, just a second. I'll explain."

"There's nothing to explain. I've got to get to Denver. You are *not* reversing course."

"I . . . have no choice. We've got to repair this mistake, and fast."

"Captain McKay." She paused and took a deep breath while

unsuccessfully trying to make eye contact with him. His eyes were on the center panel, his hands clasped together, as if bracing for what she had to say.

"Look, Captain, as a representative of your contractor, NOAA, I'm essentially ordering you not turn this plane around. Drop me in Denver first. Then you can fly back to Miami or wherever you want."

Scott McKay sighed and studied a small scratch on the center console, just aft of the transponder panel. McCoy was the type of woman who excited and infuriated him. Forceful and feminine at the same time, with a soft oval face framing her startlingly large brown eyes, her shoulder-length black hair swept behind her ears. Even the khaki jumpsuit-flight suit she wore was carefully tailored and accentuated her trim athletic body. He'd been aware of the tiny hint of perfume she wore, and it compensated in a way for her abrasive attitude back in Miami. He'd been disappointed, he realized, that he couldn't seem to charm her into compliance.

Now, of course, he really didn't care. There was only one person he wanted to mollify, and that was the NOAA contract officer in Washington.

He looked around at last and met her gaze, trying to see her only as a customer.

"Dr. McCoy, you don't understand. Back in Miami we left the main courier pallet we were contracted to deliver to Denver. Your pallets are on board as a courtesy."

"You can go back after you drop me," she replied.

Scott shook his head before she finished. "No. Denver is more than two hours from here. It would take an extra six hours to get back to this precise point."

She was shaking her head vigorously in response. He could feel her hair whipping the air inches from his head.

"Captain, that courier pallet is no longer time-critical. Mine, however, are."

"I'm sorry, Dr. McCoy."

"If you reverse course on me, I'll personally see to it that you lose that damn contract!"

Scott let his gaze drop to the center console again as he fought a tidal wave of conflicting emotions. Linda McCoy didn't understand what was happening to them, and he wasn't sure he wanted her to know the embarrassing facts of how close they were to financial oblivion. Yet, the temptation to strike back was too great. He looked up at her again with a tight smile and a small flash of vindictiveness.

"You'll cancel our contract?"

"I'll certainly try, if you insist on this."

"Well, Doctor, the threat rings hollow. You know why? Because if I *don't* turn around, I *will* lose the contract. That phone call was from one of your bureaucrats in Washington, who was nice enough to inform me that because we left the main pallet back in Miami, if we don't get back there in the next two hours, he'll cancel us. I have no choice. But I'll tell you what I *am* going to do, and I'm sorry if it doesn't meet with your approval. We're going to fly back to Miami, and as soon as we unload and refuel and pick up the right cargo, we're flying you directly to Denver—but not before." He looked back down at the console, seeing nothing in particular. "It could easily be our last significant act as an alleged airline. I don't have any confidence that they'll forgive this mistake."

Jerry Christian sighed audibly at the comment, and Linda McCoy looked puzzled.

"Last act?" she asked.

Scott nodded. "Without the proceeds from that contract, we are, quite simply, out of business." The words made him sick to his stomach, but they needed to be said. There would be no hope without it.

"If I can't make the lease payment on this airplane next week, the whole thing's up in smoke. Right now, I don't have the money. I was counting on the NOAA check, and frankly, I have the sick feeling that guy back in Washington has no intention of forgiving us. Something in his voice tells me we're already history."

"Scott!" Doc Hazzard's reproving tone from the right seat cut him short. "It ain't over till it's over."

"Got an extra thirty grand you could loan me, Doc?" Scott said with a snort as he turned back forward in the seat, already regretting his tone. Doc didn't deserve that.

Linda McCoy fell into uneasy silence. The copilot read back a revised clearance and began turning the 727 toward the southeast.

Scott sat back, his eyes focused on nothing, his mind surveying the damage. What was going to hurt the most would be the smirks of those who had laughed at his idea to begin with, especially some of the bankers who had ignored his M.B.A. degree and sneered at the "paltry" sum of three hundred thousand as insufficient start-up capital. The house in Central City and the money was all that he had left of his father, and now the money was gone. He had dreamed of turning it into millions.

Scott pictured his father, stern, often unyielding, but loving, always able to let a sudden smile burst like sunshine through storm clouds. Scott had worked hard for those flashes of paternal approval, and success would have equaled the same thing.

Perhaps, though, there was still a chance. Maybe he was misinterpreting things.

Scott shook his head at the surrealistic thought of failure. Salvation had seemed so close just a few days ago. He wondered whether he should stay in Central City if he had to shut it down. Maybe he could apply again to United Airlines. Maybe this time he'd be lucky.

Scott could see Jerry's crestfallen face in his peripheral vision, and his thoughts turned to his two friends, his only employees.

Doc Hazzard would be okay, of course, no matter what happened. The thirty-three-year veteran captain from Pan Am would always land on his feet—and always with a beautiful woman in tow. Doc was amazing. No, he was far more worried about Jerry Christian, who had a family to support and nothing to fall back on. He'd do his best to help Jerry find something else. If they folded, there would be enough cash in savings to pay Jerry's rent and his own for a few months, and by then, maybe something would turn up.

"Captain, I'm very sorry to hear this." Linda McCoy said at last, her tone a bit softer. "I had no idea it was that critical. I . . . suppose I can hang on while you do what you have to do."

Scott nodded his head without looking back, but Linda McCoy leaned forward, around the side of the captain's seat.

"The NOAA contract is it, then? You've no other options to stay afloat?"

Scott McKay shook his head as he lifted the Flitephone receiver from its cradle once again.

"None that I can see," he told her quietly, deciding to omit the details. He pulled a slightly rumpled business card from his shirt pocket and punched the phone number into the keypad, dreading the necessary follow-up conversation with the Miami freight forwarder. Perhaps he could calm the man down. He'd had enough people disappointed in him for one day.

NOAA HEADQUARTERS, WASHINGTON, D.C.—
12:45 P.M. EDT

It had taken only one call to the Air Force's Air Mobility Command for the logistics officer to find a quicker solution than waiting for ScotAir to return. An Air Force C-141 cargo jet was preparing to leave Fort Lauderdale empty, bound for the West Coast with an Air Force Reserve crew aboard looking for gainful employment. Their headquarters had agreed to divert the huge cargo jet to Miami to pick up the stranded NOAA pallet just as word came that everyone in the U.S. government within the Beltway could go home before the hurricane hit.

There was one remaining task. A vengeful little delight he was definitely looking forward to, considering the aggravation he'd been caused: a final conversation with the captain of ScotAir 50, whose outfit was obviously too unreliable to be working for Uncle. For the second time in fifteen minutes he pulled up ScotAir's number and reached for the phone.

UNIVERSAL AIR FREIGHT FORWARDERS, MIAMI
INTERNATIONAL AIRPORT—12:50 P.M. EDT

The operations manager had known for several hours that he was personally responsible for the misloading of ScotAir 50. Not that he would ever admit it, of course. He replaced the telephone in his office feeling somewhat relieved that the crew themselves thought they were at fault. Best to keep it that way.

He'd been shorthanded on the morning shift, so a brief delay in sacking an incompetent employee had seemed reasonable. He decided to say nothing and let the man work through lunch, but an overly chatty dispatcher had tipped the employee when he punched in for the morning shift that he was going to be canned.

By 11 A.M., the operations manager had discovered that every load his employee had touched in the previous hours had been purposefully scrambled. With an incredible amount of energy from the rest of the work force they managed to unsnarl the mess, with one exception. Before noon the government-chartered ScotAir flight had hauled the wrong pallet into the air and departed for Colorado.

The shipper whose pallet ended up aboard ScotAir found out about the mixup about the same time NOAA's representative discovered their time-critical shipment had been left behind by the same crew.

The shipper was an older woman scheduled to accompany her cargo personally, which meant it must be something of significant value. That possibility made the operations manager even more nervous, especially considering it was his mistake her pallet had been shanghaied in the first place. Her large, heavy, palletized crate had been hauled in from someplace in South Miami around 9 A.M. and the woman had arrived a few minutes later to execute the paperwork and pay the fees. She'd left for a while before her flight was due to arrive, but returned in plenty of time—only to find that her pallet had disappeared.

From the first she had been coldly assertive in that quiet, intense way that always scared him. People with such assurance were best taken seriously, and he knew only too well what would happen if she did, in fact, file a lawsuit as she threatened. He'd be history at Universal.

The first challenge had been figuring out which crew had flown away with her cargo. The second challenge was contacting them, especially since his calls to the office phone back in Colorado for a company called ScotAir kept terminating in the usual irritating voicemail runaround.

The real challenge, though, was figuring out how to get the woman's pallet reunited with her and on its way to Washington, D.C., in time. He was well aware of the major hurricane moving in from the Atlantic and threatening the nation's capital, filling CNN with reports of impending disaster. There didn't seem to be any way the ScotAir 727 crew could return to Miami in time. On top of that, word had come that the Air Force was going to take the abandoned NOAA cargo in the next half hour, leaving little reason for the 727's crew to fly back in the first place. He'd been agonizing over what to do when the ScotAir captain called.

The idea of diverting the ScotAir crew to Tallahassee to join up with their inadvertent client was his. A small stroke of genius, he assured himself, even if the 727's captain did reject the idea at first. The ScotAir captain had said he was going to return and dump the woman's pallet, and that was that.

The operations manager had taken a deep breath and tried again. "If you want to avoid a lawsuit, you'd better meet her somewhere else," he told the captain, carefully avoiding any reference to shared liability. "I'd suggest Tallahassee. Listen, Captain, this lady's hopping mad and ready to sue if she and her stuff don't get to D.C. ahead of that storm. You can't do it if you come back here."

"How," the captain had asked, "can we arrange that fast to get her northbound?"

"Already taken care of," he had announced. "She's at the terminal now, waiting for my confirmation to board. We'll pay for the ticket."

When the ScotAir captain agreed and terminated the connection, the manager picked up a handheld radio from the desk and spoke the call sign of the man he'd dispatched to the passenger terminal with the woman.

"Luis? Go ahead and put Mrs. Henry on the Tallahassee flight as planned. Give her an extra twenty dollars so she can take a cab from the terminal to the air freight area. The plane she'll be looking for is a Boeing 727, ScotAir Flight Fifty."

When the acknowledgment came, he replaced the radio and looked at his watch. A frantic FAA inspector had shown up a few minutes earlier demanding a list of the cargo flights they had worked that morning, and the list they'd handed over had been done in great haste. As operations manager, he knew he should have checked it for mistakes, but there wasn't time. He had no idea why the FAA seemed so upset, though normally he would have been curious. Certainly it wasn't about the vengeful employee he'd just fired. That was too petty a matter for the FAA. No, something unusual was going on around the airport.

He needed a break, and it was lunchtime, after all. He made a mental note to verify the accuracy of the list after lunch. Whatever the feds were worried about wasn't his problem.

5
· · · ·

Vivian Henry paused as she entered the Tallahassee terminal, wondering if someone—such as a representative for Universal Air Freight Forwarders—might have the decency to be waiting to escort her to the freight dock.

No one, however, seemed interested in her presence.

She'd hardly noticed the flight from Miami. There was too much else to think about, including Universal's outrageous negligence. The whole episode had rattled her badly, since losing that pallet had seemed like a final personal insult—especially when they told her a government agency was behind the whole mixup.

So they'd done it to her again. She'd reached that conclusion for a moment back in Miami, emotion overwhelming logic. An internal rage from the two-year battle over her annuity had engulfed her—until she discovered the agency was NOAA, and that they, too, had been victimized by Universal's mistake.

Vivian walked quickly through the security checkpoint toward the exit doors, ignoring a man in an expensive suit who courteously held a door for her.

She pushed open the adjacent door herself.

The man hesitated, shrugged slightly, and studied her as she passed—a tall, elegant woman with a shoulder-length mane of chestnut hair pulled back around her ears and allowed to fall. The well-cut dark blue suit and heels she wore emphasized her slender feminine shape and patrician bearing. She was probably forty-nine or fifty, he concluded, smiling as he held the visual memory of her in his mind—unaware he had just underestimated her age by more than a decade.

Vivian spotted the taxi queue and moved toward it. She'd begun to take pride in her appearance again in recent months, and she knew she often attracted male attention. Yet, for some reason, her need for anonymity on this trip was visceral, and she felt a small shiver of relief when the man at the door moved away without speaking. She was ashamed of having to come crawling back once again to do Rogers' bidding, ashamed that she had no choice but to perform for the money.

The fact that the air freight terminal was within a mile angered the cabbie, who had "waited in line a long time," he'd snarled, "for a better fare than this." He slapped on his meter in a gesture of disgust and burned out of the baggage claim area into a light rainstorm, muttering in what sounded like Farsi.

Strange, she thought. *I hadn't noticed from the airplane that it was raining.*

Vivian forced herself to think through the next few hours. Even if the aircraft was waiting as promised, she would likely face more problems on arrival in Washington. She'd called from Miami to reschedule the flatbed truck, but she wasn't convinced they were going to show up as promised, and even her contact at the Pentagon had sounded put-upon. He couldn't understand why she kept insisting the crate be delivered directly to the officer in charge of the Pentagon's basement storerooms, rather than shipped to a nearby Air Force base or some other large storage facility.

"In the interest of national security," she'd told him, following Rogers' script precisely.

"Well," he had said, "I can't meet you later than 6 P.M. I'll stay that long, but that's it."

They haven't a clue as to what I'm bringing them, she thought. *No one ever thought he'd succeed.*

Of course, there was always the chance he *hadn't* succeeded, and the Medusa Weapon was nothing more than one last gesture of contempt by Rogers Henry—a useless mockup sent as a last insult to the men who'd exiled him into early retirement. They could study it for months, maybe years, before discovering it was a hoax, and Rogers was very capable of hatching such a plan. She couldn't be sure, of course, but the idea that he could have actually developed the Medusa Weapon by himself still sounded ludicrous. They would have no choice but to spend months and many millions of dollars inspecting the mockup, and perhaps even building a real one and testing it at astronomical expense in some remote corner of the globe.

The cabbie wrestled his vehicle into another high-speed turn, skidding on the wet pavement, delighted that he'd thrown his passenger to one side of the backseat. He tromped heavily on the gas pedal to make sure she didn't miss the point, then rocketed down a service road toward the freight facility as he stole a look at her in the rearview mirror—disappointed that she seemed lost in thought and oblivious to the wild ride.

Vivian cringed at the thought of how Rogers would have reacted to the cabbie's conduct. He would have picked a verbal fight, drowning the cabbie in a tidal wave of rhetorical insults the man would have had no hope of understanding.

She didn't miss such scenes. Her former husband had been capable of hurling intimidating, withering verbal abuse at anyone, including his wife.

Especially at me, she thought. She certainly had the psychological scars to prove it.

It startled her to remember that Rogers had been dead and buried for two years. But in some strange psychological twist of the mind, she found herself regarding the palletized crate as his coffin. With its delivery to the military brass, she could, hopefully, be rid of him at last.

Vivian realized the cab had stopped and the driver was holding the door for her with no courtesy intended.

"Six-fifty," he said curtly in his heavily accented voice, obviously anxious to get back to the terminal for a more substantial fare.

Without comment she placed the exact amount of six dollars and fifty cents into the man's hand in her own gesture of contempt and walked toward the entrance of the metal building, shielding her head with her hand against the rain. She barely heard the cab door slamming behind her and its screeching departure from the parking lot.

ScotAir's Boeing 727 was waiting as promised, the three-engine jetliner sitting sideways to the freight facility as a fueler disconnected his hose from beneath the right wing.

A sandy-haired young man with the four-stripe epaulets of a captain had been pacing around the front office. He was of medium build and broad shoulders, athletic, with a wide mouth and easy smile set in a handsome face. She had the feeling she'd seen him before, but the whisper of recognition was vague and distant.

The young captain brightened as she entered. Before noticing the lines around his eyes, she judged him to be in his mid-twenties—which seemed young for a captain.

No, she decided, *mid-thirties—and young enough to be my son.*

He moved rapidly toward her with an outstretched hand. "Mrs. Henry?"

"Yes."

He shook her hand firmly and looked at his watch simultaneously. "I'm terribly sorry about the cargo mixup," he began. "Just for the record, I truly don't think it was our fault, but however it happened, if we're going to get you to Washington, we'd better get going. I assume you know there's a huge hurricane threatening D.C. and we only have a limited window."

"And you are?" she asked, a bit put off by his rapid speech and lack of introduction.

"Oh, I'm sorry. I'm Scott McKay, the . . . captain." For a second he'd intended to add the word "owner," but he was speaking to someone who'd threatened to sue him, and by next Monday the title of owner would apply only to the empty shell of what used to be his airline. No, it was better to let her think of him as a mere employee.

"Any luggage?" Scott asked.

"Just this overnight bag," she replied, holding up a small tote bag. "You mentioned that hurricane, Captain. How much time do we have?"

Scott bit his lip as he glanced at a sheaf of papers covered with numbers.

"Well, I'd say if we're off the ground in the next twelve minutes, that puts us into National Airport about an hour and forty minutes later. I figure it'll take us forty-five minutes to get your pallet off, get you on your way, get us refueled, and get back in the air. That's a bit under two and a half hours, and the winds are forecast to be blowing around thirty knots in D.C. within the next two hours, *if* the storm doesn't speed up. So we're time-critical."

He gestured to the door and she moved in that direction, ducking her head under the proffered umbrella when they were outside.

"I've heard this hurricane is unusual," she said. Noise from another jet sitting fifty yards away with its engines running began to overwhelm their voices.

"I'VE NEVER SEEN ONE THIS HUGE!" Scott shouted at her. She nodded, and he continued.

"IT'S CALLED HURRICANE SIGRID, AND IT'S OVER EIGHT HUNDRED MILES IN DIAMETER! WINDS NEAR THE CENTER ARE . . ."

"WHAT?" she yelled.

"WINDS ARE ABOVE TWO HUNDRED NEAR THE CENTER!" Scott handed her the umbrella and motioned her up the slick, rather unstable boarding ladder which had been placed at the forward entry door, waiting until she was at the top before bounding up behind her.

Safely inside, Vivian Henry asked him to repeat the answer.

"I was saying," Scott began, "that the winds are horrendous near the center, above two hundred knots. If that eye hits the Delaware coast, it'll blow away Rehoboth Beach and half the Jersey seashore to the north."

"But can we make it to D.C. in time?" Her eyes were wide with alarm. They were racing both the clock and a killer hurricane.

Scott took a deep breath as he saw her expression. "I can't promise we can, ma'am, but we're certainly going to try."

"Please . . ." she began, then hesitated, as if recomposing her words. "I . . . would rather not go into details, but please understand that it is of the utmost importance that I reach Washington this afternoon with my shipment."

How can I tell him how much I want this to be over? she thought.

Scott McKay could feel the urgency in her words, and her anxiety was unsettling, distracting him enough to leave his answer sounding less than confident.

"We'll . . . do the best we can, Mrs. Henry."

WASHINGTON, D.C.—2:25 P.M. EDT

At noon the federal government in Washington began shutting down in the face of Hurricane Sigrid. The emergency closure, however, was having no effect whatsoever on the rapidly escalating workload of the National Security Council staff.

Stanley Shapiro, the President's National Security Advisor, decided to walk over from the West Wing to the NSC's main offices in the adjacent Executive Office Building as soon as it became apparent a genuine terrorist threat might have been detected in Florida. With the President on his way to Japan for an international trade summit, the situation was being relayed to Air Force One. The White House Chief of Staff snagged Dr. Shapiro for a hallway briefing as he was leaving his West Wing office.

"Right now, it's a mess," Shapiro began. "You've been briefed on what that Navy monitoring outfit in Miami thinks they detected, right?"

The Chief of Staff nodded.

"Okay, while Langley is working on targeting the *who*, FBI is working with the Pentagon and the FAA to find out the *where*, and NRC is working on *what* material was detected, but the bottom line is, we may already be too late. We may have already lost the trail."

"I was told all the airplanes were being called back to Miami."

The former Princeton professor shook his head no, causing his trademark bow tie to wobble, an image the tightly buttoned-down Chief of Staff had always found irritating. "They didn't discover it in time. Some planes had already landed at their destination, others had to refuel first, and thus could have had the material removed. Eight flights, I think, were returned and taxied past that detector with no results. But the radioactive package could have been in a truck or a car as well, and we're not even sure we've accounted for every aircraft yet. It's a needle in a haystack."

The Chief of Staff leaned against the wall and studied the floor for a few seconds before looking up. "Anyone considered putting that detector on a plane and flying it around the country?"

"I'm told it won't work in the air without special equipment no one has time to manufacture. I'm also told an airborne version had been canceled in some Pentagon budget revision several years back, and so far we don't have a detector in orbit."

"Naturally the Pentagon would take advantage of the moment to get in those digs. So where are we?" the Chief of Staff asked. "What do we do?"

The National Security Advisor shook his head and pursed his lips before replying. "I don't think anyone knows *what* to do. It's terrifying. We've got everyone up to and including Justice involved. There's not a lot of bickering, but there's not a lot of coordination, either. Everyone's absolutely astounded that our worst-case threat may actually be happening, and if so, it's a real nightmare, because I'm told those readings were strong enough to confirm one thing for certain: Someone out there has enough unregistered illegal weapons-grade material to build a thermonuclear bomb. We have to assume they also have the hardware and the expertise to build a device to use it."

The Chief of Staff snorted. "Hell, even Tom Clancy told everyone how to do it several books ago, not that I read his stuff."

"Bottom line? We have to assume someone out there is planning to detonate a nuke somewhere in the United States. CIA says they'll support that conclusion."

"Good God!" He whistled, low and long. "How much power are we looking at?"

The National Security Advisor shrugged. "God only knows. I'm told anything from a kiloton to megatons. Enough to wipe out any one of our cities. There's no precedent for this. Well"—he hesitated—"there *is,* sort of. You're aware of the Iranian the FBI snagged in Dallas in the mid-eighties with a briefcase full of radiation?"

The Chief of Staff nodded. "Yes. At least the fact that they had enough fissile material, as its called, to construct a bomb, and the fact that they had a workable trigger. We never knew the target." He sighed and shook his head sadly. "I remember warning that it was just a matter of time before this happened. I gave a speech many years ago—even before the Dallas incident, while I was still in the Senate—about nuclear proliferation leading inevitably to an American city being destroyed by a nuclear fireball to further some maniac's cause. It was a dire warning, carefully designed to shake up the audience and make them angry enough to pressure some of my colleagues who were trying to cut back the FBI's funding. But you know what, Stanley?"

Shapiro raised his eyebrows in response.

"The truth is, I didn't believe it myself! I didn't *really* believe that we'd ever face that possibility."

Another car squealed to a halt outside the Navy trailer. The FBI agent behind the wheel spoke a few more words into his cellular phone and punched the disconnect button. He leaped from his car and bounded through the door of the trailer.

"Okay, people, we've inspected every aircraft we can inspect, I'm afraid," he announced. "There's no one left to intercept, and we're batting zero. Any creative ideas will be appreciated."

One of the men inside had turned around. "They got the Salt Lake flight, too?"

The agent nodded. "On arrival. They found nothing, provided our people were looking for the right things."

The Navy officer who had originally commanded the trailer was sitting at a small desk to one side. He turned toward the senior agent now and nodded a brief greeting before turning back to the papers spread out before him. He was obviously searching for something, the senior FBI agent realized, and he was apparently frustrated at not finding it.

The senior agent moved quietly to the Navy officer's side and took a quick look at the documents he was studying. On the top of the stack was the rapidly prepared list of flights that had taken off from Miami International about the time the gamma ray readings dropped to zero. And sitting next to them were a stack of cargo manifests from the various freight forwarders on the field showing everything that had been shipped as cargo during the same time period.

"Something puzzling you there, Commander?" the agent asked.

The naval officer looked up, scratched his cheek, and frowned slightly, then pointed to the manifests.

"Something doesn't fit." He got to his feet and picked up the papers, pointing to the top sheet as he brought them closer for the senior agent to see.

"There was a shipment of high-priority pallets for NOAA which was to have gone out to the Denver area on a 727, but apparently an Air Force cargo jet, a C-141, landed here and took that load for NOAA, according to the notes from whoever talked to the forwarder. I know you intercepted that flight."

The FBI agent nodded. "We had him land at Richards-Gebaur Air Force Base near Kansas City. We found nothing, of course. Just that one pallet belonging to NOAA. The Air Force crew confirmed they were pressed into service when a contract flight failed to show. They weren't happy."

The commander was nodding again, almost rhythmically, as he sat down and pulled more papers toward him. "Right. Right."

The agent pulled up a folding chair and straddled it backward. "So what's bothering you?" he asked.

The commander looked at him before speaking. "I . . . may be wrong, here, sir, but I think there's yet *another* cargo departure that isn't listed on the tower log."

"That shouldn't be possible," the FBI agent replied, following the commander's index finger.

"I agree, but the freight forwarder also lists a second NOAA shipment in his inventory as of this morning. Instead of the one pallet which left with the C-141, however, this one is a two-pallet combination, also bound for Colorado. Now, we know where the single pallet went. It left with the Air Force. But suddenly that mysterious second set of two pallets disappears from the list. So where'd the other pallets go, or were there ever really two shipments to begin with? For that matter, if there *was* a second shipment, was it really a pair of NOAA pallets or someone taking advantage of NOAA's presence to ship something else under an alias?"

The agent rose to his feet and leaned over to look at the papers more closely as the commander continued.

"See the tower log here? There appears to be a double entry for Northwest Nine-Ninety-Four. See how one is crossed-out, as if the tower controller realized he'd accidentally put the same flight down twice? That time corresponds almost perfectly with our reading drop. Now, suppose that crossed-out entry was really some other cargo flight carrying those two mystery pallets out of here, and the controller simply made an error with the call sign? They're human, too. They do make errors, and obviously someone wrote down the same flight twice."

The senior FBI agent turned immediately to an FAA inspector a few feet away.

"Charlie, could you find out if there was a flight plan out of Miami filed about this time for a cargo flight whose call sign doesn't show up on the departure log?"

The FAA man nodded yes. "Miami Center's computer should

have a ready record of all the flight plans that were activated. It'll take a few minutes to get and compare. If that fails, we could always pull the tower tapes and listen."

The FBI agent pointed to the papers on the table. "Call the center, please. If there was a departure the tower didn't log, we need to know what airplane it was, and where it is right now."

The commander rose to his feet again beside the senior agent. "You know," he began, "two pallets of cargo could, rather easily . . ."

"Contain a package of plutonium?" the agent finished. "Commander, even a briefcase is big enough."

In less than five minutes the FAA inspector hung up the telephone and swiveled around to catch the senior FBI agent's eye.

"You were right!"

The Navy commander rose from his seat. "You found something?"

"One flight *did* slip by us. A Boeing 727 belonging to a tiny cargo outfit out of Colorado Springs. ScotAir. He left at exactly the time that Northwest flight was entered twice."

The FBI agent turned rapidly to an assistant. "Call the forwarder who handled the NOAA stuff and find out if they put anything on that 727." He turned back to the FAA inspector. "Do we know where he was going?"

"Yep. He was flight-planned to Denver, Colorado."

"Bingo!" was the reply.

6

• • • •

Pete Cooke breathed a sigh of relief as his flight slowed and turned off the main runway. The landing had been hard enough to register on the Richter scale, but the pilots of the McDonnell-Douglas MD-80 had done an outstanding job of negotiating the advance winds of Hurricane Sigrid. After all, they were down in one piece, and as a pilot himself, Pete had been well aware that the two airmen up front were fighting exceptionally wild winds all the way to the ground.

Through the window the *Wall Street Journal* reporter could see the trees along the Potomac whipping crazily as his flight taxied south toward the terminal. The angle gave him a clear view of the runway they'd just assaulted—Runway 36—and a clear view of a tiny commuter plane struggling through the last part of its approach to the same ribbon of concrete.

It was a small twin-engine Jetstream, being kicked around rather dramatically by the heavy gusts. Pete found himself leaning forward to get a better look, sympathizing with the passengers aboard the little craft who were probably clutching airsick bags by now. As they passed over the runway threshold, a massive gust rolled the turboprop into a dangerous forty-five-degree bank, and, just as suddenly, the wings leveled. Pete expected to see the pilots begin a go-around maneuver.

Instead, amazingly, they continued their landing attempt.

The massive crosswind was blowing the Jetstream off center-line, but the pilots kept coming, determined to make the landing work. They were halfway down the runway and poised to make a normal touchdown, but the aircraft suddenly dropped through the last ten feet, coming down hard and partially sideways. The left main landing gear immediately collapsed in a shower of sparks, whipping the Jetstream around violently to the left. Still moving at more than a hundred miles per hour, the aircraft dragged its left wing, pushing its nose and right main landing wheels sideways against the runway surface until they, too, collapsed, leaving the craft to spin to a halt several thousand feet away in the middle of the intersection of Runway 36 and Runway 33—effectively shutting down Washington National Airport.

Looking back through his window in shocked disbelief, Pete Cooke saw doors and hatches fly open as the passengers and crew scrambled safely onto the concrete. Despite the sparks, there was no fire.

Thank God! he thought.

Pete fumbled with his tote bag beneath the seat in front of him, groping for the new handheld radio scanner he had begun carrying. His hand finally closed around it and he yanked it out and quickly punched in the memorized frequency for Washington Approach Control.

The runways wouldn't be usable until the damaged Jetstream was removed, but dozens of flights were headed for Washington National. They were going to end up in one massive airborne snarl of diversions and holding patterns, and both the reporter and the pilot in him wondered how the Washington Approach controllers were going to sort out the mess with a monster hurricane approaching.

ABOARD SCOTAIR 50—3:45 P.M. EDT

ScotAir 50 was forty miles south of the Beltway when word came that Washington National Airport was closed.

"How long a delay?" Doc Hazzard asked the controller.

"No information on that, ScotAir. I'll advise when I know. For now, I can give you a holding clearance or send you to Dulles Airport or Baltimore."

In the left seat Scott McKay shook his head in agonized disbelief.

Just when I think it can't get any worse, it gets worse!

He mouthed the word "hold" to Doc, who nodded and punched the transmit button again.

"We'll take the hold, Approach. We need to get into National as soon as possible, but we do have enough fuel to wait."

"Roger, ScotAir Fifty, you're cleared direct to the Georgetown radio beacon to hold as depicted at one-zero thousand feet, right-hand turns."

Doc adjusted the volume control on the communications radio, then turned to check his work.

"Dammit! Scott, we've got to get these radio heads changed. I grabbed the wrong one again."

Scott's eyes shifted to the VHF radio control heads. The two were mirror images of each other, the result of Jerry scrounging a refurbished radio when the original equipment delivered with the old leased 727 had broken. Each radio head had two volume knobs, one for air traffic control, the other—usually kept at zero volume—for checking navigational signals. But the number one VHF control head had the important volume control on the left, while number two VHF had it on the right. It was constantly confusing, and more than a few times they'd had the embarrassing experience of flying along for twenty minutes out of touch because the wrong volume knob had been turned down.

"Sorry, Doc. We'll get it fixed as soon as we can."

Jerry had leaned forward. "About the holding pattern. We weigh a hundred and seventy-two thousand pounds, guys," he announced. "That's a holding speed of two hundred forty knots."

Doc repeated the holding instructions and dialed in the radio beacon while Scott guided the Boeing to the left, his right hand retarding the throttles to slow to a speed of two hundred forty knots, trying not to focus on how much he just wanted to be finished with this flight. The desire to crawl off and lick his wounds in private was strong. The impending collapse of his airline—and his dream—was just too painful.

The holding pattern was an invisible racetrack in the sky. They would fly in one direction for a minute, turn right one hundred eighty degrees to fly in the opposite direction for another minute, then another right turn to repeat the exact same path, for as long as they had extra fuel.

Jerry Christian leaned over the center console and handed Scott a slip of paper covered with fuel figures. The 727's tanks had been filled in Tallahassee at a cost of eight thousand dollars, and somehow ScotAir's company credit card had been accepted one last time. At least that would get them all the way to Colorado.

"We've got forty-seven thousand pounds of fuel remaining," he counseled, "which gives us about an hour and a half of holding time before we'll have to depart for Denver. But if we changed our alternate to, say, Louisville, we could hold here in D.C. for over four hours."

Scott was already shaking his head no.

"In four hours we don't want to be anywhere close to here, considering the rate that hurricane's coming ashore."

Doc Hazzard spoke up. "I just monitored the weather for Dover Air Force Base, almost due east of us on the coast. This is not good, folks. The winds are already howling at over seventy knots." Doc glanced to the left at their new passenger, who was sitting in the same seat Dr. McCoy had occupied earlier, the observer's chair right behind Scott. Five-foot-five Linda McCoy had taken one look at five-foot-eleven Vivian Henry back in Tallahassee and decided there was no way the older woman could fold her long legs into the second jumpseat, a tiny affair sandwiched between the observer's seat and the back cockpit wall. Linda had moved immediately to the smaller seat.

Vivian Henry was restraining herself from asking the obvious questions, but her face betrayed deep worry, and the copilot leaned in her direction to explain what was blocking the runways below. She listened carefully before replying in a quiet, firm voice, "They can reopen their runways, then, in an hour and a half?"

Doc nodded, knowing it was no better than a wild guess. "They'll have to get permission from the safety board and the FAA to move the wreckage, but they can do it if they hustle."

Linda McCoy's face was too expressive to hide the dark worry she was feeling. She leaned between Jerry Christian's seat and the observer's chair. "I'm not a meteorologist," she began, "but I can tell you we'd better not underestimate this storm. The winds down there are going to get worse. Don't assume it's going to follow the pattern of any previous hurricane."

Something in her tone caused Scott to turn around.

"Why, Doctor?"

"This is a new breed of storm—one of the effects of global warming. Atmospheric science is my field, and I can tell you that the engine that's fueling that storm is a hotter ocean, and more heat coming out of the oceans means more energetic storms. You may have noticed in the last few years how hurricanes seem to be getting stronger, and more fearsome? Well, this is one of that new breed, and the worst is yet to come."

"You're scaring me, Dr. McCoy," Doc said, forcing a chuckle.

"I'm trying to," Linda replied. "I want you to understand that a cyclonic monster eight hundred miles in diameter has immense power. I don't want you fellows to underestimate its intensity. I *especially* don't want you to underestimate it if you're planning to land in it with *my* tail aboard."

From the engineer's seat Jerry Christian tried to suppress a smile as he watched the captain's eyes, waiting for the inevitable, possibly sexist remark about Dr. Linda McCoy's shapely tail. He knew Scott too well. He knew he'd be unable to resist, and for just a second the anticipation made him forget the inner panic he'd felt for the last few hours.

But there was no smirk on Scott's face, and no reaction, so profound was his distraction. The silence made Jerry feel even sicker, the hollow desperation welling up inside like the day more than a decade ago when he'd stumbled out of the flight simulator in Minneapolis knowing he'd blown his last chance to pass his copilot check with Northwest Airlines—an exam he had to pass to stay employed.

Jerry studied the captain's face, trying to sense his thoughts, realizing why the silence dismayed him so: If Scott McKay had lost his puckish sense of humor, it really was over.

Scott turned around as far as he could and tried to look at Vivian. "Mrs. Henry, we could probably land at Dulles Airport right away, if you wanted to change your destination."

The image of a flatbed truck came into her mind.

"I've already arranged my transportation for Washington National Airport, and that was a struggle. I'd much rather go to National."

"Okay," Scott began again, "but let's say Washington National doesn't reopen. We've got to plan for that."

Vivian sat in high-speed thought for a few seconds. If they couldn't land at National, Dulles did make sense, even if it took a day to get another truck dispatched.

"I think," she began, "what I'd like to do is wait and see if National opens up in time, if you can do that safely."

Scott thought about it before nodding in agreement. If he had come this far and burned up this much fuel to satisfy her, he could burn a little more. "Okay, let's say we'll give it forty-five minutes. If National doesn't reopen, we'll land you at Dulles, and I'll help you arrange transportation before we head west."

Vivian acknowledged the plan with a weak smile, the words of her Pentagon contact replaying in her mind: "I can't meet you later than 6 P.M." Rogers Henry had left extremely detailed instructions. "Once the shipment has arrived in Washington," he had written, "it must be delivered immediately to the Pentagon within the hour. *This is very important!* Security demands it!"

She had not concerned herself with why. He had never authorized her to question his judgment, though so long ago when they'd first met at Lawrence-Livermore labs, there had been no need. She was a young engineer specializing in weapon assembly techniques, starstruck to be dating the resident *wunderkind,* the rising star of theoretical physics. His judgment seemed beyond question until they married, and the kind and caring young husband began metastasizing into a monster determined to maintain total control at home.

She shuddered now to realize that even after his death, Rogers' iron will could control her thinking.

MIAMI INTERNATIONAL AIRPORT—3:50 P.M. EDT

The senior FBI agent in charge in the makeshift command post in the Navy trailer was irritated. It had taken much too long to relay the distressing news that the missing cargo flight, ScotAir 50, was *not* on the ground at Denver International Airport, after all. He had been worrying about how their cargo should be examined, and how it could be tracked down if any part of what they had flown from Miami had left the Denver airport. The possibility that ScotAir 50 might have diverted somewhere *other* than its planned destination of Denver had occurred to no one.

And *that,* he concluded, was poor planning on his part.

This time the word came back in minutes.

"Okay, I understand," one of the FAA men was saying to the phone as he held up his right hand in a wait gesture. "We may need to contact him. Get me a direct line to that sector controller, please. Yeah, I'll hold."

"What?" the senior FBI man asked. *"What?"*

The FAA inspector took a deep breath and shook his head. "I'm not sure you're going to believe this."

"Try me."

"The one aircraft in the United States we most suspect of carrying material that could be used to construct a nuclear bomb?"

"Yes?"

"At this moment, it's in a holding pattern over Washington, D.C."

ABOARD SCOTAIR 50—4:00 P.M. EDT

Doc Hazzard excused himself for a quick walk to the back of the aircraft.

"I can only watch us bore circular holes in the sky for so long without a break!" he explained as he slid his barrel-chested frame from the seat with surprising ease.

Within a minute, however, he was back, a quizzical expression crinkling his weather-beaten forehead.

"Uh, Dr. McCoy, you said several hours ago that you've got batteries and things ticking away in your equipment, right?"

Linda McCoy studied Doc's face before replying. "Yes. Why?"

"Well, I hate to tell you, but there's an electronic alarm going off back there."

Scott looked around at Doc, who shrugged his shoulders.

Linda followed Doc out of the cockpit and down the narrow passageway on the left side of the compartment, aware of a high-pitched sound that seemed to be rising in intensity as she moved aft. The Boeing 727 was cruising through bumpy air at low speed with very little engine noise, which let the warning horn echo from everywhere in the cargo compartment at once. She scanned her memory of the things her team had packaged back in McMurdo Sound in Antarctica, but nothing, as far as she could remember, could make a noise like that.

"It's coming from your second pallet, I think," Doc offered as they moved back slowly alongside the cargo.

"I can't imagine what that could be," she said, her head cocked to try to locate the source of the high-pitched sound, which had become almost deafening.

Doc Hazzard tried putting his head against the side of the pallet, while Linda squeezed past him, realizing that it was getting louder as she moved aft.

"Doc, that's not coming from my stuff! It's coming from the last cargo position." Linda pointed toward the rear of the cargo cabin.

Together they moved carefully alongside Vivian Henry's shipment and stepped behind it, and as Linda reached out to steady herself with one of the cargo straps, the noise changed at the same moment to an urgent electronic warble, causing both of them to jump.

"What on earth?" Linda asked.

Doc backed up and stared at the pallet briefly. "Wait here," he said. He motioned toward the front of the aircraft and Linda watched him disappear up the narrow passageway, returning in less than a minute with a startled Vivian Henry, who moved around her pallet slowly, her eyes wide and fixated on the large crate beneath the heavy-duty cargo straps and plastic sheeting.

"What's in there, Mrs. Henry?" Doc asked.

Vivian stared at Doc in uncomprehending silence for a few seconds, then suddenly shook herself awake.

"I . . . I don't know. I don't know what could be making that noise." Her voice seemed distant against the loud electronic warble.

"What's *in* the crate, I mean?" Doc tried again.

"My husband instructed me," she began, "to bring this to Washington personally. It's something I'm not supposed to discuss, but it's very important to our military . . . to the United States."

Doc Hazzard moved slightly in front of her, trying to look her in the eye.

"Mrs. Henry? Was there supposed to be anything running, or turned on, in there?"

Vivian took a deep breath. "No. It's a mockup. A dummy."

"If we got your husband on the phone, could he tell us?"

"He's deceased."

"What . . . was his business, Mrs. Henry?"

"He was a government scientist, before he retired."

"What kind of scientist, Mrs. Henry? What area?"

"Physicist," she replied in a small voice.

Doc felt off-balance all of a sudden. A jolt of apprehension had come with the title of "physicist," as if the word invested the pallet's unknown contents with more sinister possibilities. He shook off the feeling and tried again. "Is there anyone your husband worked with who would know about this?"

Vivian's eyes remained on the pallet as she shook her head, slowly at first, then with rapid back-and-forth jerks.

Linda had been watching her carefully, especially her eyes. It was obvious that Mrs. Vivian Henry had absolutely no idea what was in her own pallet. Or could it be that Vivian was just a good actress? If so, what was she hiding? A small, cold chill began to ripple down Linda's back.

"Okay," Doc said, "I think we better open it up."

"*No!*" Vivian Henry's reply was instantaneous, but her eyes remained glued to the pallet. "He left strict instructions . . . that . . ."

Doc put his large hands on her shoulders and slowly turned her around to face him until their eyes met.

"Mrs. Henry, something inside your pallet is sounding a warning. It's trying to tell us something, and we're a commercial cargo aircraft in flight. Unless your husband left specific instructions about what to do if you heard such a warning, we've got to figure out what this alarm means. Okay?"

She looked at him blankly.

"*Okay?*"

Her eyes dropped to the floor. "Okay."

Doc motioned to Linda, and together they began removing the cargo straps, using a penknife to cut through the side of the heavy vinyl covering, exposing a crate within.

"Hold on a second." Doc disappeared up the passageway again, returning quickly with a crowbar. He tried to control the creepy feeling that the alarm, which kept changing in pitch, was very much beyond his control. The nails screamed as he hauled them out of the wooden crate. The back panel finally gave way and fell, causing all three of them to step back as it clattered to the metal floor of the 727, revealing the crate's contents.

Facing them was a large stainless steel container. It was rectangular, but with rounded edges at each of the corners. The rear panel was over six feet wide, but only the surface of the metal was visible within the opened crate. There were no stickers or decals—no markings of any kind—only the outline of what appeared to be a removable panel approximately twenty-four inches square located about three feet up from the bottom along the left-hand edge.

Linda McCoy reached out to the panel, but the pattern of the electronic alarm changed before she actually touched it.

When she pulled her hand back, the alarm reverted to its previous warble.

"This thing's got a magnetic field sensor responding to us!" Linda said. "Why, I wonder?" She looked briefly at Vivian, who seemed frozen in place, her eyes riveted on the container. Doc stepped forward, braving the change in sound to run his hand along the panel.

There were four Phillips-head screws holding the panel in place, and Doc produced a small screwdriver, finding them easy to remove. When the last one was free, he pulled the panel loose and handed it to Linda.

The glow of a TV screen within spilled from the cavity as soon as the panel was open. Doc leaned close and noticed a foldout computer-style keyboard and number pad mounted below the screen. There was a message on the screen directing him to press the "Enter" key on the keyboard.

He did so.

Instantly the alarm stopped as a line of text appeared on the screen.

THE CURRENT LOCATION OF THIS DEVICE IS 38 DEGREES, 52.5 MINUTES NORTH LATITUDE, 77 DEGREES, 03.5 MINUTES WEST LONGITUDE.

The numbers were changing slightly as the 727 moved over the ground, and Doc realized there had to be some form of inertial navigation system inside, tracking their precise position.

Without prompting, a second block of text suddenly appeared.

WARNING! THE FACT THAT THIS DEVICE IS NOW LOCATED WITHIN THE PHYSICAL CONFINES OF THE PENTAGON HAS BEEN DETECTED AND LOCKED IN MEMORY. ANY ATTEMPT TO MOVE THIS DEVICE FROM ITS PRESENT LOCATION—OR ANY ATTEMPT TO DEACTIVATE—WILL RESULT IN INSTANT DETONATION!

7
. . . .

The voice of the Washington Approach controller was terse.

"ScotAir Fifty, I've been handed a telephone number in Miami you're to call immediately. Do you have a phone aboard?"

Scott felt off-balance. He'd never heard an air traffic controller order a pilot to make an airborne call. He wished Doc was back in the cockpit.

Scott punched the transmit button. "Ah, roger, ScotAir Fifty does have a telephone. Who's requesting the call?"

"I don't know, ScotAir," the controller began, "but you need to call this number immediately. I'm told it's an emergency."

The controller relayed the number and Scott punched it into the Flitephone handset, his mind whirling through a variety of apocalyptic possibilities as a man answered on the other end, listened to the name ScotAir, and identified himself as an FBI agent. Scott felt himself shudder within.

"We've been trying to find you, ScotAir. You were in Miami this morning at the same time some undocumented hazardous material was shipped out. We think that material may be on board your aircraft."

The memory of Linda McCoy's pushiness in getting her two pallets aboard suddenly flooded Scott's mind, almost blocking the agent's words. They hadn't really verified her identity, had they? They hadn't even inspected her pallets, once he'd agreed to take them.

"We need you to land immediately," the agent said.

The visual memory of Mrs. Henry's single pallet also crossed his mind. He knew even less about her.

Scott realized the agent was still talking, and he wasn't paying attention.

"I'm sorry. Say again."

There was a pause in Miami. "I said we'll have the appropriate people ready to meet you to examine what you've got on board. You haven't unloaded anything since you left Miami, have you?"

Suddenly, for some reason, he felt guilty. All they'd done wrong was load someone else's pallet, and that was an innocent mistake. Yet the fact that an FBI agent was asking him questions at all was vaguely terrifying.

"No, sir," Scott answered. "It's all still aboard. But I need to know, are we in any danger, if what you're looking for is really here?"

Silence.

"Sir? Did you hear me?"

He could hear the phone being shifted from one hand to another in Miami, and at last the FBI agent's voice returned. "Ah, Captain, I doubt you're in any immediate danger, but I can't say for certain. If the . . . items . . . we're looking for are on board your airplane, it depends on how well they're, ah, packaged."

More links and connections raced through his head, none of them comforting: *Miami . . . drug dealers . . . drug-making equipment . . . hazardous carcinogenic chemicals . . . What if we're carrying illegal drugs?*

Scott heard his own voice as if it were disembodied. "Okay. Where do you want us to land? We're waiting to get into National, but right now it's closed."

There was a worrisome hesitation on the other end. Scott could hear voices before the agent spoke into the handset again.

"Okay, stay in your holding pattern. What phone are you on?"

Scott passed the number of the aircraft's Flitephone.

"Keep the line open, Captain, and I'll call you back as soon as we've decided where to bring you down."

"You do realize there's a hurricane moving in here?" Scott asked.

"I . . . wait a minute." The agent began. Scott could hear someone talking in the background. "Okay, Captain, what did you say?"

"I said there's a hurricane moving into the D.C. area. Whatever we do, we're going to need to do it fast. One of my clients wants her cargo to go to National, but if it doesn't reopen soon, the winds are going to go out of limits."

"You've got just one shipment on board, right?"

"No, sir. We've got two. One's going to Denver, Colorado. The other was loaded by mistake this morning. We're delivering it to National."

More background discussion. Scott realized he'd flown beyond the end of the holding pattern. His right hand found the autopilot controller and began a right turn to reverse course. Even at ten thousand feet and two hundred forty knots of speed, the turbulence was getting worse, and the old 727 was bouncing around with an irritating consistency.

The agent's voice filled his ear again. Scott thought he detected fatigue. "Okay, Captain, we're going to need to inspect everything you've got aboard. Right now, we're considering bringing you down at Andrews Air Force Base. Hang tight until I've got final word. I'll call you right back."

The sound of the cockpit door being flung open was punctuated by the sound of the FBI agent disconnecting.

"Scott!" Doc Hazzard laid a large left hand on the younger pilot's shoulder, turning him partly around with a startling roughness. "Scott, we've got a problem." Linda McCoy stood in the doorway, he noticed, her face ashen. Mrs. Henry was nowhere to be seen.

"What?"

Doc flung himself in the copilot's seat and began strapping in. "Dr. McCoy will take you back there. I'll watch the bird. I don't know what to make of it."

"*What*, Doc? What the hell are you talking about?"

Doc Hazzard grabbed the yoke with his right hand and turned toward Scott.

"That warning horn? It was coming from Mrs. Henry's shipment. There's a metal container in that pallet. It looks like stainless steel. I opened an inspection hatch and found a TV screen inside with a message you've got to see. Scott, this thing may contain a bomb! And it's got an inertial navigation system in it that may be malfunctioning. It thinks it knows where it is, but it doesn't know precisely."

"Doc, for God's sake, slow down! Tell me that again. There's a huge container back there with some sort of message and you think it's a *bomb?*"

Doc shook his head as he scanned the instruments, trying to make sure he knew where they were. "You'll understand when you look at it."

"What's this about an inertial navigation system?"

Doc turned to him. "It thinks we're in the Pentagon. Rather, it thinks *it's* in the Pentagon."

"Well, we flew *over* the Pentagon before we started holding, but what does that have to do with . . ." The word "bomb" was beginning to sink in.

There was true panic in the copilot's eyes, Scott noticed. For eight months nothing had seemed to rattle Doc Hazzard. He was always steady as a rock. But now he was shaken.

"Doc, does Mrs. Henry know what's inside that pallet?"

Doc shook his head vigorously. "Not a clue. She says her husband was a government physicist. Whatever that is back there, he built it. I can't get anything else out of her, except that he's dead and left instructions for her to take it to the Pentagon. It's supposed to be a mockup of some sort. That's all she'll tell me, and she looks pretty scared."

Linda McCoy's hand gripped his shoulder with surprising strength. "Captain, please follow me back. I'm really worried about this." Her voice carried a tense urgency as well, and Scott scrambled out of the seat to follow her through the cockpit door.

Vivian Henry had steadied herself against the turbulence by holding on to a small handrail above the windows, but she was aware of little more than the container before her. She'd recognized the look of alarm on the face of the young female scientist several minutes before, then had seen it consume the copilot as well. They seemed unable to tell her what they were seeing, so she'd stepped forward and looked for herself at the small screen inside her ex-husband's creation. All she could see on the screen was text, but in her head she could hear the familiar snarl of her deceased husband's voice reaching out for her again with the horrid clarity of a can't-get-away nightmare.

What does he mean, "detonation"?

Maybe it was a burglar alarm of sorts, she thought in a frantic search for a benign explanation. She looked at the screen again. He obviously meant those words to be threatening. Once the shipment was within the Pentagon complex, Rogers Henry had devised a plan to keep it there.

Perhaps that's it! The threat is just a ploy to make sure they really study the mockup.

Nothing would happen. Nothing would explode. Vivian knew Rogers had always been passionate about defending his country. He would never attack it.

Doc Hazzard and Dr. McCoy had disappeared toward the cockpit, leaving her alone with her husband's handiwork. For the first time a cold, haunting shroud of fear began to cover her mind with an unexpected sense of helplessness and resignation. The old feeling of being cornered by him in some other impossible position, her back against a wall—often with his hands around her throat— came back with chilling familiarity. So many times she had assumed she was about to die at his hands—so many times she was sure he would carry out his threats. Until she'd mustered up enough courage to leave him, she'd grown used to feeling helpless and being resigned to her fate.

But there were other people involved this time, she reminded herself.

Vivian Henry looked out the nearest window, trying to shake the feeling of impending doom. Rogers had stopped appearing in her nightmares some time ago, but the rancid, electric feeling of impending attack had returned. It was a feeling she knew all too well. For years she'd had nightmares about his stalking her, nightmares she relived night after night with the visceral presence of pure hate reflected in his eyes when they fastened on her. His pupils would become tiny little pinpoints, and she would be transfixed, unable to move, until she awoke in total confusion.

She stared, mesmerized, at the partly exposed metal canister, sensing her ex-husband at his most sadistic.

Linda McCoy reappeared with the captain, both of them with averted eyes and strained faces as they looked inside at the glowing TV screen. She heard the young captain inhale sharply.

They would think her responsible for Rogers' threats, Vivian concluded. They would think she planned this, especially when they discovered she, too, had worked at Los Alamos.

APPROACH CONTROL FACILITY, WASHINGTON
NATIONAL AIRPORT—4:15 P.M. EDT

Pete Cooke had programmed his handheld radio scanner to intercept the paired frequencies used by the air-to-ground Flitephone system. It had been a random choice made months ago while researching a story on corporate jets, but when he overheard the Washington Approach controller's request for ScotAir 50 to call Miami on a Flitephone, he realized he could monitor both sides of the call. The opportunity was too much to pass up.

Pete stood toward the edge of the arrival lounge and listened through an earpiece until the call between the captain of the cargo aircraft and the FBI agent in Miami had concluded. He stood in thought for a moment. What could the FBI possibly be looking for?

The aircraft was still in a holding pattern somewhere overhead. The research project that had brought him to Washington could wait, he decided.

Pete walked as fast as he could through the heart of the terminal to the FAA's Washington Approach facility. A voice interrogated him through a small intercom on the wall, identified him as a licensed pilot who wanted to visit the facility, and buzzed him in. A supervisor checked his ID and then led the way to the controller working ScotAir 50.

"He's waiting for us to reopen the airport," the controller explained as he adjusted the speaker over his head so Cooke could listen.

Pete held up his scanner. "I was listening when you gave him that phone number, and I locked in on the call."

"You can do that?"

"It's on the airwaves. It's not private."

The controller held up a finger and issued instructions to one of the flights under his control before turning back to his guest. "What was the call about?"

Pete filled him in. "He may be requesting a vector to Andrews in a few minutes. Whatever the FBI thinks he may have on board, it's got their undivided attention."

"Drugs, you think?"

Pete started to reply, but the controller was already back on microphone issuing more instructions to his flights. Drugs were an easy assumption, but why would the FBI alert the crew if they suspected the crew of smuggling? And why was the FBI involved instead of DEA?

No, he concluded, drugs didn't make sense.

The controller let go of his microphone button and tried again. "You think it's drugs, then?"

Pete shook his head. "No. Something tells me it's far more serious."

FBI HEADQUARTERS, WASHINGTON, D.C.— 4:15 P.M. EDT

A growing number of people had been filtering into a small conference room near the deputy director's office since the FBI's Miami agents had taken charge hours before. The news that the most likely target was a Boeing 727 now circling the Beltway jolted the collection of agents and staff personnel into a team, and with word of the call between the Miami agent in charge and the captain of the cargo aircraft, the FBI took control of the situation.

Assistant Director Tony DiStefano began a quick briefing to bring everyone up to date. Notepads, steno books, and telephone consoles were strewn everywhere, along with three portable notebook computers hooked up to phone lines.

"Okay, the Navy tells us they've got another neutron sniffer at Patuxent River Naval Air Station just south of here, and the reason that's important is because we won't know whether the nuclear material that set off the Miami machine is on board that 727 until we subject it to another neutron bombardment. A bunch of our FBI people happen to be at that naval air station right now, attending some sort of terrorist workshop. They couldn't get conference space at Quantico, so all the experts will be there. Problem is, the Navy doesn't have a cargo aircraft at Pax River that can fly the sniffer to Andrews. It's about eight feet square and weighs over a ton, and they're going to put it on a flatbed truck and rush it there with a light-and-siren escort. Should take about ninety minutes. George, you talked with Andrews?"

A silver-haired man toward the end of the table spoke up.

"They'll let them in the back gate. The parking place for the 727's all arranged."

"Sir, we've got other problems." A woman in her mid-thirties was holding up a pencil for attention as she rested a telephone receiver on her shoulder.

"Go ahead, Donna," the assistant director replied.

"CIA is yelling that we shouldn't rule out foreign involvement . . . they're sending several of their people over here from Langley. The Nuclear Regulatory Agency is lobbying the National Security Council staff to participate, and the FAA is about to start a turf war over who can order this airplane to land and where. Alcohol, Tobacco, and Firearms is demanding a role in this. They say they have some nuclear terrorist experts as well."

The FBI assistant director threw his head back and snorted before looking back at her. "Screw 'em! We're in charge. We're going to get that airplane on the ground, get the sniffer in, and find out whether they're carrying nuclear material. If so, then and only then will we turn it over."

A younger agent in shirtsleeves had been on the phone. He stood up now and held out the receiver.

"Sir?"

"Yes?"

"I've got the Air Force's Pentagon command post on the line. A Major General Goddard, I believe. He says he has the President's authority to tell you to forget bringing that airplane anywhere close to Andrews with suspected nuclear material on board."

ABOARD SCOTAIR 50 — 4:15 P.M. EDT

The cargo cabin of his 727 was too noisy, so Scott McKay ushered Vivian Henry and Linda McCoy back to the cockpit before trying to talk. With Linda standing beside him next to the engineer's seat, he waited until Vivian Henry sat down sideways in the first observer's chair. The leading edge of Hurricane Sigrid had already moved across the Beltway, and the ride at ten thousand feet was increasingly turbulent. Both Scott and Linda braced themselves against the continuous irritating motion.

"Mrs. Henry, this may be serious," Scott began.

She nodded, her left arm resting on the back of the empty captain's seat as she rubbed her temple.

"I know," she said quietly.

"While you were back there . . ."

"Please call me Vivian," she added.

"Okay. Vivian. While you were back there, an FBI agent called from Miami." Scott glanced back at Linda. "Dr. McCoy, you don't know this yet, either."

"Linda," she said.

"Okay. Vivian. Linda. We're carrying cargo for both of you. Linda, I don't know what's inside yours. You do. Vivian, you say you do *not* know what's inside yours, but there's a frightening threat on that computer screen back there. The FBI tells me they've been searching all morning for a package of some sort which contains hazardous material that came through Miami while we were there. They seem to be convinced we're carrying it." Scott turned to Linda again, whose eyes had turned wide with concern. She straightened up as if challenged.

"Not in my stuff! There's nothing in my cargo which could be called hazardous in any way. What are they looking for?"

"I don't know. He wasn't specific. I don't think he wanted to tell me over a radiotelephone, but I thought for a moment . . . until you came up about Vivian's cargo . . . I thought, you know, Miami might equate to drugs and chemicals."

"No way," Linda said again. "I've had my things under my personal control since leaving McMurdo Sound."

Scott turned to Vivian. "Vivian, I need you to tell me everything you can about what your husband might have built, and why you're here in the first place. Why were you shipping this thing to Washington? What could it be? Why is the Pentagon mentioned?"

Vivian Henry met Scott McKay's gaze and looked at him steadily as Linda McCoy's voice echoed in his ear.

"Vivian, I was watching you back there. I got the feeling you don't have a clue what's in that container. Is that suspicion accurate?"

Vivian's gaze shifted to Linda.

"I . . . thought it was . . . something else. I didn't expect it to be powered or have a computer inside."

The 727 hit a patch of moderate turbulence, the wild bouncing causing Scott to lean forward and search the sky ahead before standing up again and looking back at Vivian.

"Do you know what it *is,* though?" Scott pressed.

"I can only theorize," she began, "that Rogers, my ex-husband, has created a dangerous, boorish plot—and put me right in the middle."

Scott raised his hands in a gesture of puzzlement. "Plot? What do you mean, 'plot'? Who *was* he? What was his specialty?"

Scott was aware of Doc on his right as the big copilot leaned to the left to hear the answer. Jerry Christian had swiveled his chair to the front and was sitting quietly forward, his hands clasped in front of him as he watched Vivian's eyes, glancing only occasionally at the windscreen as the turbulence continued.

Vivian Henry took a deep breath. "Very well. Let me try to tell you what I do know, because right now, I'm . . . confused and mortified that I'm . . . that what I've done is worrying everyone. And now it seems maybe there's good reason to worry. I'm . . . I'm beginning to get frightened."

She looked at Linda, then back at Scott, her voice softer than before, her words filtering through a veil of embarrassment.

"My husband, Captain, was a government nuclear physicist— the one who discovered the theoretical existence of a phenomenon he named the Medusa Effect, a destructive continent-sized convulsion of electromagnetic energy."

"The *Medusa Effect?*" Scott asked, turning to Jerry, then glancing at Doc.

Both shrugged.

Vivian nodded. "Rogers claimed it was the ultimate EMP, or electromagnetic pulse, and that it could destroy a modern society's ability to communicate, compute, transmit electricity, or use electronic circuits of any sort."

"I've heard of EMPs," Jerry said.

"The Navy was always trying to make our electronics resistant to any EMP the Soviets might create," Scott said.

"This was in the 1960's," she continued, falling silent for a few seconds as her eyes strayed to Doc's, then down to the floor. She took another deep breath as her right hand came up to her chest. "I'm sorry, but I'm very upset about this."

Linda McCoy gently placed her hand on Vivian's shoulder.

"Please go on, Vivian. We need to know."

Vivian looked at Linda and tried to smile. "Rogers was ahead of his time. He knew we would eventually become dependent on computers and computer codes, and that the United States had to develop Medusa first or risk being neutralized or blackmailed."

"So," Scott added, "what we've got aboard may be some sort of electromagnetic pulse generator?"

"Not exactly," Vivian said. "It's a mockup, but I suppose he wanted to be dramatic and embarrass me one last time."

"Why would he want to do that?" Jerry asked.

Vivian's eyes seemed to be looking through him as she weighed how much to say about the abusive genius who had been her husband and captor for so long.

"He . . . could be very cruel to me," she said at last.

"Vivian, did this thing come from a government lab somewhere?"

She shook her head no.

"Then where?" Scott asked.

"From our garage. Let me explain. In 1977, they terminated his research program near Denver, dispersed his research team, and when he refused to give up trying to design Medusa, they labeled him psychologically unreliable and retired him. We moved to Florida, but he was single-minded. He kept researching on his own and built his own lab there in our garage. This mockup, I believe, was constructed there."

"But what is it a mockup *of*?" Scott asked again.

"The object of his life's work," she said simply. "It's a mockup of the apparatus which creates the Medusa Effect."

"And he ordered you to bring it in person to the Pentagon?" Scott's voice carried an incredulous tone. He glanced at Linda, who was staring quietly at the elegant woman in the jumpseat.

"It's a bit more complicated than that," she said without emotion. She looked toward the cockpit door and gestured in that direction.

"Vivian," Scott prompted, "I still need an answer to the basic question. What kind of apparatus creates the Medusa Effect? A bomb? I mean, that thing is threatening to detonate. A bomb detonates."

Vivian Henry looked up again.

"I don't really know. It was a hopelessly complicated explanation I could never quite absorb. My background was nuclear engineering, but this is theoretical physics. Anyway, all I'm sure of is what's supposed to trigger the whole process."

"And that would be?"

She didn't respond.

"Vivian?"

She looked up again sharply, took a deep breath, and exhaled before answering.

"To create a Medusa Wave, you first need a thermonuclear explosion."

8
• • • •

One of the sixteen men and women working telephones and computer terminals in the tense atmosphere of the conference room spoke a few words into a receiver and turned to the man in charge.

"I've got him. Line three, sir."

Tony DiStefano, the assistant director of the FBI, flashed a thumbs-up sign and grabbed a telephone.

"ScotAir?"

"Yes?"

"You're"—he consulted a hastily scribbled note—"Captain McKay? Scott McKay?"

"Yes. Who're you?"

DiStefano identified himself and the fact that FBI headquarters in Washington had taken over control of the crisis.

"Okay," the pilot said. "What do you want us to do? Since you're in D.C., you know the winds are getting pretty high."

"We know, Captain, but we're going to bring you down at Patuxent River Naval Air Station. You know the place?"

The mention of the Navy's flight test center some fifty miles southeast of the Beltway on Chesapeake Bay was startling. "I know it well, but why Pax River?" Scott asked. It would be even closer to the oncoming hurricane.

"Because," the FBI official replied, "that's the only place close enough that has the equipment to examine your cargo."

Tony DiStefano braced for the question he knew would crackle through the pilot's mind. A few seconds of silence passed before the captain replied.

"Ah, Director DiStefano, was it?"

"Yes, but that's *Assistant* Director. I'm under the Deputy Director."

"Okay," Scott began. "Your man in Miami said you were looking for hazardous material. Now you want us to fly closer to that hurricane because you've got special equipment at Pax River. What *kind* of equipment, Mr. DiStefano? What is it, exactly, that you think we've got on board?"

"Captain, I'd rather not . . ."

"No, dammit! I need to know what I'm dealing with up here. I haven't checked the winds at Pax River, but they've got to be scary by now. Before I go try to land there, I want a straight answer. What on earth do you think we've got on board this airplane?"

In the cockpit of ScotAir 50 Scott McKay realized he was holding his breath. Dr. Linda McCoy was standing beside him, trying to listen.

Somehow the FBI already believed that the contents of Vivian Henry's cargo were dangerous, but *how* dangerous? If Vivian's cargo was really nothing more than a mockup being used in an elaborate hoax as she believed, why was the FBI involved?

Or could the contraband be in Linda's cargo without her knowledge? After all, her stuff came in from South America.

When the call began, Linda McCoy pointed to the handset and Scott kept the receiver turned slightly so she could press her ear against the edge of it and hear, too, her face occasionally touching his as they stood in the small aisle way behind the flight engineer's seat trying to brace themselves against the continuous turbulence. Somehow the feeling of her hair on the side of his face—the nearness of her—was comforting.

Scott realized he was shaking slightly inside. The suspicion that he was dealing with something far beyond his control was making it difficult to stay focused. He would have to tell DiStefano about the container and the screen and the warning messages, but first he needed to know precisely what it was that had spooked the Federal Bureau of Investigation of the United States.

Tony DiStefano's staff was used to his progressive signals of internal upheaval, from the rhythmic patting of his bald head to the rubbing of his brow. For the last few seconds he'd progressed to furiously rubbing his eyes as he tried to decide how much to tell the captain.

If I want this guy's complete cooperation, I've got to be straight with him.

DiStefano took a deep breath, steadied himself, and picked up the receiver again.

"Captain, based on some very sophisticated detection equipment at Miami and what it recorded this morning when you left, we believe there's something in your airplane that may be extremely dangerous, ah, nuclear material."

DiStefano could hear another voice, a female voice, murmur something in the background before the captain replied.

"Uh, Mr. DiStefano, when you say nuclear material, do you mean something like plutonium?"

DiStefano glanced at his resident nuclear expert, an agent who had been directed to listen in on another extension. The man nodded.

"Yes, Captain, that's exactly the category we're talking about. Are you familiar with such material?"

"Only as a layman."

Tony DiStefano motioned to the agent to get a pen and pick up the extension. "Captain, by the way, can you give me the full names of everyone on board, including your two passengers?"

Scott passed all five names. They were entered in the FBI's computer system immediately and several other agents shot out of the room in pursuit of background information. DiStefano cleared his throat and repositioned the phone to his ear. "Okay, please head for Pax River as fast as you can. You'll be met on the ramp there by one of our people and a Navy captain. Cooperate fully with them."

"Mr. DiStefano?"

"Yes?"

"There's . . . something else," Scott began. "There's something you need to know . . . something strange that's been going on up here."

Scott held the microphone as his mind raced through the problem.

What do I say now? Do I just blurt out the possibility that we might have an activated thermonuclear weapon aboard that could incinerate millions of people in the next few seconds and vaporize Washington, D.C., in the process?

"Go ahead, Captain, I'm listening."

"Okay, bear with me, please. This is very odd."

APPROACH CONTROL FACILITY, WASHINGTON
NATIONAL AIRPORT—4:20 P.M. EDT

Pete Cooke said nothing to the controller as he listened to the new Flitephone conversation between ScotAir 50 and the FBI. He slid into an extra chair as quietly as possible and stayed out of the way behind the controller's console as he began scribbling notes. The fact that FBI headquarters and an assistant director were involved raised the stakes even more.

But why did they want him to go to Pax River? The explanation had left Pete stunned.

My God, plutonium! No wonder the FBI is working the case.

Pete wrote down the names of those aboard as they were being passed to the FBI. The name of Dr. Linda McCoy seemed familiar, but from where he wasn't sure. For a few seconds he was so absorbed in trying to place her that the captain's words about "something strange" nearly passed unnoticed.

The captain was describing a pallet of cargo he had aboard—a metal container and a screen displaying a message the captain slowly repeated word for word.

WHAT?

Pete pressed the earpiece deeper into his ear, straining to hear every word as the pilot described the warning on the screen.

He reread his hastily scribbled notes, wishing his handwriting had not deteriorated so much in previous years.

"WARNING! The fact that this device is now located within the physical confines of the Pentagon has been detected and locked in memory. ANY ATTEMPT TO MOVE THIS DEVICE FROM ITS PRESENT LOCATION—OR ANY ATTEMPT TO DEAC-TIVATE—WILL RESULT IN INSTANT DETONATION!"

Detonation! My God, what does that mean?

Pete stood up and moved silently behind the controller, mentally comparing the position of ScotAir 50 on the screen with the approximate position of the Pentagon.

They were significantly different! The aircraft might have passed over the Pentagon, but it was holding between eight and eighteen miles away now, and the thing in the cargo compartment of ScotAir 50 didn't seem to know it.

Pete sat back down, his mind racing: *Suspected plutonium . . . a message threatening detonation . . . the FBI is involved . . . a large metal container on a cargo aircraft . . .*

My God in Heaven, they've got a live nuke flying around over D.C.!

The temptation to run to the nearest phone and call his editor was strong, but was it the right thing to do? The story was breaking in front of him, but the next edition of his newspaper was fourteen hours away. This was probably one for the broadcasters, but it was highly likely that he was the only reporter in the country who had any idea what was going on just a few miles away.

But what *did* he know?

Pete could feel his heartbeat accelerate. It was suddenly very warm in the otherwise slightly cool control room.

Suppose this is a test, and I panic everyone in the country into thinking there's some sort of nuclear bomb flying over the seat of government of the United States. Maybe I've missed something.

The consequences of getting it wrong were too thunderous and frightening to contemplate.

The voice of one of ScotAir's pilots coming from the controller's overhead speaker cut through the shock, reaffirming that at least part of the conversation he'd overheard had been real.

"Ah, Washington Approach, ScotAir Fifty. Sir, we need an immediate vector to Patuxent River Naval Air Station, and the latest weather there, if you have time."

The controller shot a questioning glance back at his guest. Pete Cooke moved the chair forward and tried to sound normal.

"The FBI's ordered them to land there," he explained simply.

The controller nodded and turned back to the scope as he picked up a tie-line to arrange the clearance and get the weather.

"Roger, ScotAir Fifty. I have your request. Stand by, please."

ABOARD SCOTAIR 50—4:25 P.M. EDT

The wail of a new electronic warning horn from the cargo compartment reached the cockpit just as the revised clearance to Pax River was coming through. Doc remained at the controls with Jerry backing him up in the engineer's seat as Linda led the way to the back with Scott and Vivian following. This time the noise was many decibels higher in volume, and different in tone.

Linda swung around the rear of the container and pressed forward to read the screen as Scott approached on her heels, almost losing his balance as the 727 bounced through the turbulent air.

She touched the screen and the horn stopped instantly.

"The screen is changing," she said.

Scott pressed in beside her to read the message.

WARNING! THIS WEAPON IS NOW FULLY ARMED. ALL ANTI-DISARMING SAFEGUARDS ARE ACTIVATED. ONE PERSON—MRS. VIVIAN HENRY—POSSESSES THE ABILITY TO DISARM THIS WEAPON, PROVIDED SHE DOES SO IN PERSON WITHIN THE NEXT FIFTEEN MINUTES. IF NOT DEACTIVATED WITHIN FIFTEEN MINUTES, FINAL COUNTDOWN SEQUENCE WILL BEGIN.

The symbols 00:15:00 appeared and began counting backward.

Scott motioned Vivian over and she, too, pressed forward to read the words—which changed once again.

THE PRESENCE OF VIVIAN HENRY HAS BEEN DETECTED.

She jumped back. "How? How does it know I'm here?" Her voice was alarmed and almost indignant. Linda McCoy moved to her side and took her arm to calm her down. "He could . . . *it* could . . . be guessing."

A deep male voice boomed through the cargo cabin without warning, causing Vivian to feel trapped and doomed.

"Vivian, as the screen says, I can detect your presence. Are you curious as to how?"

Vivian gasped audibly as her left hand flew to her mouth, her eyes wide with fear.

Linda glanced at Scott, who looked at the container.

"There's a large speaker down there, I guess," he said. "That's either a tape or a computerized voice."

Linda turned to Vivian. "Is that your husband's voice?"

She nodded, breathing hard, as the voice began again, full of sarcastic expression and oily self-confidence. If it's a computer synthesizer, Linda concluded, it was very advanced.

"Step forward, Vivian, my dear, up to the screen. If the people gathered here want you to disarm this weapon, and I'm sure they do, all you have to do is enter some numbers. It's a simple task. Even a brainless idiot like you can do it."

Vivian remained rooted to the spot.
The computerized voice resumed with an angrier tone.

"STEP FORWARD, VIVIAN! I know that's you. The pacemaker your doctor implanted in 1991 was modified by me. It contains a special transponder so I could always locate you electronically. I know you're here, and I'll know if you try to leave, and if you try to leave, I'll detonate this device instantly."

"It's a digitalized voice, Vivian!" Scott said.
Vivian seemed transfixed, her hand over her mouth.
"It's not him, Vivian," Linda added. "It's a thing your husband programmed."
Vivian pulled away from Linda and squared her shoulders, then moved slowly back toward the screen. When she was within a foot, the voice resumed.

"Vivian Henry, you are the last chance every computer, database, telephone and communications switching center, and every other electronic circuit within two thousand miles has of remaining functional. If you screw this up, you'll doom Washington, D.C., the Pentagon, Washington National Airport, Arlington, and the economy of the United States to ruin. But to disarm this device, simply reach in, put your hand on the keypad beneath the screen, and key in our old four-digit PIN number from our joint banking account."

Vivian slowly inserted her hand, the familiar PIN numbers running through her mind over and over. Her stomach was twisted up in fear, and her hands were shaking, but she forced herself to push each number deliberately.

Linda McCoy stood a few feet away wondering what Rogers Henry had been trying to accomplish. If the threat was real, and if he was going to permit it to be disarmed, why the game? Why force his ex-wife to remember an old PIN number with the penalty for mistake being a nuclear detonation?

Why, indeed, unless he was toying with her.

"VIVIAN!" Linda yelled, starting toward her. "STOP!"

"What?" The final number had already been keyed as she turned toward Linda.

"He's setting you up to get it wrong!"

An ear-splitting blast of electronic sounds filled the compartment, followed by a new small beeping sound and the sarcastic digitalized voice of Rogers Henry once again.

"You entered the wrong PIN number, Vivian, so the countdown to detonation will now begin. This whole thing is your fault, Vivian.

Vivian turned back toward the device with an overwhelming feeling of rage. He had done it to her again! Even from the grave, he had set her up to take the blame for everything that went wrong, no matter how obvious the ploy. She felt a guttural scream begin in the back of her throat as she flung herself at the thing and pounded it with her fists.

"NO! NO, NO, NO, NO, NO!"

Linda McCoy moved toward her. "Vivian!"

"One-six-five-five! I got it right! I punched it in right, you son of a bitch!"

"If you hadn't left me, Vivian, there would have been better ways to introduce this weapon, and better ways to punish the fools in the federal government who tried to prevent the building of this weapon. Oh, by the way, say hello to Medusa. This sample proof-of-concept version is a twenty-megaton-yield nuclear device, specially built by me. Just in case anyone has any question about what's happening, let me make it clear: The U.S. military canceled my project, now, thanks to my stupid ex-wife, I'm going to cancel the rotten core of the U.S. military, and the nation can start over. The generals have precisely three hours and thirty minutes from this moment to

*evacuate Washington and the twenty-five-mile radius this
weapon will destroy. If there's immediate compliance, up to
one million lives can be saved, although I fully expect Medusa
to kill millions more, most of them, no doubt, useless bureaucrats. And, of course, there will be no way to protect against
the Medusa Wave this will create, nor prevent at least a million
more deaths from radiation poisoning in the next few months.
Perhaps future generations will thank you, Vivian, for stupidly
triggering Medusa. After all, the Pentagon and all of Washington, D.C., has outlived its usefulness. Think of this as a very
effective way to reduce the size of the federal government.*"

Scott and Linda moved in on either side of Vivian, taking her
arms and moving her back, away from the embodiment of Rogers
Henry, as the voice began again.

"*I detect you have moved a short distance away, Vivian. If
you move more than fifteen feet away, detonation will occur
instantly, and you will take a million more innocent people
with you who might otherwise be saved. You will remain here
and die in less than three hours and thirty minutes, or you can
die trying to walk away and murder more. Your choice, Vivian.*"

"Let me sit here. I'll stay here," Vivian told them as she sank to
the metal floor of the 727.

Scott looked at her in confusion. "You said it was a dummy! A
mockup! That's probably still the case, right?"

Vivian shook her head as Linda knelt beside her, feeling the
chill of the cold floor. "I'll find some blankets, Vivian, if you want
to stay here."

"I have no choice," she said. "He's thought of everything. He's
won again. He always said I'd never get away from him. He said
he'd kill me. Now he will."

"Is that true, Vivian, about the pacemaker?" Linda asked.

She nodded. "I have one. The date's right. A transmitter inside
would explain a lot of strange things."

Scott knelt beside her as well. "Vivian, he's already made a
mistake. He said it would explode if it left the Pentagon. We're

more than eight miles away from the Pentagon and moving constantly. It probably *is* just a mockup."

She was staring blankly at the device, but shaking her head in a slow resolute manner.

"That was wishful thinking, I'm afraid. I gave you false hope."

Linda and Scott looked at each other.

"What do you mean?" Scott managed.

She looked up at the young captain.

"I was married to Rogers Henry for thirty years. In all that time, I never once knew him to bluff."

9
• • • •

Pete Cooke left the Washington Approach Control facility as ScotAir 50 prepared to depart the holding pattern for Patuxent River Naval Air Station. This was a major story, and he needed to be there when the aircraft came down. But how? He needed privacy and a telephone to figure it out, and, he decided, an airline club room would do nicely.

Pete pulled out his membership card and headed for the American Admiral's Club, the small scanner still firmly plugged in his ear with the frequencies set to the Flitephone channels.

If he decides to start using a cellular telephone up there, I'm screwed! Pete thought. His scanner couldn't pick up cellular frequencies.

It took only a few minutes on *The Wall Street Journal*'s 800 line to New York to round up two researchers, his secretary, and another reporter and get them on the same speaker phone. Avoiding the impression that he was becoming paranoid was another matter.

"Someone's circling D.C. with a live nuclear bomb? But there's been nothing on the wire, Pete. What's your source?"

"Things do exist, Hillary, that have not been reported on the wire services. My sources are the actual phone calls between the FBI and the aircraft. I've been monitoring them. All of them."

Pete could hear the murmur of voices back in New York.

"Okay, listen up, everyone," he began. "This could be nothing, but it could be an incredibly major story I've stumbled upon. I need background help immediately. I need anything you can find on a scientist named Rogers Henry. He died two years ago in Miami, Florida, but I have nothing else on him. Wife's name is Vivian Henry. Also, I need information on a Dr. Linda McCoy. I know nothing about her, either, but her name rings a bell." He passed the remaining names of those on board just as the Flitephone frequencies came alive again.

"Gotta go. They're making another phone call from the plane. Call my cellular when you've got something."

FBI HEADQUARTERS, WASHINGTON, D.C.—
4:40 P.M. EDT

Tony DiStefano grabbed the proffered receiver and recognized the voice instantly.

"Captain McKay? What's up?"

"I was just getting ready to leave the holding pattern, sir, when . . ."

"Kill the 'sir' stuff, okay? Call me Tony."

"Okay. Ah, Tony, the bomb . . . I don't know any better way to put this . . . has started a countdown to detonation. The countdown is at a little less than three hours and thirty minutes. That's . . . ah . . . 8:01 P.M. There's a recorded voice back there too that says it's a twenty-megaton weapon that will vaporize everything within a twenty-five-mile radius. You remember what it threatened would happen if it was taken away from the Pentagon?"

"I remember. Remove it, it blows. But you said you were already between eight and eighteen miles away from the Pentagon as you flew that holding pattern. If the bomb was telling the truth, you'd be gone already. Obviously it knows you've left the Pentagon's coordinates."

"But, Tony, what if the bomb has a tolerance range of, say, twenty miles? If I stay within twenty miles, it's okay. If I fly twenty-one miles away, it detonates. I'm worried about going any farther. It's talking about killing millions of people and blowing away the entire capital. If this thing goes off while we're flying, the altitude of the burst will kill even more, and could blind anyone who makes the mistake of looking up."

"Calm down, Scott. Let's take this one step at a time."

"I'm trying to, but this scares the hell out of me. I'm certainly not anxious to die, but if I do, I sure don't want to be responsible for incinerating a few million people and two hundred years of American history. If we try to fly any farther from here, it may detonate."

"Whoa, fellow! We're not even sure it really *is* a bomb . . ." Scott's earlier words finally sank in. "Wait a minute, Scott. What do you mean, it's started a countdown? Tell me everything that's happened."

Tony DiStefano listened to Scott McKay summarize the events in the rear of the 727. He covered the mouthpiece with his hand long enough to whisper to one of the other agents in the room. "This is now a terrorist situation. Understand? We're classifying this now as domestic nuclear terrorism."

The sudden force of a high wind gust rattled the windows of the room they were in, causing everyone to look outside. Trees were whipping violently and sheets of rain were striking the windows periodically, announcing the arrival of the hurricane's leading edge.

Tony DiStefano closed his eyes for a few seconds and thought hard. He couldn't focus on the potential loss of life. He had to deal with the situation unemotionally.

"Has it said anything more about its position?" he asked.

The pilot's voice came back instantly. "No. But it is clear now that one of the aims of this maniac Rogers Henry was to torture his wife. She's back there now, by the device. It says it will detonate if she gets more than fifteen feet away. He's made her pacemaker into kind of a transponder. It knows where she is."

"Her *pace* . . ." Tony was rubbing his eyes again. "This thing makes a lot of detonation threats, doesn't it? Scott, it seems less concerned with where it is, than with making sure she's by it, right?"

"Seems that way, yes."

"Then . . . I think it's safe to leave. I know that's easy for me to say . . ."

The thought flashed through Tony's mind that an immediate detonation would begin with the line going dead and an incredibly bright light outside. Within seconds, he and the FBI building he was in would be literally blown away by the shock wave of the explosion.

He tried to shake off the chilling personalization of the threat and continue.

"Ah, Scott, I really think if it was telling the truth, you know, 'Take me away from the Pentagon and I'll blow,' you'd already be gone. Get the controllers to send you out to the southwest as fast as possible. Don't come back over the Beltway, because, well . . ."

"I know, just in case we're wrong. You're in D.C. too, right?"

"That's not the point, Scott, but, yes, I am."

There was a moment of silence from ScotAir, and Tony felt his heart skip a beat until McKay's voice returned to the line.

"I guess the people who'll meet us at Pax River are ready for this, huh, Tony? To disarm it, I mean?"

"We'll get them ready, Scott. Just get yourself there safely."

There was a hesitation from the aircraft.

"Tony, have you ever heard of a Medusa Wave?"

"A what?"

"Mrs. Henry, his ex-wife, told us he was working on something called the Medusa Weapon, or the Medusa Effect. It's an unbelievably large electromagnetic pulse. This device is claiming to be that weapon."

"We'll check it out, Scott. I can hardly think of anything worse than a twenty-megaton nuke over the White House. Can you keep this line open?"

"If you'll pay the bill." The pilot chuckled on the other end. "Yeah, we'll keep it open. I'll hand it over to Jerry, my engineer, as soon as he's finished getting Pax River weather. The winds a few minutes ago were gusting up to seventy knots."

"You can still land in that, right?"

"If the maximum crosswind doesn't get too high, yeah, I think so. But . . . it could get sporting."

"Define 'sporting,' Scott."

"Well, risky."

"How risky?"

The hesitation from ScotAir 50 was palpable.

"Well, if the crosswind is *too* severe . . . I mean, even a Boeing 727 has its limits."

PATUXENT RIVER NAVAL AIR STATION, MARYLAND—
4:45 P.M. EDT

Word reached the commanding officer of Patuxent River Naval Air Station that once again the plans had changed. It was bad enough that he'd had to prepare his people for the worst hurricane the base had faced in its history, but to have the FBI send him a civilian airliner with suspected nuclear material aboard solely because there were FBI experts at a conference on his base was just too much. There had been no directives from the Navy Department, just directives from the FBI, which wasn't even bothering to ask for his assent.

Yet, to keep peace between federal departments, he'd have to be diplomatic and help them out.

The unwelcome news that something more than stolen plutonium might be on board was flashed over from the command post as he stood behind his desk and scowled at the dark clouds and high winds already pummeling his field.

His yeoman appeared in the doorway holding a notepad and a wide-eyed look of disbelief.

"What now?"

"Sir, the FBI says they're not sure, but there might be a chance they've got an actual nuclear weapon on board that aircraft."

"WHAT?" He let the word reverberate around the walls of the office for a second as he tried to focus on what that really meant. "Good grief! What is it, some stolen military nuke?"

The yeoman was shaking her head. "No, sir. Apparently a home-built. And it may be armed."

"That does it!" the commander growled. "Any directives from the Pentagon about this?"

"No, sir."

"Then it's my decision?"

"Yes, sir."

"Call him back, the FBI agent you were speaking to. Tell him permission denied. Tell him they'll land that airliner here only over my cold dead body. We don't do armed ticking nukes at Pax River."

The yeoman smiled and nodded with enthusiasm. "Yes, *sir!*"

AMERICAN ADMIRAL'S CLUB, WASHINGTON
NATIONAL AIRPORT—4:45 P.M. EDT

After passing the details of the latest phone call from ScotAir 50 to his team in New York, Pete Cooke sat hunched over one of the desks in the American club room with his computer connected to a telephone jack. He had quickly logged onto the Internet and fired off search requests looking for any information about a scientist named Rogers Henry and a thing called the Medusa Effect.

His cellular phone rang again while he was waiting for answers, this time with Ira, the leader of his New York research team, on the other end.

"Pete, I've E-mailed a whole file of stuff on EMP weapons and the Medusa Project. Can you log in and get it?"

"Yeah, in just a minute. Give me a quick overview."

"Lord, Pete, I'm not sure you realize the significance of what you've stumbled on. This is terrifying stuff!"

"How so?"

"Well, to start with, do you have any idea what a twenty-megaton explosion over Washington, D.C., would do?"

"A vague idea."

"You'd be instant history, for one. But so would several million others. The entire city would be uninhabitable for many years. Millions would die within a year in terrible agony of radiation poisoning. Hiroshima had thousands of half-dead burn victims. We'd have millions. The number of people permanently blinded by an unexpected airborne blast could number in the hundreds of thousands. The fallout would spread on the winds of that hurricane all over the Southern United States, and, essentially, the entire U.S. government infrastructure would cease to exist."

"Good Lord!"

"The human agony would be unfathomable, Pete. That's just the beginning. You told me this guy Rogers Henry claimed to have developed a Medusa Wave weapon? Well, that might be correct. Dr. Rogers Henry was, in fact, the lead scientist on an EMP project throughout the sixties until it was canceled in 1977. Some of the information is deeply classified still, but you'd be astounded how much of it is now declassified and floating around various databases."

"What, exactly, *is* a Medusa Wave?"

There was a whistle from the other end. "Any nuclear explosion will create an electromagnetic pulse, but the Medusa Project was trying to design a bomb that would trigger a much larger, continent-wide secondary wave which could immobilize electronics, electric systems, communications, even electric motors, and ruin a gazillion computer chips over an entire continent. If the theory was accurate and such a device could be built, a sustained electromagnetic wave pulse like that could cripple all of Europe, or North America."

"You mean, where computer users would lose data?"

"How about five orders of magnitude worse. No, I mean where they'd have to replace every damn computer chip, disk drive, modem, or other piece of hardware completely. Every cellular phone and every computer-chip watch. Anything with a silicone chip is essentially destroyed. Turned to stone. That's where the name Medusa came from. Silicon chip sees Medusa, silicon chip turns to useless rock. Anyway, even if the hardware isn't ruined, a Medusa Wave would be crippling because it would also insert extra ones and zeros in computer codes which happen to be flowing through a processor as the event occurs."

"Meaning?"

"Meaning it doesn't take much to crash a major computer program these days. Remember the huge telephone system crash several years ago on the eastern seaboard?"

"Yeah, I do," Pete replied. "1991, I think. But as I recall, that was a programming error, not some outside electronic pulse."

"That's right. Some technician in an office down in Plano, Texas, inserted a total of three lines of code in a multimillion-line program one fine afternoon without testing the effects, and the entire East Coast switching system crashes."

"Okay, but what . . ."

"You know how they fixed it?"

"How?"

"Nothing else would work, so they just took out the three new lines of code and restored what was there before. Like magic, it ran again, but no one knew why. The whole program runs on these incredibly complex computer languge codes. They couldn't debug it because no living human being could decipher the monster their operating system had become. It's far worse today, and phone companies are not alone."

"How does that relate to this?"

"Vulnerability, Pete. Most communication systems, manufacturing systems, banking and financial systems have so many millions of lines of that kind of computer code, and so many patches to that code, no one has a prayer of understanding the whole thing.

Insert a few extra ones and zeros somewhere in there and it's like tampering with human DNA: God only knows what you're going to get!"

"You're saying that if a weapon like this went off . . ."

"Well, in addition to the small inconvenience of killing millions of Americans and wiping out every significant building in Washington, D.C., including the White House and the Capitol, killing most of the U.S. government, and creating human misery on a scale never experienced on this planet, the stock markets would come to a screeching halt, bank records would disappear, nothing could be processed, and the computer equipment itself would be ruined. We couldn't get any money, elevators would stop, hospitals would shut down, even sophisticated airliners would come out of the sky because their engines won't run without their computer controls. All phones would be down, so we couldn't even call in to yell at each other. No radar, no air traffic control, no pacemakers, no money, no services, no anything. And, Pete, it could take *six months* to just get all the computer systems replaced and running again, even if all the databases could be reconstructed. Pete, if this thing is real, even if it explodes offshore without hurting a soul, its electromagnetic effect will hobble this country."

"Good Lord!"

"To say the least. And there's more. You remember what a house of cards our international banking system has become? The whole rickety thing depends on computers to keep everything kited properly. Take the computers and the international communications away and the U.S. of A. is out of the game. We're talking theoretical worldwide financial collapse. Please, Pete, tell me this is a joke."

"It's not a joke, Ira," Pete replied. "I wish it was. Of course, we don't know it can really create all that havoc . . ."

"You'd better pray that thing doesn't go off *anywhere* then, buddy, unless you're on the barter system."

"Ira, do me a favor. Make sure all of you keep a tight lid on this. Seriously. I don't want to be responsible for creating a panic."

"But what if it's true? What if this nut really figured out the physics and this is the real thing?"

"I still don't want to create a panic."

"You already have. *I'm* panicked! I'm headed for the cash machine downstairs as soon as we hang up, and then I'm going to go cower in the lowest basement in the city."

"Don't take this wrong, but you don't count."

"Understood, Pete, but if Uncle Sam doesn't warn people, shouldn't we? At the very least, they should be evacuating D.C. Shouldn't we call our friends at the networks, or something?"

"We have friends at the networks?" Pete asked sarcastically.

"Well . . ." Ira's voice trailed off.

Pete sat in thought for a few seconds, trying to imagine public reaction to news of such an impending catastrophe.

"Only when we're sure, Ira. Only when we're absolutely sure."

ABOARD SCOTAIR 50—4:50 P.M. EDT

"Doc, I'll spell you for a few minutes if you want to stretch." Scott looked over at the copilot, who nodded and pulled his large hands away from the yoke as the Boeing bounced its way through the roiling air currents.

"You've got her," Doc replied. "Autopilot's engaged, we're on vector heading two-zero-zero, as discussed, more or less level at ten thousand, given the turbulence."

"Roger."

"I'm gonna go check on Mrs. Henry. Bellow on the PA if you need me."

"Doc." Scott looked up at the veteran pilot as he hesitated halfway out of his seat.

"Yeah?"

"If she's got to stay back there, I guess we'd better strap her down somehow."

Doc nodded. The use of a cargo strap for a seat belt would be undignified, but with the aircraft bucking in the turbulence and the potential violence of the landing ahead, the prospect of having her catapulted into the ceiling was not acceptable.

"I was thinking the same thing, Scott."

Jerry Christian turned around as Doc moved past his chair. "You need help?"

"Naw. I'll take care of it." He patted Jerry on the shoulder as he glanced back at Linda McCoy, who was sitting in the observer's seat watching with a question in her eyes as he moved toward the door. "Doctor, you stay put. Two of us moving around in this turbulence is enough. You strapped in?"

"No," she answered, looking down at her seat belt, which was hanging loose.

"It'd be a good idea to get it on."

Doc left the cockpit and scrambled down the passageway toward the back of the cargo cabin and around the edge of the device built by Rogers Henry.

Vivian Henry was sitting cross-legged on the aluminum cargo floor, staring at the metal face of the thing, an unfathomable expression on her face. The sight of a large man moving into her peripheral vision startled her momentarily, and she looked up at him with the expression of one in pain slowly recognizing the presence of a friend.

Doc was startled as well by the sight of her. For a fleeting moment warm memories of his maternal grandmother flooded back from early childhood. He'd traveled from his Arkansas home to spend several summers with her. Jenny, the pillar of society in Rockport, Maine, and the unyielding force that had held his family together through the Depression years, before he was born. Her dignity and femininity had stayed intact through the roughest of times, and the pictures of her as a strikingly beautiful woman holding her six-year-old grandson reminded him of Vivian Henry. He still missed Jenny. Her warmth and her wry sense of humor had been legendary in Rockport.

But this was someone else sitting like a prisoner before him, someone he didn't know, regardless of how familiar she seemed—someone who was roughly his age, and only a year or two younger than the eternal image of his grandmother he carried in his memory.

"How're you doing?" he asked, feeling suddenly self-conscious. How *could* she be doing under the circumstances? What a dumb question!

"I would prefer to find the 'off' switch as soon as possible," she said simply, her eyes drifting back to the device that had become her captor.

"Anything new?" Doc asked.

She shook her head. He briefed her on Pax River and the impending landing in high winds. "Vivian, we don't have seat belts back here in the cargo cabin, so I'm . . . going to have to use a cargo strap to hold you secure. It could get quite rough."

Her eyes latched onto Doc's suddenly. "Is there somewhere remote you could take us, and unload both this monstrosity and me, and get away?"

Doc knelt beside her and put his right hand on her shoulder.

"I . . . don't know, Vivian. Right now, we just need to get ourselves to someone who knows how to disarm it."

"He's dead."

"Pardon?"

"The only person who knew how to disarm it was Rogers, and he's dead. Believe me, I know. I worked with him for years at Los Alamos. I was an engineer helping his team construct the exotic things they designed, but he knew more than all of the rest of us combined on the subject of triggers. He knew all the tricks for arming and disarming and invented most of them. If he decided this wasn't to be disarmed, there will be no way to disarm it." She was trying to remain calm, but he heard a small catch in her voice and realized she had choked back a sob before quickly regaining control. She waved her hand at the device as she struggled to maintain her composure. He decided not to call attention to the effort.

"Vivian, I've been wondering about something. I can't figure out how this thing could sit for two years with the batteries remaining fresh. I mean, it has to have batteries."

She took a slightly ragged breath. "When I entered his workshop last week for the first time, I noticed there was a wire in the back going into the wall. I should have been suspicious, but I was trained not to question anything he did, and I never thought of it until now. It must have been a power cord, but I didn't realize it at the time. I don't know what I thought it was."

The moment of silence seemed awkward, and he found himself searching for something to say as they both looked around in response to a particularly severe jolt of turbulence.

Doc cleared his throat. "You know, I think this has to be an elaborate bluff. I mean, he'd need plutonium to make this Medusa Effect work, wouldn't he, and you don't just waltz down to the corner 7-Eleven for a container of plutonium, right?"

The reassurance had no effect. Her eyes looked deeply into his, the anguish showing clearly. She looked back at the device for the longest time, the sound of the engines and the slipstream their only audible companion until her voice reached his ears again.

"I told the captain," she said.

"Pardon?"

She looked him squarely in the eye. "Rogers never bluffed. The fact is, he *could* have obtained plutonium, which means that we must consider this a live nuclear weapon, capable of killing millions of innocent people. I can't even imagine the damage it could do, even if the Medusa Effect doesn't work."

The words hit Doc Hazzard like a body blow. Up to that moment the possibility that they were flying around with a genuine nuclear bomb had been unlikely.

Remote.

But in an instant his confidence crumbled.

"Vivian, you said it was a mockup! You were convinced."

She shook her head slowly.

"I *was* convinced. But I was wrong."

10

. . . .

This is becoming unmanageable.

Tony DiStefano realized the three agents trying to update him were not going to stop talking simultaneously.

"Hey! *Hey!* HEY!" He held up his hand to silence them and waited until all eyes in the room were on him and all voices had paused in midsentence.

"If we don't do this in an orderly way, we're going to screw it up!" He looked at the three people waiting with papers in hand and pointed to them one by one.

"Bill, you first. What do you have?"

"Weather report at Pax River. It's getting worse."

"Okay. Donna, how about you?"

"Background information on the Henrys. You won't believe it."

"Don't editorialize. And, Jim?"

"Jake."

"Sorry, Jake. How about you?"

"The Navy's decided he can't land there."

"Where? He can't land where?"

"Pax River. The commander there has closed the base."

"Dammit! Okay, Bill, Donna, stand by. Jake, who passed *that* word?"

"The Navy command post at the Pentagon. They're still holding."

"Get them for me."

The agent immediately handed Tony a receiver and punched a blinking light on the telephone console. The conversation was short and tense. Tony replaced the receiver and turned back to the agent called Jake.

"Call the director's office and tell Janie, his secretary, I'm on my way there. I need the director to work on the White House Situation Room, NSC, and the Secretary of Defense to force the Navy to get that base reopened. We don't have time to screw around!" He whirled toward the other two agents who had been waiting to brief him.

"Donna? Call the aircraft. Tell the captain—his name is Mc-Kay—have the air traffic people put him in some sort of holding pattern near Pax River and wait for instructions."

"Should I tell him they closed the base?"

"Yes. But tell him I expect to have it fixed in a few minutes. Then find that open line to the Situation Room and brief them." Tony headed out the door, then came back.

"Bill."

"Yeah?"

"Follow me down the hall and tell me about the weather on the way."

The man leaped to his feet and headed for the door. "In a phrase, it's going to hell!"

WASHINGTON NATIONAL AIRPORT—5:01 P.M. EDT

A chorus of jet noise outside the American club room heralded the reopening of Washington National Airport and caused Pete Cooke to look up in surprise. The rain had abated somewhat, but the winds were rising steadily, the heavy gusts even rocking some of the jetliners as they prepared for pushback.

There was no way to get to Pax River in time. He had tried unsuccessfully to hire a helicopter before hearing that the Navy had closed the base. He would stay at National instead and keep digging while hoping his scanner continued to pick up the calls to the 727.

Pete scowled at the telephone. "Come on, come on! I don't have all century!" Ira had unearthed the name and number of Dr. William Barker, a long-retired coworker of Rogers Henry after a frantic search through the *Journal*'s own archives. The physicist was living in suburban Maryland, and with any luck, the man might even be home.

A woman answered, her voice suspicious as she reluctantly summoned her husband. He listened carefully as Pete Cooke identified himself as a *Wall Street Journal* reporter calling from Washington trying to find out more about Rogers Henry, the scientist.

"I worked with Henry for over a decade," Dr. Barker said. *"For* him, actually. You know he's dead?"

"Yes, sir. Two years ago, if that's correct."

"That's right. Pancreatic cancer. From diagnosis to death it took less than nine months. Why are you asking about him?"

Pete closed his eyes and made a hip-shot decision.

"Doctor, I need your help in understanding something that's occurring right now, this very moment, over suburban Washington. I have reason to believe that before he died, Rogers Henry constructed an operating model of the weapon you helped him work on."

"What?"

"Yes, sir. I also have good reason to believe that weapon is at this moment armed, in an airplane over the Washington, D.C., area, and on the verge of . . . detonating."

Silence.

"Sir?"

"You say you're from *The Wall Street Journal?"* Dr. Barker asked.

"Yes."

"Your name's Cooke?"

"Pete Cooke. That's right."

"Your home office know what phone line you're sitting in front of right now?"

"Ah yes, but . . ."

"I'll call you back."

The line went dead. Pete stared at the phone wondering whether to redial the physicist's number or give him a few minutes.

Of course! He'd be well trained to never pass information unless he initiated the call. He'll call New York to check on me.

Pete dialed Ira's number in New York and alerted him to pass on the club room number in Washington the second the scientist called.

Within two minutes the phone rang with the physicist on the other end.

"Is this Pete Cooke?"

"Yes."

"Okay. This is Bill Barker again. I'm satisfied you are who you say you are. How much do you know about the Medusa Project?"

"Only the name and the fact it involved an attempt to generate an electromagnetic pulse."

There was a sarcastic laugh from the other end.

"Pulse, hell. Any five-and-dime nuke can generate an EMP. We were working on the ultimate weapon for modern warfare, a bomb that would competely shut down a computer-based country."

"Did you succeed?" Pete shot back.

There was silence on the other end for so long, Pete began to wonder if the line had gone dead.

"Are we on deep background here? Do I have your word you won't quote me?"

"If you want to be on background, Dr. Barker, you've got my word."

"Mr. Cooke, I signed the usual oath not to talk, and I sure don't want to go to jail, but frankly I'm not sure what is and isn't classified anymore. Anyway, I won't tell you *how* to do anything, but I will tell you that *we* truly believed we were on the threshold of an incredible breakthrough when they canceled the project."

"Why did they cancel it?"

"Because Jimmy Carter decided to throw a bone to the Soviets. *He* didn't think we were that close and he wasn't willing to spend the money to find out. The Soviets *did* believe we could do it. In fact, they were terrified, so they pressured the devil out of Carter to cut us off, and the little wus capitulated. I mean, we were right *there*! Trembling on the brink. A few more months of running calculations, one round of field tests to see if we could create a tiny secondary effect, and I truly think we might have validated the theory."

"Could Rogers Henry have completed the work on his own?"

The answer came without a second's hesitation. "If the theory was right, yes. They kept all the notes when they threw us out, but I'm sure Rogers had duplicates of everything. I always suspected he was violating the rules about keeping personal files, even taking equipment home. After all, the Medusa was *his* baby. He had the knowledge, he had the myopic drive, he just didn't have any way of proving it worked without actual tests, which would have been risky. But he's been dead for two years. So tell me, Mr. Cooke, what in hell did you mean about there being a working model over Washington ready to explode?"

Pete filled him in on everything he knew so far, including the puzzling fact that the device seemed to think it was in the Pentagon. He heard the receiver being moved to the physicist's other hand, and a long exhaled breath.

"My God! After all this time, I would think . . . Well, I don't see how. I mean, the man's been dead for two years!"

"Interesting," Pete replied. "I expected you to say that Henry couldn't have obtained the plutonium."

There was a short, sharp laugh on the other end. "Oh, believe me, Mr. Cooke, Rogers could have squirreled away enough plutonium. Remember he was the boss, the head of the program. He could have taken anything he wanted over time. It's the question of *why* he'd want to build a real weapon I can't answer. I mean, what possible motivation would he have had?"

"That's . . . what I'm asking you. We know his ex-wife is the one who arranged to ship the weapon."

The shock on the other end was palpable.

"*What?* You say Vivian is involved?"

"That's right."

"How?"

"She's aboard the aircraft, and if I heard correctly, the device is programmed to detonate if she moves more than fifteen feet away from it. Killing her seems to be a part of the plan."

"Oh Jesus, he *was* serious!"

"About what, sir?"

Another long pause. "About murdering his ex-wife. The last time I talked with Rogers was three years ago. He had called me with some screwy question about where we'd obtained certain parts years ago. I remember thinking it was an odd request. I almost asked him if he was building his own bomb as a hobby, but he didn't have much of a sense of humor. I did make the mistake of asking about Vivian, though. She was a classy, beautiful woman— one of our engineers at Los Alamos, in fact, when he married her. I was always convinced that Rogers was abusing her. I'd always figured that someday she'd get enough and leave him. Anyway, after I asked casually about Vivian, it took me an hour to get the bastard off the phone. All he wanted to do was rage and tell me how much he hated her for leaving him, how evil *she* was, and how she had plotted to destroy him, which was ridiculous. He wanted her dead."

"So he has . . . he *had* . . . a reason to hurt her, Dr. Barker?"

"In *his* twisted mind, yes. He told me outright how much he wanted to kill her, slowly and painfully. Told me he dreamed of it. I thought it was just steam. I *hoped* it was just steam. I mean, this man had been a responsible world-class scientist. Just the thought of him trying to blow up Washington along with several million people to get his wife is beyond surreal!"

"Doctor, that brings up a key question: Do you think he was capable of doing just that? Was he capable of attacking his own country with a nuclear weapon?"

"Oh jeez!"

The reply was awash with disgust, followed by silence. Pete hurried to fill it. "I mean, was he that unbalanced?"

Dr. Barker's voice came back, low and steady. "Could he have set a nuclear trap for his wife and ignored the incredible human damage it would have caused? I doubt it. I can tell you he was well aware of what the blast over Hiroshima had done, and he had always professed to be horrified at the carnage the Japanese suffered for being slow to surrender. Hiroshima was his motivation to build a weapon that would kill a country's economy, not its people. But that was before our program was terminated, and before he began going very strange on us."

"So was he capable of mass murder?"

"How the hell can anyone know that, Mr. Cooke? I know he hated Vivian. I know he hated the Department of Energy and the Department of Defense. I know he hated President Carter—we *all* referred to him as Jimmy the Small. But if Rogers really succeeded in creating a Medusa weapon, he would know the incredible damage that the triggering nuclear blast could do, not to mention what the Medusa would do to everyone who has as much as a bank account. He would have known that a Medusa Wave would go far beyond just vaporizing the military puzzle palace and devastating D.C." The physicist's voice trailed off. "You said twenty megatons. You do realize what an airborne twenty-megaton thermonuclear bomb would do to humans below, don't you? You do know that's the engine of a Medusa Weapon?"

"Yes, I know."

"Lord! You say they're right now flying over *Washington?*"

"Actually, sir, they've sent them to Patuxent River Naval Air Station about fifty miles south."

"That's still too close! They've got to get that airplane far, far away, immediately!"

"So"—Pete pushed—"you can't be certain that he's capable of doing all this?"

"You misunderstood me, Mr. Cooke. I *can* be certain." Pete heard an ominous, deadly serious tone come into William Barker's voice. "That's what's scaring the living hell out of me," Barker continued. "When I remember the pure hate in Rogers' voice, I have to tell you I wasn't talking to a sane man. Could Rogers have planned something like this? Yes. Sadly, the answer is yes."

FBI HEADQUARTERS, WASHINGTON, D.C.—
5:05 P.M. EDT

In the midst of the ringing phones and tense voices filling the conference room with urgency, the brief absence of one FBI agent had gone unnoticed—just as the young agent had planned. Hearing that ScotAir 50 was being sent to Patuxent River Naval Air Station left him no choice, since his sister and two young nieces lived on the base. While his brother-in-law was safely overseas in Rota, Spain, the lieutenant commander's family was sitting innocently in the flight path of an armed thermonuclear device.

He had to do something.

The agent shut his office door and pulled out his handheld cellular phone to dial his sister's home number in Pax River. It took four rings before her voice reached his ear.

"Hello?"

"Jolene? This is Tom. I've only got a second. Are the girls both there?"

"Why are you whispering, Tom?"

"Listen to me very closely," he said. "You've got to grab the girls, get in the car, and head out of there *immediately.*"

She protested. There were endless reasons not to leave. The

wind was already at gale force, the rain was terrible, they needed to watch the base house for wind damage . . .

"JOLENE! For Chrissakes, listen. Get out of there! Go north as fast as possible. Head for the summer cottage in New Jersey, but move."

He felt the risks increasing exponentially. He was on a cellular. A cellular could be monitored by anyone, including other departments of the FBI. It was only slightly less risky than an FBI office phone.

It was obvious she wasn't going to budge without a reason, and time was running out. With little more than a second's hesitation he filled in the blanks of what was headed their way, and what it could do.

And the protests stopped.

"My God, Tom, it's *armed*? Why haven't we been told?"

"They can't evacuate everyone. Jolene, we're wasting time! Get the girls and go. Don't tell a soul why. Just go. Now. Please!"

"Okay. Okay, we're gone."

"Keep your car phone on," he said as an afterthought.

But the line was already dead.

SILVER SPRING, MARYLAND—5:10 P.M. EDT

Dr. William Barker—the former coworker of Rogers Henry—had listened to Pete Cooke's thank-you and replaced the receiver in a state of shock. How could Rogers have built a Medusa alone? And if he really had, how could he use it for such evil purposes—for *mass murder*?

The retired scientist looked around suddenly, as if afraid he was being watched. What should he do now? Should he tell the government? They already knew. Should he call the media? But Pete Cooke *was* the media, he reminded himself. Or should he concentrate on trying to find some way to protect his computers and disk drives?

He refused to consider an airburst near D.C. There wouldn't be time to prepare for that or run anywhere. No, if they were sending the bomb to Pax River and it detonated there accidentally, he would live through it, but the electronic destruction would be incredible. The Medusa Wave, however large or small, would destroy every computer-based service he depended on.

The bank accounts should be first. Cash out everything. In a few hours it might be too late.

This can't be happening! He realized he had actually considered the possibility he was dreaming.

Another disturbing memory kept nagging at him. The reporter had asked if he might know how such a device could be defused.

"If Rogers didn't want it defused," he'd told Cooke, "it will be impossible to defuse. He knew virtually all the tricks."

That meant, of course, that if it was counting down . . .

The fifth ring reasserted the telephone's presence on his consciousness, and he grabbed the receiver, surprised to hear the voice of another alumnus of the Medusa Project.

"Did you see the E-mail I sent you in the last twenty minutes?" the caller asked.

"No. Why?"

"Someone's surfing around the Internet asking frantic questions about the Medusa Wave and about Rogers. Any idea what's up?"

"You won't believe it."

"That's what you used to say at Sandia Labs back in Albuquerque, and my response is still the same: Try me."

FBI HEADQUARTERS, WASHINGTON, D.C.—
5:10 P.M. EDT

Tony DiStefano thanked the FBI director and charged out the door to resume his mission, thankful that a heated debate had finally concluded in the basement of the White House. The question that had momentarily convulsed the senior advisors of the executive branch was whether the government of the United States really believed the device aboard ScotAir 50 was an armed nuclear weapon which could, in fact, detonate.

"So, do we believe, or don't we?" Tony had asked as the director replaced the phone.

"We believe. According to the Situation Room, it is, it can, and if those nuclear wizards at Pax River can't defuse it, it will. At least we're getting it fifty miles south of here, but if that damn thing should somehow go off while they're working on it . . ."

"So the base commander is overruled?"

"The base commander is toast if he tries to interfere. The Navy finally ordered him to stand aside."

Tony had started for the door before the director's voice stopped him.

"There's more, Tony."

"Oh?"

"According to the National Security Council, we are officially even more panicked about the possibility of a Medusa Wave."

"Really? I know almost nothing about the Medusa Project, or Medusa Waves."

"We've got a briefing package coming over by secure fax from, I think, the Energy Department. We don't know if such a thing exists, but we have to assume it does. The important point is that a Medusa Wave would be designed to cripple computer-dependent societies."

"And we, of course . . ."

The director's head was bobbing. "Are an incredibly computer-dependent society. The NSC supposedly has an old study from the late sixties on what it could do to us. It was pretty grim even back then before personal computers, Tony. Today it's far worse. In the late seventies we were hardened against a major electromagnetic flux, or whatever they call it. I'm told we've gotten lax."

"Is the FBI still in control of this?"

The director sighed. "I'm in the middle of a turf war, but for the moment, we're calling the tune and the Navy's dancing. Soon as you get that jet on the ground, I'm sure we'll lose control to the NSC and the Situation Room and the Pentagon."

ABOARD SCOTAIR 50—5:10 P.M. EDT

Jerry Christian handed the latest weather slip to Scott McKay as Doc Hazzard returned from the cargo cabin. Scott studied it for a few seconds and shook his head as he glanced up to brief the co-pilot.

"Winds are now three-six-zero degrees at forty-eight knots,

Doc, gusts to sixty-five, and that's a forty-degree crosswind to Runway 32, but a sixty-degree crosswind to Runway 6."

"What about Runway 2? That's almost perfectly aligned with the wind."

"It's closed."

Doc slowly let himself down in the right seat and fumbled for the seat belt, his eyes on the swirling mass of dark clouds ahead. He glanced at the glowing radarscope, which was tracking cells of heavy rain and turbulence in all directions between their position and Pax River some ten miles to the east. The 727 was bucking in moderate turbulence now, and even reading the instruments was a struggle.

"Scott, I don't know about this . . ." Doc said, the sound of his long sigh audible over the clatter of rain hitting the windscreen. "She's going to be hard to handle down there."

Scott nodded. "Jerry and I were looking at the wind charts. It's out of limits, but not by much. Doc, what I'm thinking is, if I angle the airplane from the downwind side of Runway 32 to the upwind, rather than trying to land straight down the middle, we'll be so slow over the ground I can probably get her stopped okay."

"And if not?" Doc shot back.

"Well, if not, then we'll go off into the grass and probably be out of business next week."

Doc snorted and shook his head. They were out of business next week anyway.

"What if we jostle that thing enough to set it off? What if we crash? Will it detonate?"

"I don't think so," Scott replied.

"We're landing at, what, a hundred and twenty knots?"

"We weigh one hundred sixty-five thousand pounds. For a normal flaps-thirty landing, that's an approach speed of one hundred forty knots," Jerry added.

Scott glanced back at the engineer and nodded a thank you. "Okay, one hundred forty minus about fifty knots of headwind equals one hundred knots. I've driven a go-cart almost that fast before."

"Yeah, but with two terrified passengers and a ticking nuclear bomb aboard?" Linda McCoy added from behind Scott's seat.

Startled, he struggled to turn his head far enough to see her. He'd forgotten she was there.

She wasn't smiling.

"Linda, that's slow enough to get us stopped without major damage, even if we end up in the grass."

Doc adjusted himself in the seat and ran his hands gently over the control yoke. "Bottom line is, we've got no choice." He looked Scott full in the face. "You ready, Captain McKay?"

Scott nodded.

"Okay." Doc keyed the microphone and declared ScotAir 50 ready for the instrument landing approach to Runway 32 just as the 727 penetrated a hailstorm, the deafening sound of hailstones impacting the aluminum skin of the Boeing making conversation momentarily impossible.

A shattering sound like the crack of a rifle amplified several dozen times shot through the cockpit, accompanied by an incredibly bright flash of light. Scott could hear Linda gasp behind him as adrenaline filled his own bloodstream.

"Lightning strike!" he managed to bellow back to his right. "Not dangerous!"

"Just frightening as hell," Doc added.

As quickly as it began, the hail ended.

"Come right, Scott. That's a nasty cell three miles ahead," Doc said.

"Tell the controller to give us an intercept to final from the south side of the straight-in nonprecision course."

Doc nodded and pressed the mike button as a second flash of lightning filled their eyes and ears.

ABC NEWS, NEW YORK—5:10 P.M. EDT

The tip to look at an Internet "chat room" called U-235 came by phone from a friend at Columbia University forty blocks to the north. It took less than a minute for the ABC investigative correspondent to pull a rapidly moving discussion onto the computer screen in his office.

ROCKETDOC: HEY, EMC, THE MEDUSA PROJECT FAILED, REMEMBER? MEDUSA CAN'T HAPPEN. BAD SCIENCE.

EMC: COULD AND HAS, OR IS, HAPPENING. WE'RE IN IMMENSE DANGER THIS MINUTE FROM THE PROTOTYPE! I'M NOT KIDDING!

A3: WHO'S IN DANGER?

EMC: CERTAINLY ANYONE NEAR WASHINGTON, D.C., BUT ALL OF US ON THE EASTERN SEABOARD, AND IF IT WORKS AS DESIGNED, ALL OF NORTH AMERICA. I'M IN BOSTON, BUT IT'LL STILL FRY MY CHIPS UP HERE.

A3: B.S.! WHO'S MAKING SUCH AN ALLEGATION?

EMC: I AM. IT'S ON AN AIRBORNE CARGO JET IN FLIGHT OVER D.C. IT'S ACTIVATED AND IT'S SET TO GO OFF IN A FEW HOURS. THE GOV'T IS TRYING TO KEEP IT SECRET, BUT IF IT EXPLODES, THIS FORM OF COMMUNICATION WILL CEASE, AS WILL ABOUT FIVE MILLION PEOPLE!

ROCKETDOC: OKAY, I'LL BITE. WHAT ARE YOU WAXING HYSTERICAL ABOUT?

A3: HE'S GONNA TELL YOU IT'LL DESTROY YOUR COMPUTER CHIPS!

EMC: WHAT IT WILL DO OUTSIDE THE BASIC BLAST ZONE IS DESTROY COMPUTER CHIPS AND GARBLE BASIC OPERATING CODES ALL ACROSS AMERICA. ESPECIALLY ROMS.

ROCKETDOC: HEY, EMC, HOW IS IT THAT YOU HAPPEN TO BE THE ONLY ONE WHO KNOWS ABOUT ALL THIS?

EMC: I JUST TALKED TO ONE OF THE ORIGINAL PROJECT SCIENTISTS AT SANDIA. HE'S A FRIEND. SO HAPPENS, I WAS ONE OF THAT GROUP, TOO. BEEN THERE, DONE THAT, SEEN THAT, GOT THE T-SHIRT. SATISFIED? BY THE WAY, ARE YOU GETTING THE MESSAGE THAT THE THING THAT DRIVES IT IS A THERMONUCLEAR AIRBURST? WE'RE TALKING ABOUT IMAGES OF ARMAGEDDON HERE! I CAN'T UNDERSTAND WHY THEY'RE NOT FLYING THAT JET SOMEWHERE OFFSHORE THIS INSTANT.

A3: SO YOU'RE NOT KIDDING?

EMC: I'M DEAD SERIOUS.

A3: I'M IN BALTIMORE, AND I'M OUT OF HERE.

The correspondent leaned over his keyboard and fired a volley of keystrokes into the discussion using his usual screen name.

RESEARCH-R-US: s'cuse me, gents, but could someone please explain "medusa wave" and "medusa project"?

For nearly a minute the screen remained unchanged. The possibility that all three participants had fled somewhere else in the face of a stranger ran through his mind, but at last a new line appeared.

EMC: don't know you, "research," but state your phone number and i'll call you.

The correspondent typed in the network's 800 number and his extension and sat back to wait, his mind occupied with the details of a story he'd done about Los Alamos and Sandia Labs, and what was developed there.

Part of his mind was still tracking the hoped-for phone call when it dawned on him what he'd done.

"Damn!" The correspondent launched a number two pencil across his small office. The automated voice on the other end of the 800 number would tell the man he'd reached the ABC Network. Undoubtedly he'd hang up before dialing the extension. Surely he'd be reluctant to talk to the media.

He turned back to his computer to offer a direct collect call number at the same moment the phone rang. He snatched up the receiver.

"So ABC wants to know about the Medusa Project. I guess it's time."

11

• • • •

The lightning was almost continuous now, illuminating the soggy countryside below with ghostly, staccato flashes reflecting off an eerie landscape of dark forests bisected by small roads carrying long lines of rain-smeared headlights creeping northward.

Dr. Linda McCoy's fingers dug into the armrests of her observer's seat as the 727 lurched through another narrow band of severe turbulence. With each encounter she could see the two pilots struggling to keep the plane upright, while her stomach churned and her mind reeled. The storm, she realized, was terrifying her more than the bomb in the cargo cabin.

Linda watched Scott's right hand shove all three throttles to maximum power as the bottom once again dropped from beneath them. He seemed incredibly calm, yet she could feel the stress in his voice each time he spoke. He was obviously frightened and trying hard not to show it.

If he's scared, she concluded, *I'm scared!*

The sound of the air traffic controller's voice clearing them to begin an instrument approach to Pax River was like music to her ears, especially after they'd been told minutes before that the field was closed.

Just a little bit longer! she told herself as the cockpit rocked and bounced massively, sending chills up her back and bile into her throat.

She'd never experienced anything like this, not even on bush flights in remote parts of the world. She couldn't control the terror that was taking over. At that moment a sudden pitch-up slammed her downward in the seat as the 727 rammed into a massive column of rising air and just as suddenly staggered into a vicious downdraft. She wondered how much more the aging aircraft could take.

Face it, girl, she told herself, *you might not get out of this alive!*

Her thoughts flew to her home in Colorado. She should have been there by now. She thought of her cat. She thought of her parents. She thought of Christa McAuliffe on the doomed space shuttle *Challenger* and wondered if she'd felt the same panic as it exploded.

Scott McKay's voice cut through her preoccupation like an electric jolt.

"Flaps fifteen!" he barked suddenly to Doc, his voice almost lost in a brief rematch with a column of hail.

"Flaps fifteen set," Doc replied instantly as his left hand positioned the flap lever to the appropriate detent. "Engine anti-ice on. Your localizer is tuned and identified, Scott."

"He cleared us to three thousand feet?" Scott asked.

Doc nodded. "That's right. Three."

"Gear down. Landing checklist. Flaps twenty-five."

She watched Doc's hand snap the gear handle to the down position and heard the instant sound of high-speed air rushing somewhere beneath their feet as the nose gear door opened. The main landing gear would be coming out as well, some eighty feet behind them.

Linda's eyes darted from Doc to Scott to Jerry and back again. They were calm. She should be calm. But how could anyone be calm with such violent shaking and banging around? They were barely in control of the plane—and that thought sent her terror to new heights.

The approach controller's voice cracked over the speaker above her head.

"ScotAir Fifty, fly present heading, cleared approach to Runway 32, maintain twenty-five hundred feet until on course inbound, and contact the tower now."

"ScotAir Fifty cleared approach, twenty-five hundred until on course," Doc repeated. "Cleared approach, Scott."

"Roger. Set me up on the inbound course now. That's three-three-zero. I'm gonna hold an extra thirty knots for wind shear."

"I'd recommend a little faster, like a plus forty knots," Doc said.

Scott glanced quickly at the copilot, then over his shoulder at Jerry. Somehow Linda was aware of Jerry nodding, though she couldn't take her eyes off the windscreen ahead.

"Okay, plus forty," Scott agreed as he reached forward to reposition a small white plastic pointer on his airspeed indicator.

Doc toggled the radio again to make contact with the control tower, and the controller's voice came back weak through the overhead speaker as a burst of lightning-caused static crashed across their ears.

". . . cleared to land. Winds are, ah, three-five-five at fifty-five to sixty, gusts greater than twenty knots above that. The runway is open for you, ScotAir, but landing is at your discretion."

"Understood, Patuxent tower," Doc answered, his head going forward immediately to read the instruments, his voice raised against the deafening sounds of heavy rain. "Okay, Scott, we're at fifteen hundred, five miles out. That's the final approach fix. We're cleared down to four hundred feet."

Jerry Christian's voice chimed in from the engineer's seat. "The navigation radio's monitoring good and steady, and the runway's in sight at about ten o'clock."

"This is one helluva crosswind!" Scott said, his voice little more than a constrained squawk as his hands moved the control yoke ceaselessly to keep on the glide path and localizer course to the runway. "We're crabbing nearly thirty degrees to the runway!"

"Scott, be ready for a go-around," Doc said. "Don't press it! We've got the fuel!"

Linda felt like a rag doll being tossed around in a washing machine. She heard the strain of Doc's voice as he began calling out parameters and talking almost nonstop.

"Speed's plus forty-five knots. You ready for flaps?"

"Yeah. Flaps thirty."

"Roger. Flaps thirty."

"Set final speed. I'm continuing down to the minimum descent altitude. Field in sight ahead. Let's call it a visual."

"You want the wipers, Scott?" Doc asked as he moved the flap lever to the final setting.

"Yeah!"

Doc snapped on the windshield wipers, which began making

a terrible racket, almost drowning out his voice as he ran through the six-item landing checklist. The words "Checklist complete" were spoken just as a huge bolt of lightning lit up the landscape ahead.

Linda heard a gasp from the direction of the flight engineer's seat. "That hit the tower!" Jerry Christian said.

"Sonofabitch!" Doc added, punching the transmit button. "Pax River tower, you still there?"

No answer.

"Eight hundred feet, and you're forty knots above marker speed," Doc intoned.

"Are they there?" Scott asked, his eyes riveted on the instruments.

"No, but we're already cleared to land," Doc replied.

"Okay."

"You're six hundred feet now, plus thirty-eight knots."

"Okay."

"Speed is plus thirty-four and . . . That's a wind shear, Scott! It jumped up ten, maybe twenty knots . . . No, it's *more* . . . !"

"I can feel it!"

Scott's right hand was pulling back the throttles as Doc's left hand covered his. "Not too much! Don't pull off too much!"

"What's my speed?"

"We're four hundred feet, speed plus, ah, almost fifty."

"I gotta slow down!"

"Scott . . ."

Doc's voice trailed off as the airspeed rapidly increased another twenty knots, the sound of the slipstream roaring at them with greater authority every second.

"This could be a microburst, Scott!" Doc's words echoed in Linda's ears as the Boeing 727 flew through the precise midpoint of a massive rapidly descending column of air.

In an instant the forty-knot headwind became a forty-knot tailwind. Suddenly the wings had insufficient airspeed to produce enough lift to keep them airborne, and the seventy-five-ton airplane shuddered and began falling.

Linda gripped the armrests, her heart in her throat. This time there was no hint of the climbing sensation she'd felt on the other side of each downdraft. This time they were falling.

She heard a sharp sound from Scott's throat, but no coherent words. In her peripheral vision she could see Doc equally stunned as Scott shoved the throttles forward all the way to the firewall, making an audible impact against the stops.

It was Jerry Christian's voice from behind that found the words. "WIND SHEAR! MAX POWER! PULL UP! PULL UP!"

"Doin' it . . ." Scott managed.

"Airspeed is one hundred. Scott, we're sinking!" Doc yelled.

"I know it!"

"Two thousand feet per minute!" Doc's voice filled her ears as the captain responded.

"Max power!" Scott replied. Doc's left hand followed the throttles, but they were already as far forward as they could go.

Doc's eyes took in the radio altimeter, which dutifully read their exact altitude above the ground. The pointer was moving down through the last digit above zero.

"One hundred feet, Scott. PULL!"

"I am!"

The runway rushed at them as Scott hauled the yoke back into his chest. Linda felt the jet respond in pitch, the deck angle increasing suddenly as the tarmac and the grass alongside the runway raced up at them from a thirty-degree angle to the left. If they hit like that, she thought, they'd explode in a ball of fire!

"BACK! BACK! Up to fifteen degrees!" Doc yelled.

Scott gave a quick nod. His voice wouldn't come. The 727 banked right, rolling right, into the wind. The ground was still rushing at them. He had to get the wings leveled! The controls felt mushy, as if the big jet had no more performance left to give.

"I'm trying . . ." was the best he could manage.

From the perspective of the two men in the control tower the shattering impact of the lightning strike accompanied by an incredibly bright light had momentarily wiped out their awareness of anything. Both controllers realized simultaneously that they were lying on the floor without a clear memory of how they got there. They rose quickly to their feet as the lights of ScotAir 50 punched through the black clouds on the approach end of the runway.

"Radios are off-line!" one of them said.

"What's he doing?" the other replied, gesturing toward the end of the runway. The approaching jetliner appeared to be almost hovering off the end of the airport, its nose pointed not down the runway, but toward the bay as the pilots fought to stay aligned in the powerful crosswind.

Without warning, the jet began dropping at a frightening rate, its nose pitching up as it gained speed toward the ground.

"What the . . . ?" One of the controllers grabbed the microphone and punched the button hard, his finger protesting in pain, oblivious to the fact that the radios were not working.

"ScotAir, go around! GO AROUND!"

"Microburst!" the other announced, watching the nose come up even higher as the engines wound up to full power, the angry smoke trails of maximum thrust pouring out of the tail end of the Boeing.

"He's gonna hit!"

Scott felt the welcome thrust of the Boeing's tail-mounted engines kick the small of his back as he pulled on the yoke, his eyes riveted on the attitude indicator as the airspeed began to rise. An eerie calm had engulfed him, a feeling of being along for the ride and not in control—as if he were standing off to one side and watching the struggle to stay airborne with nothing more than detached interest.

"Ten feet, Scott!" Doc's words broke through. Scott could see trees in the distance to the left, buildings to his left, the grass along the runway flashing by in his peripheral vision. They seemed just inches above the ground.

"One hundred thirty knots and rising!" Jerry announced.

Scott continued to concentrate on what was only the bare hint of a climb, just as a massive gust from the left caught him by surprise.

Instantly the right wing dropped as the 727 weathervaned into the wind. The sound and feel of metal scraping concrete and the sudden lurch of the jet to the right as the right wingtip dragged the runway in a shower of sparks was amplified in the cockpit.

The wings were full of fuel. He had to stop the sparks and the impact.

Scott yanked the control column back hard, instinctively rolling the yoke to the left slightly to lift the wingtip off the ground.

The right wingtip rose from the runway at the same instant the tires of both main landing gear thudded onto the surface at nearly a forty-degree angle, the massive force dragging the Boeing's nose back to the left with a wobbling, shaking effect that Scott had never felt before.

The nose gear impacted the runway a second later as Scott once again hauled the yoke as far back as he dared, feeling the wind pick up the right wing. He fought to keep the wings level amidst the squeal of protesting rubber, realizing they were about to dig the left wingtip into the soft ground alongside the runway.

Everything in his mind was unreeling in slow motion. If the left wing hit, it would embed itself and yank them to the left until the aircraft rolled sideways and broke up in a massive explosion of fuel and flames. He had to get off the runway!

Jamming the rudder almost full right, the control wheel full right, and the yoke in his gut, Scott felt his ship suddenly leap off the surface and stagger back in the air. It seemed to take forever for the side-to-side shaking and vibrating to cease.

Doc's voice cut through.

"Scott! Come back right!"

A voice in his mind had been screaming the same warning. The control tower was off to their left, and they were drifting over the grass toward it, the tower cab still hundreds of yards away, but growing steadily in size in Scott's side window.

He looked at the airspeed. It was hovering above one hundred thirty, the push of the seat cushion in the small of his back confirming they were accelerating. He had to have speed to climb, speed to bank away from the tower, speed to get out of ground effect . . .

"Gear up," Scott ordered. "We've got to take the chance it's not damaged."

Doc grabbed the gear lever and moved it to the up position. Scott banked harder to the right, correcting the path of the jet as he tried to nurse it above the altitude of the control tower structure.

A wall of rain and hail and virga descended like a curtain from the east end of the airfield and engulfed them as the 727 clawed for altitude, rising finally above the height of the tower cab and into the fury of the storm.

"Scott, we've got an unsafe gear indication on the left main, but I think it's retracted. I think we can ignore it for now," Doc called out.

"Gear door, or the gear itself?"

"The main gear itself. There's a procedure we could do later to see if it falls out. I'll leave the handle up for now. That'll keep it pressured to the up position."

"Yeah, not now," Scott said.

Doc raised the microphone to his mouth and looked at the captain. "Where do you want to go?"

"Get me a clearance back west, somewhere out of this. Let me get stabilized and I'll talk to the FBI guy again. I don't know where we're going, but I sure as hell don't want to try *that* a second time!"

Jerry Christian's voice rang in from behind.

"Amen!"

"Agreed," Doc added as he pressed the transmit button and said, "Washington Center, ScotAir Fifty, request." He glanced around at Linda McCoy, who had remained silent, and noticed her death grip on the arm rests and the bloodless white skin around her tightly clenched lips.

She saw his glance and returned it with not even a flicker of a smile.

Doc nodded at her and closed his eyes in a momentary gesture of empathy.

"It's okay, Doctor."

She barely heard him and swallowed hard, aware of a rasp where her voice should be. Her lips felt parched and she realized she had been holding her breath. The big copilot was watching her with concern, and she finally acknowledged him.

"What?" she asked.

"I said it's okay. Relax. We're still airborne."

"That," she said softly, looking directly at him, "is precisely the problem."

FBI HEADQUARTERS, WASHINGTON, D.C.—
5:15 P.M. EDT

Before ScotAir 50 began its approach to Pax River, a series of phone calls had connected the FBI agents at the Pax River meeting with the common purpose decided upon back at FBI headquarters: The occupants of ScotAir 50 were to be arrested, detained, and secured, all in accordance with standard procedure for hijackings, using the assumption that the hijacker—or terrorist—might be posing as one of the passengers or crew. The good guys could be sorted out later.

When the arrangements were complete and the Boeing 727 was within a few miles of the field, Tony DiStefano plunked himself in a chair to listen to the background briefings.

"Okay, Donna. What've you got?"

The tall, attractive woman with large glasses he'd worked with for years sat in a swivel chair next to him and consulted a yellow legal pad overflowing with notes.

"For Dr. Rogers Henry, not many surprises, Tony." She outlined his pioneering background in nuclear weaponry, Los Alamos during the Manhattan Project, Sandia, Denver, Lawrence-Livermore, his security clearance, which had been amazingly still intact at his death, a brief history of the Medusa Project and its dismantling, and the lack of any negative remarks on Henry's human reliability file with the National Security Agency, the organization which issued security clearances for Americans in sensitive government research.

"That's it?" Tony asked.

"He had a small police record in Miami after retirement. Two arrests for suspected spousal battering. Both times the wife refused to press charges: 1986 and 1988. Two speeding tickets. No wants or warrants other than those."

"And the wife?"

"An entirely different matter. Remember, Tony, this man died two years ago, okay? The wife's alive right now and on that aircraft."

"Okay. Meaning what? Does she have a record of some sort?" He arched an eyebrow at the I-know-something-you-don't-know smile spreading across her face.

"No criminal record, and not even a traffic ticket, but listen to this. She met her husband while working at Lawrence-Livermore Labs in California as a nuclear engineer, then married him while working for the government at Los Alamos. She designed assembly methods at Livermore and worked on trigger production design at Los Alamos. In other words, this girl knows her way around nuclear weapons."

"So"—Tony raised both hands in the air in a gesture of mild frustration—"where is this going?"

"Her husband has been dead for two years. Since he isn't

around, he doesn't have a motive for threatening his country with an alleged bomb."

"Okay."

"She, however, does."

Tony came forward in his chair. "What do you mean?"

"The wife's got a whale of a reason to hate the government, and maybe the military. Five years ago she divorces her husband. In the divorce, she's awarded half his retirement, and a survivor annuity, which is considerable money. She lives reasonably well on the retirement income until her ex-husband dies. Then she files for her survivor annuity, which should roughly equal what she was getting for her share of the retirement. But those wonderful humanists over at the Office of Personnel Mis-Management find a typo in the court order and cut her off. I've dealt with OPM, too. They're incompetent idiots. Anyway, OPM happily declares her annuity award invalid, and since the husband is dead, they won't let her go back to the divorce court for a corrected order, even though the annuity was clearly hers. It's an outrageous decision, but she fights the OPM for the last two years and gets nowhere. Just a month ago a U.S. Court of Appeals turns down her appeal without comment and permanently takes away her annuity. This week she puts her home on the market, perhaps because she can't pay the overdue property tax. Today, suddenly, she ends up on an airplane over Washington, D.C., with a mysterious device, alleged to be nuclear and said to be ticking."

"*Alleged* to be nuclear? Donna, you're forgetting the readings in Miami."

"No, I'm not. We're just *assuming* the nuclear material that caused those readings is on that airplane. In fact, there are other alternatives, as you pointed out. Several other airplanes weren't searched in time, and trucks went out in all directions from the airport in the same period. Bottom line? We could be chasing the wrong fox. It could be a coincidence. This scientist's wife gets ready to pull off an airborne extortion with a nonexistent weapon, and by dumb luck some terrorist ships some plutonium through Miami at the same moment."

"That's a real stretch."

"Then maybe it's real. The bomb, I mean. That is also a possibility with her."

"Not plausible, Donna. This is a widow running out of money, so she spends her remaining funds to blow up the world? I don't smell suspect here."

Donna leaned over to put her face in his as she aped a Brooklyn accent.

"Hello-o? The husband is dead, Tony. For two years now. *Still* dead! The only living human with a motive is Vivian Henry."

Tony smiled and studied his shoes for a second before looking back at her.

"Okay, then where's the demand for money? There've been no demands."

Donna straightened up, her eyes still flaring but her voice more subdued. "Maybe it's coming. Maybe that *is* a real bomb and she's suicidal and intends to take out as many as she can to pay back official Washington. Who knows?"

Tony raised the palms of his hands to stop her. "Okay, okay. She has a motive, but we don't know that she's got the intention, the anger, the capability . . ."

"Oh, she's got the capability, all right. As I told you, she worked in the nuclear bomb arena at Los Alamos and there's every reason to believe she knows how to construct a dummy nuke. I just talked to the Nuclear Regulatory people out there. They're pulling her files, but they confirm that someone with her pedigree married to a key physicist like Henry would probably be able to build a real one by herself as well. It's plausible, Tony. On top of that, we've got talking computers issuing threats on that airplane, and she uses computers extensively."

"How do you know *that*?"

"The standard sweep. She has accounts with CompuServe and America Online and uses them daily. We checked her account billings and they're pulling all her records."

Tony got to his feet and walked to the window, shoving his hands deep in his pockets as he thought through what Donna had said. He had thought of everyone aboard the ScotAir jet as a victim. What if the perpetrator *was* aboard pretending to be a victim? What would her plan be? What would she want? Money? Or maybe she was suicidal.

Tony turned. "Has she ever threatened violence?"

"We don't know yet. We've secured the entire file from OPM,

so after we comb through it, I should be able to tell you if there's anything in writing, and to buttress that, we're trying to reach some of the OPM employees who dealt with her."

Tony turned from the window. "Okay, there's one problem. The bomb thinks it's in the Pentagon, and I got word a few minutes ago that she had, in fact, hired a flatbed truck to take her cargo— the bomb—from National Airport over to the Pentagon. The OPM is downtown, a couple of blocks from the White House. Now, if I wanted to blow away the OPM, why would I take my bomb to the Pentagon?"

Another agent had been listening quietly. He moved forward slightly and raised a finger to take the floor.

"I think I can answer that."

Tony DiStefano cocked his head slightly. "Go ahead, Bill."

"I've been digging into her background, too. Vivian Henry waged a quiet but rather energetic campaign in the late seventies to get the Energy Department and the White House to reactivate her husband's research project. She lobbied extensively on Capitol Hill, wrote letters to the editors of various defense journals, and from at least one archived news report was very bitter over her husband's being put out to pasture."

"But why the Pentagon?" Tony tried again.

"Because the young presidential advisor responsible for convincing the President back then to kill the Medusa Project—an individual Mrs. Henry called a Machiavellian liar in a Senate hearing— now has his office at the Pentagon. These days, however, he goes by another title."

"Which is?"

The agent smiled. "Secretary of Defense."

Tony nodded thoughtfully. "And a nuclear detonation at the Pentagon would get OPM too, not to mention the rest of us."

"That's right," Bill agreed. "Hell hath no fury . . ." The agent suddenly glanced at the more senior female agent and stopped in midsentence. She smiled at him, knowing the words he'd choked off, and why.

"Like a *woman* scorned, you were going to say?"

He nodded sheepishly.

"Believe it!" she said.

12
. . . .

With the rising wind from the approaching hurricane rattling the aging windows of her tiny apartment, a senior
clerk for the Office of Personnel Management sat at her
kitchen table and wondered what could be important enough for
her boss to bother her at home. After all, they'd closed all government offices early on account of the bad weather, and that should
be that. She'd always refused to work off the clock. She wished she
could quit altogether! Her section was an unhappy collection of
lousy managers and brooding workers, most of whom she couldn't
stand. None of them had the right to chase her down at home, least
of all her stupid manager. She probably shouldn't even return his
call. She could lie tomorrow and say she was visiting her mother.

But his wimpy voice had sounded even more frightened than
usual on the answering machine tape. No, she decided. He could
make trouble. She'd better call him back.

She punched in his office number while shaking her head. If
he'd changed his mind and wanted her to come back to work for
the afternoon, he could forget it. He knew the rules!

"This is Doris. You called me."

"Doris! Thank heavens. The FBI needs to talk with you immediately about a recent annuity case. Wait. I'll get the number."
There was a pause and she heard the rattling of paper. He gave her
the telephone number and the name without further comment, and
she disconnected with a small knot of fear rising in her stomach.

What'd I do? Why do they want to talk to me?

She'd never talked to the FBI before. Even though she was sure
she hadn't done anything wrong, the thought of talking to them
frightened her. Maybe someone was setting her up to make a mistake.

But her boss had said immediately.

She dialed the number. A polished female voice answered and identified herself as the FBI agent whose name she had written down. She gave her name tenuously.

"We appreciate your calling, ma'am," the FBI woman said. "We need immediate help with some background information about a woman named Mrs. Vivian Henry. I realize you're at home, but do you remember this woman?" The agent explained the history of the denied annuity while Doris closed her eyes and rubbed her forehead with a pudgy finger, as if trying to massage the memory to the surface.

Vivian Henry. Probably one of those divorced women looking for a government handout, she thought. She was tired of such women, whining and pleading on the telephone for OPM to make exceptions and help them. A few might be deserving of help, but she just knew most of them had only themselves to blame for marrying bastards and hiring poor divorce lawyers who couldn't get the annuity award papers right. *She* didn't get any free handouts, and as far as she was concerned, all the pampered little ex-wives could damn well go out and work for a living like she'd had to all her life. Screw 'em! Screw 'em all!

The FBI agent's voice snapped her back to the present.

"Ma'am, does the name ring a bell? Your supervisor told me you handled this case personally and spoke with the woman."

Several names and faces swam before her memory, all of them involving appeals and desperate women and more urgent work to prepare the OPM's folders for the government lawyers. Whenever someone appealed an OPM decision, everyone had to work harder to make absolutely sure that it wasn't overturned. The agency would go to any lengths to win, she knew, even if they knew they were wrong.

"I don't know. I process lots of 'em," she said.

"Well, would you remember if such a woman had ever threatened you?" the FBI agent asked.

Threatened. That's different!

The face of an obviously pampered, snobbish woman holding a fur coat coalesced in her mind, a condescending, demeaning look on the woman's face as she'd stood to leave. What were the words?

"You'll regret this!" the woman had said to Doris. "I'll see to it!"

"What do you mean?" Doris had countered, feeling off-balance and defensive.

The woman had gestured contemptuously to the surroundings of Doris's tiny cubicle at OPM headquarters and tossed several of her official letters back on the desk.

"You uneducated pig! You can't even write an intelligent letter, you probably didn't finish high school, you haven't understood a single thing I've said, and you think *you're* going to interpret a court order that determines my financial future? This is a stupid farce! I'll tell you what you're going to do. You're going to approve this claim in full or pay the consequences."

Doris remembered getting to her feet with shaky legs, her face contorted from embarrassment and anger. She hated confrontations, and if the woman hadn't been blocking the entrance to the cubicle, she would have just walked out and left her.

"If *I* say your claim's no good," she had stammered, "then . . . then that's that, whether you think I'm smart or not. Rules're rules. I'm just following the rules."

It was then that the woman had leaned very close so no one else could hear. Her voice had been a furious hiss.

"You cancel my benefits, you ignoramus, and I'll cancel *you,* and make a smoking hole out of this place in the process."

"You . . . you're threatening me!" Doris had said, trying to sound threatening herself and not succeeding.

"No. Not a threat. A promise."

The woman put on her elegant ankle-length coat and disappeared down the corridor, leaving Doris speechless.

That must be the one they're looking for!

"Ma'am?" the FBI agent's voice was in her ear again.

"Huh?"

"I asked you if you'd been threatened?"

"You mean like, 'I gonna hurt you if you don't do what I say'?"

"That's correct."

"Yes."

"Yes? In other words, you *were* threatened by this woman?"

"I been threatened, yes."

"But was it by Vivian Henry?" the agent asked.

Doris thought about that. Her memory for names was not good, but she did remember being belittled.

Henry. Vivian Henry. Yeah. That's the bitch. She turned the name over in her mind several times. She remembered the Henry case. The court order had a flaw in it. It had been easy to deny the annuity.

"Yeah. It was Vivian Henry."

"Tell me what happened and what she said."

The clerk smiled to herself. Invisible worker bees didn't get revenge very often.

ABC NEWS, NEW YORK—5:30 P.M. EDT

The hurricane battering the East Coast from New Jersey to the Carolinas was scheduled to take up most of the thirty-minute evening network newscast. Live shots from the coast, along with interviews ranging from meteorologists to atmospheric scientists knowledgeable about global warming, were being lined up as ABC prepared to show the country what was happening in graphic detail.

Something new, however, was pulling away more and more members of the ABC News team. Word had come from the Washington bureau that something unrelated to the weather was presenting the White House with a new crisis.

"The usual denials, of course," the ABC correspondent in D.C. was saying to his counterpart in New York on a speaker phone as a growing number of people gathered around the main news desk, "but one of our best sources in the White House confirmed the Situation Room is in full operation, and the crisis is some sort of domestic terrorism threat."

"We have only one source for this story, then?"

"We have two, but they're only telling me that something's afoot and it *might* involve a nuclear threat."

"How about the other networks?"

"Nothing from the other nets, but we do have a real break. You know how cellular phones can suddenly shift frequencies and leave you listening to someone else's conversation?"

"Yeah. I've had that happen."

"A staff member for Senator Campbell called up one of his friends here fifteen minutes ago wanting to know what we knew about a nuclear emergency at Patuxent River Naval Air Station. Seems he overheard a frantic call from someone around here to a woman at Pax River, telling her to take her daughters and hit the road north. We've checked. There *is* an evacuation of the base going on, and a civilian cargo plane did make a touch-and-go in high winds there just a few minutes ago, but the official word from the base is the evacuation is because of the hurricane."

"Is that plausible?"

"Hardly. They've had a day's warning to evacuate and nothing happened. Now that the winds are howling, it doesn't make much sense to be moving the base."

"Do you have scanners down there that can monitor the aviation frequencies? We've got this Internet stuff about a nuke flying around Washington, and now your report of a civilian bird doing a touch-and-go at the Navy base. I'd sure like to know if it's still in that area. If it is a nuke, millions of people are at risk."

"I'm acutely aware of that, especially since I'm one of them! Yeah, we have a scanner, and we're monitoring. I'll let you know. What have you found out there in New York?"

A senior producer for *World News Tonight* slid quietly into a chair at the same table and motioned to the correspondent to continue.

"We've got a retired nuclear scientist who worked on the Medusa Project. He's described the whole thing and says one of his good buds was called a half hour ago by a reporter for *The Wall Street Journal* who said he'd been monitoring phone calls from that airplane. We're trying to track the reporter down now, but this thing is beginning to sound both credible and scary. Did you get the summary I sent you by E-mail?"

"Looking at it now. Has the fifth floor made a decision yet?"

The reference to the executive suite in ABC News headquarters caused glances around the table.

"Not yet. They're standing by. We're trying to determine the national security risks of this, too. We'll be ready for a live break-in if necessary."

ABOARD SCOTAIR 50—5:30 P.M. EDT

Vivian Henry had closed her eyes through the worst of the gyrations over the Pax River runway, glad of the cargo strap holding her to the floor of the airplane. When the landing gear retracted and the aircraft began climbing, she realized they were changing plans once again.

She wasn't close enough to the screen on Rogers' monstrosity to read the numbers as they ticked by the remaining time, but she was sure that approximately two hours remained. They would need every minute.

Somehow the crew would have to be convinced to get the airplane on the ground so they could escape and leave her there. And she had to prevent any attempts to defuse it, since the results would be obvious.

But until someone came back to check on her, it was just she and the device. She wasn't supposed to move more than fifteen feet, away, and she had no intention of trying.

FBI HEADQUARTERS, WASHINGTON, D.C.—
5:35 P.M. EDT

Tony DiStefano looked up from the briefing sheet he'd been reading to see Donna standing impatiently in front of him again.

"Gotta hear this, Tony. Right now! The captain of ScotAir Fifty is holding for you on line four, but you've got to hear this first."

"Shoot."

She slid into an adjacent chair and began talking rapidly, her hands moving in dynamic cadence to her words. "We found a worker at OPM who dealt with the Henry case. Mrs. Vivian Henry threatened the worker."

Tony replaced the briefing paper and sat back, searching her eyes. "How long ago?"

"She came storming into their office to complain about the annuity denial over a year ago, but remember that it was just a few weeks back that her appeal was finally rejected."

"This OPM person is sure?"

"Oh, she's sure, all right. Mrs. Henry apparently gave her an earful she'll never forget."

Tony let out a deep sigh. "You really believe this woman could pull off all this, Donna? With the airplane and the device and everything?"

Donna nodded solemnly.

"Okay," Tony said, reaching for the phone. "Vivian Henry

now becomes our prime target, and since she could theoretically overhear our conversation, I can't say anything to the captain."

"He may already know. She may be holding them hostage."

Tony leaned toward the phone, but Donna raised her hand to stop him from punching up the line to Scott McKay.

"What?" He asked impatiently.

"ScotAir?" She pointed to the phone. "We just heard he can't get into Pax River. He almost crashed trying. He's pretty shaken up and wants to go west somewhere."

Tony DiStefano sighed again as he shook his head and jabbed a finger at line four.

WASHINGTON NATIONAL AIRPORT—5:35 P.M. EDT

Pete Cooke had been straining to hear the latest conversation between the feds and ScotAir when the phone in front of him rang. He answered it without thinking, puzzled at the unrecognized voice on the other end.

"Pete Cooke?"

"Yeah. Who's this?"

The man identified himself as an ABC News correspondent just as the voice of a young woman came through his earpiece telling ScotAir's captain to stand by.

"ABC?"

"Yeah."

"What . . . why are you calling me?"

"You're apparently working the same story we are. You've got sources, we've got sources, the story's immediate and big, and we're looking for confirmation."

"What, exactly, are you talking about?" Pete asked, knowing instinctively the response would be knowledgeable.

"There's supposed to be a live nuke over Washington, D.C., that threatens computer chips and computer systems nationwide—in addition to possibly killing a few million people in an unprecedented thermonuclear blast. You just talked to a retired scientist about it and he gave you a lot of details. You may have others. Look, Pete. You're print. We're broadcast. Your deadline's tomorrow. Ours is now. We need confirmation, and you may need the same. How about sharing?"

Pete held the receiver with his left hand and began rubbing his eyes with his right. So it had leaked already. *How* in the world? Had one of his people talked in New York?

The word "confirmation" made its way to his consciousness. "Only if we're sure," he had cautioned Ira. Maybe this was the last tumbler in the lock. Maybe ABC could provide the corroboration he needed to be sure.

"Tell me yours first," Pete said. "If it fits, I'll share."

"Fair enough. You have a pen?"

"I do."

"Let's start with a strange report from Pax River."

13
••••

Jerry Christian extended his lanky frame as far forward as he could from his flight engineer's seat and gently placed a bony left hand on the captain's shoulder. Scott was fumbling with the Flitephone receiver, trying to get it back in its cradle after terminating the latest conversation with the FBI. The severe turbulence was gone, but the Boeing was still bouncing and lurching as it flew westward, away from the hurricane's worst winds and toward an uncertain destination—the red "unsafe gear" warning lights still shining in their faces.

"Scott, we've got twenty-nine thousand pounds of fuel left. That's no more than three hours' flying time, depending on where you want to go. Could be a lot less if we stay at low altitude."

Scott McKay glanced back at the engineer and nodded.

"What's the word from the feds, Scott?" Doc asked, gesturing toward the Flitephone. "I take it they were less than happy we couldn't get into Pax River."

"Okay, here's the deal. Our FBI friend wants us to fly to Mc-Guire Air Force Base in New Jersey, enter a holding pattern, and wait for that group of experts from Pax River to get there. The Navy's going to load them in a Navy transport and fly them there. I wish them luck with those winds!"

Scott could see his engineer's head shaking in his peripheral vision. He turned slightly to the right. "What, Jerry?"

The response was wide-eyed and impassioned. "Why on earth would they choose McGuire? McGuire's far too close to New York and Philadelphia, and it's probably being battered by the hurricane as badly as Pax River. Even if that Medusa Effect thing or whatever it's called isn't real, my God, we're flying around with a twenty-megaton thermonuclear bomb that could kill, what, ten million, twenty million? Are they crazy?"

"Obviously they don't think we're going to blow up," Scott replied.

Jerry's eyes were flaring. "Can you imagine what we're dealing with here? What if that thing goes off while we're over New Jersey? The radiation bloom alone would cause millions of cancer and radiation deaths all over the East Coast, birth defects for decades, blindness, and worse. But if it can also produce that Medusa . . . what did they call it?"

"Wave. It's called a Medusa Wave," Scott said.

"Yeah. If it *can* create that sort of disruption, why would the FBI or anyone else want it even closer to New York banking centers?"

"Good point," Doc agreed instantly, his eyes still glued to the instruments as he brought the 727 through fifteen thousand and began to level off at sixteen thousand feet.

The voice of the Washington Center controller filled their headsets.

"ScotAir Fifty, I see your level off at sixteen. Turn right now three-zero-zero degrees, and state your intentions."

Doc looked over to the left seat as Scott picked up the microphone and stopped, his eyes studying Doc's.

"Suggestions?" Scott asked.

Doc shook his head and sighed. "I guess not." Scott strained to glance at the engineer. "You, Jerry?"

"No," the engineer responded. "I don't know what else we can do but work with them. But McGuire . . . I don't understand their logic. Maybe you should call them back."

Scott requested vectors direct to McGuire and took the new clearance as the copilot banked the aircraft toward the new heading and clicked on the autopilot. Doc ran his large right hand over his partially bald head and turned slightly in the seat, aware that Scott was waiting to confer with them both.

Doc caught himself glancing at the empty jump seat behind Scott where Linda McCoy had been sitting until a few minutes before. Over his protests about the turbulence, she had beaten a rapid retreat to the cargo cabin to check on Vivian Henry as soon as they'd climbed to a safe altitude. Doc suddenly missed her, as if her absence made a frightening dilemma even more lonely. He sensed they all felt her absence as Scott, too, glanced at the empty jump seat.

"I . . . feel like we're on some sort of out-of-control ride, guys. The situation is controlling us, but I don't know what else to do. I've worked around nuclear bombs before on aircraft carriers, but I've never had a live one strapped to my butt, not to mention the responsibility for God knows how many millions of lives riding, at least in part, on what we do. I mean, what if they can't defuse it? What do we do then?"

"Let's review what we've got, Scott," Doc began, counting off the points on the fingers of his right hand. "One, that device back there could be a dud, but neither we nor the government can take that chance. Two, if we assume it's real, then we've got less than two hours and thirty minutes left before it goes off, and if we're not at least, say, fifty miles away when it does, we're dead, too."

"Three," Scott broke in. "None of us knows how to defuse the thing, so we've got to do whatever's necessary to get this aircraft to an expert who knows how to stop the countdown. You agree? I mean, since we can't dump cargo from a 727 in flight, the only other course of action is to land somewhere and transfer the bomb to a C-141 or a C-130 and drop it at sea to protect the population. If it weren't for this dammed hurricane, there'd be enough time, but, God, every minute we're flying around the eastern seaboard, we're almost terrorists ourselves! Can you imagine what the average person down there would think right now if they knew what we had up here over their heads?"

"Wonderful image for our little company, eh?" Doc asked.

"Tell me about it," Scott replied. "Can you imagine discovering that there's a plane flying nearby with a small object inside that could burn all the flesh off your body even from twenty or thirty miles away? To hell with the Medusa Effect, a live nuke is enough to get my undivided attention."

Doc nodded.

"And what happens if, as you pointed out, Scott," Jerry said quietly, "we get on the ground at McGuire and the experts can't defuse it or move it? What then? We'll be the infamous crew who brought it within range of New York and Philly."

Doc had been leaning to the left over the center console. He moved upright, deep in thought, as Scott gestured toward the rear of the Boeing.

"I know that, if nothing else, they can blow up our airplane with the bomb still in place. Even burning it would work."

Doc looked startled.

"Blow up . . . ? That defeats the purpose!"

Scott was shaking his head. "It wouldn't trigger a nuclear detonation. That's the military way to dispose of a nuclear weapon to keep it from falling into enemy hands. I remember the briefings from the Navy. You burn it or set a high explosive charge to detonate the high explosives inside the bomb. That wrecks the nuclear triggers before anything nuclear can occur. The only problem is, you scatter radioactivity. You'd expose the plutonium core. We'd have to get ourselves well clear of the airfield before they did that."

"That would do it, then," Jerry said, sounding relieved. "If they can't turn the thing off, they can blow it up safely." He laughed briefly, without humor, adding, "After we have it on the ground and are away from this aircraft, of course."

Doc Hazzard was shaking his head sadly. "You're forgetting something, fellows."

"What, Doc?" Scott asked.

"How about Vivian? She can't move more than fifteen feet away or the thing goes off."

All three men fell silent for several seconds until Jerry broke the silence.

"Well, we're not really sure her dead husband is . . . or was . . . telling the truth about how far she can get from the bomb, are we? Maybe it will detonate if she goes too far, maybe it won't. We just can't be sure."

"Can we take the chance?" Scott asked. "We know it can track her, but would it give us another warning?"

Doc glanced back at the instruments to assure himself the autopilot was performing properly, then looked back, nodding. "Yeah. Yeah, I think there would be. The bastard wanted to torture her. He wouldn't just let it end like that. He'd warn again and again, just to keep her scared."

"So," Jerry added, "you think if they can't defuse it, we could test the pacemaker threat by moving her away from the thing in increments?"

"It isn't aware it's been moved from the Pentagon," Scott said. "We're well away from there and we're still alive."

Doc pointed to the controls suddenly and then to the captain.

"Scott, one of us needs to go check on those two. I had Vivian strapped down, but I'm worried about Dr. McCoy walking around back there."

Scott began throwing off his shoulder harnesses and unfastening his seat belt. "I'll take a look. We scared the living hell out of Linda trying to land back there."

"We scared the living hell out of *us* trying to land back there!" Doc said.

"Before you go, Scott," the flight engineer said, "there's something else we should all consider."

Scott recognized the tone instantly. Whenever something passed from the serious to the critical, Jerry's voice underwent a subtle transformation, his eyes echoing the depth of an unspoken concern.

"What, Jerry?"

Doc settled back into his seat.

"I hate to bring this up, but we've been so busy considering Vivian a victim, we haven't even thought about the alternative."

"What alternative?" Scott asked, perplexed as to where this was heading.

"I like Vivian. I hope this isn't true, but . . ."

"*What,* Jerry?" Scott prompted. Doc, too, had looked around over his left shoulder to read the engineer's expression.

"Okay, suppose . . . just suppose . . . that it wasn't her dead husband who thought all this up. Suppose she's the one. Remember, he's been dead for two years. Would anything be different?"

Doc snorted and rolled his eyes. "That's idiotic, Christian!"

"Wait . . ." Scott held his left hand up to quiet Doc's protests. "You mean you think she might be behind this, Jerry? But *why* on earth? To accomplish *what?*"

Jerry was shaking his head again. "I don't know why. I'm not making a case. I'm just suggesting an alternative explanation we hadn't considered."

Scott and Doc exchanged glances as all three men fell into a silence broken immediately by the ringing of the Flitephone.

Tony DiStefano was on the other end. After less than a minute of conversation, Scott replaced the receiver once more, a puzzled expression on his face.

"What?" Doc prompted.

"Change thirty-seven," Scott said. "Seems they figured out that

Jerry was right, and McGuire's too close to New York and Philly, so we're to fly south now to Seymour-Johnson Air Force Base in North Carolina."

Doc was shaking his head in disgust. "Okay. As usual, no one in government can make up their minds. What else?"

"He asked something very curious," Scott continued, making eye contact with Jerry. "He asked if Vivian Henry could overhear our conversation. I asked him why. He wouldn't tell me."

EAST WASHINGTON, D.C.—5:40 P.M. EDT

The telephone had been back in its cradle for five minutes before Doris remembered something significant. The shock of speaking with the FBI had muddled her for a while, but suddenly a clear image of the case file popped into her mind with the last name of the woman who had threatened to blow up the OPM prominently stenciled on the side.

It wasn't Henry. The fur-clad bitch's name was Watkins! So she wasn't the same one the FBI woman had asked about.

Doris sat for a moment on her threadbare living room couch and tried to concentrate, feeling even more scared than before. Maybe she should call the FBI woman back and tell her she'd given the wrong information.

Doris looked at the phone with her stomach in a knot. What if the FBI got mad at her for making a mistake? She could lose her job. She had lied to them, hadn't she?

But they don't know that unless I tell 'em.

Vivian Henry was probably just another pampered divorcée, she decided, and even if she hadn't threatened OPM, she'd probably thought about it, and that was almost as bad. After all, she *had* appealed the decision Doris had made. That made the Henry woman her enemy. She had questioned the government's wisdom and cost them time, and a court had ruled that Doris had been right all along. She remembered the ruling now. She'd felt good about that ruling. The bitch had gotten what she'd deserved, and Doris had felt important and smart. The memo had come down just last week.

The phone sat on a nearby table mocking her. *You're in trou-*

ble! it seemed to scream. *If you tell the FBI you lied to them, you're in big trouble!*

It really didn't matter anyway, did it? Doris thought. The FBI wouldn't put the Henry woman in jail for making a threat. They never jailed anyone for threatening OPM workers. Happened all the time.

If I call, I'm in trouble, she decided. *If I don't call, nothing happens to her or me.*

That made sense. It wasn't her job anyway to worry about OPM's enemies.

Doris picked up the TV remote and punched the "on" button, her mind already shifting to the sleazy talk show in progress.

ABC NEWS, NEW YORK—5:48 P.M. EDT

With Pete Cooke's information providing the missing pieces, the network's confidence level in the emerging story finally justified a break-in news report. ABC affiliates all over the nation cut to the single camera in New York.

Peter Jennings was monitored simultaneously in all the other television network news departments, as well as TV screens in the Oval Office and the Situation Room of the White House, where an instant icy silence stilled all conversation.

> *"A drama is unfolding at this moment in the stormy skies of the eastern United States involving a civilian cargo jet which we have reason to believe may be carrying an armed thermonuclear weapon. The airliner, a Boeing 727 operated by a small Colorado firm named ScotAir, was originally headed for Washington National Airport. Less than an hour ago, however, it was ordered by the FBI to land at a naval air station south of Washington called Patuxent River. Due to the rising winds of Hurricane Sigrid, the landing attempt was unsuccessful, and the aircraft is now reported to be en route to yet another undisclosed location on the eastern seaboard.*
>
> *"There have been instant denials of this story by the White House and other government agencies, but ABC's sources have been monitoring air-to-ground communications between the aircraft's captain and agencies of the government and con-*

firm that the flight crew was trying to land at the Navy base to permit a team of nuclear experts to defuse a bomb which was apparently contained in a cargo shipment. At this moment the aircraft is being sent to another location, and we are trying to determine . . . exactly where that might be. ABC News has also learned that the crew of the Boeing 727 believes the bomb is counting down toward an automatic detonation less than three hours from now.

"Now, there is more to the nature of this bomb. Aboard this aircraft, ABC sources have discovered, may be a weapon the United States tried to build in the sixties and seventies, a weapon which, if exploded over or near a modern society such as ours, would do more than kill—it would also attack the economy and infrastructure by devastating computer systems, computer-based banking and financial systems, communications networks, and even the television network you're watching at this moment."

A full description of the Medusa Project and the Medusa Effect—and the scientific uncertainty that such a weapon existed—followed, as other news services leaped for their telephones and computers to catch up.

Within fifteen minutes, similar break-in news reports had aired on all the networks and most radio stations as residents of the storm-battered eastern seaboard began looking skyward and wondering where the lethal jetliner might be.

FBI HEADQUARTERS, WASHINGTON, D.C.—
5:51 P.M. EDT

Tony DiStefano replaced the receiver with an ashen expression as several of his agents stood by, wondering what had happened.

"Donna, find a TV and turn it on. Some bastard leaked this story!" He launched a pencil at a far wall in utter disgust.

"What happened?" an agent named Bill asked.

"ABC just announced that we've got a live nuke that's set to go off inside three hours." Tony put his head in his hands.

"But, Tony," another agent began, "that's essentially correct."

"I know it, but the last thing we need is a national panic, and that"—he gestured toward the phone—"is exactly what's happening in the Situation Room."

"So we're losing control?"

"I'm not sure we want control!" Tony sat back in the swivel chair with an ashen expression and looked out the window. The angry clouds, sheets of rain, and blurred vision of trees bent at odd angles in the teeth of the storm had filled their peripheral vision for the last hour. "If that bomb goes off *anywhere* near a populated area . . . *Lord!* Thank God we've got him flying away from here, but even at Seymour-Johnson, even in North Carolina, we're talking millions of victims, even if the Medusa Wave doesn't work." Tony leaned forward, pointing out the window. "Do you know what happens to the eyes if you're unlucky enough to be looking in the wrong direction when a nuclear fireball erupts? It destroys your retina. Instantly."

"And if it is a Medusa Wave?" Bill asked.

"Then this entire country is in deep trouble." He jumped up suddenly. "Okay, let's stay focused. Here's the latest. The plane is headed for Seymour-Johnson Air Force Base at the Situation Room's insistence. The Air Force is going to evacuate the base and provide a small army of security police, some with heavy weaponry. The Pentagon has a plan in progress for getting the weapon offshore if they can't defuse it. I guess they'll let it blow up over water. How, I don't know. Not our department. We have the job of getting the captain to go to North Carolina. Our people on the ground have the responsibility for securing the crew and taking Mrs. Henry into custody. They'll need every second to work on the defusing, so the last thing we need is this woman holding the bomb hostage while she makes threats to explode it, if that's what she's intending to do." Tony surveyed the faces around him and let his eyes fall on Donna. "Of course, I'm still not convinced Mrs. Henry is our suspect. I can't figure out what she'd have to gain besides terrorizing the U.S. government."

"Revenge, Tony. She wants revenge," Donna said.

"She could be a potential suicide," Bill added. "What else does she have to live for, Tony? With what she's done already, any jury would throw away the key."

"Then we've got to figure out what she wants, and pray she

wants something we can provide, or pretend we can provide. Donna? Keep digging up backgrounds on the rest of the people aboard that plane. Maybe something we find out could help."

"Suggestion, Tony," one of the agents said.

"Sure. Go ahead."

"Has anyone searched her place in Miami with a Geiger counter? Might answer some key questions. You can't assemble fissionable material without leaving traces."

Tony stared at the man in silence for a few seconds.

"I'm embarrassed to admit I didn't think about that. Could you take care of it? Our Miami office will need a quick warrant."

"Done."

"And if there's no radiation?" Tony asked.

"There's probably no bomb."

14

• • • •

Donna reappeared with a new set of faxes.

"You ready? I've got the rundown on two of the crew."

"Go ahead." Tony sat down hard and began rubbing his forehead again.

"This is on the copilot. Name is John Turner Hazzard, nickname 'Doc,' age sixty-three, born in Conway, Arkansas, son of a Methodist minister, served in the Marines as an enlisted man in Korea, honorable discharge 1953, learned to fly on the G.I. Bill, and joined Pan American World Airways in 1956 after numerous flying jobs. Served as a Pan Am pilot and captain until the company's bankruptcy in the eighties. Earned a bachelor's degree from Southern Illinois University in '89 and an M.B.A. from Syracuse in '92. Married three times, divorced three times. No history of domestic violence. Unblemished FAA record. A few traffic tickets in recent years and an outstanding parking ticket in 1983, but no DUIs or other serious matters. No FBI record, no wants, no problems. FAA reports jobs in aviation since Pan Am are too numerous to itemize. Currently lives by himself in Colorado Springs, Colorado."

"Hardly suspicious. Height and weight?"

"Big fellow. Six-foot-four, two hundred twenty pounds at last FAA physical."

"And a Marine. Good. Who else?"

"I've got the flight engineer. Name is Gerald Donald Christian, nickname Jerry, age forty-three, born in Topeka, Kansas, no information on his family, graduated University of Kansas with a B.A. in 1975, private pilot license 1975, aircraft mechanic rating 1976, joined Northwest Airlines 1976. Terminated by Northwest in 1985 for unsuccessful performance in training. FAA record of a nonfatal accident in 1983 in a small plane, otherwise it's unblemished. He has no FBI record, no military history, no wants, et cetera. Christian is married, three children, and lives in Dallas with them. Bankruptcy filing in 1989. No DUI or other traffic offense history."

"And the captain?"

"He's recent military. It's coming. Give me fifteen minutes."

THE WHITE HOUSE—5:56 P.M. EDT

One floor above the Situation Room the National Security Advisor and the Chairman of the Joint Chiefs huddled in a hallway for an urgent private exchange. The four-star Army general had rushed over from the Pentagon ten minutes before.

At five-feet-five, the National Security Advisor had to crane his neck to look the six-foot-two-inch general in the eye, but he did so with the commanding authority of someone who has the ear of the President.

"Okay, John, we're out of earshot. What is it?"

"We've found the Special Forces people we'd need, Stanley, to fly the airplane, if we can't defuse the weapon, but . . ."

"You mean to fly it offshore, bail out, and let it detonate in the air somewhere east?"

"Yes, and the Air Force is prepared to use a cruise missile to bring it down at a safe range. Otherwise, you know, there's Bermuda out there and God knows how many merchant ships. We've even got a carrier fighting its way south around the hurricane. Damned inconvenient timing."

"So what's the problem, John? Why are you in my face?"

"We need that weapon."

The shorter man removed his glasses as if they were getting in the way of seeing the general clearly. "You *what*?"

"If the scientist who built that thing really succeeded in creating a Medusa Effect weapon, we need to know what's inside and how it works. We need to try to salvage it by defusing it instead of blowing it up or dropping it in the ocean. To go with that plan, we'd have to launch that Boeing over the Atlantic with at least one hour remaining on the bomb's clock. We estimate we can defuse it in one hour."

"John"—the White House official shook his head and clenched his jaw—"you're saying you want to play a game of chicken with an armed thermonuclear weapon on U.S. soil? Do you know how goddamned lucky we are it didn't go off over your office already? Do you realize the potential loss of life involved here? Do you realize the history-altering potential of this thing if we make a mistake?"

"I very well understand the risks."

"I'm not so sure you do. Do you also know this story just hit the airwaves? You *do* know, don't you, that we can't stall the media forever on what we're planning to do?"

"I'm aware of all that, but there's a big national security interest in this."

"And I'm the National Security Advisor, but just . . . just a second!" He raised his hand in a stop gesture. "What are you military guys going to do if you can't defuse it? Are you planning to blow it up with seven seconds remaining like James Bond, for God's sake?"

"That was *Goldfinger,* 1964, Stanley. Great movie, but Bond didn't blow up the bomb at Fort Knox, someone else came in and turned it off. If we can't defuse it, then with ten minutes left we'll detonate the high explosives and destroy it."

"And if you're wrong?"

"We've had these contingency plans for decades for stolen nukes or compromised weapons. Burning is less precise, so we've already got the high explosives en route to the base. We'll be wiring up the explosives as the disposal squad is trying to turn off the bomb's timer."

"Suppose the clock is lying? Suppose it goes off early, devastates our economy, kills a million folks in North Carolina, not to mention your people, when we could have had it go off safely over the Atlantic? You want to take that chance, John, just to study it?"

"We do. We think it's vital we have that technology."

"Why vital? We're not at war with anyone currently, in case you hadn't noticed."

The general sighed and looked down the corridor before glancing at his feet and deciding how much to say.

"Okay, Stanley, in a nutshell, by the late seventies we were pretty sure of two things. One, our major facilities—military and civilian, communications and power grids—had been hardened adequately against electromagnetic pulses from nuclear explosions. Second, we were pretty sure there was no such thing as a Medusa Wave."

"And now you're not so sure?"

"And now nearly two decades have passed and our society is vastly different. Our communications networks and just about every industry—not to mention the average American home—are dependent on computers. Most of the work we did before to harden the nation's infrastructure against an EMP in the sixties and seventies is now useless. We're very, very vulnerable to even an ordinary EMP in this country. You wouldn't even need a Medusa Wave to wipe out all the computers. Do that, and there goes the entire financial system."

"I didn't know that. I'd read about EMPs years ago. I thought we were hardened. You're saying if Medusa is unleashed, a thermonuclear tragedy is the *least* of our problems?"

"Absolutely. And I don't want to think what happens if the technology should fall into someone else's hands."

"But why, John, have you fellows all of a sudden decided a discredited theory is now a viable fact? You canceled this program two decades ago!"

"Two decades ago we didn't have anyone claiming to possess a working model. In addition, several top secret studies in the late eighties reopened the debate suggesting that the Medusa Effect was real and achievable, after all. My predecessors did nothing about it, but now . . ."

"So if it's not really a Medusa weapon, you don't need to study it, and we could detonate it offshore. But if it *is* a Medusa, we need to keep it right here so you can study it to prevent someone else from threatening us in the future. Interesting situation, don't you think?" The National Security Advisor chuckled as he rubbed his forehead. "We don't need enemies. We're threatening ourselves. Answer me one other question, John."

"Go ahead."

"Could this dead scientist really have obtained explodable nuclear material? I thought we could rely on you fellows to keep the stuff locked up."

The general let out a long sigh. The memory of a briefing many months before came to mind, a briefing only given the incoming chairman of the Joint Chiefs. It had been a frightening eye-opener relating to the past security of nuclear bomb production in the United States, and a military secret not even the White House was supposed to know: Not all the fissionable material in the military's hands was accounted for. He suspected the Energy Department had similar secrets about their stockpiles of plutonium.

"Stanley, we have to assume it's possible. Not every human reliability system is perfect, and this Dr. Henry was the chief of the project, with unlimited access. Did his superiors account for every molecule of enriched material? You'll have to ask them."

The shorter man nodded with a rueful expression as he watched his taller colleague squirm, knowing exactly what had been left unsaid.

"Okay, John. I'll relay your recommendation to the President. He may want to sit down with all of us shortly. When does the team leave Pax River?"

"Momentarily." He looked at his watch. "They should be lifting off right now."

PATUXENT RIVER NAVAL AIR STATION, MARYLAND—
5:58 P.M. EDT

The wide-eyed Navy lieutenant in the left seat of the Grumman S-3 twin-engine transport remembered launching his craft into a frightening storm from the deck of the aircraft carrier *John F. Kennedy* just two months before. With the combined speed of the ship and the forty-knot gale, the winds over the deck had been at eighty knots, less than he now faced from the land-based airport at Pax River. But then he'd had the comforting kick of a steam catapult in his back. This time all he had were the plane's engines to launch him into the teeth of a hurricane, and the task seemed slightly suicidal.

He'd received his orders at the command post by phone from the Pentagon to carry a small group to Seymour-Johnson Air Force Base in North Carolina, but no one would tell him the reason why. He'd tried to explain how dangerous the weather had become, but the admiral on the other end wasn't listening to any excuses, and no one seemed interested in his opinion. Five Navy and two FBI personnel were going to be risking their lives and his, and he didn't even know why.

Taxiing had been brutal. The aircraft had been spun around and nearly pushed off the taxiway. With a combination of brakes and power, he fought the gusts to a draw and finally got the aircraft into position at the end of the runway. He was aligned with the runway now, the wind howling at over seventy knots from the right, and it seemed he could probably just push the power up, pull back on the yoke, and lift straight up.

In any event, it would be a short ground roll.

"Ready?" he asked his copilot. A pair of frightened eyes stared at him with feigned equanimity as the lieutenant jg nodded.

He pushed the power up, verified that both engines were steady, and released the brakes. The aircraft seemed to stagger forward, then lift off suddenly, as he struggled to hold the nose down to gain real speed. They headed toward a dark mass of clouds crossing the far end of the field with pelting rain washing over them as the altimeter began to wind up.

"Gear up," he ordered. The copilot positioned the gear handle as he banked the craft to the left, heading north. The weather radar was useless, a mass of red-colored splotches covering the screen and warning of violent weather no airman should be trying to penetrate. He'd tried to make sense of the radar picture before takeoff, but the entire sky was filled with what looked like severe thunderstorm activity, and the presence of a small hooklike appendage on the end of the massive cell to the north of the field had escaped his attention—until now.

With the force of a thousand freight trains, the unearthly howl of winds spinning in excess of three hundred miles per hour reached both pilots' ears simultaneously as the Grumman entered the side of a tightly packed tornado funnel at a hundred and ninety knots and instantly flipped sideways, exceeding by several hundred percent the maximum design loads for the structure as the wings and the tail were ripped from their fittings and flung away in a cloud of aluminum parts. In the same split second, the right engine tore free, the propeller blades stitching a series of gashes in the disintegrating fuselage as it flung itself into the void. The main body of the aircraft, deprived of its structural integrity, split open and exploded into shards of metal as the bodies of those inside became lifeless projectiles in the maw of the funnel. In less than two seconds, what had been a flying machine was nothing more than a grisly rain of debris falling to the north of the base.

On the radar screens in departure control, the flight suddenly became a collection of targets, then disappeared along with the transponder. In the tower the visibility to the north was nil. Repeated radio calls went unanswered. It was nearly three minutes before the tower controllers concluded jointly that the Grumman and the nine souls on board were history.

The tower operator picked up his crash phone as the chilling sound of an emergency locator beacon began broadcasting its plaintive wail through the tower's speakers.

ABOARD SCOTAIR 50—6:01 P.M. EDT

Linda McCoy had been on her way to the cockpit when Scott McKay met her in the passageway.

"Scott!" She grabbed his arm and motioned toward the rear with a toss of her head. "It's reeling off more warnings. You need to hear this."

He followed her quickly to the rear of the third pallet. Vivian Henry was standing now, arms folded, her eyes glued to the screen a foot in front of her, but maintaining her distance, as if touching the loathsome thing would contaminate her. She glanced over as Linda and the captain came into view.

"He's repeating the same warnings now, over and over, but I don't understand."

Scott moved beside her and read the message scrolling across the screen.

I AM WELL AWARE THAT THERE ARE PLANS BEING MADE TO TRY TO MOVE THIS DEVICE. I HAVE ANTICIPATED ALL POSSIBLE METHODS OF RELOCATION AND HAVE ENGINEERED THIS DEVICE TO INSTANTLY DETECT ANY MOTION IN ANY AXIS. THERE IS NO PHYSICAL OR ACCESSIBLE SWITCH OR SENSOR YOU CAN AFFECT OR DEFEAT. IF YOU ATTEMPT TO MOVE IT, IT WILL DETONATE WITHOUT FURTHER WARNING. ALSO, DO NOT THINK THAT THE TRIGGERING MECHANISM CAN BE DEFEATED BY HIGH EXPLOSIVES OR BURNING. THIS IS NOT A STANDARD MILITARY NUCLEAR DEVICE. BURN IT OR EXPLODE ANYTHING CLOSE TO IT, THE NUCLEAR TRIGGER WILL ACTI-

VATE BEFORE THE CASING IS COMPROMISED. YOU NOW HAVE ONE HOUR, FIFTY-NINE MINUTES REMAINING TO EVACUATE THE PENTAGON AND THE D.C. AREA.

Linda watched Scott McKay step back slightly. His face carried a dazed expression and he seemed totally preoccupied.

"You see what I mean?" Vivian began. Scott didn't answer. His attention remained entirely on the screen.

Vivian turned instead to Linda. "What I don't understand is, he says it can detect movement, but all we've done since it activated is move. Up, down, sideways, and back."

"Oh Lord!" Scott's voice cut her off, and just as suddenly he looked from Vivian to Linda and back with embarrassment.

"What?" Linda shot back.

A sudden jolt of turbulence threw them all off-balance. Linda grabbed a cargo strap, but Vivian tumbled to the right and Scott almost lost his balance as he reached out to catch her. When the aircraft had steadied, he caught Linda's eye.

"It was nothing, Linda. Just a thought," Scott explained.

"How about sharing it?" she prompted.

Scott again looked from Vivian to Linda and back.

"Okay. This thing claims it can detect motion, but it obviously can't, and it still thinks it's in the Pentagon. I'll bet anything it has an inertial navigation system in there and the program froze somehow when it detected we'd reached the Pentagon's coordinates."

"Meaning?" Linda asked.

"Meaning we could throw the damn thing overboard or move it anywhere and it wouldn't know the difference." Scott looked at Vivian. "I don't know whether your ex-husband was bluffing or not. You said he never bluffed, and you may still be right. It could be his device has malfunctioned. But this damn thing sure as hell *cannot* detect motion. You're right about that, Vivian."

Vivian Henry suddenly moved forward to the open screen and read it once more. She turned with a strange expression on her face, her eyes looking beyond the captain toward the rear of the cabin.

"All those years, I believed every word Rogers told me because he decreed I had to. I think . . . I think it's time I stopped believing him."

She began walking slowly toward Linda and Scott, then past them, moving steadily to the rear of the otherwise-empty cargo cabin. She was several feet past when Scott realized what she was doing.

"Vivian! The distance to the pacemaker isn't the same thing!"

"I refuse to believe him," she said, her voice surprisingly strong and audible over the noise of the slipstream.

Scott could see Linda glance at the Medusa weapon, then back at Vivian, alarm showing clearly in her eyes.

Vivian was ten feet away and moving steadily. She passed the fifteen-foot point and continued without hesitation as Scott held his breath.

There was no sound from Rogers Henry's contraption. No indication of a response. Scott remembered Doc arguing that the pacemaker threat might be false. Maybe he was right.

Vivian was twenty-five feet away, moving steadily toward the rest rooms at the aft end of the cabin.

If that threat was a lie, too, Scott thought, *maybe we can assume the whole thing is a hoax.* He let his mind wander for a second. How would he feel if it turned out to be a hoax? How would it feel to know that they'd been goaded into trying a near-suicidal landing at Pax River for nothing?

Vivian reached the rear of the cabin and put her hand on the door to the aft airstairs. She turned then, slowly, the hint of a smile showing on her face, the first smile Scott could remember seeing since she'd come aboard.

He felt himself breathe again and heard a nervous chuckle from Linda.

Vivian held out both arms and bobbed her head to the side, as if taking a bow and acknowledging success.

"You were right, Vivian!" Scott yelled, the sound of his voice echoing in the empty interior of the aft cargo cabin until it was drowned out by another sound that originated behind them, from the direction of the Medusa device.

"Vivian Henry has moved more than fifteen feet from this device in violation of my orders!"

Rogers Henry's computerized voice boomed.

"You were warned. She must physically touch this device in the next five seconds to avoid immediate detonation."

Vivian was instantly in motion, sprinting forward, racing toward the device. She shot past Scott with wide-eyed terror on her face and threw herself at the back of it, her arms cushioning the impact as she fell against the metal surface.

"Your return has been detected, Vivian."

The voice sounded as soon as she touched the surface.

"But you disobeyed me. Detonation will now occur in thirty seconds. Reflect on the millions you'll now be responsible for slaughtering. You made a fatal mistake, Vivian."

Another disembodied sound—an expressionless computer voice—began counting backward as Linda and Scott looked at each other in helpless panic.

"Twenty-eight, twenty-seven, twenty-six . . ."

The sound of Vivian's voice rose in the background as an anguished counterpoint. "No! Damn you!"

"Twenty-three, twenty-two, twenty-one . . ."

Linda McCoy sprang into motion, launching herself at the back of the device. She pushed Vivian aside and reached inside to begin punching the attached keyboard with any combination she could think of, trying desperately to get a response.

The voice continued, relentlessly and unchanged:

"Nineteen, eighteen, seventeen . . ."

Scott felt time dilate as his mind raced ahead. They'd been overconfident, made a fatal assumption, pushed the device too far. It was too late to reconsider. There was no one to reason with. The possibility that he was about to die loomed before him as a reality.

Doc and Jerry! If they were all going to die, perhaps he owed them a few seconds' warning. There would be no time for an explanation. He might be able to reach the cockpit if he broke and ran . . .

Doc's words from a half hour before suddenly came back to him like a thunderbolt. "The bastard wanted to torture her," Doc had said. "He wouldn't just let it end like that. He'd warn again and again, just to keep her scared."

As Vivian Henry sank to her knees in tears, her fists impotently pounding the unyielding stainless steel of the container, and Linda McCoy continued punching the keyboard with maniacal determination, Scott realized it was all happening precisely as Rogers Henry had planned.

"Fifteen, fourteen, thirteen . . ."

With a sudden calm deliberation, Scott moved forward and placed his right arm through the same opening, grasping Linda's right hand and moving it off the keyboard. She looked up at him frantically, as if he'd lost his mind, as the computer voice continued unfazed.

"Ten, nine, eight . . ."

"What are you doing? Let me go!" Linda yelped at him.
"Nothing's going to happen, Linda!"

"Six, five . . ."

"We've got to stop it!" she yelled, trying to pull her arm away from him.

"Four, three, two . . ."

"It's all a bluff, Linda!"

"One."

Silence.
Linda McCoy froze. Her eyes searched Scott's for an answer. She looked at the Medusa weapon, and then at Vivian, sobbing softly on her knees.
Except for the slipstream, there was no other sound from the device for nearly thirty seconds.

Finally the computerized voice of Rogers Henry returned with a single word:

"BOOM!"

The screen returned to the original countdown in silence, the numbers 01:57:00 showing clearly.

Linda closed her eyes and wavered for a second, leaning against Scott and grabbing his shoulders for support. He held her awkwardly for a moment, then pulled her to him and hugged her tightly.

She lay her head on his shoulder, and he could feel her shaking inside.

Finally she straightened up and pulled back, discreetly clutching his hand.

"I'm so embarrassed . . ."

"Don't be," Scott said softly. "I thought we were dead, too . . . at first. At least you were doing something about it."

She searched his eyes. "How did you know?"

"Something Doc said earlier in the cockpit. As usual, he was right."

They looked in each other's eyes for a few seconds, Linda still holding on to Scott's hand, before both turned to help Vivian to her feet. They steadied her between them until she insisted on sitting down on the same blanket she'd occupied before.

"You see how it is?" she said. "He wasn't bluffing. He always wins."

Both Linda and Scott knelt beside her.

"But he *was* bluffing, Vivian. We're still alive."

"He wasn't bluffing about my pacemaker. He's still going to kill me. He just wants to enjoy it."

Linda McCoy cupped Vivian Henry's face in her hands and forced her to meet her eyes.

"Vivian, listen to me. Rogers Henry can't enjoy anything. He's dead! Understand? This is just a device he programmed, that's all. We can beat it, because it malfunctioned. It doesn't know it's been moved. That, and knowing he wants to torture you, gives us opportunities."

Vivian smiled slightly, patted Linda McCoy's hand, and looked away, unaware of the captain's puzzled expression. What opportunities could she possibly mean? What else could they do? It all depended on the group of experts from Pax River now.

Linda replaced and tightened the cargo strap over Vivian's lap. "We're going forward now," she said, "but I'll be back shortly."

FBI HEADQUARTERS, WASHINGTON, D.C.—
6:05 P.M. EDT

The news of the crash at Pax River left Tony DiStefano and his team in shock. While dozens of military and civilian employees scrambled to find someone else with expertise in defusing a non-standard home-brew nuclear device, the reality had sunk in that their best chance for defusing the Medusa Weapon had probably been lost in the wreckage of the Grumman.

"What do you want us to do, Tony?" one of the team asked quietly after he'd briefed them.

Tony DiStefano let out a long sigh and pointed in the general direction of the Potomac River.

"I just got word from the director. The Pentagon is taking over, in order to, as he put it, unify this effort. It's their game now. We just tag along and assist."

"So what's the bottom line? We get blamed for the tornado and the plane crash?" Donna asked.

Tony waved away the question with obvious irritation. "It's a turf war, what else? If it's a nuke, it's military."

"Do they know about the likelihood Mrs. Henry's the perpetrator?" Donna asked.

"You're going to make sure they do, right, Donna?"

"If that's an order."

"It is." Tony looked around, catching everyone's eyes. "Okay, we've still got to apprehend Mrs. Henry when the plane lands, but the military brass are going to have to deal with the bomb."

"You think they'll screw it up?" Bill asked.

"Were you in the military?" Tony asked.

The agent nodded.

"So was I. Air Force."

"Army here."

"Okay. Given your experiences and your knowledge of how innovative and intuitive and subtle the military mind usually is, do *you* feel confident about their handling what is probably the most dangerous single weapon and delicate detonation threat to ever show up on the North American continent?"

Bill nodded solemnly. 'I see what you mean. But there's still the chance it's not real."

"No, there's not."

The voice caused both men to turn as another agent walked in with a notepad. "Tony, I just got off the phone with the search team from Miami. They swept the Henrys' home and workshop with Geiger counters and protective suits."

"Yeah?"

"They found traces of plutonium, and a lead-lined vault in the concrete floor where this Dr. Henry apparently stored it. There was a container there, too, with NRC markings, and two spare nuclear triggers, both of them highly modified. Preliminary theory is, the registered container with that serial number, which is in deep storage at Hanford, Washington, is probably empty."

"My God!"

Donna was nodding energetically. "I thought so!" She said. "The Henrys had the means, Tony. They had the means and they had the motive. Which means we do indeed have a live one." She reached to call the Pentagon before Tony could suggest it.

15
· · · ·

The President of the United States swung his legs over the edge of the bed and reached for the wall-mounted handset that connected him to the cockpit of Air Force One some one hundred feet away. Sleeping was impossible now, though the First Lady had pulled a pillow over her head and gone back to sleep when the crisis calls began coming in ten-minute intervals.

The colonel in command of the 747 answered almost instantly.

"Jim, we're going to have to turn around. Get us back to Washington as fast as you can."

"Yes, sir. We'll need an in-flight refueling north of Juneau."

"Whatever it takes. How long to get home?"

"Over, ah, nine and a half hours, sir, approximately. We're over the western end of the Aleutian chain."

"This is going to reach a climax long before then, Jim. You've been briefed on what's happening with that 727?"

"Yes, sir."

The President replaced the interphone and glanced up at the monitor showing their current position. The small computer-generated image of the aircraft was already in a left turn back to the east.

He picked up the telephone handset again and brushed back his hair before punching the appropriate satellite line.

"Okay, Stanley. We're on the way home. Get everyone in the Starsuite and I'll meet you there in ten minutes. I've got to get dressed."

"Yes, sir."

Eight minutes later the unshaven fifty-five-year-old President entered the state-of-the-art Standard Teleconferencing Array Room, a fifteen-by-eighteen-foot walnut-paneled conference chamber designed into the lower deck of the 747, where the Secretary of State, the U.S. Ambassador to Japan, and several aides were waiting. On the other side of the polished walnut table, which bisected the room lengthwise, the National Security Advisor, his deputy, the Chairman of the Joint Chiefs of Staff, and four others had gathered. They turned and nodded as the President walked in.

The table appeared to be whole. In fact, only half of the table was actually aboard Air Force One. The other half—along with the other half of the room and the occupants—consisted of semiholographic projections produced by a massive data stream connecting Air Force One through communication satellites to an identical suite recently built next to the Situation Room in the basement of the White House over five thousand miles away.

The President looked his National Security Advisor in the eye and shook his head slightly.

"Amazing technology, Stanley. I always have to suppress the urge to shake your hand again through the screen, or wall, or whatever we call it."

Stanley nodded. "Agreed. I'd almost swear we were in the same room."

"I'm damn glad we have it at times like these. Okay, folks," the President said, looking around and indicating the various chairs, "let's get to it. What do we know, what are we doing, and where are the decision points?"

Everyone took a seat except the general, who picked up a sheaf of papers and gave a rundown of the Medusa Wave theory, the loss of the nuclear threat reaction team at Pax River, the discovery of trace plutonium in Rogers Henry's Miami garage, the FBI's conclusions that Vivian Henry was the perpetrator, and the plan for capturing Mrs. Henry and defusing the bomb in North Carolina. When the general had finished, he found the President's eyes boresighted on his.

"John," the President began, "why the hell North Carolina? Can't we find someplace more remote? We've managed to get them away from Washington, but we shouldn't be imperiling *any* population center."

"Hurricane Sigrid's even affecting Seymour-Johnson Air Force Base, sir, but the more remote locations are either too much in the grip of the storm or too far west to reach safely in the time remaining. Remember, we're severely limited by the time-to-detonation countdown the crew reports the bomb is showing."

"How much time do we have?"

The general consulted his digital watch. "One hour, forty-six minutes."

"And the time to landing at Seymour-Johnson?" the President asked.

"Around thirty minutes, sir."

"And . . . the time to defuse the damn thing?"

The general hesitated a moment too long before answering, a telltale eternity to the Chief Executive.

"You're not sure you *can* defuse it, are you, John?"

"Well, of course not, sir. This is apparently a home-built device. We have no idea until we see it, you know, whether it can be done."

"And you've lost your best people in that Pax River crash, right?"

The general shrugged. "We've lost those who were specifically trained for this sort of thing, yes. But we've found several others who know what they're doing."

"What are the risks they might accidentally set it off while poking around?"

"None, sir, in our opinion. They're being briefed to use extreme caution. They're also being briefed about Dr. Henry's expertise, and that of his wife, who's apparently carrying out his wishes and pretending to be a victim."

"And if you can't defuse it, the plan now is to blow it up in place, along with the aircraft?"

The general nodded. "We'll be wiring high explosives to it the second we secure the airplane. You understand, sir, that nuclear weapons can't be detonated accidentally. They . . ."

The President raised his hand to stop the lecture. "I was an Air Force pilot, an aircraft commander in C-141's both on active duty and in the Reserves, remember, John? I've flown nukes around for many years. I've had the briefing about emergency disposal probably fifteen times."

"Sorry, sir, I forgot."

"Go on, please."

"The base and surrounding community are already being evacuated, but if we have to blow it, all we'd get is the equivalent of a thousand-pound conventional bomb. Policing up the scattered nuclear material will take several days, though."

"What about Mrs. Henry? I was told the bomb could sense if she were more than fifteen feet away?"

"The FBI believes that's a hoax, sir, to give her leverage. In any event, we're prepared to substitute another radio to mimic whatever weak signal might be coming from her pacemaker, if, by any chance, her statements are correct."

"John, do you really believe this woman could pull off a stunt like this? I mean, do you believe she could've built a Medusa Weapon by herself?"

The Chairman of the Joint Chiefs looked around and stared at the President for a few seconds before responding. He began shaking his head. "We've formed no opinion about Mrs. Henry. We simply think we'd better treat this bomb as real."

"Spoken like a good turf player, John, but I want your personal feeling about Mrs. Henry. I didn't ask 'we,' I asked you."

"I don't have one," the general shot back.

"Then get one! You know how I feel about taking personal responsibility and hating bureaucratic bullshit, right? Anyone here think I was just blowing smoke?" The President looked around in all directions as the assembled group on both sides of the screen shook their heads and looked uncomfortable. His eyes returned to the general.

"Okay. Now, John, I want your personal assessment. I approved your taking over control of this crisis from the FBI, so you may end up having to decide this woman's fate if you can't separate her safely from her bomb. Do you really think she could pull off a stunt like this with the intention of holding the government of the United States hostage? I know she lost a pension and threatened someone at OPM. I got the whole briefing ten minutes ago from the FBI by phone. But this . . . ?" He let his voice trail off, his skepticism apparent.

"I do find it hard to believe, sir," the general answered.

The President nodded. "So do I. To me, the way the dead husband has programmed the thing to terrorize his wife sounds very strange. Is there something else going on here?"

The general cocked his head slightly. "Mr. President, I guess I'm not following you."

The President stood up suddenly and began pacing behind the other chairs on the Air Force One side of the table.

"I'm trying to anticipate the boxes we may find ourselves in within the next two hours. There are two vastly different pictures of this Mrs. Henry. One, an angry, vengeful ex-wife threatening the nation and the U.S. government, a picture that could, conceivably, include a monstrous suicide plan. The other picture, however, is of an abused former spouse conned by her dying husband into innocently taking a nuclear weapon to the Pentagon after his death, a weapon programmed to at least terrorize her if not kill her in the end.

"The Bureau thinks the woman in the first scenario is masquerading as the woman in the second scenario. Perpetrator playacting the victim. If that's true, we'll have to handle things very carefully at Seymour-Johnson. She could, for instance, drop the façade and claim she has her finger on the trigger, and if our forces don't back off or do whatever, she'll push the button long before we could get the thing neutralized. But if it's *not* true and we make a mistake in our assumption, we may waste a lot of time trying to get around her when all we have to do is ask the crew to open the doors. We're dealing with a massive, historic threat here. I don't want to lose any time because of assumptions. *That's* why I'm belaboring this. I think we've jumped to a conclusion." He sat back down with a thud.

The National Security Advisor had been conferring with the Press Secretary in the background. He stood suddenly.

"Ah, Mr. President . . ."

The President gestured for him to wait.

"One thing I need to know from you, General. We originally had a plan, I'm told, to pull the crew off, put our own pilots on board with parachutes, fly this thing offshore, let it go on autopilot, and bail out while it flies off to explode. Now we're going to try to defuse it. Do we really need that bomb's technology badly enough to risk a detonation? Is it worth that level of risk, for God's sake?"

The general was shaking his head. "We don't believe we're taking any risks of accidental detonation by trying to defuse it, but it's a Catch-22, Mr. President. If that really is a Medusa Weapon, we *must* get the technology first. If it's not a Medusa, we could easily dump it at sea with no impact on national security."

The President was shaking his head. "General, you're talking about the Wave. I'm talking about killing American men, women, and children, devastating the economy of North Carolina, blinding people, giving them cancer, and traumatizing an entire nation. I know the Medusa Wave is a far worse societal threat, but I hope you haven't forgotten the human cost if you're wrong and this damn thing detonates."

"I wasn't implying, sir . . ."

The President held up his hand. "You say our national interests demand that we try to get the technology. I hope and pray you're right, but I want you to keep the other option open as well. I want you to have a C-141 or a C-5 or a C-17 standing by, ready to go. Instead of blowing it up at Seymour, if you can't turn it off, take it out and dump it." He looked closely at the civilians in the Situation Room, five thousand miles away. "Any of those transports, as you know, can open their rear cargo doors and dump cargo in flight. If our experts decide they can't defuse it, or defusing is improbable, stop right there and fly it offshore. If there's real promise, okay, keep working with the explosives backing you up, but I'd rather dump it than run any real risk of detonation on American soil." His gaze shifted from the National Security Advisor back to the general. "John, can we get a transport aircraft in place in time?"

The general nodded. "Yes, sir. We'll scramble a C-141 out of Charleston right now. It's not far. But there's another problem."

"Yes?"

"If we blow it up at Seymour, we get no Medusa Wave. If we detonate it at sea by dumping it, we could easily get the full force of the Wave it's designed to generate."

The President sat examining the general's face in silence for a few seconds before turning to Shapiro.

"Okay, Stanley, what else?"

"Sir, we've got a public panic developing. The media is reporting an armed nuclear bomb flying around. We're going to have to say something."

"We've denied everything to this point, I take it?" the President asked, turning to the Press Secretary, who nodded.

"Yes, but they've got the Medusa Effect nailed, as well as the effects of a nuclear burst over a populated area. That's what the panic's about. Naturally the facts are becoming confused. But the switchboards are also heating up with some pretty important corporate heads demanding help on protecting their data-processing systems."

"What are we telling them?"

"I . . . well, not much. Officially, we haven't acknowledged there's a problem."

"Okay, that changes as of now. Do we have anyone with the expertise to advise what to do to protect computer systems?" The President looked around at the array of blank faces. "That's our main vulnerability, right?"

A young man in a bow tie on the Washington side of the table cleared his throat and the National Security Advisor gestured toward him. "Mr. President, I invited Dr. Ralph Jensen over here from the Office of Technology Assessment. He's an expert on EMP's." He turned toward Jensen, who looked marginally terrified. "Doctor?"

"Welcome, Dr. Jensen. Please help us out here," the President prompted. "If this thing should cause a Medusa Wave, what will we lose, and what can we advise people to do ahead of time?"

Dr. Jensen surveyed the faces on both sides of the screen and cleared his throat several times before answering in a surprisingly strong voice.

"Sir, in a nutshell, there's almost nothing that can be done if we get a true continent-wide Medusa Wave. You'd need heavy metal shielding around every computer-based device, and no one has time to do that. The silicon chips themselves in most systems will have their internal switching gates melted. If the systems are shut down, though, and no data streams are being processed, the computer tapes will, for the most part, be unaffected. You should advise anyone with a critical or big system, like a bank or stock exchange, to shut it down immediately and store the data tapes and disks as deeply as they can. All disks, tapes, and other storage media will probably survive if not being used at the moment it occurs. But all the computer hardware will have to be replaced."

"When you say 'all,' Doctor, what exactly do you mean?"

The young scientist shook his head. "I mean that virtually every silicon-based processor a Medusa Wave hits will be permanently ruined. I'm talking about each and every silicon processing circuit. You . . . also should know that late-model airliners may lose all engine power and have to make forced landings. I'd recommend all air traffic involving aircraft with computer engine controls be grounded immediately nationwide, including Air Force One, since I understand it's got computer engine controls, or FEDACs." He paused, watching the Chief Executive, who leaned forward immediately.

"Go on, please, with whatever list you have. You have the floor. We need everything you've got."

"Yes, sir. Well, I've prepared a long list here of what needs to be shut down, just in case. It's . . . rather amazing how much of our society runs on computer chips. For instance, all railroads and subways . . ." He looked up again. "Uh, let me explain that if a vehicle is under computer control when the computer microprocessors—the chips—are hit with an EMP, for a millisecond the wrong orders may be given by the dying computers, which could cause railroad switches to be thrown physically, signal lights to show the wrong thing, port facilities to go berserk, cranes to rumble off on their own or drop loads, and so on. Anything involving computers and heavy equipment has to be stopped. Ships or ferries with computer-controlled engines could get locked in full speed without the ability to shut them down or communicate with the engine room. Bridges, locks, major dams nationwide and their hydroelectric grids—nuclear power plants are especially critical, since all cooling controls could be disabled. Elevators in buildings will stop, most of them between floors. Sewer processing facilities could create tremendous public health problems with effluent spills, and pumps could either shut down or run backward, with valves opening and closing unpredictably. Nuclear naval ships are an exception, since I believe everything there has been completely hardened."

"That's the only bright spot?" the President asked with an amazed expression.

"Yes, sir. All critical hospital functions nationwide should be switched to manual backups. No medical procedures should be in progress, unless it's an unavoidable emergency. Complete loss of the nation's electric distribution grid is possible, not because of direct failure, but because of the contemporary dependency on computerized switching gear and associated relays." He turned another page on a heavily inscribed yellow legal pad. "Ah, I would recommend all heavy manufacturing facilities here and in Canada be shut down, and especially anything with critical computer-based containment controls for hazardous materials, such as refineries or facilities producing dangerous gas and liquid products. Certainly all heavy industry should be stopped immediately, because so many containment and safety controls are computer-based. Steelmaking, car assembly, food procesing, and, well, the list is almost endless. Anything with industrial robots, the same. They could do great damage to personnel as their host computers die. Even pipelines should probably suspend operations, especially natural gas pipelines."

The President had slowly leaned back in his chair.

"Good Lord, Doctor. We're talking about shutting down the entire country here, and within two hours?"

"Or sooner, sir. I'd recommend that all information-based systems be shut down immediately, and especially the financial market computers. And I need to talk about communications."

"And if this should go off, how long would it take to restart things?"

"Some facilities which can be run manually could get back up and running within hours. Anything dependent on computers would take weeks, months, maybe as much as six months, because until their computers have been rebuilt and rebooted and tested, you couldn't take the chance. Mr. President, we're talking about the instant destruction of nearly all the silicon-based processors in North America, if this is a true Medusa Wave. Even if it's only a standard nuclear-created EMP, everything on the upper East Coast will be affected the same way, if not hardened. You can't replace these chips overnight. I doubt there are enough computer chips in stock in the world to replace, inside six months, what we may lose. And that doesn't even address the cost."

"You have more, I take it?" the President asked, sounding stunned.

"Yes, sir. Communications are critical. Most military communications systems are hardened, but virtually all the geostationary communications satellites are vulnerable, as are all broadcasting facilities, all uplinks and downlinks, most telephone systems based on satellite longlines and high-speed multiplexing switches, broadcast systems, and . . ."

The President raised his hand in a stop gesture. "You're way over my head, Doctor. Tell me the end result."

"Yes, sir. Almost all telephone service, cellular service, business radio, telemetry radio systems, security monitoring systems, and other forms of telecommunication will cease. Bottom line? We go stone-deaf for many weeks, except for military command and control channels."

"My God!" the President said. He hesitated a few seconds, his index finger tapping his chin, before leaning forward suddenly.

"Okay, let's summarize the options. Stanley, you first."

Stanley Shapiro cleared his throat and held a hand out, palm up.

"First, I think we have to assume this thing is the real McCoy. If it is, I agree with the general that we do need the technology, because if it can be built, someone else is already working on it and will eventually succeed. So if we proceed from the assumption that it exists and we need it, we have to ask if it's a reasonable gamble to try to defuse the bomb to get the technology. The general tells us there is no risk. If his people can't turn it off, they can either blow it up, like a conventional weapon, or take it offshore and dump it to explode at sea. I'm assuming there's time for either option. Problem is, exploding it at Seymour would probably not produce a Medusa Wave, but dropping it at sea might. Thus, even if we decide there is no possibility of accidental detonation in North Carolina, the chance of a Medusa Wave is very high if we take the offshore option. In addition, do we tell the public what's really going on and ask for assistance in trying to power down as many critical computers as possible, or do we lie and issue calming, soothing B.S. that it was all a false alarm—at the same time we're frantically looking for a way to turn it off?"

"That's the crystallization of the issue, Stanley, but what do you recommend?"

"I'd try to defuse it, and blow it up conventionally at Seymour if that doesn't work. We're really at risk if we dump it at sea."

"Should we order an electronic shutdown, though?"

"No, sir. I think a shutdown would cause more problems than it would solve, and, in fact, we don't even know it would do that much good if the worst-case explosion occurs."

"General? The Pentagon's view?" the President prompted.

"Sir, we're confident that this can be defused or disposed of without a Medusa Wave, as Mr. Shapiro says. With such confidence, it would seem imprudent to trigger a national shutdown panic."

"Is there anyone here besides Dr. Jensen," the President asked, "who thinks calling for a shutdown is appropriate?"

The President of the United States surveyed the room, looking each individual in the eye, then spent a few seconds in thought before speaking again.

"Okay, gentlemen. I'll accept the Pentagon's assessment that the plan has zero possibility of an accidental detonation, and that we can try to defuse it or then blow it up without causing a Medusa Wave. Therefore, we'll refrain from sounding a general alarm via the media. But if something changes, I may change my mind." He arched an index finger at the Press Secretary. "Okay, Joe, work with the doctor here on telling the media what we know, except for where the aircraft is going, and reassure everyone that the device, even if real, will be defused safely."

Chairs began moving backward as the various principals and aides stood up. The President raised an index finger.

"Ah, one more thing, John."

"Sir?" the general asked.

"If there is any reason whatsoever to believe that your plans to defuse have become dangerous, any suspicion at all that it might not be perfectly safe to try, then I want the weapon dumped at sea. The sooner you make such an election, the farther out you can get it."

"Yes, sir. You said to have the aircraft standing by. We will."

"And the split second that looks like a possibility, I want us to quietly order certain things shut down as a precaution. Get the trains stopped just before the time runs out and get all air traffic on the East Coast on the ground by twenty minutes prior. Let's find a way to directly alert hazardous material companies, electrical companies, and communications companies. We won't have a lot of time, so press into service whomever you can to make this a viable contingency plan which can be triggered by one call."

The Press Secretary almost leaped to his feet.

"Sir, have you considered our legal liability in this?"

All other murmured conversations suddenly ceased as the President locked his eyes on the Press Secretary across the almost imperceptible electronic gulf between Air Force One and the Situation Room.

"What did you ask, Joe?"

"I'm questioning the legal liability the government assumes if we put out such requests or directives, especially if we alert some and not others. We can't be held liable for doing something wrong if we don't assume the duty, unless, of course, there's already a legal requirement. But if we start issuing such recommendations and damage results and this thing doesn't blow or doesn't work . . ."

"Joe, are we a private corporation here?"

The Press Secretary looked shocked. "Well, of course not, but . . ."

"We're the government, right?"

"Yes."

"Then I can't believe you would even bring this up. The government has no business concerning itself with potential legal liability. None whatsoever! We'll do everything we can to act within the law, and if anyone wants to challenge the correctness of our actions in court, that's what the courts are for. Joe, I'm sorry to pick on you, but I want everyone to understand that that question will never be tolerated in this Administration as an impediment to action by any official in any agency. Clear?"

"Yes, sir."

"Okay, get the Canadian Prime Minister and his Transportation Minister and the head of Transport Canada on the horn, brief them, and I'll talk to them after that. We need them with us on this. Share everything we have. Same with the Mexican government. Now . . ."

The President looked around momentarily. "Does the media know where we're sending this aircraft?"

"We don't think so, sir. But they've found out almost everything else."

"Okay. Prepare a short statement for me to give within ten minutes and alert the networks. I'll do a live break-in from here on Air Force One. I want to reassure everyone that we're going to disarm this thing, but I don't want to mislead anyone. I want them to know we consider it real. And get the Transportation Department moving on contingency plans. If they want to start slowing the system as a precaution, tell them to go ahead."

"Air traffic, highways, trains?"

"Whatever takes the longest to wind down. If we suddenly find we have to dump it at sea, I don't want aircraft and trains vulnerable."

The President glanced over at the general.

"John, where is the airplane right now?"

"They're currently south of Richmond, sir." The general touched a switch before him and a plot of the area and the 727's position appeared on a projected map that seemed to float in front of them. "They're beginning a descent for landing at Seymour-Johnson. The twenty-five-mile circle around the 727's symbol is the direct impact area of any blast. He's still a threat to populated areas, but he's dragging the threat area south with him."

The President seemed momentarily stunned. "John, you just got through reassuring me there was no chance of accidental detonation."

"Yes, sir, as a result of our trying to defuse it. But we still have to recognize it as a nuclear weapon. It could go off for other reasons."

The President stared at the Chairman of the Joint Chiefs and tapped a pen on the Air Force One side of the table. Several tense seconds passed before he cleared his throat and spoke. "So what about fallout, General, if that impossible occurrence should occur at Seymour?" the President asked.

"Thanks to the storm, it would rapidly sweep southeastward and out to sea. Charleston and some of northeastern Florida would be affected, but that's it for primary fallout."

"Okay," the President said, getting to his feet once again. "Keep this room hooked up, set up communications links to Seymour, including video from the tower if you can patch it through, and keep me informed. General? You have command of the situation at Seymour, but use the FBI's negotiators. Brief them on my concerns about Mrs. Henry."

"Yes, sir."

"And, John, we're all going to pray that your people know how to turn this thing off without setting it off. This is a direct order from your Commander in Chief, okay? If any doubts develop—and I mean any—I want it airborne again and headed east, offshore, instantly. I don't care how badly we want the technology, I'm only agreeing to this attempt based on your assurance that it's a completely risk-free operation. I already have my doubts. Tell your

162

commanders, do *not* press the defusing attempt one inch beyond certainty, understood?"

"Yes, sir."

The President sat back in his chair and tried to imagine the bomb flying over Washington, and what would have happened if it had gone off. He had said nothing to anyone else, but it was an immense comfort to know his wife and two daughters were aboard Air Force One and safely away from Washington.

FBI HEADQUARTERS, WASHINGTON, D.C.—
6:07 P.M. EDT

Once again Donna appeared at Tony's side with more reports.

"The rest of the crew?"

She nodded. "The captain and the scientist."

Tony leaned against a door frame. "Go."

"Okay, the scientist's name is Linda Ann McCoy, age thirty-three, born in Austin, Texas, father was a doctor, mother a university professor, she's a recognized world-class expert on atmospheric science and global warming with a long, long list of published credits, a Ph.D. in atmospheric science from the University of California at Irvine, and currently a senior research fellow at the National Center for Atmospheric Research in Boulder, Colorado, on loan to the NOAA research center also at Boulder. She's U.S. Government, in other words. McCoy is single, lives in Boulder, and was in charge of this year's NOAA atmospheric ozone research expedition to McMurdo Sound, Antarctica. She was on the way back from that when she boarded this flight in Miami a few hours ago."

"I trust she'll be suing her travel agent," Tony snorted.

Donna looked up and rolled her eyes. "I believe it comes under justifiable homicide." She dropped her eyes back to the pages in her hands. "Dr. McCoy has no criminal history, big surprise . . . no wants, no blemishes, except that she feels the need for speed a lot."

"Oh?"

"Four speeding tickets in Colorado over the last few years. The Colorado State Patrol knows her well."

"And the captain?"

"Name is Scott David McKay. Thirty-one years of age, only son of a family originally from Hutchinson, Kansas, born and raised there, U.S. naval officer through Annapolis, graduated number three in his class, highest rank he achieved was lieutenant commander, nine years active duty, last assignment, F-14 pilot assigned to the carrier *Eisenhower*. Left active duty just under two years ago, joined the Navy Reserve. Mother is deceased. Father was a corporate executive. Also deceased. No remarkable history on his family. Never married. Earned an M.B.A. while on active duty. Started his one-aircraft airline one year ago with money inherited from his father. Lives in Central City, Colorado. No FBI history. FAA record is spotless. No criminal history, no bankruptcies, no wants, no nothing. Solid citizen with a good military history, and his military security clearance is top secret and still active."

"And we already have Vivian Henry's history. Any conclusions, Donna?"

She shook her head and grimaced. "Good people, bad timing, Mrs. Henry excepted."

"There but for the grace of God, Donna . . ."

"Go any of us," she replied.

16
•••

Scott McKay flew through the cockpit door with Linda Mc-Coy inches behind and slid rapidly into the left seat, hitting his shin on the center console as the 727 plowed through more rough air above the advancing hurricane.

"Where are we, guys?"

Doc held out the Flitephone handset. "Picking our way through thunderstorms about fifty-six miles north of Goldsboro, North Carolina, at flight level two-eight-zero. Agent DiStefano wants to talk to you."

Scott snapped his seat belt in place and took the phone, the image of Linda sliding into the observer's seat visible in his peripheral vision.

"Tony, you there?" the captain asked.

"Yes, Scott."

He felt out of breath, his heart pounding. "We need to talk, Tony."

"That's why I called. Where's Mrs. Henry?"

"In the back, still, within a few feet of the bomb. She tried to get away from it a while ago . . . tried to walk to the back of the aircraft . . . but it wasn't bluffing about knowing where she was." He described the heart-stopping countdown and their conclusions about Rogers Henry's determination to torture her.

"For a second back there, Tony, I thought it was all over, but I keep wondering now whether this whole thing could be a dud, you know? I mean, I know she says her husband could have obtained plutonium to make a bomb, but could he really? I thought that stuff was far too controlled."

"Scott . . ." Tony began.

"I'm convinced the bastard has constructed something he wants us to think is real. He's a genius at covering all the bases and knowing exactly what we'd think of next. He knew how to scare us, but I wish I had a Geiger counter up here. I'll bet the needle would stay on zero."

"Scott, listen carefully to me. We searched the Henrys' home in Miami. We found the garage lab where the device was built. We also found plutonium there. The readings were irrefutable. It was a residual amount, stored in a small lead-lined vault in the floor. There was adequate shielding, remote-controlled loading devices, spare nuclear triggers, the whole works."

"You mean, there wasn't enough left to make a bomb?"

"No, Scott, originally he *did* have enough to do the job, and he did have conventional nuclear triggers. What I'm saying is, the bomb in your cargo bay is not just a threat—it's real."

The concept of blood running cold had never made sense to Scott before, but Tony DiStefano's words felt like liquid nitrogen coursing through his veins. Scott found himself unable to look at Doc, who was watching him closely. He was embarrassed and shocked to realize how much he'd wanted to believe it was a hoax.

"Ah, Tony, jeez, I sure didn't want to hear this," he stammered.

"I know you didn't, Scott. I didn't want to either. But we've got a good plan. Seymour-Johnson is open and the winds aren't very high yet, the personnel are being evacuated, and if we can't defuse the thing, we'll have to dispose of it."

Scott fell silent as several very long seconds ticked by. Doc watched his features with growing concern, wondering why all the blood in his face had suddenly rushed south. Jerry, too, was watching, aware of the fact that Linda McCoy's left hand was massaging Scott's right shoulder as she strained to keep her ear close enough to the receiver to hear the conversation.

"You mean," Scott began again with a sigh, "you mean blow it up, Tony?"

There was a pause on the other end and a chuckle. "I have your bio here, Scott. I knew you were Navy, so I should have known you'd understand the procedure. Of course, you might lose your aircraft."

"Let me get this straight, Tony, because this is what I thought, too, a while ago. I mean, I thought we might have to blow it up," Scott said, his left hand holding his temple while the other held the handset loosely to his right ear so Linda could hear. "So what you're saying, Tony, is that if the guys from Pax River can't turn it off, the military will bring in high explosives to pack around the bomb, in order to blow it up before the nuclear triggers can activate. Correct?"

"Scott, I kind of hate to say all this on an open line, you know? We think the media frenzy out there, which is growing every minute, probably originated with someone overhearing us talking on this Flitephone. But, yes, that's the plan. Standard procedure for emergency nuke disposal."

"For *military* nuke disposal, Tony."

"Okay. Meaning what?"

"Meaning we've got a big, big problem, Tony. This isn't a military nuke."

"Oh, that's okay. They're all roughly the same . . ."

"Listen to me, Tony. Please! Listen."

"I'm listening, Scott."

"The bomb gave us another message. It played back there before the episode with Vivian I told you about."

"Okay."

"The message warned that this thing is specially built to be different from a standard military nuke."

"Okay. So . . . ?"

"The screen said if anyone tries to burn or explode it with high explosives—exactly what we'd normally do, and Rogers Henry knew that—his special trigger would set off the nuclear reaction before it could be destroyed. We'd better come up with another option, in other words. If the team can't turn it off, they'll have no other ground-based options. They can't blow it up. They'd better prepare a fast airplane to dump it offshore."

"Now, Scott, look . . ."

"Tony, I'm telling you what it said, okay? I believe the bastard! When we get out of this, I'm gonna find the sonofabitch's grave and dig his rotten carcass up and stomp it to dust, but right here, right now, I believe what the device said is true. We can't burn it or explode it without triggering a thermonuclear blast and a Medusa Wave!"

"Okay, Scott. I'll relay that information to the commander at Seymour-Johnson."

Scott focused all his instincts on the FBI agent's tone of voice. Something wasn't right. He dropped his left hand from his forehead and gazed out the windscreen as he tried to dissect precisely what Tony DiStefano meant.

"Tony? Tony, you *can* control them, can't you?"

"What do you mean, 'control them,' Scott?"

"You're still in control of this thing, aren't you?"

"We're coordinating, Scott. There are a lot of governmental agencies involved, as you can imagine. Even the President's involved from Air Force One. We're just the coordinator until we get you on the ground."

"Okay . . . okay, who's in control up ahead?"

"At Seymour?"

"Yes. That's Air Force. Is there a military commander?"

Scott heard voices consulting at the FBI headquarters, then Tony's voice again.

"Well, I can't give you the rank for certain, but I believe there's a two- or three-star general who will be in charge, and he's taking orders directly from the Pentagon brass."

"I'll need his promise personally that no one will try to destroy this device by explosives. I don't give a damn about my plane. It's leased, it's insured, and I'm out of business next week anyway. But they can't try to detonate this thing."

"Scott . . ."

Scott heard the volume of his voice increase through gritted teeth. "I'm telling you, we can't blow this thing up without a nuclear disaster! You said yourself it's real."

"It is, Scott. We're sure of that because of the plutonium traces in the lab. But we have only this dead scientist's word that we can't dispose of it with high explosives, right?"

"I want a promise, Tony. I'm still a naval officer and my responsibility is to make sure this isn't screwed up. And I *do* know the military mind."

"Scott, what would you have *your* bomb say if you were going to program one?"

"I don't own one."

"No, but if you did, you wouldn't want anyone thinking they could defuse or destroy your bomb by burning or exploding, now would you? I know you're all scared up there, but keep focused. You're letting yourself believe Rogers Henry's B.S. And that's all it is."

"You don't know that. You're gambling."

"Scott, so are you, dammit!" Tony shot back. "We've got to use our heads."

Scott sighed and rubbed his eyes as he spoke again. "Rogers Henry would have programmed it to make the very same threat, whether he had a special trigger in there or not. Therefore, the presence of that threat proves nothing. He might be lying, he might be telling the truth. It's a gamble either way, so we've got to choose the most conservative bet, which is that he's telling the truth."

"I'll relay your demands, Scott. That's all I can do."

"I want that commander's personal assurance, his word, or I'm not landing this plane at Seymour-Johnson. Okay?"

"Okay, Scott. I'll see what I can do."

"Has the team left Pax River yet?" Scott asked.

Tony DiStefano had warned himself that he could neither hesitate nor sound in the least bit different unless he wanted Scott McKay to think something had happened to the nuclear terrorism team from Pax River. He carefully avoided taking a deep breath before answering.

"Yep, they've left Pax River, and another team's coming in from somewhere else at Seymour. You'll be well taken care of."

"Stand by a second," Scott replied. He turned back to the flight engineer.

"Jerry, check me on this." He relayed his theory on why Rogers Henry's device hadn't been able to tell when they'd left the Pentagon's coordinates nearly an hour before.

Jerry nodded enthusiastically. "I was thinking the same thing. He had a digital latitude and longitude input rigged to his central processor, but he probably never considered the bomb wouldn't land in Washington, therefore he used the wrong software instruction, which made the program stop accepting position data after the Pentagon numbers appeared. I'd bet anything that detector's in there right now, still running perfectly, chattering meaningless ones and zeros about our position and speed to a computer processor that simply isn't interested. All it wanted to know, electronically, was that it has reached the Pentagon, and that's where it thinks it is. We could take it to the moon and it wouldn't know the difference."

Scott relayed the analysis in less technical terms. "So, Tony, the point is, I think we'll be able to safely move it out of this aircraft, if necessary."

"Okay," Tony replied. "I'm told they've got the cargo equipment and forklifts ready to go."

"Tony, another thing. The first two pallets are important scientific gear being shipped by Dr. McCoy, who's with us. The team can work on defusing while the front two pallets are removed. They're blocking the device. Will you have them ready to do that?"

"You bet."

"And I want Dr. McCoy, my copilot, and my flight engineer to be taken immediately many miles away to a safe area. I'll stay here until we get Mrs. Henry safely removed from the weapon."

Another long pause from Washington.

"You copy that, Tony?" Scott tried again.

"Yes, Scott. By the way, you say Mrs. Henry's still in the back?"

"Yes, she is."

"Is . . . is she dictating any of this? Is she making suggestions to you, or anything like that?"

Scott looked around at the others in the cockpit. "He wants to know if Vivian has been telling us what to do."

The expression on Doc's face was pure alarm. Linda had heard the question through the handset and seemed equally concerned.

"What the hell is that about?" she asked.

Scott put the receiver back to his mouth. "Of course not, Tony. What are you getting at?"

"Just precautions, Scott. I also need to ask you whether she has any weapons."

"Weapons?" His tone was perplexed. "*Weapons?* You mean, other than a small garden-variety thermonuclear bomb? Like what, Tony, a penknife, or maybe a can of Mace? What's going on here? Has the frigging FAA been asking whether I frisked my passengers?"

"Calm down, Scott. I've got certain questions I have to ask in a terrorist situation."

"Okay, but the terrorist has been dead for two years now. We're dealing with the bastard's mechanical son."

"Did she tell you about her battle over her pension?" Tony asked suddenly.

Scott glanced around at Linda, who had sat back in her seat, her eyebrows arched. Scott slowly returned the phone to his mouth.

"Yes, Tony, she did mention it, but what possible bearing does that have on the current situation?"

"She say anything about getting even?"

"Not a thing. What are you getting at?"

Jerry's voice cut through the cockpit suddenly. "Fighters! About ten o'clock, Scott. Two F-16's."

Doc jumped as Scott looked swiftly to the left.

The two gray Air Force F-16 fighters were belly-up in a left turn, coming up on the left side of the 727 in a well-executed join-up maneuver. As the crew watched, they slid into position in formation just off to the left and slightly ahead of the Boeing. Scott had asked Tony DiStefano to stand by. Now he pushed the handset closer to his mouth.

"Tony, you guys send an escort?"

The answer was no. Scott explained who had shown up.

"I'll find out, Scott, and . . . wait . . . I do have a note about that. They've been scrambled out of Shaw Air Force Base to escort you and assist. Ah, they're monitoring 338.2, if that's a radio frequency you can use."

"It is. So happens I installed a UHF. We'll give them a call. Wish someone had let me know they were inbound."

"Sorry about that. I hadn't seen the note."

"Tony, what were the questions regarding Vivian Henry about?"

"Routine, Scott. I'm essentially working from a checklist."

Sure you are, Scott told himself. *You've just proven yourself a liar.*

FBI HEADQUARTERS, WASHINGTON, D.C.—
6:19 P.M. EDT

Within five minutes of ending the call with Scott McKay, Tony DiStefano was handed another handset, this time with an Air Force colonel at the Pentagon command post on the other end. "There are three males and one female visible in the cockpit. No second female was seen. Our guys were also startled when the captain came up on their UHF frequency. Civilian birds don't usually carry UHF. They'll maintain contact with him."

ABOARD SCOTAIR 50—6:19 P.M. EDT

Scott McKay replaced the microphone and let his eyes play over the fuselage of the lead F-16. The sound of the pilot's voice had been reassuring. Probably younger than he, Scott concluded, but he recognized the same air of clipped self-assurance and mastery of the machine he'd felt as a Navy pilot.

Tony's questions about Vivian kept gnawing at him, initially distracting him from thinking about the F-16's, but his attention soon snapped back to their presence as he tried to figure out precisely what mission they had been sent to accomplish.

The two fighters would undoubtedly stay with the Boeing until landing, though he expected them to stay a bit farther to one side during the approach. It was too bad you couldn't just point the old Boeing toward the Atlantic and transfer everyone to the sleek fighters, he thought. Such powerful aircraft, so close and so . . . lethal.

Scott moved his face within a few millimeters of the left captain's window as he examined the appendages of the lead F-16. He had jokingly asked the lead if he was armed and dangerous and received a chuckling "Negative."

But two air-to-air Sidewinder missiles were strapped to the leader's right wing, two more on his left. Scott knew what inert practice missiles looked like, and he wasn't looking at practice missiles.

These were the real thing.

Once again the liquid nitrogen began flowing through his veins.

WASHINGTON NATIONAL AIRPORT—6:19 P.M. EDT

Pete Cooke pressed his cellular phone to his ear as the taxi driver, heedless of the heavy rain, raced down the George Washington Parkway toward the FAA's Air Traffic System Command Center in Roslyn, Virginia. With ScotAir 50 now out of range, the handheld scanner was off and in his briefcase.

His research team back in New York had been monitoring massive business and industrial shutdowns all over the East Coast as Scott McKay was ordered to head for McGuire Air Force Base in New Jersey, a destination which was itself being battered by Hurricane Sigrid.

"Pete, nothing's happening at McGuire, except the winds," Ira said.

"I know it. I lost their telephone transmissions as they were changing destinations. It *was* McGuire Air Force Base, but I didn't hear the new location. I don't know where they're headed now. You've been monitoring radio, TV, and the wires, haven't you?"

"The story's rapidly taken over, Pete. ABC broke it, and now they're on live. NBC and CBS have followed, and CNN too. Everyone's having trouble finding good pictures, but the story is moving fast."

"What's the focus?"

"Three things. Whose neighborhood this airplane is threatening, what happens to that area if the bomb goes off, and then, what happens if it creates a Medusa Wave. They're pulling experts out from under every rock. It's astounding how many scientists are out there and how graphic they can be about the hopeless match between the human body and a nuclear blast. Every foot of film ever shot around Hiroshima is being shown, as well as some pretty disgusting pictures of horribly burned people staggering away in the minutes after the blast. The possibility of the Medusa Wave sending us back a few centuries is also being fully aired, though there's a lot of false information."

"Wait . . . wait a second, Ira," Pete interrupted as he leaned forward toward the front seat. "Back to the left! Not straight! We need to go *left* here!"

The cabbie looked startled and immediately threw the cab into a screeching left turn across four lanes of rain-soaked traffic to the proper exit, just as a large plastic trash can came rolling by them in the teeth of the wind. The cabbie swerved again and barely missed the can. Pete could imagine cops all over the city shaking their heads and throwing their squad cars in gear to give chase.

"Jeez!"

"You alive?" Ira asked.

"Barely. You were saying?"

"I was saying it's amazing how many scientists knew of the Medusa Wave theory, but they all apparently assumed it was impossible. Well, they sure believe it now, and they're scrambling around trying to protect themselves from what they think is coming."

"They're shutting things down, you mean?"

"Did you hear the President's announcement?"

No. When?"

"Five minutes ago or so, from Air Force One. He practically guaranteed the military would get the bomb defused with no problem, but it's what he didn't say that's significant."

"Which is?"

"He didn't say the Medusa theory is wrong, he didn't say people shouldn't shut down computer systems and industrial systems and factories, and he didn't deny what you're looking into, the grounding of all air traffic around the country. By the way, Pete, had you heard about the grounding, or are you just assuming it?"

"I'm a pilot, Ira, remember? It makes sense, but I'm not sure the FAA is going to let me in. The system command center has to be virtually hysterical by now if this is true."

"Pete, trains are being halted as well. I talked to a buddy with Metro North here in New York. All service is being shut down. Grand Central's turning ugly, and Amtrak isn't answering. We're getting reports of ships being told to shut down and drop anchor as well, but that could be the hurricane, too."

"I doubt it."

"So do I. The New York Stock Exchange and the American Stock Exchange were already closed, but we're hearing that clearings are being delayed, and even the monitors are being turned off."

"We're pulling up to the building, Ira. I'd better go."

"You know, Pete, we depend on satellite transmission, too, these days, for our nationwide editions. This thing happens in two hours, we're not going to have a paper tomorrow morning. We're not going to have our laptops, either."

"I still own notebooks, Ira. I suggest you sharpen some pencils."

"Pencils? What're pencils?"

The battle to penetrate the paranoid layers of the Federal Aviation Administration took less time than expected. Balanced reporting and years of cultivating friends within the agency—plus a list of private numbers into the heart of the FAA and the public affairs office—did the trick. If it was Pete Cooke, it was okay. Within fifteen minutes he was shown into the central control room, where one of the more harried coordinators met him at the door.

"You're putting only the computer-equipped airplanes on the ground?" Pete asked.

"We're putting the whole system on the ground. The order just came through from the Transportation Department. There're too many computers out there to differentiate. Even business jets, private airplanes, helicopters, and older passenger jets have computers scattered all over the cockpit. Of course, the hurricane had already forced some groundings for closed airports."

"This is nationwide?"

He nodded. "Canada's participating, too. Don't know about Mexico yet. We've got transatlantics and transpacifics to worry about as well. We're bringing them down all over the place. Gander, Newfoundland, Anchorage, even Iceland."

"How soon will it be complete?"

The man put his hands on his hips and surveyed the room. His collar was open, his tie askew.

"Maybe another hour. We'll meet the deadline, but getting the system reestablished later is going to be an even greater battle."

"How about . . ."

"You're welcome to watch, Mr. Cooke. I know you're a pilot. But I've got to dive back into this. Ah, off the record?"

"You know it."

"Off the record, I sure as hell hope the President knows what he's doing. There're going to be about a billion furious passengers and crew members out there for the next week at least, as we try to unsnarl this mess. But, of course, I didn't say that."

"And I heard nothing. Thanks. I'll just watch."

The controller moved off immediately and picked up a telephone, leaving Pete to meld into a corner, where he pulled out his cellular phone once again and dialed the *Journal*'s 800 number in New York.

Medusa's Child

The wing commander of Seymour-Johnson Air Force Base had been trying his best to adopt a stoic expression ever since the FBI agents and nuclear experts had begun descending on his base twenty minutes before. In his mind, he was in control of the operation, but to his female aide, Major Dillingham, Brigadier General Wally Walch had a deer-in-the-headlights look about him as he watched the frantic preparations for ScotAir 50, his thinning hair whipping in the twenty-knot advance winds of Hurricane Sigrid.

Walch could see his Air Force staff car at the far end of the main ramp. The Air Force officer placed in charge of the operation, a Colonel Peters, had commandeered it ten minutes ago on arrival from Shaw Air Force Base to the south. Colonel Peters, still wearing a green flight suit, had streaked in at supersonic speeds in the backseat of a two-seat version of the F-15. Another two-seat supersonic fighter was on short final approach, ferrying a nuclear technician in from Wright-Patterson in Ohio.

General Walch gestured toward Colonel Peters. "He needs to brief me on the plan. We don't really have any details beyond the basics."

Major Dillingham nodded, her short blonde hair now standing out almost parallel to the ground in the steady wind. Raindrops splattered occasionally around them, but most of the ramp remained dry, even with the angry clouds racing overhead and gathering in the distance.

"I'll ask him to come over here." Dillingham began striding away toward a small group of FBI agents and Air Force personnel. General Walch watched some animated gestures before she and the colonel walked briskly back to his location.

"General, sorry, there's been little time. I apologize for taking over your base. The FBI agent in charge will be with us in a second. The aircraft is around fifty miles out. He'll be on approach in ten minutes. We don't want to put him into holding if we can avoid it. The other guy"—Colonel Peters turned and glanced in the direction of the F-15 which had raced in from Ohio—"should be here in a second. He's the only nuclear expert we have left who can get here in time."

The wing commander nodded. "Colonel, I was told we had a

C-141 inbound from Charleston Air Force Base to wait at your disposal."

The colonel nodded. "Yes, sir." He looked around at the FBI team still conferring in the distance. Satisfied no one else was listening, he turned back to the wing commander. "I've been ordered to bring the 141 here and technically keep him standing by, General. That's in case we decide to dump the bomb instead of defusing it. Theoretically, we could load the bomb on the 141 and have the crew go drop it at sea. For some strange reason, however, he's just going to remain in holding near Charleston." He winked at the general, who did not respond. "I can tell you, sir, that bomb isn't leaving this base. We'll take care of the weapon here, one way or another."

General Walch looked taken aback. "I thought dumping it at sea was a presidentially mandated option if you couldn't get it defused."

"I was briefed by the Pentagon, sir, right after the Air Force Chief of Staff returned from a teleconference with the President. There was discussion that the President suggested we consider dumping if we decide defusing it in time is not safely possible. But my orders are to preserve the bomb at all costs, which means we'll use every available second to get it defused. By the time our man gets through trying, if for some reason he doesn't succeed, there won't be enough time left to fly it anywhere. In that case, we're ready to just blow it up here."

"How comforting, Colonel," General Walch said sarcastically. "I, too, spoke to the Pentagon, and my understanding was that the C-141 was to be here and standing by. You realize, of course, that the interpretation you just gave me could be considered a violation of the President's orders?"

Colonel Peters scowled at the senior officer. "General, this is U.S. Air Force Top Secret clearance stuff, okay? We're on the same team here. We're both senior Air Force officers, and like you, I take orders from our commanders at the Pentagon. I'm responsible for defusing and preserving this bomb. I'm *not* responsible for mind-reading the current political hack in the White House to try to figure out what he might think he wants. And, forgive me, sir, but for this mission, my direct commander is General Billings on the Air Staff."

The wing commander looked at Colonel Peters in silence for a few moments. "Anything I can do for you, then, Colonel Peters?"

He shrugged. "Not much at this point, except clear your base and keep an aircraft standing by to get you and your people out of here if we're within twenty minutes of detonation and we haven't turned it off."

"We've got that KC-10 ready over there," General Walch said, gesturing to the military tanker version of the civilian DC-10 sitting in front of the control tower. In the background, three more KC-10's were waiting, the last wave of the mass evacuation taking place on the base.

The colonel began to turn and walk off, then thought better of it and turned back to the general.

"By the way, sir, here's all I know at present. The terrorist is an American female. The FBI feels they can arrest her without incident, and that's the first task. Deadly force against her has been authorized, but we can't separate her from the bomb until we've analyzed and duplicated the radio signals being broadcast by her pacemaker. Once she's under control and we're sure she doesn't have a remote detonator, we'll start work on the bomb. While we're trying to defuse it, another team will be wiring it with high explosives. If we can't get it out of the 727, and for some reason can't deactivate it, then, as a last resort, we'll blow it up, along with the 727."

"What if the woman resists, Colonel?"

"That's why I need your security police, sir. The feds will do everything they can to talk her off, because the last thing we want is her holding the plane hostage with the bomb aboard. We also don't know for sure if any of the crew is working with her, so we're going to have to gain their trust until we've got firm control. But the bottom line is, get them all in custody and disarm the damn thing."

"And if it goes off prematurely with a nuclear detonation?"

Colonel Peters looked at General Walch, then at Major Dillingham, then back again.

"Well," he began, "to tell the truth, if it goes off without warning, we'll never know it in this life, unless you'd already put at least thirty miles or so between yourself and this location."

The major inhaled sharply, but quickly recovered her composure. The general's eyes widened slightly, but otherwise his features remained impassive. He said to the colonel, "I know you need to get back to the FBI group," as he gestured to the contingent of three dark-suited men standing several yards distant.

"I do, sir, yes. Wish us luck and say a few prayers." The colonel looked at his feet and took a deep breath, as if deciding whether to say anything more. Suddenly he looked up, catching Major Dillingham's eyes. "I'm told this thing will shut down the entire country, in addition to vaporizing Goldsboro, if we let it go off. I can assure you I won't let that happen."

His eyes shifted to the general, who smiled a strained smile and gestured toward his shoulders. "Probably a star in it for you, eh, Colonel?"

"Sir?"

"Amazing what it takes to make general these days. Good luck, Colonel Peters." General Walch gripped the major's arm and turned them both toward base operations across the ramp. Colonel Peters knew he'd just been insulted, but there was nothing he could think to say in response as they turned away.

17
• • • •

A s the descent began, Linda McCoy returned to the cargo cabin to brief Vivian, who seemed on the verge of tears.

"About ten minutes more," Linda told her, adjusting the single blanket protecting Vivian from the cold floor.

Vivian patted her hand in return. "I appreciate your coming back to check on me."

"I hate that you've had to sit alone back here."

"I'm so sorry, Linda, that I've involved all you good people in this mess. I had no idea . . ."

"Don't worry about it. Really. What's important is that we're in this together, and we're going to take care of it together. Okay?"

"Okay."

"Good." Linda brushed back her hair with her free hand as she knelt beside Vivian. "Now here's what I need to tell you. Our young captain's been talking almost nonstop to the FBI. They're fully aware you can't get more than fifteen feet away from this thing, but they've got a radio circuit rigged to fool it. They'll figure out the frequency and identification codes broadcast by your pacemaker and adjust their radio to mimic it. Once that's working, they can get you out of here. The bomb won't know the difference."

"You said we're near Goldsboro, North Carolina, Linda. They can't let the thing explode anywhere on the continent, and certainly not close to any cities. The government does understand this is a thermonuclear bomb that will trigger a Medusa Wave, don't they?"

"They seem to. Look, Vivian, I'll be brutally honest with you on this. Scott's trying to get their promise not to burn this device or blow it up with high explosives. He read the same message on the computer screen you and I did. He's terrified the military won't listen, because we're both convinced the thing's not bluffing. So, can you tell me anything I can pass on, any snippet of information I could give them, that would help prove your husband could have put a booby trap on this thing?"

"A booby trap . . . ?" Vivian suddenly dropped her gaze to the aluminum floor and smiled slightly as her expression brightened.

"What?" Linda asked, puzzled.

Vivian looked up, still smiling.

"The image!" she said cryptically, waving a hand at the bomb as if trying to exorcise some vision Linda couldn't see. "I . . . I'm sorry! You triggered a silly image."

Linda cocked her head slightly. "What? Tell me."

"Rogers was cruel to me, abused me, and belittled me, and in later years grew into a monster. That's all true. But in the early days of our marriage he could be hilarious, too. A dry, droll sense of humor. That's one reason I fell in love with him."

"But what's so funny now?"

"When you mentioned 'booby trap,' I couldn't help laughing. That was what Rogers called my bra."

Linda rolled her eyes and shook her head as Vivian grew serious again.

"You asked what to tell them, Linda. Tell them to look into my husband's work in the sixties and seventies. They'll find he invented the most accepted nuclear trigger mechanism and at the same time wrote at least one paper on the fact that any existing trigger could be modified to set off a nuclear detonation if high explosives were used to destroy it. He knew how. Tell Scott he's right. If they blow it up, they'll trigger the Medusa Effect."

Linda nodded. "Okay."

Vivian reached out to grab Linda's arm. "But there's more to consider here. They're going to waste time if they try to defuse it. They won't be successful, and if they push too far, they'll blow all of us off the map and unleash Medusa. There's nothing Rogers won't have thought of. Nothing. The case is welded shut, and any attempt to get inside . . ."

"*Listen* to yourself, Vivian!" Linda's voice sounded incredulous. The older woman responded instantly, as if jolted.

"Wha . . . what?"

"You sound just like those warnings your husband programmed into the computer."

Vivian looked up, then turned to study the bomb. "I guess I do," she said, absently, as her eyes locked on Linda again. "But it's because I know he's not bluffing."

"But he *was* bluffing when he said any movement would be detected, wasn't he?"

Vivian shook her head vigorously no. "That wasn't a bluff. That was a foul-up of some sort. He made a mistake, or something malfunctioned. Vastly different. We can't rely on any more mistakes."

"So what makes you think that single mistake *won't* let us find a way in?"

"He would have expected a frantic attempt to defuse it, can't they see that? He'll have known that the military couldn't just sit back and wait to see if he was really going to wipe out the Pentagon and most of Washington, not to mention unleash the Medusa Wave. He *knows* they'll have to try to get inside and turn it off. He's probably loaded dozens of warning algorhythms. Ultimately, he'll explode it rather than permit it to be defused."

"Just like he did when you walked to the back of the plane?"

Again Vivian looked at her with surprise. Linda could see confusion in her eyes.

"He . . . that may have been different. He wants to make me hurt. He wants to scare me."

"Right. So why would he want to set it off? Think about it, Vivian. Setting it off would end your pain and suffering. If he's bluffing but keeps threatening, he gets the maximum terroristic advantage. The more he can pull your chain, the more he can torture you. He blows you up, that's the end of the torture."

"But, Linda, there is a limit. Rogers knew that if someone got inside the casing with the intent to disarm it, he'd lose his leverage. He can't accept any loss of control. He'll detonate it, rather than lose control. What happened before—my attempt to walk away and his reaction—didn't do enough to threaten his control. If he detects . . ."

"If *it* detects. Your husband's dead. Don't forget, this is a thing!"

"Okay. If *it* finds *it's* about to be defused, *it* will detonate."

Linda nodded. "That's logical."

"Listen to me, Linda. You've got to convince Scott and everyone else out there making decisions that the only way to avoid this horror is to take advantage of the one mistake Rogers made, the fact that the bomb doesn't know where it is. You can't reason with this terrorist. He's dead. You can't defuse the bomb. But you can fly it over the ocean and dump it. It probably can't successfully trigger a Medusa Wave if it blows up far enough underwater."

"We've got to get you free first."

"If there's enough time, and if we find a way. If not, I'll have to go with it. I'm responsible for everyone being in this fix to begin with. But the Air Force will have to get this thing offshore and fast!"

"Vivian, Scott's arranged to get my cargo off and have Jerry and Doc and me rush away to cover. He'll stay with you until you're sprung loose from this thing, but I'll stay, too, if you'd like."

Vivian's head was moving back and forth in an emphatic no. "You'll do nothing of the sort. You take those three guys and get as far away as you can. I don't even want Scott to stay."

"I have a feeling you won't convince him," Linda said.

"He'll accomplish nothing staying with me. I don't need the hand-holding. I'd feel better knowing all four of you were a hundred miles away."

"I'll feel better knowing this thing is turned off and dismantled."

Vivian nodded, but Linda caught a quizzical look in her eyes and arched an eyebrow to ask what she was thinking.

"You know, Linda, it's funny."

"What's that?"

"You can't be more than, what, thirty-two? And Scott can't be more than thirty, yet you referred to him as 'our young captain.' I can tell you I'm pretty impressed with that young captain, whatever his age."

Linda looked slightly embarrassed. "Well, I am, too." She looked toward the front of the compartment, past the ticking bomb. "I sat behind him through that frightening approach to Pax River, Vivian, and watched him. I watched the veins in his arms and hands and how he refused to let the airplane get away from him. I was pretty angry with him at first today for various reasons, but he's . . . quite capable. I do trust him, and that doesn't come easy for me."

"Trust?"

"Trusting the male of our species. Any male." She looked at Vivian and smiled a radiant smile as she cocked her head and fluttered an eyebrow for emphasis. "Long story for later. I love 'em—I just can't trust 'em. You know, can't live with 'em, can't live without 'em, and they're too dumb to train."

"I'd love to hear your life history, Linda. I wish there was time."

"There will be. This evening, for instance. But it'll sound like a soap opera. A version of *As the Stomach Turns*."

Linda readjusted the cargo strap over Vivian's lap and gave her a small hug before returning to the cockpit. She put on her seat belt and headset as Doc read back the latest air traffic clearance and dialed in a new frequency. Without warning he glanced up and caught her eye.

"Notice anything, Doctor?"

She looked around, wondering what he meant. "You mean, other than the fighter escort?"

"Yeah. Hear much on the radio?" Doc wasn't smiling.

"No."

He nodded. "They're grounding air traffic all over the country as a precaution. The frequencies are getting quieter and quieter."

Scott turned partway around to look at her. "Linda? We're about twelve miles out, and I think they're gonna let us land straight-in without holding. When we get on the ground and stop—while we're shutting down things up here—I'd like you to go take the automatic deployment bar off the inflatable emergency slide on the front left door right behind the cockpit and open the door, being very careful not to fall out. Help them get the portable stairs positioned. Doc and Jerry will be right out. I want to see all three of you sprinting across the tarmac to the arms of the FBI, and I want them to get you out of here immediately. We'll get your equipment off as quickly as possible."

"Understood. No offense, but I can't get away from this airplane fast enough. But what about you? And Vivian?"

"I'll be okay. As soon as we've secured the bomb, I'll be right behind you. It'll be a classic 'feets-don't-fail-me-now' situation."

"With Vivian?"

"She'll be with me." He paused. "I hope."

"What do you mean, you 'hope'?"

Scott gestured to the Flitephone. "I'm . . . getting the disturbing impression they think Vivian is far more involved than she is. The FBI may want to have some extensive talks with her."

"Define 'involved,' Scott."

"Ah, I think they're unconvinced she's a complete victim. You overheard some of DiStefano's earlier questions, right?"

Linda grabbed Scott's seatback and pulled herself closer, glancing at Doc and back to Scott as she searched for nuances. "I thought those were standard questions off a hijacking checklist. Now you're telling me they suspect her?"

Scott shrugged. "I don't know, but it's not a comfortable feeling, the questions they've been asking."

Doc looked over at Linda and nodded as Scott continued.

"I'm scared to death they think we're being held hostage up here by Vivian, which is a ludicrous idea. But remember, they've never met her and she *is* the one who actually shipped the bomb to the Pentagon. I'm sure to them, with her background involving the nuclear program and her husband being dead for two years, it probably looks more than suspicious. I just don't want any trigger-happy skycop or fed down there taking a potshot at her."

Linda seemed awash in thought for a few moments as Doc's voice filled the air.

"Okay, Scott, we're descending through eighteen thousand now, altimeter two-eight-eight-six."

"Two-eight-eight-six," Scott echoed as he adjusted his two altimeters on the forward panel.

"The weather's coming forward, Scott," Jerry added as he handed Scott a small laminated card covered with grease pencil markings. "Winds are getting up there, but this weather's a wus compared to what we went through at Pax River. Three-five-zero at eighteen, gusts twenty-two. Light rain showers."

"Thanks, Jerry," Scott acknowledged.

"Scott," Linda said. He turned around far enough to see she was staring at some indistinct point on the center console, though for a second he let his eyes try to follow hers. There was nothing of consequence there.

"Yeah?"

Her eyes came up and latched on his with an almost physical impact.

"Scott, Vivian may be in big trouble if they're thinking that way."

"What do you mean?" Doc interjected from the right seat, and Linda glanced over at him.

"What I mean is, the only evidence anyone has of whether she set this up or he set this up is the bomb itself and what her husband programmed it to say."

"I'm not following you, Linda," Scott said.

She gripped the back of Scott's seat even harder, shook it slightly, and pulled herself forward, her mouth almost brushing his ear, triggering sensations he didn't have time to consider, but which somewhere inside he knew were very pleasant.

"I'm no lawyer, but . . ."

"That's why we respect you, Doctor," Doc said with a grin.

She ignored the comment. "I don't know the law, but I've had some exposure, and the problem is evidence. There's evidence up the kazoo, if you wanted to read it that way, that Vivian Henry purposefully brought this bomb on a civilian aircraft to terrorize the government. If it's a real nuke, and I think it is, there's no end to the laws she could be accused of violating. If they can't turn this thing off and analyze it—if they blow it up or dump it or destroy it—there goes the only evidence that exists showing that her husband set her up."

"You mean the computer program inside?" Scott asked.

"Yes. I mean, she could have programmed even that, but if they have the whole thing to probe and decipher, she could probably prove that he did it, and not her."

"Why, Linda? Why would she do all this? What motivation would she . . . ?"

Scott stopped cold.

"What is it?" Linda asked.

"I've . . ."

Doc's voice cut off the thought in midsentence. "Passing eleven thousand for ten thousand, Scott. I'm slowing us to two hundred fifty knots. Radar shows a bunch of returns ahead we need to steer around."

Scott nodded at Doc. "Roger. Would you take care of the radios for a few minutes?"

Doc nodded. "You bet."

Scott looked back at Linda.

"She *has* a motivation, Linda. At least in the eyes of the feds. Remember the fight over her pension? Did you know DiStefano asked me if I knew about that?"

"I didn't hear him say that. I couldn't overhear everything."

"He did. And suspiciously."

Linda McCoy let out a deep breath. "That lady is a victim, Scott. I'd bet my life on it." She paused. "I guess we're all betting our lives on it. But do you think our testimony alone—this crew and I—would be enough to keep her safe from prosecution? We all heard the device threaten and scare her."

"But that operations manager in Miami will swear he heard her threaten my crew and me to get us to come back and pick her up. She's the shipper. She arranged everything. She could have made up the story about her husband wanting her to ship the device and written the detailed instructions she said he left."

"Bull!" Linda shot back.

Scott shook his head after a few seconds of thought. He could sense Linda's shoulders slumping slightly behind him.

"Linda, maybe a lawyer would say something or see something different, and maybe there's other evidence in Miami we're not considering, but everything we've seen and heard and experienced she technically could have manipulated by herself."

"Never! That's setting her up to be an abuse victim yet again."

"*I* know that! *You* know that! But would a prosecutor accept that? Good grief, Linda, the whole nation's aware of this now! Even if nothing happens, they're gonna want as much blood as they did after Oklahoma City. Since they can't try a dead man, they'll probably go after his wife."

"No one in this country seems to understand a thing about spousal abuse. 'If she was abused,' they'll say, 'and if he was such a horrible man, why would she have done her husband's bidding, even after his death?'" Linda shook her head and sighed. "Provided we get out of this, Vivian will be in great legal peril."

"*If* the device is destroyed."

"I know. So what do we do?" Linda asked.

Scott shook his head sadly. "We land. We taxi in. We pray they can defuse this thing. And we get ourselves to a safe distance as rapidly as possible."

"I can't . . ." Linda began.

"Linda! *Linda, listen to me!* Scott's voice was full of authority, but his eyes were full of compassion, and she could see he was equally upset. "One step at a time. We'll defend her every way we can. But right now, the country needs to get its experts at that weapon back there. We mustn't forget the power of what we're carrying."

"Scott?" Doc's voice cut through his thoughts.

"Yes," Scott answered as he swiveled himself back around in the left seat.

"We'd better do this together. I've tiptoed around the buildup on the left, there, but we need to get down in altitude."

"Right. Okay, I'll take the radios now." Scott checked the frequency and asked the controller for a lower altitude as he scanned the approach procedure. He'd already briefed the approach to Seymour-Johnson, a relatively simple combination of radar vectors to an instrument approach.

He checked the mileage. They were eight miles out.

The controller responded, "Roger, ScotAir Fifty. Fly heading one-six-zero degrees, descend to and maintain two thousand feet."

Scott reset the altitude alerter to two thousand feet as Doc altered the course. There was one major duty remaining, and they were almost out of time.

"Doc, we're set up for the ILS approach." Scott turned toward Linda. "That's an instrument landing system approach, Linda. We can follow it down with great precision when we can't see." He turned back to Doc. "I've got to raise the mission commander down there. Watch the radios, please."

"Roger. Come back soon, old son."

Scott spun the frequency selector dials on the military-style UHF radio on the center console. "Seymour-Johnson mission commander, this is ScotAir Fifty. Are you there?"

A voice came back almost instantly. "Roger, ScotAir. This is Colonel Peters. Go ahead."

"Did our FBI contact, Tony DiStefano, brief you on my concerns, Colonel?"

"Yes, Captain."

Using the push-to-talk radio versus the Flitephone was a pain, Scott thought, as he pressed the transmit button again.

"Did DiStefano tell you there's no way this device can be treated like a military nuke in terms of emergency disposal?"

"You can talk in the clear, Captain. Yes, he told me you were insisting the thing will detonate if we try to blow it up or burn it."

"And you're not convinced?"

"Captain, we know what we're doing, okay? You're not a nuclear expert, nor am I, but we have someone here who is, and he'll call the shots."

Scott poised his finger over the transmit button but held back pressing it. How adamant should he be? After all, he was just guessing. They obviously knew infinitely more than he did about how to explode a nuclear warhead and what not to do.

The image of the runway ahead filled his mind's eye. In a couple of minutes they would be down and the nightmare would almost be over. The impending failure of ScotAir, the airline, seemed totally insignificant now. Just getting rid of the threat seemed the best goal in the world, and it was very close.

They'd know what to do.

Wait! Scott thought. *He said, "someone."* The colonel had referred to the nuclear team in the singular. There was supposed to be a group of experts inbound.

"Ah, Colonel, has the Pax River team arrived yet?"

Seven miles ahead, standing on the ramp, Colonel Jeff Peters felt a warning flag go up in his mind about the Pax River crash. Someone hadn't told ScotAir.

"Captain, no one survived that crash."

The long silence from the 727 raised the hairs on the back of Peters' neck. Maybe he wasn't supposed to tell them.

"Say again, Colonel? What crash are we talking about?"

"Ah, Pax River. The people who were to work on the device were in an accident a while ago, Captain. We've brought others in, however."

"The disarming team? They were killed?" Scott asked.

"Affirmative, sir."

Scott heard Linda inhale sharply behind him.

"Who else do you have?" Scott asked.

"Captain, don't worry about it. We've got a man from Wright-Patterson who zipped in here a few minutes ago. He's up to speed."

One guy? Scott thought, his mind reeling from the news.

"Scott," Doc began, "I can do this solo, but I'd prefer we do it together."

"Yeah, just a second, Doc. Keep her coming."

"Roger."

One technician to disarm a bomb designed by a scientist who had probably thought of every possible solution. And the stakes if the technician didn't know what he was doing?

Scott pressed the transmit button. He felt his voice becoming more strained and he was fighting not to let it show. "Colonel, I've got to have your personal assurance that there will be no attempt to burn or explode this weapon. I don't get the assurance, I don't land."

The reply was swift. "Captain, you have my assurance. We've got a C-141 right here on the deck and standing by to fly the bomb out if necessary."

"Good!" Scott said as he punched the transmit button again. "Roger. We'll be on the runway in a moment. You'll have a 'Follow Me' truck, I take it?"

"Yes, sir. He's waiting."

Scott changed the radio to the tower frequency as Doc ordered the flaps to five degrees.

The runway was coming into view in the distance.

It was almost over.

COMMAND POST, SEYMOUR-JOHNSON AIR FORCE BASE, NORTH CAROLINA—6:23 P.M. EDT

For a moment, the name White House Signals made no sense to the young Air Force staff sergeant who answered the phone.

Then it coalesced.

"Yes, sir!"

"We need to set up a feed of several different radio frequencies back to us here for relay to Air Force One, understand?"

"Ah, what do you mean, 'relay,' sir?"

"We need you to get very clever and find a way to commandeer at least four telephone lines out without compromising your normal functions. Each of those lines will need to be carrying the audio, in other words, monitoring a different radio channel. One for your control tower frequency, one for ground control, one for the command channel your commander is using to coordinate, and one connected to the ear of your duty officer, in case we need something else."

"I . . . think I can set that up, sir. But why?"

"Because the President of the United States wants to listen in on what's happening, and he wants it hooked up sometime yesterday. Good enough?"

"Absolutely, sir."

"So how much time do you need?"

The staff sergeant looked around at his duty officer, a major, who was watching him closely with a highly suspicious look on his face. The sergeant gestured for the major to wait. "Probably ten minutes, sir. We just have to tape a couple of receivers to the radio speakers in the command post."

"As fast as possible, Sergeant, please. Here are the telephone numbers."

Signals passed four different unlisted numbers with a Beltway area code and a master number, in case they were disconnected.

"I'll need to brief my commander," the sergeant said.

"No, you start working now. Tell your commander to talk to me on this line right now, please."

"Yes, sir." The sergeant turned to the major with a fleeting feeling of superiority. The power conferred by relaying such a call was invigorating.

"Major? The White House would like a word with you on line four."

Rewarded by the appropriate look of panic on his commander's face, the sergeant quickly turned back to his console to begin the process of jury-rigging the system.

ABOARD AIR FORCE ONE—6:26 P.M. EDT

Twenty-five minutes after he'd left the Starsuite, the President returned, summoned by an urgent request from his Chief of Staff to review the alarming progress of Hurricane Sigrid.

"Okay, folks, we can convene this session of Disasters 'R' Us," the President said seriously.

"We've arranged a tie-in with the National Hurricane Center in Miami, sir," the Chief of Staff said, "because this thing is already chewing up the Atlantic coast to a degree we've never experienced. You need to see the latest satellite photos. We're already bracing for the disaster declaration requests."

The President raised his hand. "Before you switch over, give me an update on the 727."

A deputy stepped forward with a sheaf of papers and a headset, which he removed.

"Uh, sir, the aircraft is on approach to Seymour-Johnson at this time. We've got two F-16's with him. The base is under the same hurricane watch, but it's the downwind side of the storm, so the winds are reasonable. They've evacuated the base . . . the last few tankers are leaving right now . . . and I'm hearing that the bomb defusing expert has arrived."

"Can he handle it?" the President asked point-blank.

The deputy shrugged. "No one knows, sir. At least he's there."

"Are you monitoring communications at the base?"

"Yes, sir. Control tower, ground, command radios, several other channels. We couldn't get video hooked up, but we'll be piping everything else through to you on your request."

"As soon as we're finished with the weather."

"You ready for that, sir?"

"First, how much time have we got? What's the time to detonation?"

The deputy checked his watch. "Approximately one hour and thirty-five minutes."

The President sighed audibly. "And the media situation?"

"Sir, the country is, in a word, terrified. We're getting reports from all over of businesses frantically shutting down their computer systems, all sorts of last-minute bank transactions, communication switches overloading, and that's all in addition to the disruption of shutting down the national air system, trains, and so on."

"My little speech didn't do any good?"

The Press Secretary stepped into view. "On the contrary, I think it helped a lot because it eliminated doubt about whether the threat was real. I'll tell you this, though. Outside of Washington, which is still in shock that a bomb was flying over their heads, the prospect of a Medusa Wave is scaring people far more profoundly than the basic reality of what a thermonuclear explosion would have done to D.C."

The President nodded. "This would be Hiroshima times fifty if it detonated over any populated region, even without the Medusa Wave. As I said earlier, let's keep in mind what a terrifying prospect this is, even if it's only a thermonuclear bomb." He looked down, unsmiling, and shook his head in wonder at his own reference. "Good grief, what a thing to say! *Only* a thermonuclear bomb.' "

The President looked over at his aide. "Okay, switch me over to Miami."

The Washington half of the Starsuite dissolved into an electronic kaleidoscope for a few seconds and then returned with the identical interior, this one occupied by several new faces in Miami, including Peter Ronson, the director of the National Hurricane Center, who rapidly introduced himself.

"Dr. Ronson, this is not accusatory, okay? But earlier today I was told in no uncertain terms that this hurricane was headed north and would probably miss us entirely. Suddenly it's mauling the mid-Atlantic coast and said to be poised to do us unprecedented damage. What happened? I wouldn't have left for Japan if I'd had any idea it would be this bad."

"Mr. President, big hurricanes can take unpredictable turns, and that's what happened here. We just didn't expect it to turn west so suddenly. This is a killer storm of unprecedented proportions and power. A level-five hurricane. The worst. We measured the cloud coverage of the storm at nearly a thousand miles in diameter, but the storm really is an eight-hundred-fifty-mile-diameter monster, with winds near the center now approaching two hundred and five miles per hour. We've seen hurricanes with extreme winds near the center like this, but never a storm with this kind of scope and breadth. Atmospheric pressure near the center is below two-seven-point-eight-zero inches of Mercury. This is a direct result, in my humble opinion, of global warming, sir. It's being fueled by increased heat coming out of the oceans."

"I appreciate the unique aspect, Doctor, but tell me what it's going to do to us now."

The director touched a button and a full-color satellite map swam into view in front of the President. Another adjustment caused the map to take on three-dimensional form, with the various altitudes of the clouds clearly conveyed from space.

"My Lord, what a picture!" the President exclaimed. "Is this live?"

"Yes, sir. The picture comes from *Nimbus Eight,* which we launched last year, and it is live. Sir, this hurricane has already washed a storm surge of thirty feet of water into the upper New Jersey coast, and nearly thirty-five feet around the southern New

Jersey coast. Cape May through Atlantic City north to Asbury Park are already being mauled and devastated. The boardwalks will undoubtedly be destroyed in their entirety, and the damage to waterfront properties will easily be in the tens of billions, and that doesn't include industrial facilities, ferry docks, fishing vessels, et cetera. Delaware Bay is building up a huge tidal surge, and we expect massive near-total devastation from Rehoboth Beach, Delaware, down to Ocean City, Maryland. The eye is aimed right now almost dead-on at Chincoteague Island near Wallops Island, Virginia. If the speed holds, and we expect it to, the heart of this monster will roar ashore with sustained winds of over two hundred miles per hour in another six hours. The Washington, D.C., area is already being battered, but things will get far worse. We expect winds in D.C. before this is over to hit one hundred miles per hour steady state, with gusts of one hundred and twenty-five miles per hour. Chesapeake Bay is in trouble as well, with storm surges and extensive flooding virtually guaranteed. Virginia Beach, Norfolk, and points south all the way to Kitty Hawk will get hit badly, with unprecedented beach erosion and flooding, but nothing like the areas to the north. Even New York City will get gusts of over a hundred miles per hour, if the storm doesn't veer off to the north."

The President of the United States sat back in his chair, shaking his head slowly and sadly.

"Anyone know the situation with ocean traffic?" he asked at last.

Another man moved to the director's elbow. "Mr. President, seas in the heart of the storm are running forty to sixty feet. Two freighters are in trouble, and the Coast Guard fears they've sunk. One other, a Panamanian-registered freighter, is out of contact. Bermuda has sustained heavy damage, and the British are sending help already. Power and communications there were pretty much obliterated by the winds. As for our ships, one of our aircraft carriers, the USS *Eisenhower,* has had to divert around the southern edge of the storm, but they're essentially in it now and battling some pretty high seas to the south, here." A laser point flared on the map at the southern end of the so-called Bermuda triangle.

"How about the area around Goldsboro, North Carolina?"

"They'll get high winds in the seventies before its over, but their main threat is tornadoes and, later tomorrow, flooding over a wide area."

The men in Miami fell silent as they watched the image of the President contemplating their display from the interior of Air Force One a little under five thousand miles distant. For all practical purposes he was a few feet away, and when he moved suddenly, they all jumped.

"Gentlemen, thank you for the comprehensive update. Oh, one thing, Dr. Ronson."

"Yes, sir."

"You're aware of our airborne nuclear crisis?"

"Yes, I am."

"And you're aware it's coming to a head at Seymour-Johnson Air Force Base near Goldsboro?"

The director nodded.

"Okay . . ." the President began and then hesitated, contemplating his fingertips as they drummed the top of the conference table.

"Sir," the director said, breaking the silence, "you'd like to know about the track of any fallout, should that thing detonate?"

The President looked up and caught his eye for a few very long seconds. The director could see deep fatigue there.

"Exactly."

"South over South Carolina as far down as Charleston, but then out to sea to dissipate over the Atlantic."

"That's something at least."

"The outcome is in doubt, sir? There's a chance it won't be defused in time?" the director asked tenuously.

The President got to his feet and smiled a very thin smile.

"Let's just say a few prayers would be in order . . . and appreciated."

18

. . . .

Jerry Christian had finished his portion of the before-landing check and swiveled his seat to the forward position when Scott leaned toward him suddenly.

"I hate to have you do this, Jerry, but I've gotta know something. Go back and take another look at that thing. See if you can find any way they could penetrate the shell without drilling or using a welding torch. I didn't see any seams or any panels, other than the one we opened."

"Most of it is inside that crate," Jerry replied.

"I know. Hurry. I need your best guess."

"Why, Scott?"

"No time to explain. Just do it, please!"

Jerry tossed his seat belts aside and disappeared through the cockpit door as the three-engine jetliner settled onto a five-mile final approach, the winds and turbulence rocking it slightly as the speed settled down to a relatively sedate one hundred seventy knots.

I just assumed they would have all the answers. Scott chided himself. *I just assumed they'd have the experts. I might've just assumed myself into a corner here, and they're about to screw this up!*

"Gear down, landing check, flaps twenty-five," Doc intoned. Scott reached over and lowered the landing gear handle before remembering the previous unsafe indication on the gear doors.

"Doc, we forgot the gear indication . . ." Scott began.

A sudden lurch and muffled crunching sound echoed through the cockpit. Both pilots looked at the gear indicators. The nose and right main were showing a green light apiece, indicating down and locked.

The left main gear was showing red.

"Oh jeez," Doc said. "I forgot about that. We must have really damaged it back there at Pax River."

"Why don't we retract and re-extend it, Doc?"

"Hold it!" Doc said. "That could make things worse. How about those fighters out there? Could they take a look at it?"

Scott nodded. "Good idea. Where are those F-16's?"

"They've broken off to the right."

Scott dialed the air-to-air frequency in the UHF radio once again and keyed the microphone.

"F-16 flight from ScotAir Fifty. You guys still there?"

The voice of the lead pilot came back immediately.

"Roger, ScotAir. Go ahead."

"We've got an unsafe gear indication on our left main. Could you come under and take a look at it? We'll level off here and do a low approach to the runway, straight ahead at a thousand feet."

The F-16 lead pilot agreed and began maneuvering to the left as Doc leveled the Boeing at a thousand feet and Scott informed Seymour tower what they were going to do.

Scott could see the F-16 move in from the right and disappear behind them. Thirty seconds ticked by before the lead fighter pilot's voice came over the radio.

"Okay, ScotAir, your left main gear appears to be undamaged and appears to be in the same position as the right one. Your left landing gear door, the one attached to the left main gear, looks like a big dog's been chewing on it. The bottom edge is broken and ragged, and it's partially hanging from its mounting."

"We've got two larger doors on the belly. Are those both closed?" Scott asked.

"Yes, sir, they appear to be. The one I'm talking about is actually attached to the gear strut."

Jerry had returned to the cockpit in time to hear the exchange. In one fluid motion he put on his seat belt and leaned forward over the center console.

"Scott, first try recycling the gear."

Scott nodded and told the F-16 lead what they were going to do and what to look for.

"Gear up, Doc."

He pulled the gear handle up, and once again the left main showed an unsafe red.

"Gear down."

Doc positioned the handle, and the lurch and muffled noise once again reached their ears.

"You're back in the same position, Captain," the F-16 pilot told him. "It looks to be down and locked in the same position as the right one."

"But"—Doc was pointing to the warning lights—"it's still showing unsafe."

Scott turned to Jerry. "Worst case?"

"It collapses on landing and we have trouble steering. It's probably safe, Scott. I thought I felt it lock, so maybe the microswitch is screwed up."

"Should we give it a try?"

Jerry nodded. "Yeah, just favor the right side and be prepared for a collapse."

"Roger."

"Scott, about the bomb."

"Just a second. Doc, tell the tower we're going to make right closed traffic and stay visual, then just circle us around to the right and realign with the runway."

Doc nodded as he reached for the radio.

"Okay, Jerry. Tell me what you saw."

"Scott, every inch of that damn thing is welded shut, except the hatch where the TV screen and keyboard are located. The only way in is to cut the metal with a cutting torch, or drill in, and it looks like the shell is case-hardened stainless steel. You could burn your way in, all right, but the heat of a cutting torch will be easily detectable, and I'll bet anything the diabolical inventor has it filled with heat sensors. He would have expected exactly that sort of attempt."

Scott nodded. "There's no way one solitary technician's going to penetrate that thing undetected." Scott looked back, searching Jerry's face. "You agree?"

"Yeah. It's also repeating the same warnings about not trying to explode or burn it. I forget the exact words, but something regarding an electronic nuclear trigger."

Scott watched Doc begin the right turn over the airport. He chewed his lower lip for a few seconds before looking back.

"I think we've got to assume it's telling the truth that any attempt to blow it up will be fatal, to us and a million others. That leaves one thing: Dump it at sea."

"That's what Vivian said," Linda interjected.

"And if they won't do it?" Jerry asked.

"Then, old friend, we're all toast."

FBI HEADQUARTERS, WASHINGTON, D.C.—
6:26 P.M. EDT

Tony DiStefano held his hand over the receiver as he looked at Donna and rolled his eyes. His whisper could be heard across the room, but not over the line.

"God help us, we've drawn Attila the Hun as our agent in charge at Seymour-Johnson."

"Who?" Donna asked, looking from Tony to another male agent and back.

"Harold Hanks, special agent extraordinaire," Agent Bill Watson explained to her. "You've never met him?"

Donna shook her head. "Not that I'm aware of."

"You'd remember. Combine the self-importance of a Douglas MacArthur with the paranoia of J. Edgar Hoover and the linguistic arrogance of William F. Buckley, and then issue it a badge."

"Jesus!" Donna mumbled under her breath.

"Oh yes, Him too."

"The perfect senior bureaucrat, in other words."

Bill nodded. "In the field without a clue."

The others could see Tony's jaw muscles working as he struggled for composure, his voice carrying an artificial niceness. "Harold, is that you?"

There was a pause, and another look of disgust crossed Tony's face like a fast-moving cloud.

"Okay, I understand Agent Hanks is busy, but would you tell him that headquarters would like a word with him if it isn't too much trouble? You see, that's why we issue you guys these cellular telephones."

Tony suddenly shook his head in utter disgust. "This is *FBI* headquarters! Your fripping boss! You see, this could come as a shock, but I believe the ID card in your badge wallet says FBI, not the Harold Hanks Agency, and since we'd sorta like to talk to Agent Hanks for purposes of, oh, I don't know, maybe coordination, it would probably be a good career move for you to HAND THE DAMN PHONE TO HANKS NOW!'"

Tony's face was turning a shocking shade of red.

"Jesus H. Christ!" he snarled to the small group gathering around him as he held his hand over the receiver again, then removed it.

"You're damn right I'm being sarcastic!"

Tony pulled up a swivel chair and plunked himself in it as a voice came on the other end.

"Harold? Tony DiStefano in D.C. So sorry to tear you away. I need to make sure we're singing from the same songbook, okay? First, where is the . . . okay, on final approach. Harold, you're going to have to play this very, very delicately. We do not believe Mrs. Henry is in the cockpit, and . . . Harold, I know you've been briefed at my direction already, but now I'm briefing you in person, understand? We do believe that you can talk in the clear to the captain, either on the UHF radio or on his Flitephone. No, I said you CAN. Did you get that Flitephone number? Okay, it should work down there if you need it. Here's the thing I'm most concerned about. I'm afraid that crew may be on Mrs. Henry's side. I don't think they realize what a beef she's had with the government, and I get the feeling they think she's incapable of pulling this off herself. That could lead to real problems if she starts calling the shots directly or indirectly, and it could lead to their interference if they thought we were abusing her by making an arrest. Your . . . yeah, Harold, I'm aware of that. Our job is to assist the Air Force commander in getting his men to the bomb as fast as possible. Do what you have to do, but don't let procedure get in the way of getting them to the bomb."

Tony closed his eyes, propped an elbow on the desk, and began rubbing his head. "Harold, I'm not implying anything. Look, we've had this discussion before. I don't like you a whole helluva lot and you don't like me. That's a given. But professionally, I'm telling you to do whatever's needed, but don't let standard procedure get in the way of getting the Air Force in possession of that weapon. We'll be standing by. Yeah, good luck."

Tony stood up and poised the receiver high over his head with eyes flaring, as if he was about to slam-dunk it onto the desk. He froze in position then and let his eyes shift to the others as they watched and held their breath. Tony let a deliberately maniacal smile spread slowly over his face, then raised both eyebrows.

"Just kidding." He lowered the phone to its cradle, shaking his head. "I remember thinking the character of Major Frank Burns on *M*A*S*H* was a ridiculous caricature. No one could be that officious, that stupid. But there he is, in the flesh, about to handle the most delicate assignment in recent FBI history."

"What you're saying is . . ." Donna began.

"We're probably screwed," Tony finished.

SEYMOUR-JOHNSON AIR FORCE BASE, NORTH CAROLINA—6:31 P.M. EDT

Scott flared the 727 and pulled the power off as the plane settled toward the runway. He walked the right main gear and then the nose gear on and gently lowered the left main wheels to the concrete as he pulled out the speed brakes and thrust reversers. When it was apparent the left main was holding, Scott let his eyes take in both sides of the runway—and the apparent preparations being made for them in the distance.

"We'll roll to the end of the runway, Doc."

"Roger."

Angry clouds were whipping by overhead with occasional bursts of rain, but the effects of Hurricane Sigrid were just beginning, and the visibility was still good enough to see clearly from one end of the base to the other. Scott slowed the three-engine jet to a five-mile-per-hour taxi speed as the red lights marking the end of the runway surface came under the nose.

The tower controller verbally pointed out the dark blue pickup truck with the lighted FOLLOW ME sign waiting on the taxiway adjacent to the end of the taxiway as Scott transitioned his left hand to the nosewheel steering tiller and guided the jet off the end of the runway, where he braked smoothly to a stop.

The men in the FOLLOW ME truck began moving out ahead, then braked to a halt, obviously confused. After a few seconds, one of them emerged from his cab to wave at the 727 to continue.

But Scott had no intention of moving just yet.

"Seymour ground, ScotAir Fifty. We're going to remain here for a minute until I get something worked out. Keep all vehicles and personnel clear. Tell your 'Follow Me.' "

"Roger" was the only reply.

Scott reached for the UHF military frequency radio and keyed his microphone on the same command frequency he'd used while inbound.

"Colonel Peters, you still there?"

There was a moment's hesitation.

"Ah, roger. Peters here."

"Colonel, exactly where are you planning to park us?"

"ScotAir, the 'Follow Me' will take you there. We've prepared a spot in kind of a revetment area to the west side of the field. It's the hot area for this base."

Scott could see the area clearly from the cockpit. The site had been selected for one reason, and that was frightening him.

"Colonel, we're trying to defuse a nuke here, right?"

"That's correct, Captain."

"You guaranteed there'd be no attempt to blow up this weapon, right?"

"I said we'd do everything we can to defuse it, Captain."

"The hell you did! You said I had your assurance that there would be, and I quote, 'no attempt to burn or explode this thing,' but now you want me to taxi to an area prepared specifically *for* the purpose of containing explosives. If the bomb we've got aboard goes nuclear, it doesn't matter where on the base we're parked, the whole place is vaporized. That means there's only one possible reason for trying to send us to the hot cargo area: You've decided to ignore my warnings and blow it up anyway."

There was a hesitation before the answer came.

"Those are standard preparations for hazardous material, Captain. I'm told you're a military man. You ought to understand such things. It should also have occurred to you by now that we need to defuse the damn thing you're carrying because we need to know what's inside."

"You need to know what's inside? I'll tell you what's inside, Colonel. THERE'S A FRIGGIN' THERMONUCLEAR BOMB IN-SIDE! We clear on that point?"

"We don't have time for this, okay? Just understand that your country needs to know how that weapon works."

"Colonel, you're not going to be able to defuse this thing or study it. We've barely got enough time for you to go dump it at sea!"

"That's not your choice, ScotAir, that's ours. If, for some reason, we can't defuse it, then dumping is an option."

"Colonel, where is the C-141?" Scott shot back. "I know what a C-141 looks like, and I don't see one on this base."

"He's inbound, Captain. He'll be here in a few minutes."

"You told me he was on the ground already and standing by," Scott reminded him.

"Ah, I'm sorry about that, Captain. There's been so much to get done before you got here, I got ahead of myself. Look, time is short. Please follow the truck and get over here so we can get started."

Linda saw Scott shake his head before he remembered to punch the transmit button.

"I want to talk to the man who's going to try to defuse this thing."

There was silence for a few seconds, then a new voice on the radio. The colonel could be heard protesting inches away.

"Captain? This is Special Agent Harold Hanks of the FBI. Your aircraft and all persons in it are under the jurisdiction of the federal government at this point. I have the appropriate warrants. You will follow the colonel's instructions to the letter, and you will do so immediately."

Scott wet his lips and glanced at Doc, who inhaled sharply.

"Now it begins, Scott," Doc said.

"What?"

"We've lost control, and God help us if they haven't been listening."

Scott pressed the mike button again. "Agent Hanks, I want to know precisely what you want us to do when we reach the parking site."

"I understand the woman is not in the cockpit with you," Hanks shot back. "If that's wrong, if she is up front but can't hear me, flash your landing lights and put your flaps to full down."

"Oh my God, I knew it," Linda said from the jumpseat. "They're all wrapped around the axle thinking Vivian's a terrorist."

Scott raised his right hand for silence.

"No, she's not in the cockpit, and she can't hear us, Agent Hanks."

"Okay. Understood," Hanks said. "Don't alert her. If you can open the forward left door as soon as you get parked, our team will come aboard and take her into custody."

"Hanks, this is the captain. Mrs. Henry is not, I repeat, *not* the instigator of this. She is a victim. There is absolutely no need to arrest her or treat her as an enemy."

Jerry leaned forward suddenly. "Tell him we've got only one hour and twenty-seven minutes left."

"Okay." Scott nodded, keying the microphone again. "Hanks, I want to speak to the man who's here to disarm this thing. We've got less than an hour and twenty-seven minutes to nuclear detonation."

"Captain, this is Colonel Peters. We can let you talk to him when you're in the parking place. We don't have time right now."

Two staff cars could be seen moving along the taxiway toward the waiting 727's position. A third vehicle, a Humvee, was following at a distance.

Scott punched the button again. "No, Colonel, until the doors are open and the engines are shut down, I'm in command of this aircraft, and you will listen to *me*. We're wasting time. Put on the nuclear technician. Now!"

The voice on the other end was growing exasperated. "Captain, dammit, I'm ordering you to start taxiing and get that crate over here!"

"The technician first, Colonel."

"Or what, Captain? Are you threatening us?"

Scott held the microphone in his hand for what seemed an eternity as Linda and Doc and Jerry watched him and held their breath. Finally he raised it to his mouth again and punched the transmit button.

"I'm sitting here with a live thermonuclear weapon which can create an electromagnetic wave devastating enough to shut down the nation for months, in addition to killing maybe a million people in the local area and making North Carolina the only state that glows in the dark without benefit of electricity. Even the President, I'm told, is aware of this situation, and you fellows want to sit there and play games with *me*? You're going to put the technician on right now! I hold all the cards until this airplane is parked, understood? This is my airplane. Even the federal air regulations confirm that. You guys are nothing but unidentified voices on the other end of the radio until I determine otherwise. Now, you want to explain to your superiors that you screwed this up because of some macho-man power play over who's in charge? I'll bet you anything there are ears listening to all this at far more distant locations, and they're going to be second-guessing your every decision. So . . . stop arguing with me and comply. *Now!*"

There was a hesitation before the radio came to life again. The speaker was obviously fumbling with the radio. The sound of his hand searching for a grip on the handheld transceiver came through loud and clear.

"Uh, this is Technical Sergeant Bill Clevenger, sir. You wanted to talk to me?"

"What training have you had in defusing nonmilitary terrorist nuclear weapons, Sergeant?" Scott asked.

"Ah," the voice began, then stopped. The radio went quiet. Scott could imagine both the colonel and the FBI agent firing instructions on what to say. Finally the transmitter was keyed again.

"Sir, I'm trained to defuse all types of military nuclear weapons. I have had no specific training in nonmilitary, but I know all the basic equipment, and I'm qualified to defuse any incendiary device."

Scott keyed his mike. "Good answer, guys. But here's the problem. This thing is in a stainless steel case that's welded closed with no seams, and I've got every reason to believe it's completely surrounded inside with heat sensors and other intrusion sensors. In other words, there's no way to get in to defuse the mechanism. You can't explode it or burn it because it will trigger a nuclear blast, and that leaves only one thing: Get it off this bird and on a C-141 and dump it at sea. That's what I was trying to tell you a while ago. Only problem, you lied about the 141, and we don't have time to manufacture one."

"Well, I'll tell you what, Captain." The Colonel's voice sounded helpful and thoughtful and cooperative. "We've got KC-10's evacuating from this base and we'll just hold one on the ground here and use it."

Doc and Scott both snorted simultaneously as Linda looked on in puzzlement.

Scott jabbed the transmit button. "Colonel, we're not fools. You can't dump something out of a KC-10 in flight any more than I can dump it out of this airplane. If you haven't noticed, the cargo door is on the side, not in the back."

"Sorry, you're right. I was just trying to find a solution. At least the 141 is inbound, Captain. I give you my word."

"Your word is awfully suspect at this point, Colonel. By the way, stop those vehicles from coming any closer to me. NOW!"

There was silence for a few seconds, but the two staff cars and the Humvee suddenly stopped a few thousand feet ahead.

Doc Hazzard looked over at Scott, his voice strained and short. "What're you thinking, Scott?"

Scott was breathing hard. Perspiration beaded on his forehead.

"I . . . don't know, Doc. But I do know what's about to happen. I know damn well they're not going to listen to us. They'll promise me anything, but when they get us out of here, they'll put Vivian in chains, poke around for a while looking for a hatch in the bomb casing, then blow up the airplane and trigger the bomb and the Medusa Wave. At the very least, they'll blow themselves, and us, and Goldsboro off the map."

Jerry leaned forward at the same moment. "Whatever you decide, Scott, I'm with you."

"Me too," Doc said.

Scott licked his lips again and glanced at all of them, then looked around at Linda.

"Okay. This is what we're going to do. Linda?"

"Yes?"

"We're going to drop the rear stairway. I want you and Jerry to get out of here. Doc, you too."

"No fucking way. Excuse the language," Doc shot back.

"Same for me," Jerry said.

Scott was shaking his head side to side, his eyes almost closed. "Listen, dammit! I don't see any other way out of this . . ."

The voice of the FBI agent interrupted.

"Captain, we're wasting time, and if you fail to comply with appropriate dispatch, we're going to ultimately indict all of you on charges of felony obstruction of justice, harboring a felon, terrorism, air piracy, jaywalking, and everything else we can possibly put in an indictment. I suggest you move immediately or you'll end up a permanent resident of Leavenworth."

Scott inclined his head toward the distant ramp and snorted. "Has a real persuasive way with words, doesn't he?"

"Arrogant bastard!" Doc interjected. "Air piracy? How can we hijack ourselves?"

Jerry bobbed his head in agreement.

"What are you planning, Scott?" Linda asked, her voice low and steady, an island of calm in a storm, the feminine serenity helping him to focus as he turned to her with the sound of the FBI agent in his ears again.

"Captain, you either respond now, or we'll physically interdict your aircraft!"

Scott waved his hand at the windscreen. "I'm not interested in suicide, but somehow we're going to have to do this ourselves. I can't let them set off a nuclear blast because of their stupidity. Maybe we can negotiate with them if we're back in the air."

"ScotAir Fifty, this is Agent Hanks. What, precisely, do you want? If you're issuing demands, kindly state them."

Scott jabbed the transmit button down. "You're damn right I'm issuing demands, Hanks. I want the full assurance of the FBI, the Air Force, the President, and the United States government that no attempt will be made to blow up this device. You understand me? You've got to dump it at sea, or you're going to create a historic disaster! Do you clowns understand what I'm saying? If you try to explode this weapon, it will cause a full nuclear detonation and a Medusa Wave!"

The agent's voice came back almost instantly in what seemed a snarl. "You're attempting to second-guess experts, Captain. I believe we know what such a weapon will and will not do."

"Experts? We're talking one well-meaning sergeant who'll need six months just to analyze the casing around this thing. I'm second-guessing second-guessers!"

"I'm not going to give you any assurances, Captain, other than the fact that our man knows what he's doing, and we'll take care of it. It's not your responsibility anymore."

"That," Scott said with a verbal snarl, "is where you are sorely mistaken."

"Stop being a cowboy, Captain. You're getting in the way, and *you're* going to be responsible if we can't get it disposed of . . ."

The voice ceased in midsentence, and Doc and Jerry realized that Scott had turned off the radio.

Linda knew Vivian's position was impossible. She knew the mentality of the men on the other end of the radios, and she knew deep down that Scott was right about any attempt to disarm Rogers Henry's Medusa weapon.

Quite simply, there was only one choice.

She leaned forward, gripping the back of the seat, and put her lips next to Scott's ear. "Forget the rear stairs. Let's get the hell out of here!"

Scott swiveled his head toward Jerry. "Fuel?"

"Enough," Jerry answered, quickly checking his gauges.

Scott half-turned toward Linda. "I can't take you with us! I . . ."

With a fluid sweep of her right hand, Linda reached out and gathered the throttles and shoved them forward about halfway.

"You can and you will."

Scott jerked his head around to look at her in amazement.

"You're sure?"

"I'm sure."

"Linda, I don't know that we're going to get out of this. You had no responsibility for bringing that thing along. You . . ."

"Stop talking and GO!"

He hesitated for a moment as their eyes met, then nodded. "Okay. We're outta here."

The Humvee had started moving again, passing the two staff cars. It was highly likely they had a machine gun on board and orders to shoot the tires.

Scott's left hand jammed the steering tiller to the left as the engines began winding up. The nose began moving left, back toward the runway, which was clear ahead. His right hand was on the throttles now, waiting for the aircraft to align with the runway.

"Tell them we'll taxi down the runway and exit at midfield."

"What?" Doc said, startled.

"We're buying time," Scott shot back.

Doc grinned. "Right." He punched the transmit button for the ground control frequency, trying to sound resigned and suppress the excitement and fright that was gripping all of them.

"Okay, Seymour tower, ScotAir Fifty's going to taxi back down the runway here to go to the parking site. Tell the 'Follow Me' we'll pick him up at the midfield turnoff."

"We'd prefer you use the taxiway, ScotAir," the controller replied.

"It's better if we use the runway, tower."

"Okay, approved as requested."

On the taxiway the Humvee suddenly braked to a halt once again. There would be confusion, Scott knew, as messages were passed back and forth and the FBI agent and Air Force colonel tried to convince themselves they had won the battle.

"Set max power. Just estimate the EPR," Scott said.

"Two-point-one-three!" Jerry called out, having already computed the values for setting the power.

The big Boeing began rolling forward. Scott knew the men on the ground would be caught by surprise. By the time they passed fifty knots, the colonel would figure out they were doing something more than just taxiing.

"Eighty knots!" Doc called out.

Simultaneously, the radio came alive.

"ScotAir Fifty, you are not cleared for takeoff! Abort your takeoff! Men and equipment on runway!"

"Yeah, sure," Scott muttered.

"Vee One . . . Vee R," Doc called as Scott pulled the yoke back and flew the 727 off the runway. There would be a frantic attempt to unsheathe guns, and maybe even some ill-advised small arms fire, but they had the advantage of surprise.

"Positive rate, gear up."

"Gear up," Doc echoed as his big hand pulled the gear handle to the up position.

"I'm going to pop into the clouds off the south end, Doc, then come left to almost due east and drop down a little to stay out of radar. Make sure the transponder is off."

The almost frantic voice of the tower controller was in their ears.

"ScotAir, you've made an illegal takeoff! Return your aircraft to this airfield immediately! Acknowledge!"

"Change the damn frequency, Doc," Scott ordered.

"With pleasure."

"Time on the bomb is one hour, twenty minutes, Scott!" Jerry said. "And we've got twenty-six thousand pounds of fuel left, enough for about two hours of cruise flight with some low altitude."

"Just a quick question, Scott," Doc said.

"What?"

"Where, exactly, are we going?"

Scott looked over at Doc and shook his head.

"Toward the Atlantic. As far away from people as we can get."

19

•••

As requested, the Air Force chief master sergeant in charge of the on-board communications systems summoned the President back to the Starsuite as soon as the multiple radio frequency monitors had been established from Seymour-Johnson Air Force Base in North Carolina. The exchanges between the on-scene Air Force commander, the FBI agent in charge, and Scot Air 50 had boomed through the suite for ten minutes as they waited for the Chief Executive to finish a vital phone call to the worried Canadian Prime Minister and return. Wide eyes and silence now greeted the President as he walked in moments after the Seymour-Johnson control tower tried to order ScotAir 50 back to the base.

The President looked at the electronic map covering the Starsuite's video wall and did a rapid scan of every face in the room.

"Okay, someone want to fill me in on what's happened? Everyone in here looks spooked."

The Secretary of State sighed and gestured to the map, speaking in a slightly hoarse and weary voice. "The bomb situation has taken precedence over our Hurricane Sigrid. The Air Force and the FBI just forced the pilot of that aircraft into a corner, and he apparently decided he had to solve the problem by himself. He took off without permission, and he's not responding to radio calls."

The President sat down carefully.

"How, exactly, did this happen?"

"By the FBI agent using the subtlety of a Nazi storm trooper in declaring his intention to arrest the woman with the bomb, and by the Air Force commander refusing to listen to the pilot's extreme concern that they can't just blow up the bomb without setting off a nuclear blast. The Air Force commander also lied to the pilot—as well as to you."

"Lied?"

"Lied. You told them to have a C-141 standing by, correct?"

"I did."

"The Chairman of the Joint Chiefs promised you he would do so, and a message fifteen minutes ago to us confirmed that everything was ready. The on-scene commander told the captain of the inbound 727 the C-141 was already on the ground, but instead, it has been kept circling at a distance. In fact, it was only fifty miles north of its base at Charleston. The fact that there was no C-141 there seems to have prompted the 727 captain, at least in part, to leave."

"What?"

"The captain obviously believes the only safe disposal method is to dump the bomb at sea. Oh, but there's more! I took a call a few minutes ago from the wing commander at Seymour, a brigadier general. He was very upset, and I told Signals to patch him in. Know what he told me?"

"No, but I can understand wanting to keep the 141 away until they're ready to load. The general who called is the commander who decided to keep the C-141 circling?" the President asked.

"No, this is the wing commander who was forced to let a colonel from Shaw zip in and take over as on-scene commander."

"Sour grapes, perhaps?"

"Perhaps. He said he's retiring soon anyway, and he knows he's jumping the chain of command just a tad to call the President, but he felt you needed to know immediately of a brief exchange he had on his ramp a little while ago with the colonel who took over his base. It seems our good colonel had no intention of using the C-141 or keeping the dumping option open, despite your orders. Want to hear the quote?"

"You bet I do!"

The Secretary of State consulted his notes.

"This is very close to verbatim. The colonel said to him: 'I am responsible for defusing and preserving this bomb. I'm *not* responsible for mind-reading the current political hack in the White House to try to figure out what he might think he wants. I only take orders from the Air Force.'"

The President was shaking his head from side to side and grinding his teeth as the Secretary of State continued.

"Ask and you may or may not receive, depending on whether the Pentagon thinks you know what you want."

"Goddammit!" The President lunged for the intercom as the Secretary leaned over to speak directly in his ear.

"This is exactly what I've been trying to tell you about for the past six months. They're out of control over there. They'll tell you anything. Remember what I taught you and your classmates several years ago at Georgetown? The civilian sector cannot remain in control of the military if the military thinks that its responsibility includes lying to and manipulating the civilian sector to further its own purpose, regardless of how noble that purpose might be."

The President nodded. "I remember clearly."

"They've become professional liars. You've refused to believe me on that point. But here's a classic example."

The communications sergeant answered the intercom.

"Jim? Switch us back to the Situation Room and find the Chairman of the Joint Chiefs and the commander of the Air Combat Command immediately."

The President leaned back with a ferocious look of anger on his face, his fingers drumming the table. "Dammit, where are those poor bastards going with that bomb? What do they think they're doing? And how can we salvage this in time? We've got to answer those questions, and then I'm going to relieve a few Air Force people of their ranks, their pensions, and their damned heads!"

The Secretary of State sat down quietly, carefully avoiding the look of satisfaction he so dearly wanted to wear.

ABOARD SCOTAIR 50 — 6:45 P.M. EDT

Scott had the aircraft in a left bank on instruments.

"Jerry, I've got a question for you."

"Shoot."

"Any way you could jury-rig the main cargo door to open in flight?"

Scott was aware of Doc staring at him from the right seat, and aware of the deep silence from the engineer's seat.

Jerry found his voice at last.

"Even if I could, and I don't know for sure, the door would rip off and probably take the tail with it. It's part of the structural integrity of the fuselage when it's closed. I'm not even sure we could stay airborne with it open."

"Hey, if Aloha Airlines could fly a convertible 737 in 1987 with most of the top gone . . ."

Jerry nodded, a frightened look on his face.

"We couldn't open it in flight without major problems, Scott. We might be able to fly with it off, but I don't have the tools to get it off. That's a heavy door."

Scott looked at Doc. "Okay, get out the maps. See if there's an airport we can land at and maybe rig something up, take the door off, dump Linda's stuff out, anything. Jerry, try to figure out how we could get the door off the airplane fast and leave it behind."

"We don't have much time," Doc said. "You mentioned negotiating with them once we were in the air. Maybe that's best."

Scott nodded. "If I could get survival gear and a parachute, I could land long enough to dump all of you out somewhere, set the aircraft eastbound on autopilot, and bail out."

"You'd never get out the door," Jerry protested.

Scott was shaking his head vigorously. "Yes, I could. I wouldn't go out the side door, I'd go out the aft airstairs, and before you tell me we can't open that in flight, I know we'd need to sledge-hammer that in-flight lock off first, but it could be done. Jumping off the rear stairs is not a problem. If D. B. Cooper could do it, I can do it!"

"Who?" Linda asked.

"A hijacker," Doc explained, "back in the seventies. He took his loot and a parachute and jumped off the rear stairs of a Northwest Airlines 727 south of Seattle. That's why they put the in-flight lock on all 727 aft airstairs to prevent anyone from opening them in flight and jumping out. Worked, too. There was never another Cooper caper."

"Doc, what's the minimum safe altitude here?"

Doc pulled open one of the aeronautical maps and consulted several figures. "Twenty-eight hundred feet, Scott. Come up to three thousand and we'll clear everything."

"Right now I'm going down to the weeds."

"You think farm people down there won't notice a 727 at treetop level?"

"I'm not worried about farmers. I'm worried about those two F-16's back at Seymour. They were refueling after we landed. We caught them flat-footed, but they'll be after us in a few minutes."

"So what?" Doc asked.

"So what? Those were live Sidewinders they were carrying, Doc. Didn't you notice?"

Doc shook his head in mild shock. "Lord, no, I didn't."

Scott brought the big Boeing down through five hundred feet and held the speed to two hundred fifty knots in what felt like a barnstorming maneuver. Groves of trees and soggy fields and the occasional highway shot beneath them as he steered an easterly course and hand flew the jetliner through increasingly rough winds and growing rain showers. The ceiling ahead was getting lower. He would need to climb back into the weather shortly and navigate by radar, hoping the storm cells would mask the radar skin echoes of the 727.

"We should have thought to demand parachutes back there," Jerry said.

Scott shook his head. "They would've shot the tires or the engines or both. They wouldn't have complied anyway, and I couldn't threaten to set the thing off to force compliance without branding us all as terrorists."

"They'll brand us as terrorists now," Doc added.

"Scott." Linda's voice reached his ear. "They said they had a C-141 nearby. I know it's got a rear cargo door and they can dump cargo from it in flight. If they weren't lying—if there really is one around here somewhere—couldn't we divert him to a coastal runway and transfer the cargo? Couldn't we find somewhere they're not ready for us, somewhere they can't get a reception committee to in time? Even if we can't switch cargo, I'll bet they'd have parachutes aboard."

"Good idea, Linda," Doc said. Scott nodded in agreement.

Jerry raised his hand. "I've got their in-flight frequencies. Let me see if I can raise the guy if he's really out there."

"Using the UHF?" Scott asked.

"Yeah. Be right back."

"Someone needs to tell Vivian what's happening," Scott said.

"I'll do it," Linda volunteered. She threw off her seat belt and slipped out the cockpit door as Scott banked the jet sharply to the left and then back to the right to avoid a small series of hills.

The turbulence was getting worse by the minute as they flew deeper into the fringes of the hurricane. The bouncing and bumping was graduating from irritating to uncomfortable, an all-too-familiar sensation.

"Scott." Doc pointed to the windscreen and the scene ahead of them. "We're risking some nasty weather ahead at this altitude. Remember, we're flying back into the hurricane."

"I know it. But we need some distance before showing them a radar target."

"They'll know we're headed toward the ocean, Scott. It doesn't take a genius to figure that out."

Again Scott banked sharply, this time to the right, then brought the heading back to due east as he half-turned to Doc once again.

"Doc, hunt for an airfield on the coast, even something a little southeast along the coast in South Carolina. Anything with enough concrete to land for a few minutes. Jerry's still working the C-141 search."

Linda reentered the cockpit as Doc fought to unfold another map. Scott glanced at her and noticed that she was nursing her elbow. "What happened?" he asked.

"Nothing. It's just kinda hard to stay on your feet with a plane bouncing around like this. Anyway, Vivian's okay. Terrified as the rest of us, but okay. The screen back there says one hour, fourteen minutes remaining."

Scott nodded. "Linda, we're going to find an airfield to land on. We're going to open the cargo door and shove your pallets out on the concrete and try to drop the door, if I can find two parachutes. Can your stuff take being dropped?"

She leaned forward and smiled thinly. "When compared to the potential of my equipment surviving a nuclear detonation, a mere ten-foot drop to concrete is nothing. Yes, it can take it."

"You're going to get off there, Linda. So are Doc and Jerry. I'll get the plane going east, and then parachute out with Vivian and hope the damn bomb will rant and rave at her in absentia long enough to put some distance between us before it blows. You can get the Coast Guard to come look for us. I'll steer exactly zero-nine-zero magnetic and try to jump no more than twenty miles out."

"Right! Let me get this straight, okay? You're going to bail out of a 727 in the midst of a hurricane in late afternoon without a raft. This is a plan, McKay?" Linda asked, chuckling sarcastically. "I thought you had a plan."

Scott looked around with a surprised, almost hurt expression, completely missing her humor.

"I . . . I'm sorry, Linda, you insisted . . ."

She rattled the back of his seat. "I'm kidding, Scott! But we've got to think of something less suicidal. I'm growing accustomed to the back of your head. I'd hate to see you lose it."

ABOARD AIR FORCE ONE—6:48 P.M. EDT

The Chairman of the Joint Chiefs of Staff of the United States stood ramrod straight on the Situation Room side of the Starsuite as an angry Commander in Chief standing thirty-nine thousand feet over the Pacific Ocean read him the riot and sedition act in a tone of voice that hardly needed microphones to carry to Washington. When the President paused, his face crimson, the Chairman looked at the desk momentarily, then back at the President.

"May I speak candidly, sir?"

"You're going to be a goddamn civilian in the next ten seconds if you *don't* speak candidly, John!"

"Yes, sir. I relayed the orders precisely as given. I take full responsibility for our failure to get that C-141 on the ground, but, speaking to you personally, I'm as blind-sided and angry as you are, sir."

"Fix it, goddammit! The first priority is to win the heart and mind of that 727's captain before he blows our economy and himself—and God knows how many other Americans—off the map! I don't know how the hell you're going to do it, but do it, and keep me informed minute by minute. And, John?"

"Yes, sir?"

"When this is over, I don't want the hide of some first lieutenant. Remember I was an Air Force officer, too. I know how the secret brotherhood works, and how all the colonels and generals find lower-ranking scapegoats at the first sign of trouble."

"Sir . . ."

"Remember the Iraq helicopter shoot-down back in 1994? The President was lied to. He was told that one little captain in an AWACS was the only one responsible for the screwups and lies of a dozen or more senior officers. Bullshit! You're *not* pulling that on my watch! That colonel at Seymour is fired and retired and relieved as of this instant! Now, there's a wing commander who's going to get a commendation and a promotion for jumping the chain of coverup, but I want the professional scalp of each and every senior officer who had the slightest shadow of an idea that my C-141 order was going to be thwarted. Anyone who tries to cover for anyone else is going to be cashiered. Is that clear?"

"As crystal, Sir."

ABOARD SCOTAIR 50—6:49 P.M. EDT

The sound of Jerry's voice rising in excitement as he spoke to someone on the radio caught their attention. Scott looked around as Jerry flashed a thumbs-up. "I've got them!" he said quickly, returning to the radio. "Reach Two Six Six, this is ScotAir Fifty. Please listen closely."

Jerry gestured to the UHF radio. "Go ahead, Scott. They're listening."

Doc shot a puzzled look at first Scott, then Jerry.

" 'Reach'? What in the world is *that?* C-141's are 'MAC,' aren't they?"

Scott shook his head. "Some idiot four-star general changed the call sign from 'MAC' to 'Reach' because he liked the slogan 'Global Reach.' "

Scott punched the transmit button. "Reach, you were heading to Seymour, right?"

"That's affirmative, ScotAir."

"Okay, we've changed that mission. You were to rendezvous with us, weren't you?"

There was a hesitation, and Scott bit his lip hard enough to draw blood while he waited for the reply.

"Ah yes, ScotAir, our mission did involve you."

"Roger, and you have a minimum crew on board to take our cargo and dump it airborne to the east, correct?"

Another hesitation, but the young pilot in the Lockheed C-141 obviously had accepted the fact that whoever he was talking to knew his mission.

"Affirmative, ScotAir."

"Okay, listen up, please, Reach. We don't have enough time or fuel to return to Seymour. I presume you're carrying parachutes and survival gear?"

"Yes, sir."

"Good. All we need is to get two of those chutes and survival gear, and we'll just head this bird over the water and parachute out of it. Can you suggest an appropriate airfield? We need creative thinking right now. Time is running out."

"Sir, the Myrtle Beach area isn't too far to the southeast."

Jerry was nodding. "There's a perfect civilian field north of Myrtle called Grand Strand. Runway's about six thousand feet long, and there are several ramps. It's right on the coast."

Scott keyed the microphone. "We'll take Grand Strand, if you know where that is."

"We know that one, ScotAir. Stand by, please. We'll call you back."

He'll now call his command post for orders, Scott realized. The next response should tell it all.

20

••••

With a furious President waiting for answers in the Starsuite aboard Air Force One and an embarrassed and equally furious Chairman of the Joint Chiefs of Staff pacing around the communications consoles in the Situation Room at the White House, the rattled Secretary of Defense and ashen-faced Secretary of the Air Force conferred in one corner of the Pentagon's dark, two-story, wood-paneled War Room. A new round of calls laced a tightening net between Seymour-Johnson Air Force Base and the Pentagon as the storm inside the Pentagon echoed the intensity of the growing hurricane outside.

The on-the-spot presidential sacking of Colonel Jeff Peters had shocked everyone, but as three other senior officers—two major generals, and a lieutenant general—were removed from the command post and interrogated by the Chairman of the Joint Chiefs of Staff on a secure line from the Situation Room, a frantic attempt was being made to contact the crew of ScotAir 50. A patched-in radio call from the aircraft commander of the C-141 who had talked to ScotAir came through at the same moment, instantly stopping every conversation in the room.

"Uh, sir, I said that ScotAir Fifty has called us on a UHF frequency. He wants us to meet him at Grand Strand Airport, which is north of Myrtle Beach, South Carolina. He wants parachutes and survival gear. He's proposing to head his aircraft east and bail out. I need orders, please. How should I respond?"

The commander of the Air Combat Command, a four-star general named Ralph Kinney, held up a finger for time and picked up the secure tie-line to the Situation Room to inform the Chairman of the Joint Chiefs of the details.

"What, precisely, does the President want us to do in this circumstance?" General Kinney asked. "I don't want any more of his wrath, so what do we do?"

"What we do, Ralph, is ask him ourselves. Get to the Starsuite on your end."

In less than a minute a split transmission turned the other side of the President's airborne Starsuite into a split screen, with the Situation Room on one side and the Pentagon command post on the other.

"Where are we now with respect to detonation time?" the President asked.

"Less than an hour and ten minutes, sir," General Kinney said.

"If he lands on a coastal runway, do we have any way of transferring the bomb to the 141?"

Both generals conferred with their aides and looked back at the President as General Kinney replied.

"I'm told the C-141 does have a small K-Loader aboard, but they're unsure how fast they could get the bomb transferred. So the answer is, probably not."

"Okay, so what do you two suggest now?"

"Mr. President," General Kinney said, "we were proceeding on the assumption that we could explode the bomb in a non-nuclear controlled detonation using high explosives. The captain of that aircraft is adamant that the bomb's mechanism is different. He's convinced we'll set off a nuclear blast if we do so. That's apparently why he elected to leave Seymour-Johnson."

The President scowled and waved his hand angrily in a gesture of dismissal. "I know all that. So what do we do now? We've only an hour or so left. Is there any possibility of disarming it, as we originally intended?"

The general shook his head once more. "Sir, again, the 727's captain is virtually convinced that the device is sealed and booby-trapped and impossible to defuse in the time remaining."

"Well? Is he right?"

"He . . . may well be, sir. We've only got one expert available."

"And you couldn't figure this out earlier?"

The general shook his head as he looked at the President. "Sir, we're doing the best we . . ."

"Why the hell didn't you guys come to this conclusion a half hour ago?" the President asked, his eyebrows flaring.

General Kinney slammed a leather notebook down on the table in front of him with obvious disgust and sighed. "I honestly don't know, Mr. President. If I did, I'd tell you. With all due respect, sir, I do know we're wasting time with hindsight evaluations and over-the-shoulder management."

"Ralph!" The Chairman of the Joint Chiefs was glaring at the electronic image of his four-star subordinate at the Pentagon.

The President ignored the Chairman's attempt to muzzle the Air Combat Commander and swiveled his chair aboard Air Force One to bore-sight his eyes on General Kinney.

"General, I take it you're disagreeing with my level of participation in this thing. Speak up."

The Chairman of the Joint Chiefs of Staff looked alarmed and raised his hand.

"Ah, Mr. President, I don't think . . ."

"Let him speak, John. I never fault anyone for being frank." The President looked back at General Kinney. "Go ahead, General."

"Sir, I know you were an Air Force pilot, and I know you made colonel in the Reserves, but with all due respect, you were never an active-duty senior officer on the Air Staff, and frankly, I don't think you understand what we've been facing in this crisis."

The President leaned forward. "You're right, General, we're wasting time, so I won't belabor this. Like any other general officer in the Pentagon citadel, you've come to think no one else understands what you do, least of all fuzzy-headed civilians, and least among those, politicians. I appreciate your candor, but understand this clearly. I'm more aware of what goes on at your level than you are because I've been a member of the working brotherhood and know well how dysfunctional the vertical military structure really is. To get to the Air Staff requires more than discipline. It requires a willing suspension of personal integrity, a willingness to lie to your commander, and a willingness to embrace the dangerous idea that the military is justified in lying to the public, the Congress, and the President, if necessary, to preserve its ability to function as it believes necessary."

"Sir, I think that's excessive and slanderous."

"But all too true. General, I'm your worst nightmare. I completed all the professional military courses like the War College, as well as Command and Staff. I'm a charter member of the brotherhood who knows all the secret handshakes, yet rejects the code of silence. May I remind you that the President is the Commander in Chief? I'm watching the forest while you're minding the trees. That's why our freedom depends on continuous civilian control of the military, and I happen to be the first Chief Executive in the last forty years with enough professional military experience to understand both sides. We'll get into your collective screwups on this thing later. And, no, General, I'm not micromanaging. I'm simply the first Commander in Chief since Eisenhower who can't be snowed."

General Kinney reined in his anger and glanced down at the table to compose himself before squaring his shoulders and looking back at the President.

"You asked for our recommendation, Mr. President?"

"I did."

"I recommend we forget trying to disarm the bomb and concentrate instead on how to dump it as far out in the Atlantic as we can. To that extent, we've got two pilots with Special Operations background available at Seymour-Johnson. They're already on a KC-10. They have parachutes and survival gear aboard, and they can be sent to wherever the 727's captain wants to meet them. They volunteered earlier. One even has Boeing 727 experience."

"What?" the President asked with mock surprise. "You mean to tell me that one of these pilots is a ratty Reservist?"

The general paused and swallowed hard before replying. "Yes, sir. An airline pilot."

"Fancy that," the President replied, raising an eyebrow. "The Reserves actually being capable of a unique contribution." He leaned forward, his voice dropping back into a serious tone. "I guarantee you fellows are going to be utilizing a lot more Reserve contributions in the near future. Go on."

The general cautioned himself to stay in control and continued.

"Our plan, if you could call it that, was to transfer the bomb to the C-141, but if it looks like it's going to take too long, we could get the civilians off the airplane and have our guys do what the civilian captain was proposing: Fly it east and bail out when they're a safe distance from the coast."

"Wasn't there a problem about a pacemaker? The scientist's ex-wife's pacemaker?"

"The FBI still thinks that's a hoax."

"I'm underwhelmed with the FBI's performance here, too. What if they're wrong?"

"Well . . . we could, perhaps, carry the woman with the team and have her bail out as well."

"And if it isn't a bluff, won't the bomb detonate as soon as she leaves the airplane?"

General Kinney turned to an aide, who whispered something urgently in his ear.

He turned back suddenly. "I'm told the FBI did have a plan in place to match the pacemaker's radio emissions so they could get her out. I think that kind of got lost in the arrest planning."

"So," the President said, "you could get that radio device there, as well?"

"Well . . ." Once again the general turned to confer with the aide, an Air Force lieutenant colonel, before facing the President again. "Yes, sir. In fact, they've already launched aboard a different KC-10 tanker. We can divert them wherever the 727's captain desires. We've also got those same two F-16's headed out to help. They're armed, in case the jet needs to be shot down after the pilots bail out."

The President nodded. "Okay, do it. Get moving. Use whatever additional support you need. You can take it from here, but the policy decision is simply this: Forget diddling around with the damn thing, just get it out over the Atlantic and dump it before it goes off. Try to get it past the edge of the continental shelf. Save the civilian lives aboard that Boeing, including the woman's. We can sort out who did what to whom later."

He got to his feet and disappeared out the door of the Air Force One Starsuite, leaving the Chairman of the Joint Chiefs and the commander of the Air Combat Command looking at each other electronically across a gulf of eight miles between the White House and the Pentagon.

"You heard him, Ralph," the Chairman said. "If you need me, I'll be here looking for a sword to fall on."

The general simply nodded and turned to the occupants of the command post, who were already issuing the appropriate orders and talking to the pilots of the C-141.

It took nearly six minutes for the pilot of the C-141 to come back on the radio, his voice now more cautious than before.

"ScotAir, we confirm we can meet you at Grand Strand. There's enough concrete for both of us."

"Great," Scott replied. "Any idea what the weather's doing there?"

"We'll check with flight service. Is that where you want to go?"

"We've got no time to play games, Reach. I know you've consulted your command post. Are they going to let you help us?"

"Ah, sir, I'm instructed to help you as fast as we can."

Scott looked at Doc and raised his eyebrows. "As *fast* as they can?"

"He has his orders and he's scared," Doc said.

"I'll agree with that," Scott replied, punching the transmit button again.

"Give me the coordinates of Grand Strand, Reach."

The other pilot read off the latitude and longitude figures and Doc punched them into the flight computer.

"Got it," Scott told them. "If you'll head there immediately, so will we. Please get the parachutes and survival packs ready. We're almost out of time."

The C-141 pilot's voice returned.

"Sir, the Air Force command post at the Pentagon is now controlling this situation. They want us to let you know that we do have a K-Loader aboard. There might be time to transfer the, ah, bomb, and dump it from this aircraft without the loss of your aircraft or danger to your people. Is that an acceptable plan? Over."

Doc was nodding and Jerry flashed a thumbs-up sign. Scott could hardly believe it. A K-Loader! The special diesel-powered vehicle could lift cargo pallets out of a 727 and insert them in a C-141. Exactly the vehicle they had expected to find at Seymour-Johnson, and the very piece of equipment needed to get Linda's pallets out of the way and get the bomb moved to the back ramp of the C-141.

If they worked fast, there might be just enough time.

Linda permitted herself a small smile. The cold, hard knot in her stomach hadn't relaxed since their near crash at Pax River, but for the first time there seemed to be a way out, except for one detail.

"Sounds like a plan," Scott said.

"Wait a minute, Scott," Linda said. "We're forgetting again. If the bomb goes out the door without Vivian's pacemaker, it may go off before it hits the water."

Scott keyed the microphone again. "Reach, has your command post informed you of the problem with our passenger who can't get more than fifteen feet from the device?"

"That's, ah, the pacemaker problem, ScotAir?"

"Roger that."

"Yes, sir. I was instructed to tell you they have a radio on the way to take care of that."

Scott sighed and turned to Linda. "Tell Vivian, will you? They're going to match the radio emissions as they'd planned to before."

Linda nodded and headed for the back once again as Doc banked the 727 in the direction of the chosen airfield.

"Reach, how long before you arrive?" Scott asked.

"Where are you, ScotAir?" the C-141 pilot asked. Scott hesitated. He considered polling Doc and Jerry for advice, but the prospect of handing the bomb off to the C-141 was a powerful draw. Scott reached down to the flight computer and punched up the coordinates being generated by the global positioning satellite system. He punched the transmit button and relayed them as Doc looked up in alarm.

"Roger, ScotAir. We'll be there just about the time you arrive if you're doing two hundred fifty knots."

"Affirmative, Reach. You land first, okay?"

"Ah, whatever you'd like, sir."

Doc had been watching Scott's face.

"You sure that's wise, Scott? You just told any fighters in the area precisely where we are, and that C-141 crew is being controlled by the same group that tried to lure us into a trap before."

Scott shrugged. "I was thinking about that. But even if they *wanted* to shoot at us, they couldn't, because they couldn't guarantee the bomb would be exposed to a powerful enough external blast to destroy it, that is, even if they still believed the thing could be blown up without a nuclear blast."

"What makes you think they've changed their minds on how to handle this?" Doc added. "Someone wanted that bomb intact, wanted to arrest Vivian, and wanted to completely disregard what we were telling them. Scott, why would they change their minds now, just because we escaped?"

"I . . . don't know, Doc."

Jerry had leaned over the center console to join the debate. He nodded suddenly.

"Doc's right, Scott. We're trusting them all of a sudden. They could be laying a new trap up ahead. We land—*blam*—we can't move this time. Blocked runway, guns at our heads, and no time left. They could be rushing the same blasting materials from Seymour right this minute. The only difference is, as we disappear in a mushroom cloud, Goldsboro will have more of a chance. Of course, Myrtle Beach is toast, not to mention the danger to the rest of the country."

Doc was nodding. "Yeah, we're dead, a twenty-five-mile radius of the United States is a smoking nuclear radioactive hole with the ashes of one helluva lot of people, and if that isn't enough, Medusa will help finish off the economy," Doc finished.

Scott looked at both of them quietly. "So what's the alternative, guys?"

Jerry thought he heard a small quiver in Scott's voice, but the captain was trying hard to stay composed, even as he peered over the abyss.

"Should we drop in somewhere else?" Scott continued, his voice constrained. "Without the parachutes, it's a suicide mission no matter what. I . . . sure don't want to . . . die, but if we don't get their help, I see no other alternative but to kick you off and go it alone. It would be ridiculous for all of us to go. I mean, it wouldn't necessarily be a kamikaze mission. There *would* still be a thread of hope that the countdown might end and nothing would happen."

"You know better than that, Scott," Doc snapped. "I think we all know better than that. They found nuclear material, remember? They spotted it in Miami and they found it in the Henrys' home. You don't plant plutonium on a dummy bomb."

"Okay." He took a deep breath, but it came out somewhat ragged. "So, guys, help me here," Scott said. "We're up against it. Do we run, or do we trust them?"

There was an intense silence that lasted for what seemed like an eternity as Linda reentered the cockpit and quietly took her place behind Scott. The extreme seriousness of the moment was apparent and she said nothing as her eyes watched the resigned expression on

Jerry's face and the suppressed emotions becoming readable on Doc's far more weathered features.

A long sigh came from Jerry Christian. "You're right, Scott. Without their help . . ."

"But if they trap us," Doc said, "even if we got away in time, the idiots would probably detonate it trying to examine it."

"Your vote, Doc?" Scott asked quietly.

Doc shook his head and began to laugh, a rueful, sarcastic, resigned laugh. "McKay, there were a lot of things about this outfit you didn't tell me when I signed on!"

Scott smiled. "Yeah, I'm a dirty, lying, rotten rat of an employer, but answer the question. Run or play?"

"We don't have a choice," Doc said as he studied Scott's eyes. "We have to trust them."

"Unless . . ." Jerry began.

"Yes?" Scott turned to look at him.

"Unless we *see* some evidence that they're setting us up. Scott, you told him to land first. Let's circle at a distance, in the clouds if possible, stay low and out of radar. Let's make sure that C-141 is on the ground."

"And if it isn't, they've set a trap, and we leave immediately. Good idea," Scott said.

Jerry nodded. "We'd get the hell out of there. To where, I don't know, but we go."

Scott turned to Linda without a smile.

She closed her eyes and raised her hand as she nodded. "I heard. I understand. And I agree."

"We'll get you off this aircraft, Linda. I couldn't live with myself if . . ."

"If you killed both of us simultaneously?" she chuckled. "If you do, I'll see to it NOAA never hires your company again."

At that, Scott turned almost sideways in his seat as Doc watched the 727 respond to the gentle corrections of the autopilot. They were plowing through bumpy air and occasional moderate turbulence, the radar showing red blotches of heavy rain showers and thunderstorm cells ahead, but they had all been concentrating so hard, the rough ride had gone unnoticed.

Scott's eyes found Linda's, and they looked at each other without speaking, as if neither had seen the other before, their thoughts running through a lifetime of images and wishes and always coming back to the same shared reality: *I may end this life within an hour in the company of this person.*

Doc busied himself with the airplane and Jerry with his panel, but both were aware of the sudden silent bond that had formed between the man in the left seat and the attractive young woman a few inches behind him.

Reluctantly, Scott broke the lock and turned back to the instrument panel, aware that his heart was beating a little faster.

21

• • • •

General Kinney, head of the Air Force Combat Command, sat on the corner of the communications console in the command post and listened to the latest assembled intelligence. Located near the War Room, the Air Force facility was festooned with video monitors, telephones, maps, and intense young enlisted personnel working side by side with a cross-section of officers on a dizzying variety of assignments. A sandy-haired Air Force major in a perfectly pressed uniform stood ramrod-straight before the general, a sheaf of papers in his hand as he snapped out the facts he'd been asked to provide.

"The KC-10 carrying the two pilots who can fly the 727 will reach the airfield first, sir. The C-141 will be a few minutes behind them, and the second KC-10 about ten minutes after that with the radio gear for the pacemaker."

"And the F-16's?"

"They're approaching Grand Strand right now. We still don't have a radar track on ScotAir, but the coordinates he gave us show him here." The major pointed to a spot on an aeronautical chart spread out before them. "They'll get there about the time the C-141 arrives."

"The 141 crew knows they'll have only a ten-minute window to get that K-Loader positioned?"

"Yes, sir. They say their loadmasters swear they can do it. They said they'll have to break every procedural rule they have, but they can do it."

"Let's hope they're right. When that bomb's countdown hits

forty minutes, they've got to be airborne, whether it's the 141 or the 727."

"If it's the 141, sir, it'll be awfully tight. At top speed they'll be able to cover only about a hundred and sixty miles before dumping, and they'll need every minute to race back west to avoid the blast."

General Kinney got to his feet and motioned the Secretary of the Air Force toward the command post's Starsuite for another update.

SANTA FE, NEW MEXICO—7:01 P.M. EDT

Alerted an hour before by a frightened colleague in Washington, the senior scientist who was once responsible for providing the administrative support for Rogers Henry's Medusa Project frantically pulled the third of four aging file boxes from a closet in his den and rifled through the folders in search of one that was little more than a vague image in his memory. It had been, what, twenty years? Perhaps longer, he mused, since the last impassioned plea for reinstatement of the Medusa Project had arrived from Dr. Rogers Henry in Miami.

He had never opened it because he'd known what was inside: more pleas, more theoretical musings, many of them crossing the line into classified information. The others he'd seen had to be burned, and each time Rogers had been warned sternly about writing down ideas and postulations that were the top secret property of a government that refused to let him complete his research.

Nothing! He slid the lid back in place and reached for the last box. It had to be there.

Logically, he knew, there was probably nothing in the folder that would shed any light on what Rogers Henry had apparently built and somehow deployed two years after his death, but he had to know. His friend in Washington was frightened of what would happen if the military tried to dispose of the weapon.

"Is it possible," the friend had asked, "that somewhere in the files Rogers might have left a clue about the trigger he's used?"

At last the folder popped into view, thick with papers and yellow with age. He yanked it from its cardboard sarcophagus and stood up, aware of his protesting knees and a sudden lightheaded feeling. As much as he loved Santa Fe and its constant autumn tinge of sweet piñon pine burning softly in a thousand fireplaces, he would never get used to the seven-thousand-foot altitude.

He moved quickly to his easy chair and plunked down, his fingers working at the unbreached seal on the package Rogers Henry had sent so long ago. There was another package inside, another folder, this one sealed with what aviators called speed tape, a heavy aluminum tape used on the exteriors of aircraft. It yielded after several attempts to peel it back, and he pulled the forty or so pages out and placed them on his lap as he fumbled for his reading glasses.

"You must tell me in a call or a letter or some form of positive contact if you read this!" Rogers had written. "If you don't make contact, I'll assume you have not seen it, and I'll proceed accordingly."

What the hell does that mean? He wondered. *Strange that Henry somehow knew I might not read anything more.*

Time had dimmed the memory of their exchanges. Perhaps he had told Rogers that nothing more *would* be read.

The letter's first page rehashed old territory, but on the second page Rogers had laid out in detail a series of formulas and calculations laced with physical drawings of a strange design. He looked closer, realizing with a sudden thrill that it was, indeed, a form of nuclear trigger, and a radical departure from the traditional models that . . .

"Oh my God!"

The seventy-two-year-old scientist grabbed for the phone and fumbled with the number he'd written down.

The number rang four times before it was answered.

"Max?"

"Yeah."

"You were right. Louis here, in Santa Fe. Rogers sent me the plans for this thing twenty years ago. I never opened it. Max, you're right. It's the one he talked about."

"Slow down, Louis. You mean an instant trigger?"

"Yes, yes! Put high explosives around it, no matter how close you get, this thing creates an instant critical mass. You can't defeat it that way."

"I thought so. I'd better try to get through to the Pentagon. I know some people over there."

"Max, there's something else, though. And they need to know this immediately."

"Go ahead."

"Looking at his diagram, there's one vulnerability to the trigger that can be defeated easily, if they have the right equipment. Forget explosives, forget timers. Block the magnetic neutrality of the mechanism with a large magnetic field, and it can't work."

"A magnetic field? How large?"

"You know the size of the electromagnets used in junk yards to pick up scrap metal?"

"Sure."

"Depending on the thickness of the metal shroud around his bomb, that would do it."

"You're sure of this?"

"It's a quick read of what I see, but it's very obvious to me. It's a brilliant design, but that's its weak point. He even points out the flaw in the papers he sent, but says . . . or said . . . that no one would ever figure it out in time."

Two thousand miles distant, the retired nuclear scientist named Max looked at his watch and sighed.

"Louis, he may have been right. There's only an hour left."

ABOARD SCOTAIR 50—7:02 P.M. EDT

The turbulence was getting worse by the mile as the Boeing 727 flew deeper into the fringes of the same hurricane that had nearly killed them at Pax River. Weaving around vicious thunderstorm cells and at least one radar return that looked frighteningly like the curved signature of a tornado, Doc had done the flying as Scott worked with the maps, keeping the plane at a safe altitude as they raced to close the distance to Grand Strand Airport, also known as North Myrtle Beach.

"Fifty-nine minutes left, Scott," Jerry told him from the engineer's seat. "And, God knows, I pray we don't need this information, but I *do* know a way—a messy way, but a way—to get power to the cargo door in flight if we wanted to open it. And if I'm wrong, I can manually pump it open from the ventral stairway in the back."

Scott shook his head as he kept his eyes on the radar display.

"Thanks, Jerry, but it doesn't look like we'll need to do it, after all. It seemed like a good idea until you pointed out we might not have a tail to fly with if that door ripped off."

"Oh, it'd rip off, all right. And in the process it could flip us out of control."

Scott waved the idea away without looking back. "Not a problem. We're not going to do it." He turned to the copilot.

"The airport's about fifteen miles ahead, Doc."

"I know," Doc replied. "I'm going to start a wide circle to the right and stay below one thousand feet. I'll try to get us close enough to see it without being seen."

Doc pulled the throttles back slightly and lowered the nose to bring them out of three thousand feet to a lower altitude. The landing gear warning horn sounded again, as it did each time the throttles were pulled back with gear up unless the horn cancellation lever had been pulled in advance. Jerry cursed softly and flipped the lever at the foot of the center console, silencing the noise. He was almost always ahead of the horn. It was unusual to hear it and a matter of pride for him to stay ahead of every throttle movement.

"How many radars do you think have been watching us?" Jerry asked.

"A bunch," Scott replied, "but with all this weather clutter, the returns off our fuselage are intermittent at best. They may think they see us, but they won't know for sure. Now, if I had the type of radar I used to have in my F-14, we could have seen that C-141 fifty miles out or more."

"There's a break in the clouds coming up to the left, Scott. See anything?" Doc asked.

A large, angry thunderhead was dumping sheets of rain to their left, but as the 727 passed the core of the rain shaft, a distant glimpse of the airfield came into view. Scott struggled to make out anything on the ground.

"I'm . . . not sure, Doc. I see the runway, but I can't make out anything on the field."

"I'll get us closer."

The fleeting image of another airborne object far ahead came into view and disappeared again, all in a heartbeat.

"Wait. Doc, I think I saw our friend up ahead. If so, he's maneuvering for a straight-in from the south for Runway 5."

Doc nodded. "I'll bring us left. Soon as we get through these rain shafts, you may be able to get another look. That'll bring us within five miles of the field, too."

Scott placed his chin on the dashboard and began a disciplined search pattern with his eyes, trying to look for movement against the field of rain and angry clouds ahead. There was some lightning, but for the most part the backside of the hurricane was still fairly benign as long as the eye of the massive storm was still offshore.

Another brief glimpse of the aircraft came and went.

"Definitely a big airplane, Doc. It's gotta be the C-141."

"Anything to the left on the field?"

Scott diverted his eyes toward the airport where Linda McCoy was looking. She leaned to the left to put her eyes almost on the glass of the captain's-side window. A short yelp from Linda brought Scott's attention fully on the airport as it suddenly popped into clear view.

"What do you see?"

"Several buildings and . . . two small airplanes about midway down the field, by the runway, on the southeastern seaward side."

Scott walked his eyes toward the location. There were indeed two airplanes on the taxiway. They were small, with swept-back wings and a familiar fuselage . . .

Oh jeez. Scott thought. "Doc, those are F-16's," he said out loud. "They got here ahead of us. Probably the same guys."

There was silence from the right seat. Scott looked over at Doc, puzzled by the silence. He was staring straight ahead, open-mouthed, and Scott's eyes followed his gaze between pillars of clouds several miles ahead to where the distinctive shape of a large military aircraft could be seen clearly making an approach to the same airfield.

Scott heard a sharp intake of breath from Doc, and then from Jerry, who had also spotted the airplane. He felt his heart freeze in midbeat and his stomach implode into a chasm of sudden hopelessness—their earlier words replaying in his mind: *If it's not a C-141, it's a trap.*

There was no mistaking the shape or the gray-and-white markings of the airplane, now clearly visible ahead.

It was a KC-10.

"It's a setup," Scott said quietly.

There was a silent nod from the right seat and a whispered "Oh my God!" from Linda behind him as the seconds ticked by.

Scott felt cold and clammy and dead. He hadn't believed they could lie to him again. What naïveté. The Air Force and the FBI and God knew who else in the government all seemed bound and determined to examine the weapon until the last moment, then detonate it themselves. No one would listen to his warnings. A KC-10 couldn't carry a K-Loader and deploy it without ground equipment that would never be available at such a civilian field. A KC-10 couldn't load the bomb and couldn't drop the bomb. The C-141 had been the last option, and now that option was gone. Now they had no choice but to deal with the bomb themselves. To do anything else would doom a staggering number of South Carolinians to a gruesome death—some instantaneously, some over time.

"What do you want to do, Scott?" Doc asked softly, wanting to hear verbal confirmation of what he already knew.

"What can we do? We already considered everything, right? We can't let this thing go off onshore, and those idiots will do exactly that if we land. Myrtle Beach is just south of here."

There was no dissent.

Scott nodded. "Let's get out of here. Try to stay hidden, but let's go."

He didn't need to state where. They already knew where.

Scott reached down and turned off the UHF radio that had been the link to the C-141.

They didn't need it now. They were entirely alone.

ABOARD AIR FORCE ONE—7:08 P.M. EDT

Word that a retired government nuclear scientist had called in to warn the military how to disarm—and how not to disarm—Rogers Henry's Medusa weapon had flashed through the Air Force command post to the Situation Room in seconds, and then across the continent through the Starsuite to the President.

Traveling at five hundred miles per hour at thirty-nine thousand feet, the President sat in a desultory funk on the Air Force One side of the conference table, waiting for news as the countdown approached one hour. On the wall to his right, a weather screen was giving ongoing information from several sources on the storm's progress as it lashed across the eastern seaboard. He was acutely aware of the damage Sigrid was inflicting, and part of his mind worked on proper responses to the devastation. But the main focus of his thinking was a lonely 727 with five souls on board struggling to survive what might become an unsurvivable situation. The horror of what would happen to the country if the Medusa Wave was unleashed was something he couldn't concentrate on at the moment.

As General Kinney, the commander of the Air Combat Command, relayed word that a frenzied search was under way for a large electromagnet to rush to the coastal airport called Grand Strand, a young wide-eyed aide appeared at his elbow and handed him a piece of paper. The general scanned the page and looked sick, a change of expression the President of the United States caught immediately.

"What's the note, General?"

The general sighed and removed his reading glasses to rub his eyes as he spoke. "Sir, the 727 is not responding to radio calls, and air traffic control radar thinks they spotted him flying just south of Grand Strand and heading off east over the ocean. According to the note, an observer at the airport visually acquired them in the same place. This was about four minutes ago."

The President came out of his chair. "How could that happen? He agreed to land! Was the C-141 there?"

The general motioned several other officers and aides into the President's field of vision. "Just . . . just a second, sir."

A fifteen-second exchange ended with the Air Force Chief of Staff turning back to the Chief Executive and squaring his shoulders. "Sir, the two F-16's had landed and were on the field, and one of the two inbound KC-10's was on approach and is now on the ground. The C-141 is still about fifteen miles out."

The President stood in silence for a few seconds, running the facts over in his mind and trying to imagine what the obviously panicked aircrew of the 727 was thinking.

He sighed at last and rolled his eyes at the ceiling. "Of course. He saw the KC-10 and the fighters. He didn't see the C-141. You hadn't told him about the KC-10's, had you?"

More quick conferencing and a hurried radio call to the C-141 before the general turned back to the Air Force One side of the Starsuite.

"No, sir. He had not been told."

The President sank back down in his chair.

"Those poor bastards. They thought we were trying to trap them. They're headed east?"

"Yes, sir. Apparently."

"Call them! Explain what happened. Get him back!" the President snapped.

"Sir, we're trying everything to contact him. He's not responding. With the hurricane and the weather, radar returns are difficult for the controllers to sort out, since he has his transponder off. He's been flying, we believe, at low altitude, but he was last spotted as an intermittent target headed east over the Atlantic."

The President stared in silence for an uncomfortable period of time before replying, "He's going to try to dump it himself!"

"No, sir," the general responded as he studied the table.

"Why not? What else could he be planning? You're not suggesting a suicide?"

"Sir, that's a Boeing 727 with a side cargo door. I'm told it can't be opened in flight, and even if it could, you can't jettison cargo in flight."

"Then where is he going?"

"Mr. President, to his death, apparently." The statement was spoken without emotion or inflection, but the general felt very cold inside. Whether from fear of presidential reprisal for further screwing up the operation, or from the impending loss of a few hapless civilians about to perform a selfless act, he couldn't tell. He just felt cold and sick. He thought of his son, a young airline pilot based in Seattle. That could be his son out there, about to sacrifice his life for his country. That's what they were doing, of course. That was the only explanation. Anyone who'd flown jets in the modern Air Force or Navy knew well what a simple nuclear bomb could do to a civilian population.

"General, did you hear me?"

The general snapped to attention suddenly. "No, sir, I'm sorry."

"I said let's get those F-16's in the air. Don't you think we should chase him down? Try to make contact?"

The general nodded. "We've already given that order, sir. But we should also be prepared to shoot him down if he turns back toward the coast too late for us to dispose of the bomb."

It was the President's turn to go slightly numb. Shoot a civilian cargo airliner down? He would have to issue the order if the plane decided to return and it was too late. The F-16's would be too close to survive the nuclear blast that would result from any missile impacting the aircraft. Apparently, thanks to the scientist in Santa Fe, there was no longer any doubt that such an explosion would be nuclear.

"Ah, General, the electromagnet idea. Could we get one to that airfield? If so, could the fighters get him back there, and if there was enough time, even ten minutes to turn it on, would that do the trick?"

"All unknowns, sir. We'll work on it."

"General?"

"Sir?"

"How many people did you say are aboard that airplane?"

A thin man in civilian clothes stepped into the frame and introduced himself as FBI. "Five persons, sir." He reeled off the names and professions, and the fact that the captain had been a naval aviator.

The President nodded. "Thank you." Then he turned back to the Air Force Chief of Staff, who had come in quietly to stand beside General Kinney. "How long do we have now?"

"Less than an hour, Mr. President. If they get much more than twenty minutes offshore, there won't be enough time left to bring them back."

22
• • • •

A bout the cargo door, Jerry," Scott said suddenly. "Get ready to tell me again how we could do it."

"Whenever you're ready, I've got the systems and maintenance manuals open back here."

"A few minutes more."

Scott banked hard to the left and flew northeast for precisely two minutes before turning back to the right and flying southeast as he dropped the 727's altitude back to five hundred feet.

"Scott, our fuel is not infinite," Doc said.

Jerry was already leaning over the center console with the aircraft's performance manual. "We need to get higher, much higher, if we're going to get any range. We've got thirteen thousand pounds of fuel remaining. That's barely enough for ninety minutes at cruise, Scott, but if we stay low like this, we're talking an hour, tops, before we flame out."

"There are fighters back there," Scott said in a steady voice. "They were brought in to hold us on the ground, but they're armed and dangerous, and I bet they'll be chasing us within minutes. If they find us now with no time left, they're liable to get mindless orders to just blast us out of the sky if we won't return. Who the hell knows what those fools in the Pentagon are thinking? We've got to stay low to the water for at least another twenty minutes."

"That's about eighty miles," Jerry said, "and we're flying farther into the hurricane. It's going to get increasingly rough down here."

Scott nodded. "All right. The cargo door. How are we going to do this?"

Jerry took a deep breath and let it out slowly before answering.

"Okay. Normally we have to be on the ground to get power to the cargo door. While we're in the air, the 'Open Door' switch won't work. However, I've got two possibilities. The cargo door has its own hydraulic system. I've just got to find a way to hot-wire the electric motors and pumps, but I think I can shunt the wiring to get around the ground sensing relays. It won't be pretty, but I think I can do it. The *other* way is simply to open the rear cabin door. The manual pump handle and selector valve is back there, and I could manually pump it open."

Scott sat in thought for a few seconds. "To get through the back door we'd have to depressurize, and I'd rather delay that as long as possible. How long to hot-wire it?"

"Ten minutes, tops. But that's not the real challenge."

"Go on."

"Once we get the circuit powered, we've got to guess at what airspeed to use for opening, because we want a high enough speed to rip the door off, but not one so high that the door takes most of the top of the fuselage with it."

"What do you mean, Jerry?" Doc asked over his shoulder. "You mean, like that United Airlines Boeing 747 that lost its cargo door and nine passengers south of Honolulu in 1989?"

Jerry was nodding vigorously. "Yes. Exactly. We've got some substantial advantages over that situation, though. For instance, they were pressurized when their door blew. We won't be. That makes a big difference in the opening force. Second, their cargo door was much larger in area, and it flopped into a high-speed airstream. They were zipping along at two hundred eighty knots at twenty-three thousand feet. We'll be low, around, say, five thousand feet, and our door's smaller. When their door blew open, it did so with so much force that instead of pulling loose at the hinge, it peeled the skin of the aircraft back like a tin can. If that happens to us, the fuselage structure could crumple and we could theoretically break up in the air."

"Which, when translated, means we'd be theoretically dead," Linda said. "Wonderful prospect."

"Our most likely problem isn't that," Jerry added quickly. "It's either having the door damage us as it leaves or having it stay on the airplane."

"I don't understand," Linda said. "I mean, I know it's not important that *I* understand . . ."

"Yes, it is, Linda," Jerry reassured her. "You need to know what we're dealing with because we're going to need your help every step of the way."

"You've certainly got that," she said.

"Okay," Jerry continued. "If the door opens but stays on, it becomes a giant air surface influencing the control of the aircraft. The ailerons and elevators and rudders out there are all much smaller than the cargo door. If it opened and partially came off the hinge, so it wasn't aligned with the fuselage anymore, and if it, say, was cocked fifty degrees to the relative wind . . . the air flow streaming by . . . Scott and Doc might be unable to maintain control."

"And if it tears off?" Linda prompted.

"It could hit the T-tail and damage it, destroy it, or create some other massive control problem we couldn't overcome. In addition, it could feed debris into any or all of our tail-mounted engines and leave us with engine failures, or fires."

"Oh, is *that* all?" Doc grinned, shaking his head. "Piece of cake!"

GRAND STRAND AIRPORT, NORTH MYRTLE BEACH, SOUTH CAROLINA—7:10 P.M. EDT

With engines running, the lead F-16 pilot had remained in his cockpit monitoring the radio, his wingman sitting just to the right. The short supersonic dash from Seymour-Johnson Air Force Base had been ordered seconds after the Boeing 727 departed without clearance, and they had used a lot of their fuel in the process—a fact that was worrying both of them.

One of the KC-10's had already landed and taxied by, but there was no sign of either the C-141 or the civilian 727, and that was strange.

The major checked his watch. The other transport aircraft should have been there by now.

He looked at his wingman and gave a palms-up sign of puzzlement. The winds had picked up in the past few minutes, and intermittent rain showers were alternately pelting them with rain and small hail, which also had him worried. He glanced at the fuel gauges again, calculating how much fuel they were burning. They

had to keep the engines running, since there was no ground equipment at the civilian airport to get them started once they shut down,
but the engines were drinking fuel every minute.

"Shark flight lead, this is your number two on button three."

"Yeah, Two."

"What, exactly, are we supposed to do? We don't have enough
gas to go very far offshore, unless we take a tanker with us. Do they
expect us to escort that C-141 out to sea?"

"I haven't a clue, Two. Maybe we're here for moral support."

AIR FORCE COMMAND POST, THE PENTAGON—
7:12 P.M. EDT

"We can't reach the F-16's, sir," the Air Force senior master sergeant explained. "They lost radio contact with their command post
when they landed at that airfield. We're calling one of the tankers
right now to relay the orders."

A two-star general threw a pencil across the command post and
muttered something obscene between his teeth before looking back
at the startled sergeant.

"Just . . . do your best."

"Yes, sir." The sergeant pulled up another telephone receiver
and punched one of the buttons on the console before him, caution-
ing himself not to shake his head or otherwise react to the general's
outburst.

A lieutenant colonel had been waiting briefly for the general's
attention. He now pulled him into an urgent huddle.

"Sir, there *is* a magnetic crane in Myrtle Beach, about twenty
miles from that airport. The power supply is part of the thing, and it
is self-propelled, but . . ."

"Great! Something's finally going right!"

"No . . . sir. The crane can only travel at ten miles per hour.
The way I figure it, there's virtually no hope of getting it there in
time. It's a simple time and distance impossibility."

Medusa's Child

Pete Cooke's reportorial instincts had cautioned him against leaving the FAA facility, though he was tempted to do so. There was a nation in frantic motion just outside. At first, residents of the Washington–New York corridor had been in shock and wondering where to run against the possibility of a nuclear detonation over their heads, unsure whether it was real. But when ScotAir 50 and its lethal cargo had been reported heading away from the Beltway, the public's attention turned to the Medusa Wave the media kept describing. People began frantically shutting down computers nationwide and protecting memory and monetary systems as the winds from Hurricane Sigrid began to do real damage to the eastern seaboard.

But Pete's instinct told him to stay put. The core story was ScotAir 50 and how Scott McKay was dealing with the nightmare that had engulfed his plane barely two hours before.

He'd lost his exclusive track on the flight when it flew south and out of range of his radio scanner. He had picked up bits and pieces of reports since then, of course, most of them relayed through the constant phone calls from Ira at his office back in New York. But staying in the air traffic control facility had provided the best intelligence as ScotAir moved south. Several of the men in the control room had tossed him strategic crumbs of information as the drama progressed. He'd been witnessing their efforts to put all air traffic over the continental United States on the ground within ninety minutes.

What a story! Pete thought. *I'm in the midst of the biggest, most unprecedented shutdown of American airspace in modern history.*

Earlier, someone had come by to tell him ScotAir 50 had indeed been headed to Seymour-Johnson Air Force Base as had been rumored. But then reports circulated that suddenly it had left, and a frantic phone call to the FAA system command center from Washington Center confirmed that the Air Force was now aggressively searching for the 727.

Pete looked at his watch for the hundredth time in the last half hour. He had programmed one of the digital functions to count backward to the detonation time announced on Rogers Henry's weapon.

The numbers now stood at 00:49:00 remaining.

He sat back in a swivel chair and tried to think. The voice of Scott McKay was still in his ears, and he wondered what could possibly have happened. Was he down? Was he running, and if so, to where?

"Pete?"

One of the facility directors had appeared beside him. Pete hadn't heard him coming.

"Yes?"

"We just got word from the Pentagon that they need help tracking ScotAir."

"Where do they think he is?"

"Heading out over the Atlantic. They think he's going to try to dump the bomb himself, which means he might get it as far as two hundred miles out before it explodes."

"Can he do that? Can he dump it in flight?"

"From a Boeing 727, you mean?" the director asked.

"Yeah."

"Not a chance in the world. What's worse, two hundred miles won't have much of an effect on a Medusa Wave."

"So you're still shutting down the system?"

"No choice. When that thing goes off, any aircraft flying that's got a single computer circuit on board is in trouble."

"You'll make it in time, though?"

He nodded. "We will. But God help us if we don't have the computers to restart the system tomorrow."

GRAND STRAND AIRPORT, NORTH MYRTLE BEACH, SOUTH CAROLINA—7:13 P.M. EDT

Within two minutes of the call to get airborne, both F-16's lifted into the storm to the north off Runway 5 and contacted their command post directly.

The orders were simple: Find the ScotAir 727, try to establish radio contact, and try to get him to return.

"We're limited on fuel, sir, to about twenty minutes out."

"That's not a problem," the lead was told. "You've only got fifteen minutes in which to find him anyway. If you can't locate him and turn him around in that time, the only task left may be to make sure he doesn't return."

Linda McCoy felt like a broken record in bringing it up, but once again the men around her in the cockpit of the Boeing 727 had forgotten a frightening truth about the specter holding Vivian Henry hostage.

"Even if the device can't sense motion," Linda told them, "if we get it overboard, it will sense that Vivian isn't beside it. I'm no nuclear scientist, but I do know we'll need a thirty- to fifty-mile headstart to be safe when it goes off. Without her, it may go off a lot sooner." The washboard turbulence was becoming more difficult to deal with, and Linda tightened her grip on the back of Scott's seat for support as she partially leaned over the center console.

"I was kind of hoping," Scott said, "that we could rely on it to bluff and bluster for a while before exploding. But you're right. We could get everything else accomplished, only to get fried by that little problem."

A sound of metal against metal caused Linda to turn toward the flight engineer's panel. Jerry was partly wedged to the right of it, lying on the floor, his long frame barely contained in the lateral confines of the rear cockpit. He was holding a flashlight and working on the lower part of an opened circuit breaker panel, using two heavy gloves from his flight bag for insulation against electrical shock.

"Don't touch me," he warned Linda, "and if I accidentally latch onto a high-voltage wire, stay back."

Linda looked back toward the two pilots.

"Is there any way we could rig a receiver to find what frequency she's broadcasting on?"

"The extra circuit in her pacemaker, you mean?" Scott asked.

Linda nodded.

Jerry's voice wafted up from the floor. "If I had a scanner and a lot of time, maybe, but not here and now."

Scott sighed loudly enough to get her attention. "Linda, I'm afraid we're working with some limited possibilities. With or without her signal, the bomb may go off when it impacts the water. If so, there's nothing we can do. We'll experience a few seconds of intense light, and that will be that."

They fell silent as Doc continued banking left and right through the increasing turbulence, holding the aircraft at around five hundred feet over the cloud-shrouded Atlantic only intermittently visible below.

Linda unbuckled her seat belt. "I'm going to see if Vivian has any ideas about the pacemaker's frequency. Anything might help."

She stepped over Jerry and opened the cockpit door, aware, somehow, that Scott was watching her. She paused at the door and turned to look at him, surprised at his fleeting smile and the small thumbs-up gesture. She smiled in return and moved into the cargo cabin feeling strangely calm inside.

SHARK FLIGHT—7:18 P.M. EDT

There was no choice but to use afterburners for the first few minutes, in order to catch up with the 727. Logically, the lead pilot had decided, a civilian crew trying to get as far away from the coast as possible and out to sea would head due east.

He set his course in the same direction.

The fighter's radar had a range of more than two hundred miles, but it was cluttered with returns now from massive waves rolling across the storm-tossed Atlantic for a hundred miles east of the Carolina coast. Echoes from two Coast Guard aircraft had popped up a bit to the south, but there was no sign of the Boeing. The two fighters had pulled their engines back to normal cruise when a lone echo began strobing on their scopes, moving first to the northeast, then to the southeast, and showing very low to the water.

"That's got to be him," the major said on the intercom frequency. "It looks like he's trying to evade detection."

He plotted an intercept, electing to fly almost directly over the airliner at ten thousand feet, then drop down into formation with him.

The major looked at his watch again. He had been given ten minutes.

He had less than five left.

The target reversed course once more as the major began his descent, flying entirely on instruments with his wingman hanging in five feet from his right wingtip. The single-engine fighters were being tossed around rather substantially, but the intermittent hail was worse. The impacts of the hailstones pummeling the Plexiglas canopy sounded like gunfire.

The two F-16's slid below one thousand feet and the pilots began catching glimpses of the water. At five hundred feet the forward visibility improved slightly, and they closed cautiously to within three miles of the target using nothing but radar before spotting the Boeing.

The leader used a hand signal to alert his wingman, then pushed up the throttle slightly, indicating they would come from the right side and slightly below.

ABOARD SCOTAIR 50—7:18 P.M. EDT

Linda almost expected to see Vivian sleeping when she returned to the back of Rogers Henry's bomb.

Instead, she was writing frantically.

"Let me guess. That's a complaint to the airline about the bumpy ride and the lousy dinner?" Linda teased.

"Especially the dinner." Vivian's smile was more apparent than before. "No"—she gestured to the sheets of paper in her lap—"I'm being positive. I'm writing down everything that's happened, so I can clearly recall it later."

Linda briefed her on the plan for the cargo door and her worries about the pacemaker.

"Vivian, did you have any idea he'd jury-rigged your pacemaker?"

She shook her head. "No, but I remembered something a while ago I'd forgotten. Most pacemakers don't drive TV's crazy, but mine always did."

"TV's? The signal, you mean?"

She nodded. "Not always, but every now and then when I'd get close to a TV, there would be this jumbled pattern of visual noise across the screen which sort of pulsed every few seconds. And then there were his harassing phone calls. He always seemed to know when I was back at my apartment, or for that matter, wherever I was. I'd begun to think he was following me twenty-four hours a day or had hired detectives."

"But it was the pacemaker beacon?"

"Apparently." She nodded. "It would explain things. It would also explain why I had to have the battery replaced so soon."

"I . . . know a little about radio . . ."

Linda had knelt beside Vivian, but a sudden lurch of the aircraft knocked her backward, her legs flying unceremoniously upward while she flailed for a handhold. She picked herself up and then sat down, vigorously rubbing what would be a nasty bruise on her thigh where she'd hit one of the cargo floor rollers.

"Ouch!"

"Hold on to my cargo strap, Linda. You were asking me something."

"Yeah. I was hoping against hope, you know, that we might find a way to do what the military said they were going to do, and that's turn on some other radio that would emulate the signal of your pacemaker."

"So we'd have time to get away after we dump the bomb?"

"That's right."

"You don't need to worry about that," Vivian said quietly.

"But we may, Vivian, because it may not bluff this time when it senses you're not there. It may . . ." Linda paused as she studied Vivian's face and began to discern her meaning.

Vivian had been looking at the floor with her lips pursed. She glanced up suddenly with a look of grim determination.

"There is . . . a better way, Linda."

Shock consumed Linda's features and the young scientist raised her hand in immediate protest.

"Vivian! You're not going to think that way! There's no way in hell anyone of us would consider letting you go overboard, just to . . ."

Vivian shook her head. "No, no, no! I'm not planning suicide. But I'm not going to let Rogers defeat me so easily this time. No, Linda, that's not what I was going to say at all."

"Well . . . *good* . . . because I . . . wasn't going to let you."

Vivian reached out her right hand, took Linda's wrist, and began moving it back toward her chest. Linda pulled back slightly, an uncomfortable expression crossing her face, but Vivian tugged harder, her left hand simultaneously fumbling with the buttons on her blouse.

"The pacemaker, Linda. I want you to feel where it is. Have you ever seen one before?"

Linda shook her head. "No."

"Here. Don't be shy. Place your hand on it and feel around the edges. See how close it is to the surface of my skin?"

Linda obeyed, then withdrew her hand self-consciously.

"Yes."

"Well, I figured it out a little while ago. Don't you suppose there's a first-aid kit aboard this craft?"

"I . . . yes. I'm sure there would be. Why?"

"Because you're going to perform some minor surgery on me and remove that thing."

"I'm *what*?"

"You heard me. We're going to take it out, then we're going to tape it to Rogers' bomb, and then, for all its stupid little silicon brain knows, I'm going out the door with it."

Linda looked from the device back to Vivian.

"Can we *do* that?" Linda asked. "Won't you run the risk of a heart problem?"

She chuckled. "I daresay I'd run a slightly greater risk of a heart problem if we set off a thermonuclear explosion. No. I will do fine, dear, and it's just a small incision. The pacemaker will slip right out. I'll direct you. I just can't do it myself."

"Vivian, I'm not medically trained."

"Have you ever had first-aid training?"

"Well, yes, but surgery is a tad different."

"Have you ever had to deal with an extremely bad cut or bleeding injury that required you to take instant, decisive action?"

"Yes. My brother almost cut off his fingers once, and I was the only one there."

"How'd you hold up?"

"Fine, until later. I got sick later."

"Okay, then this will be easy."

Linda's startled expression slowly dissolved into a tenuous smile. She reached out and placed her hand on Vivian's shoulder. "You're a pretty tough cookie, you know that?"

Vivian glanced at the bomb, then back at Linda, and smiled.

"You know, I'm beginning to think I really am. And after all those years of believing I was helpless. How about that?"

23
....

The President had been pacing almost constantly for the previous ten minutes, driving not only his aides in the Air Force One Starsuite close to distraction, but also those on the Situation Room side of the telecommunications connection as well.

"That's the downside of this technology," a White House staffer had whispered to a colleague when they were able to slip into the hallway for a few minutes. "Even when the man's four thousand miles away, we get to watch him pace and fret and frown as if he's across the table."

The President repeated his previous traffic pattern and ended the pacing with a heavy landing in one of the plush swivel chairs emblazoned with the presidential seal. He reached for the intercom button to the cockpit.

"Where are we, Colonel?"

"About a hundred miles west of Skagway, and about thirty minutes from meeting the tanker for refueling, sir."

"Thanks."

He turned his attention to the screen and the military aide on the Situation Room side, a chief master sergeant who was wearing a headset and writing furiously.

"Chief, what's *your* latest information?"

The impeccably groomed NCO straightened up and pulled off the headset.

"Sir, the F-16's have spotted him. They're moving in right now to try to get him on the radio."

"Where are they?"

He checked his notes. "Approximately eighty-five miles east of the shoreline, sir, over the Atlantic."

"And how much time left?"

"Forty-three minutes."

The President sat in his airborne chair aboard Air Force One and drummed his fingers for a few seconds as the chief master sergeant stood ramrod-straight some four thousand miles away in the basement of the White House and watched him. The Situation Room was buried too far down in the White House complex for anyone within to hear the wind howling outside, but Washington, D.C., was beginning to suffer real damage as the winds rose above a steady seventy miles per hour. Dilapidated slums a mere eight blocks from the Capitol to luxurious homes in Georgetown began to shed shingles, doors, shutters, and windows.

"Chief," the President said suddenly, "hook me in again with the Starsuite at the Pentagon."

"Yes, sir." A quick incline of his head to the communications specialist working the master control board, and the other half of the airborne Starsuite switched to the Pentagon. The President suppressed a chuckle. His order had been carried out so fast, the personnel on the Pentagon side had not been alerted the President was "coming" back. Suddenly the Commander in Chief was staring at them across the conference table, projected into the room as if physically sitting there. The reaction was a slightly wide-eyed jump as several officers turned and tried to look as if they had expected him all along.

"Fellows, get your bosses in here, would you?"

The two-star Air Force general appeared, flanked by a colonel and followed by a three-star.

"Check me on this, gentlemen, but if I'm reading my watch right, even if our fighters turned him around right this second, he's twenty-five minutes from the ramp at Grand . . . where was it?"

"Grand Strand, South Carolina, sir."

"Right. You agree with the time? Until we get him parked, I mean?"

They consulted their watches and each other and quickly nodded. "That's a reasonable estimate, sir."

"Okay. That would leave less than twenty minutes to detonation. Even if we just raced our two pilots onto the airplane and pulled the civilians off, and even if we could instantly solve the pacemaker problem, it would take five minutes to get airborne again at minimum. That's less than fifteen minutes of flying until it goes off. Guys, there's no way in hell we're going to get this plane far enough from the coast if we bring it back now."

The generals exchanged glances.

"We know that, sir," General Kinney said, "but we haven't been able to come up with another solution. The only alternative is to let them go."

The President grimaced and looked away in thought for a few seconds before replying. "I hate to do that. We're sending these folks to almost certain death. But there's no choice left, is there?" He sat in contemplative silence for a few more seconds before coming forward in his chair.

"Okay. I want you to call the guys in the F-16's and tell them . . . tell them it's time to turn around. If they've made contact with the captain, find out exactly what he's planning to do and wish him godspeed."

"Yes, sir."

"General, also have the pilots tell that captain, if they can . . ." He looked around at an aide on the Air Force One side of the room. "Is there any way I could talk to them directly?"

One of the colonels in the command post stepped forward slightly.

"Sir, you mean the 727?"

The President nodded. "Yes. Any way we could hook up directly?"

Several quick conversations ensued on the Pentagon side before the colonel turned back to the President.

"Sir, if you'll stand by a few more minutes. Our guys are almost in formation with him. We're relaying now, and maybe we can hook something up through a VHF frequency and air traffic control."

ABOARD SCOTAIR 50—7:20 P.M. EDT

The darkening ocean and ragged clouds that continued to flicker by the copilot's window were becoming all too familiar to Doc Hazzard as they lurched through the turbulence. He had stopped looking for pursuing fighters some time ago, so the presence of two gray shapes pacing them below and to the right of the cockpit had gone unnoticed.

Doc jerked his head to the right suddenly, thoroughly shocked to see two F-16's less than thirty yards away flying in silent formation with the 727 as it bucked and bounced its way through the low-level turbulence of the hurricane.

"Jeez! Scott, they've found us!"

Scott's head jerked right as well.

"What?"

"The F-16's. To the right, and slightly below. The lead's gesturing something."

Scott unsnapped his seat belt and shoulder harnesses and leaned up and to the right until the canopy of the lead F-16 was in view. The hand signals were universally recognizable, and he quickly read the frequency and dialed it into the UHF as he sat down and buckled up again.

"This . . . should be interesting," Scott said. "I don't see any reason not to talk to them. They're armed, and they've got our address. You agree, Doc?"

"Absolutely, I agree. Those boys could knock us down with any one of those missiles."

Scott keyed the microphone.

"ScotAir Fifty here. You up this frequency?"

The response was instantaneous, the voice the same one Scott remembered from the final approach to Seymour when they'd helped check the questionable landing gear. "Yes, sir. This is Shark Five on your right wing."

"So your orders now are to force us to turn around or shoot us out of the sky, right? Brilliant plan! Thanks to your idiot commanders not listening to us, we're going to have to do this ourselves. Get rid of the damned bomb, I mean."

"We're not under orders to force you back, sir. There's not enough time left anyway for you to return. Please confirm that your status with the device is the same. Is it showing about forty minutes to detonation?"

Linda had returned from the back and was listening. She checked her watch.

"I just checked it, Scott. Nothing's changed. It's showing forty-one minutes."

Scott relayed the confirmation.

"Sir, my command post and the White House want me to ask what you're intending to do, and if there's anything . . . I mean, I know this is pretty lame . . . but can we help in any way? We're not here to interfere."

Scott reached over and touched Doc's left arm. "I guess we can stop zigzagging now."

Doc laughed and rolled his eyes at the ceiling. "Sorry. Escape and evasion maneuvers were getting to be automatic. They were staying with us, in any event."

Doc steadied the course to due east as Scott held his finger over the transmit button and looked outside in thought before replying.

"Ah, Shark, you're talking to a former F-14 jockey over here. You can't have a lot of extra gas, so just go ahead and get out of here."

"We're fine for ten minutes more, sir."

"Look, I know this isn't your fault, but now that we've been essentially abandoned, we're going to try to jury-rig our cargo door to open and hopefully rip off in flight. Then we're going to dump the device out the cargo door and hope it doesn't detonate when it hits the water. If we hadn't been lied to back there at Grand Strand, we could have transferred the thing to a C-141, and he could have dropped it easily. The Air Force tried to spring another trap instead."

"I don't understand, ScotAir," the F-16 leader replied.

"The C-141 back at Grand Strand. There was supposed to be one there. It was obviously another hoax. That's why we're out here now on our own, with a pretty substantial chance of killing ourselves in the process of trying to dump the bomb."

"Sir, they didn't lie to you about the C-141."

"Yeah? We saw the KC-10 on final. That's when we bugged out."

"There was a KC-10, sir, that's true. But the C-141 landed five minutes after he did. I swear to you that's true."

There was silence in the 727 cockpit as Scott realized they had made the wrong assumption. There was no time to repair it now. The die was cast.

He took a deep breath and glanced at Doc, who was watching the instruments and purposefully refraining from a reaction.

"Well, you'd better get out of here, Shark. There's a chance this thing will explode when we dump it out and it loses the pacemaker signal, if you're aware of what I'm referring to."

"We are, sir. We've been briefed."

"Scott?" Linda's voice wafted in like a welcome wave from behind him, and Scott turned, eyebrows raised.

"Yeah?"

"We've got it solved," she said calmly. "The pacemaker, without Vivian, will go out with the device."

Scott turned even farther to study her expression, wondering if she was kidding.

"How?"

"She wants me to remove it. It's a simple surgical procedure, but she says we can do it and she'll be okay without it."

"ScotAir, you still with us?" the F-16 leader asked.

"Yes. Stand by just a second, Shark."

Scott gestured to the cargo cabin. "You're sure it will work?"

Linda nodded. If Vivian was sure, so was she.

Scott punched the transmit button again. "Shark, I think we've solved the problem. The pacemaker will be physically removed and attached to the device before we dump it. Impact with the water is the only variable, other than getting the door off without losing control. We've got to get rid of the two forward pallets first."

Scott thought he heard a small gasp from Linda, but his concentration was on what to say, knowing that every word spoken to the two F-16 pilots would make its way back to the Pentagon.

"When are you planning to dump it, sir? How far out?"

Scott looked at Doc, who shrugged his shoulders.

"We . . . haven't had a lot of time to plan, Shark. Let's say another hundred miles. However far we can get. We've got to get the door open pretty soon to accomplish this."

"We have a request, sir."

"Yeah. Go ahead."

"Could you come up on a long-range VHF frequency and talk to Washington Center?"

Scott agreed, took down the frequency, and dialed it in. The whole world seemed to know where they were now, Scott thought. Radio silence hardly made sense anymore.

"Washington Center, this is ScotAir Fifty."

The response was immediate.

"Roger, ScotAir Fifty. We have a radio relay on this frequency. Stand by."

What's a "radio relay" in air traffic control terms? Scott wondered.

The next voice in his ear had a familiar ring, but it didn't register at first.

"Is this . . . Navy Lieutenant Commander Scott McKay, over?"

Scott pushed the transmit button. "Yes. I'm a Reservist these days, but go ahead."

"Scott, I'm calling from Air Force One. This is the President."

Scott instantly felt off-balance, the lethal situation they were in fading into momentary irrelevance at the thought of a call from the President of the United States.

But his situational awareness returned in almost the same instant. They were carrying a nuclear weapon away from the mainland of the United States because governmental incompetence had blown all efforts to help.

The call made sense.

"Yes, Mr. President."

"Scott, you've got a difficult job ahead and I won't take more than a few seconds, but I wanted you to know you were right. We've got positive confirmation now that if we'd tried to blow up that device on the ground at Seymour-Johnson or anywhere else, the full Medusa Wave would have resulted. Your actions saved us from our own stupidity. We've screwed this up and left you out there all alone to deal with it. I'm deeply sorry you got so little help."

"I . . . thanks for confirming that, sir."

"I don't think we can do anything to help you from here, except with prayers. I'll be standing by. Good luck, Scott. Your President and your country are already infinitely grateful to all of you."

"Sir, that should include Vivian Henry. She had nothing to do with this. She's a victim."

"I understand, Scott. God speed."

They sat in silence for nearly thirty seconds before Scott reached down and flipped back to the UHF frequency.

"Shark? You fellows better get going. Thanks for the relay."

"Good luck, sir."

The two fighters peeled off to the right and disappeared immediately into the murk as Scott placed his hand on the radio control heads.

"I suppose we might as well secure the radios."

"Turn them off, you mean?" Doc asked.

"We're over the ocean, we'll be outside VHF for Washington Center in a moment, and we don't have long-range high-frequency gear. Any reason not to?"

Doc thought about it and slowly shook his head. "No, but I'd keep one of the VHF's on the emergency frequency, 121.5."

Scott nodded his head and adjusted the number one radio before turning off the number two VHF and the UHF.

"There goes our last contact with the civilized world," Scott said.

"Ain't all that civilized," Doc shot back. "Scott, we'd better get some altitude."

"Right. Take us up to ten thousand." He turned toward the empty engineer's seat. "Jerry? How're you coming with that?"

Jerry's voice came from under the engineer's station. "I've got it wired. I was just about to push in one of my jury-rigged breakers. You ready?"

"Go."

There was the small sound of a circuit breaker being pushed into place, a tiny *plink* of a sound.

"There," Jerry announced. "No sparks, no smoke. We're ready."

"Scott?" Linda said.

"Yeah."

"I . . . hadn't thought ahead. I forgot about my pallets being in the way. You can't get the bomb to the door without moving them, can you?"

Scott shook his head no.

"I . . . was pretty sure of that. Scott, I've got two years of hard work in those boxes. Is there any way we could save them?"

Scott's eyes searched hers for a moment, reading the worry there. "We blocked off the forward two pallet positions when we launched this airline, so we could have the option of putting a few passenger seats up front. If those two positions were usable, we could move your pallets forward and out of the way, but there's no way to reconfigure now. I wish we could."

Jerry had already scrambled to his feet and was brushing the layers of dust off his pants. Scott looked at him.

"Am I right, Jerry?"

Jerry nodded and looked at Linda as he pointed to the cockpit door.

"Linda, are there things in there we could pull out? If it's not an impossible size, we could tear down the pallet and relay your gear to the back and try to tie some of it down."

Linda was nodding. "Yes. There are some big pieces, but my computer tapes, the memory drives, and one of the Dobson Instruments, if I could save those, it would be wonderful. I also have a battery-powered cesium clock, but . . . that can go, I guess."

Scott had been checking time and distance equations in his head. Less than thirty-nine minutes remained.

"You'll have to move fast, Linda. We need to get that door open in no more than, say, ten minutes. The door should be off no later than fifteen minutes from now, which means you've got about fifteen minutes maximum to move your equipment."

"Then let's get going." Jerry was already clearing the door with Linda right behind him as Scott's voice reached her ears.

"I'll be back in a minute to help."

"Go on, Scott," Doc said. "I can handle it alone. You want to cruise at ten thousand?"

"Higher than that, Doc, if needed. Hell, you've been flying these things since before I was hatched. Whatever *you* think."

"We're penetrating the hurricane even more deeply. I'll try to keep us out of the red echoes, but please be careful back there. It's going to be increasingly violent." Doc looked around as he spoke, but Scott was already out of the seat and through the door. He was alone, and he caught himself glancing to the right and feeling a twang of loss that the F-16's had left.

Okay, we're climbing through eight thousand feet to level at ten thousand, Doc reminded himself, feeling suddenly isolated. *Here I am flying solo in a 727 in a hurricane over the ocean with a ticking nuclear bomb aboard. If I didn't already have some great stories for the grandkids, I will now!*

His thoughts unreeled at high speed, images of his first wife Betty and their two sons and his second wife and family flashing across his mind's eye—hating the possibility he might never see them again. Of course, they'd miss him, too, absentee father though he'd been. He loved his kids, and he still loved his wives, despite the divorces. Lucy came to mind, his third wife. Unable to conceive, thank God, since together their lives had been a whirlwind of wild sex, wild times, wild fights, and the wrong type of three-ring circus for a kid. Lucy had written just last week—E-mailed him, to be exact. She was dating again, which was good. He was glad they'd stayed friends, even occasional lovers, though if she remarried, the sex would have to end.

Or not. With Lucy, who knew? Describing her as a free spirit was an understatement.

A huge blotch of red on the radar indicating a severe thunderstorm cell appeared thirty miles ahead and Doc altered course nearly twenty degrees to the south to avoid it. The echo was so intense, all echoes behind it were eliminated, meaning there was a solid wall of airplane-eating turbulence, water, hail, and who knew what else churning out there, waiting for a hapless pilot to venture into.

Doc looked at the readout from the navigation computer. The winds were howling from behind now at over a hundred and five knots, pushing them beneficially farther over the Atlantic. He thought about the continental shelf. If the bomb waited to explode until it sank, maybe, just maybe, the water and the wall of the continental shelf could shield the mainland of the United States from the worst of the Medusa Wave.

Linda grabbed Jerry's arm just outside the cockpit and described what Vivian wanted done and what equipment they'd need. "Do you have all that?"

"Yes, we've got a well-equipped first-aid kit. Scott insisted on it. Right by the galley, here."

Jerry leaned over and pulled out the sizable metal box just as Scott came through the cockpit door.

"What did I insist on?"

"The first-aid kit. Last time I looked, it had a scalpel, Betadyne antiseptic, bandages . . ."

"How long will it take?" Scott asked.

Linda shook her head. "I don't know. She said it would be quick. I'm guessing five to ten minutes."

"How about your pallets, Linda? How much do you need to

rescue? I mean, if it's all small boxes, maybe we can relay them behind the bomb and save the majority."

"Some are vital, some aren't. I know what I need, but let's get Vivian taken care of first."

Scott shook his head. "No. Bad use of resources. Take two minutes to help us tear into your pallets to show us what to pull out, then while you operate on Vivian, we'll do our best with the equipment."

A frightening series of bumps and lurches sent all three scrambling for handholds. Instead of subsiding, the turbulence became constant and lightning flashes began illuminating the interior through the cabin windows.

"We're going to have to work fast," Scott told them. "Jerry, grab that crowbar. Do you have a knife for the plastic?"

"Yeah, and shears."

Linda moved ahead of Scott and Jerry around the side of the pallets.

"Just a second," she said, grabbing the first-aid kit from Jerry and disappearing toward the back. In less than a minute she was back.

"I told Vivian what we were planning and gave her the kit. She'll prep herself."

"Which one first, Linda?" Scott stumbled to his right and fell against her. She caught him and grabbed the strap on the first pallet for support.

"This one. My computer tapes are in a metal container back in there."

Jerry began slashing away at the thick plastic sheeting covering the cargo. As he pared it back, Scott pulled it aside and played a flashlight on the stack of cardboard and metal containers.

"How much of this needs to be moved, Linda? You need it all?"

"Not all, no." She scrambled through the plastic and began pulling frantically at the boxes until several metal canisters beyond were exposed.

"The metal carriers. All of the small ones. The big crates are too heavy. Save as many of these cardboard boxes as you can. The second pallet has mostly heavy stuff. I'll . . . I'll just have to lose it. But the boxes have my research records, and the metal canisters are vital."

As Scott helped her back out of the pallet, the aircraft took a shuddering leap to one side, knocking them all off-balance. Linda fell against Scott and his arms automatically closed around her as he scrambled for footing on the tangled plastic. He gently took her shoulders and moved her away until they were looking at each other in intimate proximity in a slightly awkward moment that seemed to linger.

Jerry waited a few seconds, then canted his head toward the pallet. "Come on, you two."

Linda pulled back in embarrassment and Scott did the same. She gestured toward the rear. "I, ah, better get back there."

"Right," Scott replied.

"I'll keep Vivian to one side so you can get past."

"Okay. Good."

Jerry's voice reached them from within the plastic sheathing. "Let's get this heavy one first, Scott."

Scott turned to help him as Linda moved toward the back, feeling somewhat self-conscious. She'd heard about attractions growing in the midst of great peril, but she'd never experienced it.

If that's what it is, she thought, chiding herself. *It's not just Scott. You care about all of these people.*

But a very persistent voice in her head was saying otherwise.

24

••••

Pete Cooke's nationwide beeper began vibrating furiously, and he pulled it out of its small belt holster and turned on the backlighting to read the tiny screen.

CAN'T RAISE YOUR CELLPHONE! CALL ASAP! IRA

Pete moved to a nearby phone and dialed *The Wall Street Journal*'s 800 number in New York. Ira answered immediately and asked why Pete's cellular phone had been turned off.

"I don't want to disturb anyone in this air traffic control facility. What's up?"

"We got a call a few minutes ago from a very disturbed fellow, another one who used to work with Dr. Rogers Henry in Los Alamos. He got your name and a number from the physicist you first talked to in Silver Spring. The name's Dr. Gene Mislowsky. He demanded to speak with you immediately. He sounded panicky."

"What about?"

"I didn't ask, but I think you oughta call him."

Ira passed the number and Pete placed the call. It was answered on the first ring.

"Dr. Mislowsky?" Pete asked. "This is Pete Cooke."

"Mr. Cooke, I wasn't sure who to talk to, but maybe you can help. I understand you were listening in to the airplane carrying the Medusa Weapon."

"Yes, I was. Earlier. They're out of range now."

"It's counting down to detonation, isn't it?"

"That's what the crew said, repeatedly."

"And they don't know how to turn it off, right?"

Pete filled him in on the abortive attempt to get experts to the weapon at Pax River and Seymour-Johnson and the apparent decision of the crew to try to dump it at sea.

"Mr. Cooke, did anyone on that airplane, at any time, mention that the bomb had a keyboard or a keypad connected to a computer? Any sort of keyboard?"

Pete thought back through the exchanges. "One of those on board, Mrs. Henry, in fact, was said to have *typed* something into the device at one point, so it had to have a keyboard of some sort. I'm sure I heard the word 'typed.' "

"That's what I thought. They're obviously running out of time, Mr. Cooke, but I've got to talk to them. I know how to shut it off."

Pete paused, unsure of what he'd heard.

"What do you mean, Doctor? You mean, you know how to open it, get inside and defeat it?"

"No no. How to walk up to whatever keyboard it has and shut it down with the entry of one single, solitary digit. One number!"

"How do you know? Did you help build it?"

The possibility that he was talking to a nut crossed Pete's mind, but he could probably validate the man's former position with one call if he needed to.

"Hell no!" Dr. Mislowsky answered. "We worked for over a decade as a team trying to develop it, but we never got the chance to assemble a prototype. Rogers Henry had a very unique approach to passwords and entry codes. We didn't discover that fact until the project was disbanded and we were all required during out-processing to disclose whatever personal codes we used during the project. His code shocked everyone. He'd been laughing at us for years."

"What was his code, Dr. Mislowsky?"

"We're almost out of time. Someone needs to get my information to that crew. Who should I call, Mr. Cooke? That's the help I need."

"Well, probably the Pentagon . . ."

"Already tried. I couldn't find the right people. No one there was going to talk to me until they checked the Los Alamos personnel file archives. Idiots! Don't they know what they're up against?"

"I . . . may know someone, if you'll tell me the disarming method."

"Okay, '1.' But I still want to talk to them myself."

" 'One'? One what?"

"The digit '1.'" There was a sigh on the other end of the line, as if the man were making a decision not to hold back. "As crazy and simplistic as it sounds, that was Rogers' security code. Everyone else was compounding multiple digits and alphanumeric combinations, and, at the time, we even had security entry pads developed that could accept up to ten-digit codes. But Rogers apparently decided the very last cipher anyone would think of trying is '1.' And, amazingly enough, he was right."

"Wait a minute! You're telling me that if those people aboard that jet will just walk over to the bomb and punch in the number '1' . . ."

"And hit 'Enter.'"

"Okay, '1' and 'Enter.' You're telling me the damn thing will simply stop ticking?"

"That's what I'm telling you."

"How can you be sure? What if you're wrong?"

"Then nothing happens and it keeps ticking. There's nothing to lose. And if I'm wrong, a single digit is hardly going to detonate the thing. Rogers only used that number to deactivate or open things. He used it as his personal cipher code, and he *never* had it compromised until the end of the program for the very same reason you're having trouble accepting it: It's too damn simple."

Pete closed his eyes and shook his head. *Nothing is ever this simple. One digit! An end to all this with one digit!*

"Stay by the phone, please," Pete told him. "I'll call you right back."

"Please hurry, Mr. Cooke."

A main corollary of Murphy's Law at work. Pete concluded. *The more simple the solution, the more difficult it is to apply it.*

He hung up the phone and looked at his hands. They were shaking slightly and he was breathing rapidly. The magnitude of the information he'd just been handed staggered him, but he forced himself to move.

Pete checked his watch, then let his eyes dart around the desk in front of him for a phone book.

Nothing.

He yanked the phone up again and tried to dial directory assistance for Washington.

A government recording chided him for not using a personal authorization code.

He dialed the FAA operator and tried to explain what he needed.

"I can't put through a toll call without an authorization code, sir."

Pete slammed the phone in its cradle and yanked his cellular phone out, punched it on, and dialed directory assistance. After nearly a minute of holding, a bored voice came on the line.

"Directory assistance. What city?"

"Washington, and this is an emergency!" Pete said in a rushed tone. "Please give me the main number of the FBI, and please *don't* use your voice machine."

"Excuse me?" she said with a snort. "Don't use my *what*?"

"Your voice machine. I just want you to read me the number yourself."

"I have to find the number first. *Sir.*"

"Okay, okay. The FBI switchboard, please."

"The *what*?"

"The Federal Bureau of Investigation in Washington, D.C. The number of their headquarters, dammit!"

For nearly forty seconds he could hear computer keys clickity-clacking at a leisurely pace in the background.

"That was the Federal Trade Commission, sir?"

"No, dammit! The FBI! Elliot Ness, J. Edgar Hoover, G-men. Surely you've heard of them."

"I'm not talking to you if you're gonna be rude, sir," the operator said in a petulant tone.

There was more sedate clicking of computer keys at a slightly slower pace.

"Hold for the number."

"NO! Don't use the automatic . . ." Pete shot back.

But she was gone and a recorded voice slowly began intoning the number in her place. Pete jotted it down, recycled the phone, and punched in the number as he glanced at his watch again, thinking uncharitable thoughts about the hiring practices of the phone company. The aircraft would be moving away from the coast at seven to eight miles per minute. Communicating with it after a certain point might be impossible.

The phone at the FBI's main switchboard began ringing, but no one answered.

The 727's probably got only VHF radios aboard, other than the

Flitephone. He'll be too far out for Flitephone frequencies, too far out for cellular frequencies. How far can the coastal air traffic VHF repeaters go?

Pete heard an operator finally come on the line. He consulted the name he'd written in his notebook over an hour ago.

"Ah, this is an emergency. Please put me through immediately to Mr. Tony DiStefano."

"Which department, please?"

"I have no idea."

"Stand by, sir."

I'm going to sound like an idiot with this information, but if he's right . . .

More than a minute went by before a now-familiar voice came on the line, this time without static.

"DiStefano here."

"Agent DiStefano?"

"Yes."

"I'm Pete Cooke, a reporter for *The Wall Street Journal*. I have a radio scanner. By accident a few hours ago I happened to find the right frequency and I overheard all of your conversations with the captain of ScotAir Fifty, Captain Scott, ah, McKay. I've been working the story since then."

"You're the bastard who broke this story?"

"No, sir, not exactly. Look, I guess I helped, but you can growl at me later. Right now, you need to know that I've been contacted by one of Dr. Rogers Henry's former coworkers, a scientist from Los Alamos who says he knows the combination Henry would have used in programming the bomb."

"What do you mean, 'combination'?" DiStefano interrupted.

"To deactivate it. To turn it off. He says Henry would have rigged this bomb with the same deactivation code, because that was his signature. He thinks if the crew punches it in the keypad on the back of the bomb, through that hatch . . ."

"How do you know about that keypad, Mr. Cooke?"

"Because, Agent DiStefano, I was listening to every word Scott McKay said to you and vice versa! Okay?"

"Oh yeah. You did say that."

"Look, we're almost out of time. Can you get this information to the crew? To McKay?"

"We're no longer in control of this, Mr. Cooke. I'll have to . . ."

"Tony, excuse the first name, but we don't have time for formality. I'll give you the scientist's name and number, but by the time you check it out, unless you've got the crew on the line, it may be too late."

"What's the code, Mr. Cooke?"

" '1.' "

There was the predictable reaction. Pete passed on the explanation as rapidly as he could and half-expected DiStefano to hang up.

"That's a cockamamy idea if I ever heard one, Mr. Cooke. A senior nuclear scientist would be cashiered if he was found to be using something a five-year-old could compromise. He may have liked the idea, but I doubt he ever used it, and I can't buy it for this thing."

"What if you're wrong? What if it's the key and we miss it? What the hell have we lost if they try it?"

There was a lengthy silence before DiStefano spoke.

"Okay, you've got a point. Hold the line. Don't go away."

"I won't," Pete promised. He leaned against the desk and looked back at the control room floor as a previously unfinished thought made its way back in his head with a startling realization.

I wonder if he's still within range of the air traffic control radios?

"Jesus Christ!" Pete said out loud, straightening up as if hit with a cattle prod. "We don't need to *call* the air traffic control facility. I'm standing in it!"

Pete kept the cellular phone pressed to his ear as he moved quickly across the room and grabbed the shoulder of a startled supervisor.

"Can you call Washington Center on your tie-line and see if they can still reach ScotAir Fifty?"

The man had been leaning over a console. He was aware of Pete Cooke as an observer from the media, but not as a demanding participant. He straightened up slowly and suspiciously.

"I could, yes."

"I've got the FBI on the other end here." He waved the open cellular at the man. "We've got vital information to get to the aircraft before he gets out of range. Please!"

The man nodded slowly with a neutral expression on his face and suspicion oozing from every pore. He gingerly picked up a receiver and punched the Washington Center line.

He turned back to Pete in less than a minute.

"They're checking that sector. They had contact with him about ten minutes ago. What, exactly, are you trying to give him?"

Tony DiStefano came back on the line.

"You still there, Cooke?"

"Yes."

Pete raised his hand in a wait indication to the FAA supervisor.

"Okay," Tony said, "I've passed that idea to the Air Force. They tell me they've had a couple of fighters pacing him, but they've broken off now, and he's been out of contact for maybe five minutes."

"Can the fighters try to raise him on the radio?"

"I believe that's what they're going to try. I'm not sure they believe this is the solution, although I told them that Henry used this same code year after year."

"Tony, again," Pete said, "at this stage, what could it hurt?"

There was silence for a second from the other end as Pete glanced at the FAA supervisor and realized his patience was waning.

Tony DiStefano sighed. "Other than a premature detonation, I suppose it wouldn't hurt to try. But come on, Mr. Cooke. The number '1'? For a security code or an unlocking code? Any idiot could figure that out."

"Well, presumably they're not idiots on that aircraft and *they* haven't figured it out," Pete said.

"Touché," Tony replied as Pete continued.

"I thought the same thing when the guy first said it, but have you ever seen a computer password that used a single digit?"

"Hell no! Of course not."

"Right. Neither have I. Therefore, anyone trying to break the code in a military cipher lock would never figure the code was a single digit. All attempts would involve multiple digits."

"But a single-digit code wouldn't be secure, now would it?"

"It would if there was a label by the keyboard that indicated a five- or ten-digit code would open it, and you had to press 'Enter' to activate it."

"This is bizarre," DiStefano said in Pete's ear as the FAA supervisor cleared his throat. The supervisor pointedly examined his watch, then glanced around the room in growing impatience.

"Tony, excuse me, could you hold?"

"Why not, *Pete*. Yeah, for a minute."

Pete lowered the cellular phone from his ear and explained the problem. The supervisor picked up the tie-line again, said a few words to whoever was on the other end, and handed Pete the tie-line.

"This is Pete Cooke. Hello?"

The voice on the other end carried a syrupy Virginia accent. "Mr. Cooke, you're asking to get hold of ScotAir Fifty?"

"Yes, sir. There's vital information we're trying to pass him. The FBI is on the other line and they've got the Air Force working on it, but I'm scared we'll lose contact with the aircraft. Do you have ScotAir on frequency?"

The man's answer came back immediately. "No, sir, we don't."

Pete felt his heart sink.

"But we're trying to raise him. Stand by on this line. We'll try several frequencies."

"Okay."

Pete heard conversation in the background and the faint sound of a controller asking in the blind for ScotAir 50.

"Mr. Cooke, if we find him, what do you want to tell him?"

Pete closed his eyes and shook his head to clear it. There wasn't time for another explanation.

"Tell him he must go to the device's keypad and press the number '1' and the 'enter' key immediately. That will deactivate the whole thing."

More silence.

"You talking about the bomb they have aboard?"

"Yes, sir, I am."

"I don't know if I can pass a message like that, Mr. Cooke. I don't know for certain who you are."

"Look, I appreciate your caution, but I'm standing in your system command center right now, and they checked my ID, and that was a supervisor who called you."

"I'm sure that's all true, but I think I need a little more."

"Do you have him yet?"

"Not yet."

"Give me a landline telephone number directly to you. The FBI will call you." The man read off a phone number and Pete pulled the cellular back to his ear.

"Tony?"

"Ah, Peter, my new best friend from the fourth estate," he said, joking sarcastically. "Yes, I'm here."

"Washington Center's trying to raise him, too. I didn't tell you I was calling from the system command center. Take this number down. Call the supervisor at Washington Center and tell him to pass the information to ScotAir when he reaches the crew. He doesn't believe me."

"Wait a minute, Cooke. I'm not sure *I* believe you."

"It's our only chance to deactivate the bomb."

"I can't order the FAA to do anything."

"Call Dr. Mislowsky. Please. Ask him, then call the FAA. We've only got a few minutes."

There was silence on Tony's end. Finally he spoke.

"Okay. Hang on."

As Tony DiStefano left the line, Pete pressed the Washington tie-line to his ear and glanced again at his watch. Several FAA men were gathering near him now, all of them suspicious but intensely interested in what he was trying to do. Everyone in the system command center was acutely aware of the drama that had been playing out between Washington and the Carolina coast.

"Mr. Cooke, you still there?" The Virginia accent was in his ear again from Washington Center.

"Yes. Right here. You found him?"

"No, sir. He's not answering. We're still trying. We figure he's at the far end of our range out there, especially in this hurricane. Does he have high-frequency radio, HF we call it, or satellite, do you know?"

"I'm a pilot. I understand the terms, but I don't know the answer."

"Well, we're going to try all the frequencies we have, including 121.5, the emergency frequency."

"Try the military emergency frequency as well. I know he has a UHF aboard."

"Okay, 343.0."

"Right." Pete could hear the sound of a pen scratching at paper as he pressed the handset to his left ear and the cellular phone to his right.

"Stand by, Mr. Cooke."

The controller put him on hold for nearly a minute before returning.

"Someone from the FBI just called to confirm what you said. We're verifying that he's legitimate, and I guess that will do it. You understand how delicate this all is?"

"Of course," Pete said, trying to keep the extreme frustration out of his voice. The man was right to be cautious and he knew it. But there was so little time left.

"No luck yet in reaching him?" Pete asked again.

"No, sir," the Virginia accent replied. "But if we reach him, I'll patch you through, Mr. Cooke. Now, why don't you just hold on there?"

"I will. I will."

Pete looked at his watch again. Thirty-seven minutes remained.

How are we going to feel, he wondered, *if those people die in a fireball, Medusa shuts down the economy, and we could have prevented it with a single digit? Have we done everything we can? Have I?*

There was another matter eating at him, and he let it find voice in his mind now. It was a vague feeling of guilt that had been nibbling at his conscience since he had cooperated so readily with ABC. It had nattered in the background and raised its ugly head once more with Tony DiStefano's none-too-kind query about his involvement in the public airing of the story.

Should he have refused to help ABC? He had told Ira they couldn't call the electronic media unless they were sure, but with ABC's information, they *had* been sure. True, the country was in an uproar because of the media reports. True, no one really knew if there was a real Medusa weapon aboard ScotAir 50. What if a Medusa Wave didn't occur? How much damage had already occurred out there, he wondered. It didn't matter that ABC had almost pieced the story together without him. He had helped. If it was all a terrible mistake, he was partly to blame.

Pete had been staring at the far wall of the air traffic control facility without seeing it, his mind racing back and forth, from the aging Boeing 727 now over the Atlantic to his office in New York.

There was still nothing but a background hum on the tie-line.

No, he concluded. He'd done the only reasonable thing he could have done. The country needed to know. It might already be too late, but they needed to get ready.

25

• • • •

The phone call from the Air Force command post at the Pentagon had been a surprise. Tony DiStefano hadn't expected a call back. After all, Tony thought, the military was in charge of trying to manage the crisis, even if they had screwed it up royally.

Of course, the performance of the FBI's man at Seymour-Johnson had been a gross embarrassment as well. They were in no position to toss mud balls at the Pentagon.

"Agent DiStefano?"

The voice identified himself as a major general.

"Yes, General?"

"You relayed that report about the single-digit code as a way of deactivating the Medusa weapon?"

"Yes, sir. Just a few minutes back."

"Was that information from a Dr. Jack Kravitz of Aspen, Colorado?"

"No. No, it was originally from a Dr. Gene Mislowsky, and it was relayed by a Pete Cooke, a reporter for, I think he said, *The Wall Street Journal.*"

"Amazing."

"Why, General?"

"Let me verify this. The shutdown cipher code was the single digit '1'?"

"Yes, sir. It was apparently an educated guess based on that scientist's knowledge of Rogers Henry. But why? Who is Dr. Jack Kravitz?"

"Dr. Kravitz is another former coworker of Rogers Henry from Los Alamos."

"Lord, they're coming out of the woodwork."

"Apparently it was a team of thirty scientists."

"Dr. Kravitz called you at the Pentagon?"

"No, sir. He called the White House and managed to talk to the Situation Room, who patched him to us. We checked the roster from the Medusa Project days, and he's on it."

"General, what did he say?"

"He confirmed it. He told us in no uncertain terms that the single digit '1' was definitely the code Rogers Henry would have used."

"Independent confirmation, then?"

"Totally, unless he's lying about not knowing the whereabouts of Dr. Mislowsky or lying about having no contact with him today. It's always possible they could be comparing notes on a theory, one reinforcing the other. But he swore that wasn't the case, and there isn't enough time left to check it out directly from our end."

Tony felt his skepticism evaporating.

My God! One digit and they're out of the woods.

He shifted his focus back to the phone. "General, I've got a reporter named Pete Cooke on another line at the FAA's facility. He says the FAA can't reach the airplane. Can you?"

"Not yet, but we're trying everything."

Tony wanted to ask what "everything" meant, but thought better of it. "Can we help you, General, in any way?"

"Yes, sir. You already have helped immensely in giving me that confirmation, but if you could also run a quick background check through your computers on those two scientists and let us know what, if anything, you find, I think that would raise our confidence level that we're on the right track in trusting this single-digit code business . . . not that we have a choice, of course."

"I'll call you back, General."

"As soon as possible, please, Agent DiStefano. We're going to have an historic national disaster of unprecedented proportions on our hands in a little over thirty minutes if we can't reach those pilots."

AIR FORCE COMMAND POST, THE PENTAGON—
7:26 P.M. EDT

General Kinney replaced the handset and leaned over the table where two other officers and a chief master sergeant were spreading out a map of the Atlantic Ocean from South Carolina to Bermuda. The level of intensity in the command post was the highest he'd seen in a decade. For the past half hour they'd been hearing reports about the economy of the United States rapidly coming to a halt, with financial institutions, markets, and clearing houses all trying desperately to secure themselves against the impending electromagnetic pulse. Aircraft were being grounded nationwide, most of them far short of destination. Freight and passenger trains were stopped in midtrack, and countless municipal facilities were shutting down.

The attempts to reach ScotAir were becoming frantic. The entire team was painfully aware they had the key to deactivating the Medusa Weapon, but couldn't use it unless ScotAir could be reached.

The general looked closely at the map. "They're flying into the Bermuda Triangle," he said.

"Yes, sir, whatever that means."

"So where are we?" the general asked his aide. "Can the F-16's make it?"

"The two F-16's that found him a while ago are headed back to shore. They would need refueling, sir, before we sent them east again. It'll simply be too late by the time they hit the tanker and turn around. We thought we could scramble some F-15's from Shaw Air Force Base, but they can't get airborne fast enough, and they only have UHF radios aboard, which makes that a questionable choice. We need someone who can broadcast on VHF and UHF."

"Any other air traffic along here?" The general traced a line roughly running due east from Grand Strand Airport and extending four hundred miles east.

Both aides shook their heads, and one replied, "All commercial air traffic has been routed way around the fringe of the hurricane. They're all probably too far away to use as a radio relay, except this fellow . . ." He pointed to a triangle with a Lufthansa call sign.

"Lufthansa's going into Miami, and he might be close enough. His company is calling him right now by satellite phone to see if he'll broadcast for ScotAir."

"I wish to hell ScotAir had a satellite phone, but his communications gear is apparently pretty basic."

"And we have one last possibility."

"What?"

"Actually, we have two, sir. We're asking NASA for help because the space shuttle *Endeavor* is in orbit right now and may be within range. They were scheduled to take live pictures of the hurricane today, so there's a chance they could help. Second, there's an SR-71 Blackbird flying over the hurricane doing some sort of high-altitude research. He's in the air now, and we're trying to reach him."

"Good! I've always been upset at the idea of parking the world's fastest, highest-flying airplane to save money. He has a VHF radio?"

"We're not sure, but it's worth a try."

A major appeared at the general's side, a deep frown on his face.

The general turned to him immediately.

"Something new?"

"Sir, the space shuttle won't be in range for two more orbits. That's about three more hours."

"Damn!" The general looked around at everyone in the room. "How much time do we have left?" he asked.

"Thirty-five minutes, sir."

He shook his head and sighed. "There's got to be a solution! There's got to be a way to reach that plane. Think, everyone. Get creative. No idea's too far out."

"General?" The voice of another officer crackled over the table. A lieutenant colonel. He was holding a receiver and looking excited.

"Yeah?" the general replied.

"The SR-71 *is* VHF-equipped. The pilot says if we'll scare up a tanker for him to head for afterward, he'll divert to the target area and try to raise the 727 from above."

"How high?"

"He's above sixty thousand feet, sir. He'll have quite a broadcast footprint."

"Where is he now? How far away?"

The general moved quickly to the colonel's side, tension and excitement mixing in his voice.

The colonel consulted his notes and spoke a few words into the phone before turning back to General Kinney.

"He says he'll be line-of-sight to that area in four minutes. He's flat-out full-throttle."

"Yes!" the general said, punching the air for emphasis and turning to his aide. "Get a KC-10 airborne or turned in the appropriate direction. Work with him." He pointed to the colonel still holding the phone, who raised his hand for silence as he struggled to hear the voice on the other end of the line.

The colonel looked up suddenly. "He's unable to patch us through directly to the 727 when and if he responds, so he wants to know in advance what the message is we're so anxious to send."

The general repeated the code and the method of entering it into a keyboard. "Just punch in the number '1.' No zeros, no decimals, just '1', and then 'Enter.' "

"That's it?" the colonel asked.

"That's it. Ask him to do it and report back as quick as he can on whether it worked."

The colonel repeated the instructions into the phone, then fell silent, realizing all eyes were on him. He covered the mouthpiece.

"I'm standing by . . . I'm patched through his command post, and through them, into a satellite connection to the SR-71 commander."

Several people, including the general, checked their watches, mentally marking the four-minute point.

ABOARD AIR FORCE ONE—7:26 P.M. EDT

The tension aboard Air Force One had been rising almost exponentially in the previous half hour, but with word from the Pentagon that a single digit might turn off the detonation sequence—and the fact that no one could reach the 727—the President had resumed pacing around his side of the Starsuite as the National Security Advisor and the Foreign Policy Advisor entered the White House side of the Starsuite.

The President stopped and looked at the two men.

"I'm going to need to talk to the Russians in a few minutes. Then the British, French, Germans, and the Japanese Prime Minister. I need to keep everyone calm if this really happens. The Russians can see a nuclear detonation within seconds with their satellites, can't they?"

Stanley Shapiro, the National Security Advisor, nodded. "We're still given to believe they can, though, thank God, we're not facing Soviets with itchy trigger fingers anymore. Now that they're our good friends, the Kremlin's all wired up with our networks. You can be sure they know the basic outlines of this story already, but what they need to know is where to expect the detonation. Sir, have you considered submarines?"

The President appeared confused. "Subs? To call the airliner, you mean?"

"No, sir." Shapiro continued, "I mean, have you considered the repercussions if that crew somehow dumps the bomb on top of a Russian sub, or anyone else's sub, for that matter."

"Lord no, I hadn't. Has the Navy . . ."

Stanley Shapiro raised his hand in a stop gesture.

"Well, sir, I've been looking into it. Both officially and unofficially, we know of no Russian subs or anyone else's subs in that general area right now. In fact, we have a carrier group trying to get to the south of the hurricane southwest of Bermuda, and they're closer than anyone else. But there is a danger you need to be aware of. Allies or not, if one of their subs happens to go down somewhere else for a reason they'd rather not discuss—and there are a lot of such reasons these days, including mutiny, gross negligence, forgetting to close a hatch, whatever—it could be very convenient to blame its loss on their friends in Washington and ask for compensation."

"So we do need to tell them immediately, right?"

"Yes, sir, but it's so late, even if they certified to us there were no submarines in that area, they could later say, 'Oops, you gave us the wrong coordinates and fried one of our boats!' "

"The Cold War is over, Stanley. It's not supposed to be so complicated anymore."

"Ah, but that's where statecraft reaches its highest form. How to hopelessly complicate the essentially simple."

"If they file a claim, we could say it was a French nuclear test," the President said with a deadpan expression.

The President picked up the interphone to the communications room aboard Air Force One.

"Set up a hot line call to the Russian President as soon as possible." He looked back up at the Situation Room side of the teleconference. "What else are we forgetting?"

"How about satellites? I was told the shuttle couldn't help, but see if we have a satellite overhead that can reach them on VHF radio frequencies. If they need authorization to change an orbit, whatever the cost, they've got it."

"I think," Stanley Shapiro began, "that SR-71 is our best hope, sir. He's working for NOAA, but under NASA's control. Call sign is Condor Ten. He'll be overhead momentarily."

"Maybe, but get on the satellite angle, too. We can't leave any possibility unexplored."

ABOARD SCOTAIR 50—7:27 P.M. EDT

The boxes and equipment culled from the first two pallets were growing into an unmanicured jumble in the rear of the cargo cabin of the 727 as Scott and Jerry labored to move as much as possible in the time allowed, while the owner of the cargo, Linda McCoy, prepared for emergency surgery.

Scott stopped for a second in the rear of the cabin and wiped his forehead. He and Jerry were sweating profusely. The task of tying down the loose collection of boxes with a cargo net would take approximately two more minutes. The net had already been laid alongside the growing stack as the constant turbulence threatened to scatter the boxes all across the cargo floor.

The sound of the PA system clicking on caused Scott to look instinctively toward the ceiling.

"Scott, we've got less than ten minutes before the door should be opened. Ten minutes." Doc's voice reverberated around the mostly empty section between Vivian Henry and the mountain of Antarctic research gear.

There was no time for modesty, Vivian had decreed. She had shucked her blouse and bra and lain down several minutes before as Linda reapplied Betadyne antiseptic to the area where the pacemaker sat just beneath the superficial fascia of the skin, above the left breast and below the collarbone.

Linda placed a small blanket under her knees as she knelt by

Vivian's right side. She'd tried to use the blouse as a drape of sorts, but Vivian had pulled it away.

"It was a very expensive present to myself, dear," she'd told Linda. "I don't want to bleed on it."

The process, Vivian had instructed, was really quite simple. The small, pocket-watch-sized pacemaker formed a flat, circular lump under the skin with a well-defined edge all around. A simple incision along the bottom of the lump running from the four o'clock to the eight o'clock position should be enough.

"As you cut," Vivian told her, "let the tip of the knife ride along the metal casing of the pacemaker. That way it'll be very clean and there's no problem gauging how far down to cut."

"Okay."

"When the bottom is exposed, reach in with two fingers and slowly slide the whole unit out from under the skin, just enough so that two wires are exposed. There's enough slack."

"The wires connect to the top?"

Vivian nodded. "Yes. That way the unit can be slid out in a downward motion."

The fact that there would be no anesthetic to deaden the area had been bothering Linda far more than the patient.

"Can you handle the pain, Vivian?" Linda had asked.

"There won't be much," Vivian had replied evenly. "It won't be comfortable, but it won't be bad."

"Maybe one of the guys has some liquor. Would you like some, if I can find something intoxicating?"

Vivian shook her head emphatically no.

"Linda, let me finish the instructions. As I said, there are two tiny wires that connect to the top of the unit. There is enough slack for them to come out with the unit and be grasped so you can disconnect them, but you do not want to pull on them any more than that."

"Why?"

"They're embedded intravenously. They run all the way to the right side of my heart."

"Oh Lord!" Linda's hand went to her mouth. "Oh Lord!"

Vivian reached out a hand to reassure her.

"You won't be affecting those interior wires in any way, unless you try to yank at them or pull at them."

"Absolutely I will not yank at them or pull at them! No way!"

She cocked her head and focused a questioning expression at Vivian.

"My God, Vivian, they're in your *heart*?"

"The other ends are. Now, calm down! All you're going to do is disconnect them from the unit when you slide the unit out, then gently place the wires back inside."

"What if they're touching? Won't they short out or something? I mean, I know I can't use black electrical tape to insulate them, but . . ."

Vivian laughed and shook her head. "The power source is the unit we'll be removing, the basic pacemaker. It doesn't matter if the wires touch when you put them back inside. My only point is, don't yank on the wires while you're disconnecting them or after they're disconnected."

"I promise. Believe me, I won't!"

"Good. That's all. Just so you know."

"I'm not a doctor, Vivian. I mean, I'm not a medical doctor. This stuff scares me."

"I know, Linda, but you'll do fine."

"What do we do about the bleeding?" Linda asked. "Will there be much?"

"No. Not much. Use those paper towels you brought from the bathroom to absorb what there is, but try not to put the towels in contact with the incision."

Vivian could see Linda's hand shaking slightly. Vivian reached out and took it again, saying, "Now, calm down. I'm the patient and I'm calm, so you've got to be calm, too. This isn't open heart surgery. A doctor has to do the same thing when it needs new batteries."

"Really? How often?"

"Supposed to be every five years or so, but in my case the batteries haven't been lasting as long. Now I know why. All right, no more delays. We're out of time and I'm getting very cold."

Linda picked up the scalpel and felt its balance as if she were going to throw it at a target. She took a deep breath and mentally reviewed whether everything had been as sterilized as they could manage. Her hand steadied, and she gently held the lump of skin containing the pacemaker with her left hand as she positioned the blade of the scalpel with her right, being careful not to let the bouncing of the aircraft influence the cut as she pushed the tip of the blade and felt it slice cleanly into Vivian's outer skin.

Fifty feet toward the front of the aircraft, Doc Hazzard looked at his watch and picked up the PA mike once again.

"Scott, we're down to five minutes now before door-open time. Suggest you finish the cargo move."

He hadn't heard the sound of a human voice for more than fifteen minutes, Doc realized, and the absence of the constant radio chatter all airline pilots are used to hearing in flight made him uneasy. In fact, he was losing his cool altogether, and he didn't like that fact.

They were taking too much time in the back. He knew he was feeling scared and maybe a little abandoned. In fact, he was irritated and distracted, as if there were two Doc Hazzards snarling at each other in his head, one logical and one pure emotion. He wanted to scream at both of them. All his career he'd been proud of his reputation of being steady as a rock under pressure. "There's grace under pressure, and there's Doc under pressure," a friend had said once, introducing him at an Air Line Pilots Association dinner, "and Doc under pressure is calmer."

He thought back to an incident twenty years ago, when Pan Am was still a vibrant company. He'd overheard a conversation around a corner in the New York pilot lounge that had made him infinitely proud. "Ol' Doc?" a young first officer had said, not realizing Doc was in the area. "I love flying with that character. Nothing ever rattles him! If the right wing fell off, Doc Hazzard would call for another cup of coffee before ordering hard left rudder and calling for the emergency checklist. Only thing gets him excited is a sexy woman. He's a sucker for females."

Still am! Doc thought. *But I guess I'm not imperturbable anymore.*

He swiveled around and looked at the closed door with rising irritation. He forced himself to focus on the instruments and the flight path. The task of picking his way through the red splotches of severe weather showing on the color radar was taking its toll. He glanced over at the radio control heads on the center console between the captain's and copilot's seats, wondering if he should turn the radios back on. The number one VHF radio *was* on, he reminded himself, and tuned to the only VHF frequency that made sense for them out over the Atlantic: 121.5, the emergency frequency, or "guard" as the military aviators called it.

Anyone trying to call us would call us on guard, he reassured himself.

Something was nagging at him. But what? There was something else he'd overlooked. It had been a fleeting thought ten or twenty minutes ago when the fighters left, but now he couldn't remember. It had been something that needed checking, such as . . .

His eyes focused on the mirror image VHF radio heads.

Number one VHF has the damn volume control on the left, he told himself. He was finally remembering, but he had to focus on it. Number one VHF was the radio they'd left on with guard frequency.

That was it. Was the volume control still up? Maybe he'd better check to see . . .

Jerry burst through the cockpit door in a frenzy of sound and energy.

"Okay, Doc, we're going to be ready in a minute. Linda's still working on Vivian back there."

Doc made sure that the autopilot was still engaged and pushing them steadily eastward before turning back to Jerry.

"We're running out of time," Doc began. "Have you and Scott talked about body angle, speed, flap settings, anything?" Doc's tone was sharp and irritated and he knew it. Venting was an unusual trait for him and it caught him by surprise, especially when Jerry's eyes seemed to flare in response. Jerry shook his head as he took a slightly grimy cloth from the small compartment beneath the flight engineer's table and wiped his forehead with it. He'd obviously been sweating profusely.

"There's been no time to talk," Jerry explained. "We've been working like dogs to get that stuff repositioned, and we got far more done than I expected. We won't have to dump much of her cargo."

"That's just wonderful, but I'd really prefer we keep the tail on the airplane, and to do that we're going to need you up here in the performance manuals and helping with some quick planning. It could make all the difference."

Jerry stopped and stared at him for a few seconds before replying in a slower, more deliberate tone.

"I'm well aware of that, Doc. You've been sitting up here using the PA for the past ten minutes, so I thought maybe you'd be working on it in your spare time," Jerry said with a rising edge in his voice which caused Doc to bristle.

"Hey! I was 'working the PA,' as you put it, Jere, because I needed to make sure you guys didn't lose track of the time."

"We weren't going to lose track of the damn time!"

"I'm glad to hear it, because that little matter of airspeed and configuration may just determine whether we're still alive in about ten more minutes."

Jerry sighed a deep, disgusted sigh, set his jaw at a defiant angle Doc had only seen a few times over the past six months, and threw the cloth to the floor.

"Doc, if you don't like the way I'm doing my job, perhaps you and all your Pan Am experience would like to take over the panel, too!"

"What the hell does that mean?"

"Well"—Jerry swept his arm in the direction of the empty left seat—"you've taken over the airplane, you seem to have all the answers, so I won't get in your way."

Scott McKay stopped just outside the open cockpit door, listening to Doc and Jerry's rising anger. He swept in suddenly and clapped a hand on Jerry's left shoulder as he moved toward the center console and caught Doc's eye.

"What's going on up here?"

Doc shook his head and snorted in disgust. "It's nothing, Scott. Just irritations. I was getting worried about the time."

Jerry arched a thumb at the copilot. "I was just stepping aside so he could run the whole show without . . ."

"STOP IT! NOW!" Scott snapped at the two older men, a furious expression crossing his face. "There's nothing going on here but our fright getting the best of us. We're a team, guys, until we park this bucket of Boeing bolts in Denver or get vaporized out here over the Atlantic. We're a damn team. That's how we started, that's how we'll end it. I'm not going to tell you to kiss and make up, but I *am* going to tell you that I don't want one more word of irritation directed at each other! Understood?"

"Sorry, Scott. My fault," Doc said, turning back toward Jerry, who waved him off.

"Forget it, Doc. Scott's right. I'm terrified."

"I am, too," Scott said. "You, Doc?"

He chuckled. "My reputation always held that Doc Hazzard is never scared. But right now, you could legitimately say that I'm scared shitless."

"Then let's focus all that nervous energy on figuring out how the hell we're going to lose the door without losing the tail, okay?"

Jerry had already grabbed the performance manual as he slid into the engineer's seat. "You got it. But first, we'd better start descending and depressurizing."

"What altitude, Jerry?" Scott asked.

"I'd recommend five thousand."

Doc shifted in his seat. "Ah, guys, I'd feel a lot more comfortable with ten thousand. You know, in case we have a control problem."

Scott looked from Doc to Jerry, who was nodding.

"Ten thousand it is."

Doc turned back to the control yoke to begin the descent with a nagging worry still bothering him that somehow he'd forgotten to do something.

To his left, the unchecked volume control on the number one VHF radio remained where Scott had inadvertently left it more than twenty minutes before: in the full down position.

26

• • • •

With an eagle eye on his fuel consumption and the amount of fuel remaining, the command pilot of one of the last operational SR-71's in the world shifted his head inside his fully helmeted pressure suit and began a left one-hundred-eighty-degree turn back to the north to stay within the radio search area. He'd already briefed his backseat companion, another pilot sitting several feet to the rear in his own cockpit. It was always difficult to read all the instruments and gain a sufficient view of the outside world through the visor of his helmet and the small cockpit windows of the Blackbird, but he was a veteran SR-71 pilot and ignoring the discomforts of what was essentially a space suit was almost second nature.

A small flash of pride mixed with anger fluttered across his mind at the stupidity of parking all but two of the Lockheed SR-71's, still the world's fastest operational aircraft. There was another reconnaissance plane, a super-secret hypersonic craft being tested in Nevada. Those few who had seen its unique smoke trail on late-evening or early-morning test flights had dubbed it "Donuts-on-a-rope." But the design had severe problems, and when the United States needed better reconnaissance than satellites could provide, once again they dusted off the Blackbird—and called him back to the saddle.

This emergency, however, was unique.

More than thirty thousand feet below, the outer reaches of Hurricane Sigrid churned away with wind speeds above a hundred and sixty knots, but the Blackbird's ride was smooth and stable as the craft slid through the rarified atmosphere at more than three times the speed of sound.

"Nothing on 343.0, Jim," the space-suited backseater said in the interphone.

"Okay. You're trying VHF guard now?"

"Roger."

The pilot moved his head slightly inside the helmet of the pressure suit, trying to loosen his neck muscles, which were tense and hurting. He checked his clock again. The detonation time he'd been given was drawing uncomfortably close, although they could traverse the two hundred miles back to the East Coast in ten minutes if there was no contact or no success after they relayed the message.

He could hear the backseater calling repeatedly.

The Boeing 727 was somewhere below, but either not hearing or not answering.

"I'll fly two more minutes north, then reverse south," the pilot told the backseater.

Again he checked the SR-71's clock. Air Force One and the Pentagon were waiting to hear from them on a satellite channel. He could try for perhaps fifteen minutes more, then a dash westbound was mandatory. They would barely have enough fuel to rendezvous with the tanker at that.

"Got something!" he heard the backseater say.

The pilot boosted the volume on the VHF and waited as the backseater called again. For a few moments there was nothing. Then there was the sound of a microphone being keyed, and again silence.

Once more the backseater called, and this time a voice came back almost instantly.

"Go ahead, over."

Adrenaline propelled by excitement and apprehension filled his veins as his unseen partner in the rear compartment of the SR-71 spoke into his helmet microphone.

"ScotAir Fifty, is that you? This is Condor Ten, calling with an urgent message."

The voice returned.

"Ah, you're calling ScotAir Fifty?"

"Yes. Is that you, ScotAir?"

Another hesitation.

"No, this is the USS *Eisenhower*. We're calling ScotAir Fifty on guard as well, Condor Ten. Sorry about that."

The pilot sighed and shook his head in disappointment as the radio calls resumed. He poised a finger over the satcom connection, and then drew back. A few more minutes, he decided. He wasn't ready yet to admit defeat.

ABOARD SCOTAIR 50—7:30 P.M. EDT

The pain was visible on Vivian's face, but she said nothing as Linda struggled to brace her hand against the constant turbulence as she guided the scalpel. She completed the incision along the edge of the pacemaker and began sliding it out. The wires were more difficult to disconnect than she had expected, and the bleeding more profuse, though it was controllable. With her hands shaking slightly, she managed to pull one, then the other, of the wires from the small unit, which she placed on Vivian's chest as she carefully put the wire leads back under the flap of skin and pushed the wound back together, securing it with a butterfly bandage directly over the incision.

Finally, with the bleeding controlled and the wound inundated with antiseptic, she put the bandage in place and let Vivian apply pressure to it as Linda helped her get dressed.

And that was it.

Amazing! Linda thought to herself.

"Thank you, Linda. Thank you eternally!" Vivian said.

"Hey." Linda smiled. "It's enlightened self-interest. I don't want that damn bomb going off when we push it out."

For the first time in hours Vivian got to her feet and stood, somewhat shakily at first, looking at the device.

"Go on up to the cockpit, Viv. I'll be right there," Linda told her.

Vivian smiled and nodded as she reached out to the sidewall for support. But after taking a step forward, she turned back. "Linda, please, please don't think me rude, but if you don't mind, I prefer my full name, Vivian, instead of Viv."

"Not rude at all, Vivian. You got it."

Linda dried off the diminutive pacemaker and carefully taped it just inside the hatch of Rogers Henry's Medusa Weapon. They should close the hatch before pushing it out, she decided, so the air blast wouldn't tear the pacemaker away.

"Okay," she said to herself. "That's done." Linda looked at her hands, surprised that they were no longer shaking. She looked at the Medusa screen once more. The time remaining continued to tick down steadily, second by second. She was also aware of her ears clicking as the pressurization in the cabin changed. Vaguely she had been aware of the engine power coming back as well.

Was this all Rogers Henry had planned? she wondered. Just a straight uneventful countdown and an historic detonation? No more tactics to terrorize his wife? He would certainly have expected an attempt by the military to defuse his weapon, but that hadn't come. No one had tried to cut into the bomb casing or heated up any part of it with a torch. Would Henry's demented thinking have caused him to believe Vivian could really have succeeded in delivering the device to the Pentagon, where she would be blown up along with it? Would he have concluded that the military could just abandon the Pentagon and Washington, D.C., and let it explode?

The answer to those questions, she knew with growing certainty, had to be yes.

Now she wondered if there was some other last-minute terror campaign waiting to be triggered by the clock as it counted backward toward zero.

Linda stepped away from the device as if it had come alive, trying to fight the feeling that it somehow knew what she was thinking.

Suddenly she couldn't get back to the cockpit fast enough.

The relief was palpable on the faces of the three men in the cockpit as Vivian Henry walked in unsteadily, sat down in the observer's seat, and reached for her seat belt as the 727 bounced its way through the turbulent fringes of the hurricane.

"Vivian! Thank Heaven you're back," Doc said.

"Amen," Jerry added.

"You okay, Vivian?" Scott asked.

She nodded and Scott continued, "We've got to finish getting this figured out."

She waved them on.

"Where's Linda?" Scott asked.

"Finishing with the first-aid kit," Vivian said. "She'll be back in a moment."

"Leveling at ten thousand, Scott," Doc reported. "Jerry, how's the cabin pressure?"

"Almost there. The cabin's at nine thousand eight hundred. We'll be depressurized by the time we can get back there."

"You'll open the outflow valve then?" Doc asked.

Jerry nodded. "No residual cabin pressure means no explosive force when we crack it open."

Doc leaned over the radar and adjusted the signal. "Lots of red areas ahead, Scott. We'll need to keep picking our way through the heaviest thunderstorm cells." He looked over at Scott. "You ready to take over?"

Scott shook his head no.

"Doc, I've been flying this airplane less than a year, and I never flew large transport category aircraft before this. You've been flying 727's *and* transport aircraft for all your career. How long for the 727, fifteen years?"

"Yeah, at least," Doc agreed.

"Okay, so doesn't it make more sense to keep you on the controls? Especially if we're going to potentially affect the flying characteristics of the bird or try to knock the tail off?"

"Makes sense to me," Jerry chimed in.

Doc looked at Scott with a raised eyebrow.

"I still need a tail to fly, Scott, but the rest makes sense."

Scott nodded. "Okay. Decided. You fly. Now, as to the door opening, our best guess is slow her to two hundred twenty knots, clean, no flaps. We're all in agreement?"

"We're agreed," Doc said.

"Yes," Jerry said. "That way, the airstream is dynamic enough to take it off the hinges, but it's likely with that steep deck angle the door could just flip safely past the tail. At least, that's what I'm hoping."

"It's a bloody guess, any way we cut it," Doc added, "but that sounds very logical to me."

The 727 impacted a small pocket of hail, which caused all of them to jerk their heads forward. But as quickly as the jackhammer sounds began, they ended.

Scott looked at his watch, then at the copilot and flight engineer.

"Ready?"

Jerry nodded as he pushed the engineer's seat out of the way and opened the cockpit door, startling Linda, who had just reached for the doorknob to come in.

"Better strap in, Linda. We're going to blow the door."

She moved past him and let Scott slide by as Doc disconnected the autopilot and pulled the throttles back to slow the aircraft. He looked back at the door as Scott moved through it, holding the door frame for support.

"Scott!" Doc yelled after him. "Wait a second!"

Scott stuck his head back in the cockpit. "Yeah?"

"Jerry can do it alone. We shouldn't imperil both of you. It may be macho, but it's not smart."

Scott looked at him for a few seconds before nodding. "You're right, Doc. I'll tell Jerry."

He disappeared into the cargo cabin and returned within seconds.

"I told Jerry we'd tell him on the PA when we're at the right airspeed." He turned to Linda and nodded approval as she maneuvered into the second observer's seat and began fastening the seat belt.

Scott fastened his seat belt and shot a worried glance at Doc, who was inching the throttles forward and holding altitude. The deck angle of the 727 was above eight degrees nose-up.

"Right there, Scott. I think we're ready."

"I'll tell him." Scott grabbed the microphone and toggled the PA switch.

He looked back at the engineer's panel, verifying that the cabin pressure differential was zero. They had almost become used to the constant moderate turbulence. The bouncing and lurching of the 727 never abated.

"Okay, Jerry, we're completely depressurized. Go ahead."

And God be with us, please! Scott thought to himself.

He glanced at Doc.

"Ready?"

Doc nodded, adjusting his grip on the control yoke.

Fifteen feet behind them on the other side of the cockpit bulkhead, Jerry checked the heavy strap around his middle, braced himself, and moved the toggle switch to the open position.

ABOARD AIR FORCE ONE—7:30 P.M. EDT

The pilot of Condor 10 was momentarily confused by the voice of the President of the United States on the other end of his satellite channel.

"Condor Ten, can you hear me?"

"Yes, Mr. President."

"Have you been able to raise him?"

There was a short delay as the signals bounced back and forth between earth stations and geosynchronous satellites twenty-three thousand miles above the Equator, connecting the Starsuite aboard Air Force One moving at five hundred miles per hour with the cockpit of the SR-71 moving at over two thousand miles per hour.

"No, Mr. President, I'm sorry to report we can't raise him on any frequency. He has to be down there, but we've tried everything we know, UHF and VHF guard frequencies, and there's no response."

"Lord in Heaven."

"What was that, sir?"

"A form of prayer, my friend. I'm afraid we're all going to need all the divine intervention we can muster in the next twenty minutes. What's your name, Condor Ten?"

"Jim Davidson, sir."

"Well, Jim, thank you for trying your best. You'd better get the hell out of there."

"Sir . . ."

"Yes?"

"We've got a few more minutes. We're going to keep trying. We're going to broadcast in the blind the instructions on entering that shutdown code."

"Your choice, but set yourself a realistic bingo time and depart on the button. Don't let yourself be caught out there if that thing goes off on schedule."

"It's that bad, then?"

"You probably haven't been fully briefed, but it's the electromagnetic pulse from hell. That's what we're facing. By the way, can you fly that Blackbird without computers?"

"Yes, sir. I'd rather not, but I can."

The President terminated the connection and pointed to another line.

"Is this Moscow?" he asked.

"That's him," the Secretary of State confirmed.

The President punched the line on, then held his hand over the receiver. "The British Prime Minister is next, and I know he's a good friend of yours, so I'll want you on, too."

The President put the phone to his ear.

"Mr. President? Sorry to bother you at this hour, but we have a serious situation we need to tell you about in detail."

27

· · · ·

The whine of the cargo door motors started the moment Jerry Christian toggled the switch to the open position, but for a few seconds—as the internal cams rotated to the unlocked position—nothing visible happened.

Suddenly the seal around the outward-opening door cracked open. Jerry felt his heart jump to his throat as the big top-hinged cargo door gave a small lurch and began to move.

There was no explosive force, no sudden blowout, just a growing strip of gray light between the bottom of the door and the cargo floor as the door moved out nearly two inches into the slipstream.

But he hadn't expected the noise. The deafening roar of the passing air frightened Jerry and he found himself fighting a primal desire to release the switch and stop the process before the slipstream took hold.

The side-opening 727 cargo door wasn't designed to withstand a two-hundred-mile-per-hour airstream. Jerry knew what was coming, but not knowing the exact moment it was going to happen—not knowing the exact angle the door could reach before blowing away—was terrifying.

The visible crack between the cargo floor and the lower edge of the door widened to six inches and kept growing. Jerry could feel the shudder of the airplane as the lower lip of the door entered the high-speed airstream a few inches from the fuselage. He saw the door stiffen against its restraints, bucking slightly as the hurricane of air began to enter the opening. He could feel it tugging sideways at the fuselage as the airstream clawed at it.

But still it held.

The big door continued to move outward slowly in a mesmerizing, almost sedate motion, as if airborne deployment were nothing out of the ordinary. The steady movement left him wholly unprepared for the soul-shattering impact of sudden motion and sound as the airstream grabbed the door at last and ripped it away from its supports. It slammed against the top of the fuselage in a sequence so violent and immediate that as soon as it was over he realized he hadn't even seen it.

In a heartbeat the big Boeing rolled violently to the right and pitched up with sickening urgency as the sound of an explosion of some sort reached his stunned ears. He peered through the gaping hole where the cargo door had been and found himself looking at angry clouds and the left wing. He felt the bank angle steepen and the G-forces increase and the nose drop.

Jerry tightened his grip on the cargo strap and willed himself to move, thrusting his body forward a few inches against the G-forces for a better vantage point. Scott and Doc were obviously fighting for their collective lives, but they were still flying. He could see the spoilers fluttering up on the left wing as they fought for control.

There!

He could barely make out the top edge of the opening without getting too close. He expected to see the clean outlines of the door sill.

Instead, he saw the door itself, or at least a large part of it, fluttering violently against the airstream as it sat at a weird angle, still firmly attached to the aft two hinges. It had been stripped clean by the slipstream of its insulation and plastic molding and partially fragmented.

Oh jeez! It didn't tear completely off!

There was something else wrong.

Fire! Out of the corner of his eye he saw the orange flicker of flames somewhere outside to the rear of the aircraft, and he knew instinctively one of the aft-mounted engines must have swallowed some of the fragmenting cargo door.

Jerry looked at the fluttering remains of the door, which was now acting like a new control surface, dangerously influencing the flight path of the instantly crippled 727. He looked out the door at the darkening clouds as they streamed by. They had all the opening they needed now to dump the weapon, but first they had to get the airplane—and the fire—under control.

The 727 continued to roll to the right as Jerry tried to hang on. He tightened his grip beyond the point of pain and closed his eyes as he felt his feet lift slightly off the floor—and realized they were upside-down.

He remembered the same feeling as a little boy on a carnival ride that had been far too violent for his age, a wheel of connected cars which started in a horizontal position, then rose to vertical. With each pass over the top, he'd been convinced he was going to fall and die, a feeling of terror he'd never forgotten.

And that same feeling was knotting his stomach now. The cargo hatch was a yawning black hole waiting to swallow him if he let go.

Doc, too, had felt the shudder of the initial opening, the first few inches of cargo door moving into slipstream. There had been a small fluctuation of the cabin pressure, then a slight rolling movement to the left before all hell had broken loose.

In an instant the attitude indicator was telling him they were rolling to the right, pitching up, and almost out of control. He thought they'd stalled when the door came open, but now the nose slid below the horizon and was pointing down as they rolled even farther to the right, the airspeed climbing above two hundred and fifty knots. He knew something was terribly wrong with the aircraft and had jammed on full power and was battling to stop the roll, but the ship had ignored him and continued rolling over on its back, accelerating nose-down in a steep right bank.

Fear had gripped Doc. *Why isn't she responding? What the hell's going on back there?*

Doc's left hand had reached out and yanked the three throttles back to the idle detent as he made the decision to let the aircraft do a complete roll—a three-hundred-sixty-degree aileron roll—and come all the way back around to a wings-level attitude before renewing his fight to get control.

The decision had taken less than a second.

Now he reversed aileron pressure from left to right, increasing the roll rate as he focused on timing his moves. He was aware of Scott in the left seat and Vivian and Linda strapped in behind him, but there was no time to focus on anything but trying to control the airplane.

The nose of the 727 was pitched down now to thirty-five degrees, the accelerating airstream making a tremendous racket from behind the cockpit as the big jet dove toward the dark waters of the

Atlantic upside-down. If he pulled back pressure at that point, Doc knew, they'd hurtle straight down and probably break up before impact.

But if he could minimize the nose-down angle . . .

As the 727 rolled through the upside-down position and continued to roll upright, Doc shoved forward on the yoke, sending all four of them in the cockpit up sharply against their shoulder harnesses.

The pitch angle stopped increasing but the roll continued until the Boeing finally came through ninety degrees and rolled back closer toward level flight.

Doc began pulling back pressure as he watched for the exact moment to reverse the controls. His eyes fixated on the blue half of the attitude indicator—the half that indicated sky and up and life—and watched for it to come through fifteen degrees of bank. Time dilation had taken over. The pace seemed almost leisurely. His mind accelerated ahead of the airplane.

Now!

He rolled the yoke back to the left, into the stops, stomping hard on the left rudder at the same time.

The aircraft yawed smartly to the left, angling the right wing more into the airflow, shuddered, and stopped rolling.

They were in level flight once again.

Thank God! Doc thought. *With left rudder and left wheel, I can hold her level. But what went wrong back there?* He pulled on the yoke, bringing the nose back to level flight.

The altimeter read four thousand five hundred feet.

The noise of the roar from behind the cockpit door was deafening, but not loud enough to mask a thunderous metallic impact that shuddered through the airframe as the 727 began what felt like a snap roll back to the *left*! He could hear Linda and Vivian both gasp as Scott shot a wide-eyed look at the right seat.

An engine fire warning bell was ringing somewhere in the back of Doc's mind, and he thought he saw Scott's hand reach out and cancel the warning. There was no time to look for a fire warning light or call for checklists. The airplane now wanted to corkscrew *left,* and Doc banged the control wheel back to the right.

"What the hell?" Scott managed to say at last.

By rolling the wheel to the right, Doc stopped the left roll at nearly sixty degrees of left bank. Slowly she was rolling right, back to level, but fighting him in a pronounced, uncomfortable slip to the right. It was like flying sideways through the air.

They were back to wings level and neutral rudder, holding altitude at four thousand three hundred feet and airspeed at two hundred sixty when the whole thing began again, starting with the same shuddering bang.

This time Doc was ready.

With full left wheel and full left rudder, he stopped the right rolling tendency and began hauling the wings back to a level attitude, degree by degree.

The 727 yawed to the left at his command.

Again the huge slamming noise rattled through the airplane, and once again she wanted to roll left.

"Of course," he said out loud.

"What?" Scott yelped.

"The damn door . . . is still attached and flopping around . . . in the slipstream!" Doc's words came through gritted teeth as he manipulated the controls, trying for level flight without releasing too much left rudder.

"Can you control it?" Scott asked. "Want some help?"

Doc nodded. "That sudden left roll was me. When the door's open, it rolls us to the right. I apply left controls and yaw us left, the slipstream changes, closes the door, and suddenly *I'm* causing us to snap to the left because the door's closed and there's no longer any right roll moment. But when I neutralize the rudder, the airflow goes back to normal, opens the door, and we're back to a right roll."

Doc looked at the center console.

"Scott, crank in left rudder trim. Try fifteen degrees. That may do it. Then we need to check on Jerry."

Scott raced to position the rudder trim wheel at the back end of the center console. As they worked to find the right combination of control pressures, the flashing red light on number one engine finally exceeded Linda's efforts to keep silent.

"Scott, is that red light important?"

He followed her finger. "My God, I forgot the engine fire," Scott said.

"Which one?" Doc asked.

"Number one. Ready on the procedure?"

Doc nodded and Scott called out the steps as he positioned the levers and switches and discharged the fire bottle, just as Jerry burst through the door.

"We're on fire, guys!"

"We know," Doc said. "Number one."

Seconds ticked by.

The red light, which stated simply "Fire," remained on.

"Thirty seconds have elapsed, Doc. It's still burning. I'll hit the other bottle," Scott said.

"Do it," Doc replied. Scott pushed the button.

Jerry gripped the back of Vivian's seat, breathing hard, working to keep his balance as the 727 bucked in the storm's turbulence. "We've got a major problem with the door. That's what you're fighting."

Doc was nodding vigorously. "It was flopping back and forth with the yaw, right?"

"Yeah. It's fragmented and hanging on the aft hinges—the forward hinges are gone. We can try to hack it off with the ax, but . . . wait a minute, guys, that 'fire' light is still on."

"Damn!" Scott said. He looked at the number one engine instruments and stopped. "Wait a minute!"

"What?" Doc asked.

"We've got zero indications on number one. No rotation, no temperature."

"It may have destroyed all the probes," Jerry said. "I saw an orange reflection. I figured it was fire."

Scott turned to Jerry, who was still standing behind the center console.

"Can you go take a look?"

Jerry nodded. "But we've got a hell of an open door back there. Can you keep her level?"

"We almost lost her," Doc said.

"You almost lost *me*!" Jerry replied. "Be right back . . . I hope. Doc, please try to keep her steady—I mean, as steady as you can." He disappeared into the cargo cabin.

He was back in less than a minute.

"Okay, I leaned out enough to see it. The fire's out, but there's no engine out there. Number one is . . . is . . . it's just gone. It's literally off the airplane."

Scott took a deep breath as Doc nodded and Linda leaned forward.

"Can we make it with two engines?" she asked.

Doc looked over his shoulder at her and tried to smile as he nodded. The effect was not reassuring.

Jerry was studying the instruments. His eyes fixated on the altimeter, which was below five thousand feet.

"My God," he said as much to himself as Doc and Scott. "We're at forty-five hundred feet! If we'd started all this at five thousand instead of ten thousand, we'd have hit the water."

Scott glanced over at Doc. "Thanks to the wisdom of Captain Hazzard over there in wanting the extra altitude, we're still alive."

Doc looked up and shrugged. "You get paranoid in your old age. More altitude and airspeed for mama and the kids."

Scott looked back at Vivian and Linda. "How're you two doing?"

"Scared out of my mind," Linda replied, "but alive. You, Vivian?"

Vivian seemed to have swallowed her fear. "That was quite a ride."

"There's more to come, I'm afraid," Scott said with a grim expression, as the plane bucked again in Hurricane Sigrid's outer grasp.

"How much time left, Jerry?"

Jerry looked at his watch, or where his watch had been.

"Jeez, I must have lost it back there." There was a haunted look on Jerry's face. "We've got to get the rest of that door off and get the pallets ready to push out. Scott, Doc, there's a good chance one or all of those pallets are going to hit us as they fall away."

Scott was already out of the left seat, motioning toward the rear. "Let's get moving. Doc, you've got her."

"Just tell me when you're about to do something back there," Doc replied as he adjusted the throttles and began a shallow climb. "By the way, Scott, my clock indicates we've got less than twenty-four minutes before detonation."

"I'm coming with you," Linda announced as she unsnapped her seat belt and got to her feet. "You'll need all the hands you can get."

Vivian began searching for her seat belt release as well, but Linda stopped her.

"There's a good reason to force you to stay here, Vivian."

"And what might that be?" Vivian asked in a strained voice.

"You've just undergone an operation without anesthesia and you're still adrenalized, traumatized, and weak. Stay here."

Vivian nodded. "Very well, Doctor. Unless you need me."

There had been no time to think about what to expect, but the sight that greeted Scott's eyes as he opened his cockpit door was somewhere beyond a nightmare.

Fifteen lateral feet of the left side of the 727 was wide open, except for the ragged remains of the cargo door, now twisted and shredded and held in place by the off-center airflow Doc was creating over the top of the jet by yawing left. Scott held his hand out to stop Linda and Jerry. He spotted the heavy cargo strap Jerry had used. It snaked off into the gaping abyss and was fluttering frantically in the airstream, slapping the edge of the door and the floor at intervals.

"I'VE GOT THE CRASH AX RIGHT HERE, SCOTT!" Jerry yelled. The noise was unbelievable.

"WHAT?" Scott yelled back.

Jerry stepped up to him and yelled, practically in his ear, "THE CRASH AX! I'LL STRAP IN AND SEE IF I CAN HACK IT OFF."

"HOW'RE WE GOING TO GET PAST THAT HOLE WITHOUT FALLING OUT?" Linda yelled at both of them.

"WE'RE GOING TO TIE CARGO STRAPS AROUND US AND BE VERY DAMN CAREFUL!" Jerry replied.

He moved past Scott and Linda and hauled in the loose cargo strap, forcing himself to be calm as he looped it through a buckle and ran it under his armpits, tightening it around his chest.

The constant bouncing and unpredictable lurching of the aircraft gave way to a more severe series of jolts as sheets of rain passed the open door in a surrealistic display. Scott had never seen rain from the open door of a flying aircraft before. Jerry could see the water break into spray as it impacted the leading edge of the left wing, which was visible just beyond the door. He put the thoughts and the images out of his mind as best he could and turned back to Scott. "WILL YOU HOLD ON TO THIS END OF THE STRAP? IF YOU SEE ME START TO TEETER OR LOSE MY BALANCE NEAR THAT DOOR, YANK ME BACK INSTANTLY!"

Scott nodded as he grabbed the strap several feet from the anchored end and wrapped several turns around his hand for leverage, adjusting his feet against the periodic lurches of the aircraft as it plowed through the hurricane's turbulent air currents. Linda moved in beside him and took the length of strap just behind, wrapping it around her hands as well. He could feel her push in tighter against him, and it was a comfortable, reassuring feeling. Both of them anchored their feet against the forward lip of the first cargo pallet as Scott held the tension on the strap while Jerry moved gingerly toward the back edge of the cargo door opening, carrying the large crash ax.

The exposed metal cargo floor was slippery with rain and spray and Jerry slipped several times as he moved aft, each time feeling a precautionary tug as Linda and Scott prepared to yank him back.

Jerry anchored his left hand on part of the overhead structure at the lip of the door and began swinging the ax at the door hinge. Each impact was a muffled crunch of metal against metal with sparks flying, but slowly he made headway.

Another rain shower passed the door, some of it spraying Jerry as he worked. The 727 bucked upward momentarily, causing him to swing wildly and impact the wrong point. He steadied himself and started again. Scott could see he was getting tired, the job of keeping his footing against the constant turbulent movements of the aircraft a trial. The swings were getting wilder and less effective.

It was time to switch places with Jerry, Scott decided, as he glanced at his watch.

No, on second thought, there was no time left. He gave a few light tugs on the strap and Jerry stopped and looked in their direction with a questioning expression.

Scott waved him forward and Jerry pointed to the ceiling, as if to say he was getting close. Scott gestured to his watch, and Jerry, understanding, let go of the overhead door lip and tried to take a step toward him, just as the aircraft lurched to the left.

The ax slipped from Jerry's hand and hung almost suspended in midair as he grabbed for it, but the sudden movement of his body shifted his center of gravity and his hand failed to close around it as he lost his balance.

In a split second he was toppling toward the abyss of the open door, powerless to stop.

Twenty-five feet away, Linda and Scott saw Jerry's lanky torso falling dangerously toward the door. Simultaneously, they gave a mighty pull on the strap, unceremoniously yanking Jerry off his feet and propelling him forward to crash face-first on the slick floor in front of them, safe but shaken.

Jerry got to his feet with Linda's help and brushed himself off. He looked at Linda and then at Scott and managed a little grin. Linda could see his hands shaking.

"THANKS!" he yelled over the noise outside. "THAT WAS TOO CLOSE."

Scott motioned them all back into the cockpit and closed the door against the worst of the noise.

"Doc, let's neutralize the rudder trim and see if you can maneuver us back and forth and make that door come off."

"Wait," Jerry cautioned. "Doc, pull both engines to idle before you do, just in case anything heads for the engine opening."

"Understood. You'd better strap in," Doc told them.

Scott was shaking his head as he reached for the top of the engineer's panel to steady himself. "There's no time, Doc. Go ahead and start the maneuver. We'll watch the cargo door from here."

"Hang on, then."

Jerry cracked open the cockpit door and partially wedged his tall frame between the last observer's seat and the bulkhead. Scott turned and held on to the flight engineer's panel with his left hand and encircled Linda's waist with his right arm as she held on to him and one of the seats. She glanced at Vivian, who appeared calm, though very pale. Her eyes were fastened on Doc.

Doc held his left foot hard against the left rudder pedal.

"Here goes!" he bellowed over his shoulder.

In a rapid stroke he let up on the left rudder and pressed the right rudder. The 727 moved in a sickening sideways motion from a right skid to a left, and the sound of the cargo door section flopping open again was immediate.

This time, however, there was no right roll.

"It's off! It's gone!" Jerry yelled.

"*Yes!*" Linda echoed as Scott nodded and grinned. He looked at his watch again and felt his heart skip a beat.

"We've got to move fast." Scott let go of Linda and leaned forward toward Doc.

"Keep her steady, Doc, with just a little bit of a right slip with right wing down. We almost dumped Jerry overboard back there before."

"I'll do my best, but for God's sake be careful."

"I'll relay word to you when we're ready to release the pallets."

Doc nodded as he readjusted the throttles, and Scott turned to Jerry and Linda.

"Okay, here's the plan. We all put on cargo straps. We've got very little time left. The first pallet can just be shoved straight out sideways. Jerry, you unlock it while we hold your strap. Then all three of us will start pushing it out. It's almost unloaded, so it's likely to flip off its rollers before it gets to the opening. Linda, just help us get it started, then hold back. We'll push it the rest of the way."

"Okay."

"We should have Doc bank left about fifteen degrees when we're ready. It should go out on its own then," Jerry said.

Scott agreed. "Excellent." He returned forward and briefed Doc on the additional procedure.

"Just let me know when. I'll need positive communication, Scott, not just a vague voice in the wind."

Scott nodded, his eyes falling on Vivian, who had been following every word with wide eyes.

She saw his look and nodded immediately. "I'll stand in the door, Scott, and relay information to Doc."

"That'll work."

Vivian unstrapped and took her position in the cockpit door after the three others had moved out and begun tying themselves into the cargo straps Jerry had prepared. Each strap was tethered to a cleat in the forward cargo floor.

Unlocking the first pallet was simple. Choreographing how to get it moving sideways to the left and out the side-opening cargo door was more complicated. Jerry directed Scott and Linda from the forward end, and together they moved it sideways on the dual-direction floor rollers until the pallet was partially out the door.

"READY?" Scott yelled.

Linda and Jerry positioned themselves on the right side of the pallet with Scott. They all crouched, preparing to shove it sideways. Scott looked forward at Vivian and nodded.

"NOW, VIVIAN! BANK LEFT!"

She nodded and disappeared into the cockpit, returning almost immediately.

They felt the floor cant to the left and the engines go to idle as

Doc banked the 727, and then, while holding the left bank, he kicked in right rudder to slip the aircraft through the air slightly and cause gravity to pull the pallet through the open door.

"NOW!" Jerry bellowed, and they all three heaved at the pallet with such combined force it seemed to shoot out of their hands and completely clear of the door.

Linda fell forward on the floor as both Scott and Jerry stumbled and caught themselves.

For a second it had seemed to hang outside the door like a separate aircraft now given its own wings, and then the forward edge canted up slightly and it rose and was gone.

Scott braced for an impact with the tail or the engines, but there was nothing. He looked back to the doorway and flashed a thumbs-up sign at Vivian, which she immediately relayed to Doc.

The engines rose in pitch again and the aircraft steadied.

Scott helped Linda to her feet and the two of them moved to keep up with Jerry, who was already unlatching the second pallet.

With some difficulty, they wedged themselves behind the second pallet from Antarctica—still piled high with boxes and canisters and restrained with a plastic-covered cargo net—and began pushing it forward into jettison position.

It barely moved.

They tried again, all three of them straining as hard as possible.

Again it crept forward barely an inch.

Scott shook his head. "We've got to get the airplane into a nose-down deck angle. Hang on."

He moved out of the small space between the pallets and made his way along the right sidewall of the aircraft—opposite the open cargo door—to the cockpit to relate the problem to Doc.

Doc looked over his shoulder at Scott. "We'll have to get the flaps out, and I'll have to lose some altitude if we want a nose-down angle."

"Then let's do it," Scott told him.

"But, Scott, if the flaps are extended while we dump the pallets, they could slam into the flaps on the left side and make it impossible to get them retracted again. You know the results of that: We'd be unable to fly fast, we'd be using far more fuel, and we wouldn't have the range to make it back to the mainland. We'd have to ditch in the Atlantic in a hurricane with no life rafts."

Scott clenched his jaw and thought for a second.

"Okay, instead of using the flaps and slowing down, how about pitching the aircraft forward, nose-down, just for a short duration? When I relay the signal, push the nose over and hold us nose-down until you hear a big thud and Vivian tells you the pallet has hit the forward stops and we've blocked it from rolling backward."

Doc was nodding. "That'll do it. I'll hold it just long enough for you to get the thing moving forward, then I'll climb back to ten thousand before we do the next one."

Scott briefed Vivian on what to do and then returned to the back, trailing his safety strap.

With all three in place again, safety straps secure, Scott leaned into view of Vivian and gave her the prearranged sign.

Within seconds the engines had been pulled to idle and the 727 was nosing down, giving the cargo floor a downward tilt. One small shove from all three of them and the pallet rolled forward smartly until it banged to a halt against the forward stops.

As with the first, they prepared to shove the pallet sideways out the door. With a steady shove, it began rolling in the direction of the opening with very little effort.

All three watched the heavy pallet slide sideways into the darkening clouds and watched as the pallet seemed to hover for a heartbeat. Then, like the first one, the cargo pallet tipped up and rose out of sight, clearing the leading edge of the wing.

Another successful jettison! Scott thought with relief.

He looked at his watch as a shuddering impact threw all three of them forward, facedown on the floor.

Oh God, Scott thought. *The pallet hit the tail!*

The 727 pitched up at a frightening rate until the sound of yet another loud metallic bang echoed through the cargo cabin. Suddenly they were weightless as the jet pitched nose-down. Then, just as suddenly, they were thrown to the floor as the jet pitched back up, each oscillation preceded by a bang.

Scott's heart sank. The pallet had hit the T-tail and had possibly taken it out.

No, he thought, *if it was gone, we'd already be screaming toward the water. There's some control left!*

The G-forces increased on the next up-cycle. Scott crawled on hands and knees toward Vivian, who was hanging onto the door frame for dear life with huge, wide eyes. Scott looked back at Jerry and Linda, both of whom were trying to make their way in the same direction. He reached the door and grabbed their safety straps and began hauling on both of them as the next nose-down excursion began.

Both Jerry and Linda this time rose weightless from the floor and began floating toward the ceiling. Scott hauled even harder on the lines, knowing what would happen when Doc once again pulled the 727 nose-up, leaving Jerry and Linda to smash to the floor. Like a scene from some orbiting spacecraft, the two came swimming through the air toward him with terror-filled eyes and outstretched hands. He caught both of them just before the next up excursion began, and they all scrambled into the cockpit.

Scott pulled himself up to Doc's shoulder, aware the senior pilot was pushing hard on the control yoke.

"WHAT HAPPENED?"

Doc rapidly glanced left before returning his eyes to the panel. The horizontal control surface on the aft end of the T-tail called the elevator, which controlled the nose-up, nose-down pitch of the 727, was giving him fits.

"Something's binding the elevator!" Doc said.

Linda, Jerry, and Vivian strapped themselves into their seats as Scott pulled himself into the left seat, fumbling for the seat belt as another thud and a sudden weightlessness floated them upward.

"It's either nose-up or nose-down. I can't get anything in between!" Doc cried out.

"Let me feel it." Scott pulled on the yoke and felt the same resistance. As the elevator suddenly reversed with the now-familiar bang, he reached up and pointed to the switches controlling the multiple hydraulic systems that powered the elevator surface up or down.

"Doc, should we try to isolate? This could be a hydraulic problem."

Doc shrugged. "I thought it was mechanical, but . . . maybe . . ."

"I'll turn off one of the hydraulic systems, the A system."

Scott flipped the switches—and suddenly everything returned to normal.

"Saints preserve us," Doc exclaimed in an aped Irish accent. "I've got full control again!" He glanced admiringly at Scott. "Brilliant move, Captain Kirk." He grinned.

"Procedural shot in the dark."

"Why didn't *I* think of that?"

"Teamwork, remember?" Scott grabbed for the seat belt release. "If you'll run the emergency checklist for hydraulic failure and see if we've forgotten anything, I'm going to go back there and jettison the bomb before it vaporizes us."

Doc swallowed hard. "Scott, please. No more impacts between cargo and airplane. The airplane may survive it, but my heart won't."

28

. . . .

General Ralph Kinney, the commander of what used to be called the Tactical Air Command, now known as the Air Combat Command, had taken responsibility for coordinating the last-ditch efforts to contact ScotAir 50 some thirty minutes earlier—and it was clear he had failed. The general scanned the multitude of television and computer monitors in the command post, closed a classified folder, and stood up with a weary sigh as he mentally reviewed what he was about to tell the President of the United States.

"General?"

A major had materialized at the general's elbow holding a telephone receiver. The general hadn't even heard the major approach.

"Yes?"

The major put his other hand over the mouthpiece. "I've got the commander of the 495th fighter wing at Seymour-Johnson on the line, sir, with a question we don't understand."

"Which is?"

"He says their two-ship flight of F-15's has gone feet wet at Mach one-point-six, requesting instructions for the rendezvous."

The general stared at the major for a few seconds. "What two-ship is he talking about?"

"I don't know, sir. I made sure his 'feet wet' statement meant they're over the water now, and he confirmed that. Two F-15's, but I wasn't aware we scrambled any."

The general took the receiver with a scowl and identified himself.

"This is Ralph Kinney. What're you talking about down there, Colonel?"

A chief master sergeant appeared from the direction of the Star-suite and waited quietly, listening as discreetly as possible to the commander of the Air Combat Command's side of the conversation.

"Where *are* these guys, and what were they ordered to do?"

Several other men and women in the command post had stopped what they were doing and focused on the general's expression, which had gone from a scowl to raised eyebrows to complete disbelief.

"Chasing . . . you mean *ScotAir?"*

The general turned and motioned his aide over, then turned his eyes to the floor as he concentrated on what the colonel on the other end was saying.

"Do they have a track on him? . . . How far out? . . . And Mach one-six, you said? They can't sustain that for long."

The general looked up to verify his aide's presence and quickly covered the mouthpiece on his end. "Get on an extension and take notes on this."

"Yes, sir," the aide responded, diving immediately for the phone on the command console.

The general looked down again as one hand climbed to his hip and the other pressed the receiver in tightly to his ear.

"No, hell no, they don't need to be armed. That's passed. What we need now is communication." He checked his watch and turned to the major, then to the chief master sergeant. "How much time left?"

"Twenty-four minutes to stated detonation time, sir," the chief master sergeant replied instantly.

The general nodded and returned to the conversation, his speech clipped and urgent. "What's their range? Do they have enough gas? Okay . . . okay . . . flash them to press on at full speed and try to join up for a visual, ah, referral, ah . . . the damn words are escaping me, but they need to pull alongside that civil cockpit and get those suckers to turn on their goddamned radios. We've tried every frequency known to man and they haven't replied. Do your guys know the message to pass?"

The chief master sergeant flashed a note in front of the general, who waved at him to wait. The message said: THE PRESIDENT IS READY, SIR.

"Okay, Colonel, now here's the big question. Why didn't we

know about your boys? . . . Well, somebody sure as hell didn't keep us informed about that . . . *What* order?"

The general listened for a few more seconds, then covered the mouthpiece and bellowed at the major, "FIND OUT WHO THE HELL ORDERED THESE F-15'S AND FAILED TO TELL THE REST OF US!"

He removed his hand from his waist and turned away from the group of officers watching him. "Okay, Colonel, relax. If you've got it in writing, we dropped the ball here. It won't be the first damn time today. We just . . . we didn't know there was any chance, and it's damn slim as it is."

He nodded a few more times before looking around the room. "Yes, they're in grave danger, and we may not get them back if that thing goes off. It's a risk we've considered, but, because we're just now figuring this out and because the command structure is involved, I want you to hang on while I get a final directly from the President. I'll be right back."

The general put the receiver down and turned to the chief master sergeant, who had just received another note.

"Is the President ready in the Starsuite, Chief?"

"He was, sir, but I was just advised he's on another call."

"How long?"

The chief shrugged. "Perhaps five minutes, sir. I looked in myself. Air Force One has gone off-line."

"I don't have five minutes!"

"You want me to try to get him back, sir?" the chief asked.

The general looked at the senior NCO and shook his head. "No."

He scratched his chin and stared at his shoes for a few seconds before picking up the receiver again. It was his decision, and he was out of time.

"Colonel, their orders are to proceed. Let's just hope and pray they can find that Boeing in time."

ABOARD SCOTAIR 50—7:38 P.M. EDT

There were twenty-three minutes left to detonation as Scott, Linda, and Jerry reentered the cargo cabin while Vivian took up position in the cockpit door.

The noise and wind from the gaping hole where the cargo door had been and the sight of rain showers flashing past along with ragged clouds in the waning light made the former passenger cabin seem foreign and strange, but the malevolent presence of the bomb made it feel surreal and threatening.

The one remaining item in the cabin was the crate containing eight thousand pounds of thermonuclear engineering, a monstrosity concocted in the workshop of Dr. Rogers Henry. It sat where it had been loaded in Miami, in pallet position five, halfway to the rear of the cabin and twenty feet behind the aft edge of the gaping cargo door opening.

Scott turned and pointed to the safety straps they had reattached to themselves.

"MAKE SURE THEY'RE SECURE!" Scott yelled over the noise of the slipstream.

Linda nodded as Jerry flashed a thumbs-up acknowledgment.

Quickly they moved to positions behind the pallet containing the weapon as Jerry unlocked the forward restraints and carefully checked the rollers. They would have to push the pallet and its contents twenty feet forward on the cargo floor rollers to get it in position to shove sideways out the door.

Jerry moved around to the aft end of the Medusa Weapon and took his position alongside Scott and Linda. He could see Vivian around the right side of the pallet.

"READY?" he asked Scott.

Scott nodded yes.

Jerry looked forward at Vivian and gave the prearranged hand signal. Within moments the engines once again wound down toward idle and the nose of the 727 began coming down.

"OKAY," Jerry prompted, "PUSH!"

Even with the floor canted down toward the front, the bomb was hard to start in motion. They strained and pushed, rewarded by a slow movement that then accelerated steadily. Doc was holding the deck angle at about six degrees nose-down, Scott figured, and that was enough.

Foot by foot the steel box moved forward, gaining a little speed, until a sudden *bang* vibrated through the aircraft as the pallet hit the forward restraints and came to a halt, perfectly aligned with the cargo door opening on the left side.

Jerry leaned down and quickly installed floor anchors to prevent it from rolling back, then stood and flashed the appropriate sign to Vivian, who once again slipped into the cockpit to relay the word.

The deck angle returned to normal.

"OKAY," Jerry yelled, "YOU TWO TAKE THE BACK. I'LL TAKE THE FRONT EDGE." He moved forward and took his position between the bomb and the cockpit door several feet away.

Scott looked at his watch once again and then glanced out the gaping door into the gathering night. The thunderous noise of the slipstream and the sight of the constant rain showers were awesome, and as he watched, the showers became a torrent of water accompanied by sudden intense turbulence.

There were several heavy bounces as the 727 ran through wild vertical air currents, followed by a tremendous updraft which lasted for many seconds as Linda and Scott steadied each other and hung on to the bomb itself for balance.

Jerry was standing on the cockpit side of the bomb pallet with his safety strap lying in some disarray on the floor as the Boeing hit a mighty series of updrafts. The sudden lurches terminated in a gut-wrenching heave of the aircraft upward, followed by an equally violent drop.

With all but the forward restraints removed, the eight-thousand-pound Medusa Weapon had no physical means of remaining attached to the floor as the 727 suddenly dropped at greater than one gravity. Jerry saw the bomb rise from the cargo rails and rollers, float for a moment over the top of the floor restraints, and begin moving in what seemed like slow motion toward the forward bulkhead. His mind raced to compute the most effective means of getting out of its way and he launched himself backward several feet, expecting to fall safely against the bulkhead.

But the safety strap had wrapped itself around one of the floor restraints a minute before. The strap tightened now against the restraint, and like a shortened leash, yanked him in a hopeless downward arc to the metal floor five feet short of the forward bulkhead.

The pallet floated toward him, looming over his feet and legs. The inevitable updraft was waiting on the other side of the downdraft, and it slammed the 727 upward with positive G-forces, leaving the unrestrained bomb free to crash to the floor.

There was nowhere to go, and no time to get free of the safety strap holding him helpless in the shadow of the oncoming pallet.

Like a surprised mouse watching the bar of a sprung trap descend with unanticipated speed, Jerry watched the pallet slam to rest on top of his legs.

Linda and Scott had been yanked from the floor by the downdraft and the cargo net they were clinging to.

When they had taken quick inventory and found themselves whole, Scott's attention shifted to Jerry, just as a strange high-pitched noise started at the forward end of the cabin. At first Scott wondered if the scream could be another warning from the weapon. It echoed from all points in the cabin.

But the realization of what had happened came as a sickening impact. His stomach churned as he realized the lower half of Jerry's body was trapped underneath the bomb, and the flight engineer was screaming in agony.

Scott saw Linda come around the edge of the pallet and heard her gasp as she saw Jerry.

There was no time to think. The pallet had to be moved. Scott looked up to find Vivian watching in horror from the cockpit door. He raced to the door and flung it open to stick his head inside.

"DOC! JERRY'S BEEN HURT. HE'S UNDER THE FORWARD LIP OF THE BOMB. WE'VE GOT TO MOVE IT!"

Doc whirled his head toward the door with true fear on his face. "WHAT?"

"PUSH OVER AND ACCELERATE, NOW! GIVE ME ZERO G FOR SEVERAL SECONDS AND ACCELERATE, WE'VE GOT TO PUSH IT BACKWARD." Scott turned and pushed past Vivian through the door.

Linda had dropped to her knees by Jerry's head and was trying to comfort the traumatized engineer. She looked up as Scott rushed back toward the forward edge of the pallet.

"GET UP! LINDA, GET UP! GET READY TO PUSH IT BACKWARD!"

She scrambled to her feet as the floor began to drop out from under them and the engines wound up to full power.

The Medusa Weapon was suddenly moving upward, as were they, and Scott saw Linda's feet float uselessly out from under her. He had managed to wedge a foot under the lip of the side rail. He pushed backward against the heavy pallet with all his might now, his foot straining against the rail.

The pallet moved up and off Jerry, but it still hung over him.

Scott had to get it back far enough before Doc reversed and pulled out of the dive. He had no more than a few seconds.

Please, God! Please, God! Scott felt himself straining beyond all normal physical limits as he struggled to move the bomb backward. For an eternity the Medusa pallet refused to budge. Finally, slowly, it rose from the floor and moved backward far enough to clear Jerry's feet.

In the cockpit—his stomach in a knot, praying he'd given them enough time at zero gravity—Doc reached the absolute limits of the dive. A few seconds more and he wouldn't be able to recover. He yanked the speed brakes out and retarded the throttles to idle as he pulled the nose up, aware of another loud *THUNK* which wafted forward from the cabin as the eight-thousand-pound bomb smashed back down to the floor.

Scott fell forward to his knees and looked at Linda, who was wide-eyed and frightened, but unhurt. Then they both scrambled to the grievously injured flight engineer. The pallet had dropped just inches from his flattened boots.

There was a crimson pool growing slowly beneath Jerry's left boot, which had been compressed like an accordion. His right boot was twisted and flattened from the side, but there was no blood.

"JERRY, CAN YOU MOVE?"

Jerry was grimacing in pain, his eyes wide with fear, his arms flailing over his head, trying to propel himself backward toward the safety of the cockpit.

"MY . . . LEGS!" he cried out. "I CAN'T MOVE THEM!"

Scott turned to Linda as Vivian appeared from the cockpit, trying to steady herself against the continuous, but lighter, turbulence.

"LET'S MOVE HIM INTO THE COCKPIT," Scott yelled.

Vivian and Linda grabbed Jerry beneath his arms and pulled backward as Scott tried to guide his legs and feet. Jerry cried out loudly in pain at the movement, his eyes closed. It was obvious that his knees and legs and pelvis had been badly broken in numerous places. It was equally obvious he would need immediate medical attention if he were to live through this.

Vivian pulled open the cockpit door and they wrestled him inside at an angle, but his long frame grossly exceeded the floor space of the cockpit and his injured legs and feet had to be left protruding into the cabin.

Scott hooked the door open and gestured Vivian toward a compartment in the galley.

"GET OUT THE FIRST-AID KIT. THERE'S A HYPODERMIC OF MORPHINE."

She nodded as Linda grabbed Scott's arm.

"WE'RE DOWN TO NINETEEN MINUTES."

Scott looked back at the Medusa Weapon. It was askew and off to one side now, sitting astride the guide rail and resting against the sidewall. The forward edge, however, was perfectly aligned with the open cargo door. If they could lift it and move it sideways, they could still dump it.

He looked at Jerry, his stomach knotting up at the thought of his employee, not to mention his friend, in such pain. What if they had to ditch? There was no way Jerry could get out without being carried, and even the movement itself could kill him.

Vivian came back with the first-aid kit, quickly found the hypo of morphine, and injected it into Jerry's upper arm through a ragged tear in his shirt. He grew quiet almost immediately.

Scott closed his eyes and shook his head to clear it. *I can't think about anything but the bomb now. I've got to put him out of my mind!*

Scott turned back to Linda and pulled her close so he could speak without yelling.

"Doc will have to push the aircraft over again, then slip left."

"Can we do it?" Linda asked. "There's only us now."

"I think so." Scott turned quickly to the cockpit and stepped over Jerry's body to brief the copilot. He was back in thirty seconds.

"I'll take the forward right edge, you take the back right side edge. When Doc floats it, we push it toward the door. When it's on the rollers, I'll yell at Doc. When he cants the floor to the left side, we push for all we're worth."

"SCOTT!" Doc's voice boomed over the PA and into the cabin. "GIVE ME A COUPLE OF MINUTES TO GET POSITIONED. WE PULLED OUT AT ONE THOUSAND FEET ON THAT ONE. I'VE GOTTA GET SOME ALTITUDE!"

Scott looked at his watch, then at Linda, who was biting her lip savagely. He leaned over to speak in her ear again.

"If it goes off on impact with the water, we're screwed. But if somehow it doesn't . . . if it doesn't go off until the timer hits zero . . . we'll have time to get away. But we've got to get it out fast."

Linda reached up and tightened Scott's restraint. He did the same for her. They could feel the aircraft climbing as sheets of water and mist passed the open door, wetting the interior continuously. They were both aware of the slick metal floor.

But they were equally aware that time had almost run out.

29

• • • •

The two-ship formation of F-15 Eagles had been gulping fuel at a furious rate for the previous twenty minutes as they streaked across the southern edge of Hurricane Sigrid in pursuit of ScotAir 50. The coordinates of where the 727 had been when the flight of F-16's had left them were passed by their command post, and by a simple time and distance estimate, the lead F-15 pilot had figured about where the Boeing would be.

The unenhanced radar return of the 727 flared on their tactical screens right on schedule. The two Eagles punched down through the fury of the hurricane and closed on the target using only radar, just as their F-16 counterparts had done. At ten miles behind the 727 they slowed below supersonic speed, and at four miles began looking in earnest through the murky twilight for the cargo airliner ahead.

There were eighteen minutes left to detonation, and both pilots knew they had been assigned what could be a one-way trip. Even if they escaped the blast, they might not be able to reach a tanker in time.

But the lead pilot had also been briefed that their mission was focused on a single, critical objective: Avert a historic national tragedy by getting the crew of ScotAir 50 to insert the single digit "1" in the bomb's computer before the countdown reached zero.

ABOARD SCOTAIR 50—7:43 P.M. EDT

Scott McKay placed his hands on the side of the Medusa Weapon as if it were a living thing, and waited for Doc's voice to signal they were ready.

If it went off on impact with the surface of the Atlantic more than a mile below, there would be an incredibly bright light—and then oblivion.

Scott glanced at the beautiful dark-haired woman next to him. She was similarly absorbed in the task they were about to perform, her face a mask of stress as she looked out the open door ten feet away. He assumed she was wondering the same things: How it would feel. How fast it would be over. What lay beyond.

Linda glanced around and caught him looking at her. Her eyes locked onto his and she smiled softly as she reached out to touch his arm, her voice necessarily loud against the ambient noise.

"WE'RE GOING TO MAKE IT, SCOTT."

He smiled self-consciously, his mind suddenly preoccupied with the thought that he should be reassuring her.

"YOU BET WE ARE," he replied.

More turbulence bounced the aircraft, sending chills down Scott's back. What if it happened again, and one or both of them ended up trapped beneath the weapon?

Why, why, why couldn't we find another solution?

Scott visualized the screen and the keyboard inside the small access hatch. They had taped it closed, but he'd been haunted by the thought that there might be a simple switch inside that would turn off the countdown and stop the bomb from exploding. Perhaps there was a code you could type in, one that Rogers Henry knew that no one would be able to figure out in time.

No, Scott reasoned, if Henry wanted to make absolutely sure no one could turn it off, either through logic or luck, he would have made certain no switch or combination of numbers or letters could stop the countdown.

But why have a keyboard if you're not going to allow meaningful input?

Still no word from Doc on the PA. The howl of the slipstream seemed to get louder, the sound of hail chattering against the aircraft's structure once again assaulting his ears.

Scott glanced at his watch. Seventeen minutes left.

His head almost hurt from the high-speed stream of thoughts, but lurking just beyond his conscious grasp was the promise of an answer. It wasn't logical that there'd be no solution.

Suppose it was something bizarre, like his wife's name, or a simple sequence of digits, like, say, Douglas Adams's "42," Heinz

"57," or Joe Heller's Catch-"22"? There were thousands of possibilities, but there was virtually no time left.

Maybe I should try anyway, Scott thought.

"OKAY, SCOTT." Doc's voice filled the cargo cabin. "WE'RE AT SIX THOUSAND AND STABLE. I'M SLOWING NOW."

Linda glanced at the ceiling of the 727 at the same time, both of them aware that the whine of the two remaining jet engines was decreasing.

"SCOTT, I'M GOING TO GO NEGATIVE G FOR A COUNT OF FOUR. I'LL HOLD HER STRAIGHT AHEAD SO YOU CAN MOVE IT BACK ON THE ROLLERS."

Scott looked forward at Vivian, who was standing in the cockpit doorway, straddling Jerry's prone form. He flashed a thumbs-up sign at her and saw her nod, turn, and yell a confirmation at Doc.

Slowly, steadily, the gravity force diminished as Doc smoothly lowered the nose of the 727. The stainless steel Medusa Weapon on its aluminum pallet shifted slightly, and Scott pushed his shoulder into its side, waiting to feel it move.

Finally it yielded.

"NOW!" he said to Linda.

They pushed hard toward the open door, feeling the edge of the pallet slide off the rail and back in place on the rollers.

Doc began increasing back pressure on the yoke at the same moment, and the weapon settled back down as the 727 pulled into a slight climb, the engines once again winding up.

Scott leaned over to Linda's ear.

"This is it! The next one is the jettison."

She nodded, and he could feel her hair brushing his face, a familiar sensation that triggered the urge to kiss her, an incongruous reaction he quickly suppressed, glad she couldn't know.

"We push together as hard as we can," he continued, "but do not go beyond the centerline of the cabin. Let go at that point. If it needs more, I'll do it."

She nodded again, and Scott pulled away and resumed his position, hands against the side of the Medusa, feet firmly planted against the sidewall of the cabin where it met the floor. He looked down and visually tracked the safety straps. Both lay on the floor, cleanly away from the weapon's path, still attached to the cleats in the forward floor near the cockpit entrance.

The aircraft pitched forward slightly again and the engines retarded to idle.

This is it, Scott told himself. Once the weapon was out, they would have only a few minutes to dash away from the impact point, praying every mile of the way.

Scott looked at Vivian, who had a questioning look on her face as she held her thumb in the air.

He nodded and returned the thumbs-up, and she once again ducked her head inside.

The sound of the PA system being triggered reached their ears. At first there was no voice, then Doc's familiar tones.

"OKAY, SCOTT. I'M STARTING THE LEFT SLIP NOW."

WOLF FLIGHT—7:46 P.M. EDT

The outline of the Boeing 727 slowly emerged from the dark clouds ahead as the two F-15 pilots pressed in toward their target.

"He's dead ahead, about a mile. Take my left wing. We'll come up on his left side from below his left wing."

"Roger" was the only reply.

The closing rate was in excess of fifty knots as the 727 began to take on detailed shape slightly above and to the right. The lead pilot could see damage to the T-tail on the right side of the horizontal stabilizer. Cables and torn metal hung from the left stub wing where the number one engine had been.

"His number one engine is gone!"

"Rog, I see it. The left side cargo door's open, too. In fact, it's gone."

The leader moved left a bit to gain the same vantage point, as his wingman followed the correction. The gaping opening where the cargo door had been, and the jagged area where the hinge had been, were perfectly visible.

"Move on up, Two, and get visible in his left windscreen at this lateral spacing. I'm going in closer to look at that door."

ABOARD SCOTAIR 50—7:46 P.M. EDT

In one smooth motion Doc Hazzard rolled the 727 into a fifteen-degree bank to the left and pressed the right rudder to keep the airplane aimed in the same direction as before. The effect was the same as tilting the floor to the left while sitting stationary on a ramp: Gravity began tugging left on everything within the fuselage.

"NOW!" Scott yelled.

Scott and Linda gave a mighty shove and felt Rogers Henry's Medusa device begin to move toward the door, slowly at first, and then with a sharp acceleration as the gravitational vector tugged it toward the abyss.

They scrambled after it, their feet working to find traction on the slick floor.

The pallet moved to the left and into the slipstream, still accelerating, and Scott decided momentum would do the rest. He fell forward on his hands and knees just past the middle of the floor. Linda had stopped in place, stooped over but standing. The pallet was halfway out and moving in slow motion as Scott glanced at Linda—and then at the safety strap tightening around her ankle.

His eyes followed the strap as it curled around the edge of the pallet, and he lunged forward to grab it and flip it away, but slipped and landed short, his hands inches from the target.

Linda was being pulled along with the departing bomb, her right foot dragged from beneath her, her left foot trying to find something to grasp as she landed on her rear end between the cargo rollers.

Scott scrambled to reach her, his legs frantically working to propel himself in her direction, his feet still slipping wildly on the slick metal floor.

The pallet entered the slipstream and moved with a sharp jerk off the last of the rollers and into space, dragging Linda's safety strap with it.

Scott heard himself yell, "NO!" as he reached with all his strength and grabbed Linda's right leg, his fingers struggling to close around the material of her jumpsuit. He felt her body accelerate toward the abyss, her hands frantically trying to find something to grasp, her leg sliding away from him.

As she slid backward over the edge, Linda lunged forward and found his hands.

The bomb and its pallet began to drop away. The safety strap that had carried her out uncoiled from the pallet's corner and fluttered free.

Scott was holding her full weight, both of his hands and wrists hanging over the edge, but he, too, began slipping toward the opening. His right foot found the corner of a roller and he worked frantically to dig the toe of his boot against the bracket holding it, but couldn't hold on. Slowly, inexorably, he felt Linda's weight pulling him into the void.

His foot touched another roller and flailed at it, but that one, too, rotated and let go.

Scott kicked his legs back and forth, trying to find something to hang on to. There was no way to remove one hand from Linda's two hands without losing her, and there was nothing to grip at the edge of the opening.

His right foot slid past another roller, his arms now hanging over the lip of the door as Linda began swinging wildly at the end of his hands, her weight testing his grip.

He could see her struggling below, twisting in the wind, straining to maintain her grip on his hands. The safety straps whipped wildly in the breeze, distracting him.

Once more he felt his right toe snag the housing of a roller, but this time it held!

Scott's body stopped sliding, his leg muscles stretching painfully as the one patch of leather on his boot held him in place. Linda's hundred and twenty pounds were becoming a dead weight, increasingly difficult to hold, let alone pull back in.

It was an impossible situation, her body dangling in midair, his own body prevented from following her into space by only a tenuous toehold on a rain-slick roller.

The Medusa device had passed under the left wing, but Scott heard a distinct metallic impact at the same moment he spotted another shape below them that looked like an F-15. There was another Eagle in his peripheral vision off to the side, neither image making any sense. His whole being was focused on holding Linda, but she was slowly slipping from his grip.

Linda McCoy's eyes locked on to Scott's and passed a silent message of resignation.

Slowly the left bank diminished as the 727 returned to level flight.

If Doc pulls up sharply, Scott thought, *I'll lose her for sure.*

But whether he did or not, Scott could feel his grip on Linda's hands loosening.

WOLF FLIGHT—7:46 P.M. EDT

The F-15 lead pilot had been flying a hundred feet beneath and slightly behind the 727's left wing to examine the open cargo door when the Boeing suddenly banked left. He had dropped the twin-engine fighter down a few dozen feet for safety and checked the position of his wingman, who was moving forward to make visual contact with the 727's captain.

What the hell is he doing? the lead pilot had wondered. The rapid movement of something large in the maw of the cargo door had escaped his notice, but as it departed the aircraft and seemed to hang in midair for a split second, the F-15 pilot realized it was a cargo pallet and it was descending directly toward his cockpit.

"Jesus Christ!" he'd exclaimed as he popped the stick downward and jerked the fighter to the left. The pallet had raked across the underside of the 727's wing and disappeared into the clouds below, barely missing his Eagle.

Adrenaline now coursed through the pilot's veins at the close call, which his wingman had not witnessed. He looked to the right at the 727's cargo door and noticed something else, something dangling from the entrance.

My God! he thought. *It's one of the crew!*

As the 727 rolled wings-level, the lead pilot moved in closer. The dangling figure was a woman, being held by a man who was himself hanging over the edge and losing the battle.

The pilot's mind was racing. Maybe he could come closer and help somehow.

No, that wasn't possible without hitting the 727.

Maybe he could pop his canopy and catch her.

No, if she let go and he missed her by an inch, she'd end up consumed by one of his engines.

Helpless and horrified, the Air Force major held his jet thirty feet away and tried to wish Linda McCoy back into the aircraft as his conscious mind arrived at a terrible reality: What had been jettisoned was probably the Medusa Weapon, and it would impact the surface of the ocean below in less than a minute with unknown consequences.

Their mission, obviously, had failed.

"ScotAir Fifty, do you read me on UHF guard?" His wingman was transmitting, trying to get the flight crew on the radio.

There was no answer.

Does the pilot know what's going on back here? Lead wondered.

The man hanging over the edge tried to pull the woman up, but the man was tiring. He could see their fingers grasping, trying to hang on.

Every professional instinct and every bit of training crackled in conflict with his emotions as a human being. There was a someone out there in trouble, and there had to be some way to help her.

But there wasn't.

It was obvious the man and woman were losing the battle.

The major had never felt so utterly helpless.

Vivian Henry had been slow to accept what she had seen as Linda went over the side, almost followed by Scott. For many seconds she had stood in frozen horror at the cockpit door, not knowing whether to run to Scott's aid or dash back in the cockpit to tell Doc.

She chose the latter and quickly stepped over Jerry.

"They're *what*?" Doc asked, eyebrows lifted, as he shallowed the bank and rolled wings-level.

"Linda fell out! Scott . . . Scott's holding on to her, but he's almost over the edge, too! Can you do something?"

"Jesus!"

The image of an F-15 swam into view in the left window over Scott's empty chair at the same moment, momentarily confusing Doc as he realized Vivian was moving toward the door.

"NO!" he yelled at her. "Don't go back there without a restraint!"

The F-15 pilot was gesturing at his helmet. Doc was trying to decide whether dumping the nose would help or hurt Scott. If he did it too fast, Scott's grip could fail. He needed to let him know, yet there was no time.

Doc fumbled to turn on the UHF radio and select the guard channel.

". . . Fifty, are you listening?" coursed through his headset as soon as the switch was flipped on.

Doc stabbed the transmit button.

"Yeah, we're here," he said. "We have a crew member over the side!"

"I can see her. A male is hanging on to her. Have you dumped the weapon yet?" the fighter pilot asked.

Maintain speed! No acceleration! Dump the bird over smoothly, not quite zero G, and maybe he can pull Linda back in!

"Ah, F-15, I'm pushing over to try to get her back in."

Doc edged the yoke forward as he began retarding the throttles.

Linda's left hand slipped from Scott's grasp, and the two of them clawed the air, trying to reconnect. For a second Scott thought he'd lost her, but he tightened the grip of his right hand beyond pain and held on until his left hand found her right and reattached.

But he couldn't pull her back in, and he was tiring, his toehold threatening to let go, though the wings-level attitude had helped immensely. The slipstream was whipping Linda mercilessly as gravity tried to pull her away.

Suddenly he felt himself getting lighter as Doc pushed the nose over, and Scott instinctively tried to propel Linda up and rearward. If he could just swing her over the lip of the door and back into the 727 . . .

But the added motion was too much. He watched her fall away from him toward the leading edge of the left wing, the decreasing G-forces causing her to float upward slightly as her body moved backward into the slipstream, their hands grasping only air.

The F-15 lead pilot deployed his speed brakes and leveled off as he watched the Boeing descend alongside him. He was seeing the 727 from a different angle now and realized there was fuel venting from a damaged spot on the forward underside of the wing. He looked closely at the Boeing as he let his Eagle lag behind slightly, then dropped down for a better look. His wingman was hanging in formation by the Boeing's left side, aligned with the cockpit. That was what he expected to see.

It was what he *didn't* see that turned his stomach. The woman who had been hanging below the cargo door was gone.

Linda McCoy knew her life was over. She flailed for something to grab as Scott's hands slipped from hers, her mind rebelling at the reality of the long, cold fall ahead of her, when her feet touched a solid surface.

As the two-hundred-mile-per-hour wind blast accelerated her rearward, the 727 had descended faster than her body, and instead of dropping below the leading edge of the 727's left wing, she was sliding over the top of it.

With a frantic burst of energy, Linda grabbed for anything to hold on to, but the rain-slick aluminum slid beneath her as the crest of the wing began to disappear in front of her, her body oozing over the top and toward the trailing edge.

A sudden, unexpected tug beneath her armpits left her stationary and facedown on top of the wing. The wind pushed her up against the side of the fuselage where the wing met the cabin structure.

The safety strap! she thought.

Linda looked sideways and upward. She could make out the outline of the cabin windows just above her. The slipstream was brutal. Her hair streamed behind her, hurting her head, and she felt as if her eyelids would be blown away.

But the safety strap was holding, still fastened to the floor anchor inside the cargo cabin.

She reached forward and closed her hands around it, trying to pull herself forward against the amazing force of the wind. Using her legs and knees, she pulled forward hand over hand until she was lying across the crest of the wing.

The 727 was pulling out of its dive and she felt herself getting heavier, her ears popping frantically as the effort to stay in place increased.

She managed to peer forward. She could see Scott through the doorway holding on to the strap, looking at her in helpless amazement, then suddenly he was gone.

She looked at the yawning gulf between the leading edge of the wing and the opening where the cargo door had been. The distance was greater than ten feet. Even on the ground, she wouldn't have been able to jump from the wing to the door. The only way back in would be to dive off the front of the wing and dangle from the strap in hopes of being pulled back in.

Impossible! Scott couldn't pull her in alone.

Linda closed her eyes and put her face down again as a swarm of raindrops battered at her, and just as quickly ended. A flash of lightning and a clap of thunder reached her eyes and ears from somewhere to the left. Maybe the flash was the expected nuclear blast—but it was only lightning and faded instantly.

I'm going to die out here! she realized. An immense sadness consumed her. There was no way she could survive for long on the wing, even if the strap held.

Scott was momentarily in shock when Linda slipped away from him, but when he saw her land on *top* of the wing, being held by the safety strap, he sprang into action with one thought flashing through his mind: *Overwing emergency exits!*

Scott dashed rearward to the overwing area, his heartbeat accelerating. He realized he'd never checked the overwing exits before, but if the exit windows hadn't been removed when they converted his airplane to carry cargo, he could open one and pull Linda inside.

He pressed his face to one of the windows and looked down. He could just see Linda's clothes blowing in the incredible wind flowing over the wing. He said a small prayer as he reached up and snapped the lever to the OPEN position.

It yielded, and in one fluid motion he yanked the exit window toward him and swung it around, tossing it unceremoniously to the center of the cargo floor.

Fifty yards to the side, the lead F-15 pilot changed to the interplane frequency and keyed his transmitter.

"Two, lead."

"Two."

"Get on button five, talk to the command post, and get the tanker headed eastbound to meet us, flight level two-five-zero. Get him out here as far as he can go. We're going to be critical on fuel at this altitude and speed."

"Roger."

Lead moved to the left and slightly below and behind the 727 to monitor the fuel leak. As his wingman joined him, he brought them slightly above the level of the Boeing's wing and realized there was something on the left wing root. The recognition of what it was caused him to gasp.

He fumbled for the transmit button.

"ScotAir! ScotAir! The woman is on your left wing at the wing root! She's on the wing! I thought she'd fallen, but somehow she's holding on up there. Do you copy?"

In the cockpit of ScotAir 50 Doc sat in shock for a second before grabbing the microphone to reply.

"Roger."

With no way to know Scott was already aware of the situation, Doc picked up the PA mike, his voice booming through the cabin.

"SCOTT! LINDA'S HANGING ON TO THE LEFT WING! THE FIGHTER PILOT SEES HER ON THE LEFT WING!"

Scott was already thrusting his upper body through the hatch into the slipstream. There wasn't a moment to spare. He knew there was nothing for Linda to hang on to on that part of the wing— except the strap, which was fraying, strand by strand, from the sawing action of the sharp door edge.

Linda was just aft of the exit window opening, her face down on the surface of the wing, her eyes closed.

He spread his legs behind him to achieve a firm anchor for his lower body, then leaned down and grabbed her shoulders.

Linda jerked her head up, shocked to see Scott suddenly appear above her.

She looked at the opening where the hatch had been, as Scott slid his hands under her arms and over the loop the strap formed around her chest. Linda's body was still straining against the strap, and just as Scott began to pull her toward him, the last strands of the cargo strap parted, the loose end snaking over the top of the wing and fluttering off behind them.

She saw the remains of the strap flash by and understood instantly. His grip was the only thing holding her on the wing now. Linda tried to thrust herself forward toward the door. She was numb with cold, her movements sluggish, and the two-hundred-mile-per-hour torrent of air was starting to freeze him as well. The angle was excruciating. He had to bend out, down, and sideways to try to move her forward toward him, and then sideways into the hatch, while trying not to be pulled completely through the window himself.

A sudden wall of rain threatened to loosen his grip as it blinded him momentarily, but he didn't need to see to pull her in. Slowly, very carefully, he inched her toward the opening, feeling her matted hair hit the side of his face as he locked his arms behind her back and pulled harder, slipping her head through the opening as her legs fought to help.

Her shoulders came through as Scott pulled himself completely into the cabin and guided her hands inside. Linda grabbed the window frame and propelled herself the rest of the way in, catapulting her body into Scott's and knocking him backward onto the floor as she fell alongside him.

Scott put his arms around Linda and held her tightly, his left hand cupping the back of her head. She held him tightly in return, neither of them able to let go.

She was shaking, shivering, windburned, and freezing cold. Her voice was hoarse. "Thank you, Scott! I thought . . ."

"I know!"

"It didn't explode!" she said.

"What?" He seemed puzzled.

Linda pulled back slightly and wiped the water off his forehead with a shaking hand. Her words came in slightly jumbled bunches as she tried to fully regain her voice.

It was no use trying to shout, so she leaned next to his ear again. "The Medusa Weapon."

He nodded his head as she pulled back. "So far, so good. We've got a few minutes left, if the timer's still working."

Scott realized with a sudden chill that the other end of the cargo strap tied around her was still hanging out the window and tugging in little jerks at her body. He quickly removed it before helping her stand. Her legs were like lead and she could barely shuffle forward. Scott put his arm around her waist and looped her arm over his shoulder. He half-carried her to the cockpit door.

30
• • • •

He's pulled her back in!" Vivian reported.

Doc jerked his head around to look at her incredulously. "They're both okay?"

She nodded, too stunned to add anything to the gesture.

Doc began a gentle climb. He reminded himself that the F-15 was still visible in the left window, just as the fighter pilot called.

"ScotAir, can you answer now?"

Doc stabbed the transmit button.

"Yeah, I'm here," he said.

"I need to know, sir, whether you dumped the weapon yet?" the pilot asked.

Doc looked back at Vivian, who was moving back toward the cockpit door.

"Yes, we have," he replied, as the voice of the lead F-15 pilot cut in.

"ScotAir, this is Wolf lead. Be advised you've got a fuel leak, sir. Left wing, about one third out from the wing root. It looks like a puncture in the forward underside. There's a steady stream."

"Oh Jesus," Doc said to himself as he looked around sharply to his right, trying to see Jerry's fuel panel. He couldn't quite read the needles.

He turned back forward and punched the transmit button.

"How bad is it, Wolf?"

"Seems to be coming out at an unhealthy rate, sir."

Doc heard the pilot pause, then address his wingman.

"Wolf Two, Wolf lead. Rejoin my left wing."

"Roger, Two," the wingman responded.

Myriad thoughts shot through Doc's mind. He *really* needed to see Scott walk through the door in person. They had dumped the weapon and it hadn't exploded on impact. That was good. That was great! That meant they had a chance.

Doc began a turn back toward the west. With two engines and the remaining fuel, he'd originally calculated they could make the South Carolina coast. But with fuel leaking from the number one tank, they would flameout somewhere over water.

We'll be left to ditch a nonpressurized, crippled airplane in a hurricane with no life rafts aboard. Wonderful! Doc thought. *The last pallet must have snagged the wing.*

"ScotAir, what are your intentions?" Wolf lead asked.

"Wolf lead, we're not going to be able to make it all the way if we're losing fuel. I'm heading toward the coast. I . . . think we're committed to a ditching."

"Understood, ScotAir. We'll stay with you as long as we can."

Doc realized he could save some of the leaking fuel by transferring it into another tank. He snapped on the autopilot and unstrapped long enough to lean up and over the back of his seat and operate the crossfeed valves on Jerry's panel to feed the remaining two engines from the leaking tank.

It was too late. The tank was almost dry.

He paused to study Jerry's face before getting back in the seat. "How're you doing?"

Jerry's eyes had been closed. They fluttered open at the sound of Doc's voice.

"I'm . . . ah . . . hurting less because of that injection, but I'm still . . . hurting, Doc."

"Hang in there!" Doc plopped back in the right seat and fastened the belt, his mind racing over a hundred thoughts at once. If they ditched, how high would the waves be? Could they ditch near a ship? How did one go about finding a ship?

He looked over at the F-15 and realized he was ignoring a resource.

"Wolf lead, ScotAir. I need your help on something."

"Go ahead, ScotAir."

"Can you help us find a ship to ditch alongside?"

Medusa's Child

News that Hurricane Sigrid had blown a passenger train off the tracks near Washington, D.C.'s, Union Station reached Air Force One a minute before word arrived that two F-15's had found ScotAir 50.

The President stood on the Air Force One side of the Starsuite and waved away further information on the Amtrak wreck after he heard that casualties appeared to be light.

"Are they talking to ScotAir? Were they able to punch in that code?" the President demanded.

The Air Force general on the Pentagon side of the screen shook his head as he consulted a single sheet of paper.

"Sir, they were jettisoning the Medusa Weapon just as our two-ship pulled up to them, before radio contact was established. It's in the water now."

"And no explosion?" the President asked.

The general shook his head no. "Not yet, at least. Remember, it could have survived the impact and still be ticking down there. It could still go off on schedule."

"How the hell could they get that out of a 727?" the President asked.

"Apparently they jettisoned the cargo door and lost an engine in the process."

"You say it could still go off," the President began. "How? What altitude was that thing dropped from? I mean, I've done airdrops back when I flew C-141's and if a parachute didn't open on a cargo pallet, it was destroyed on impact."

The general shrugged slightly and raised his hands. "We're just guessing, sir. They said the casing was steel. It's not impossible that it could have survived. If the impact did nothing more than destroy its power source, we think that alone would deactivate it and we'd be out of the woods."

"And then you'd want the Navy to go get it, right?"

The general looked up and studied the President's expression. There was a knowing look on the Chief Executive's face.

"Yes, sir, I suppose we would."

"How much time till we know?"

"Nine minutes, Mr. President."

Scott and Vivian carefully guided a shaken Linda McCoy around Jerry Christian's prone form to the larger observer's seat. Scott strapped her in and draped a coat around her shoulders before slipping into the captain's position. The noise level in the cockpit was horrendous, the temperature was uncomfortably cold, and there was no way to close the cockpit door with Jerry's injured legs sticking out.

Vivian checked the jury-rigged belt holding Jerry to the floor of the cockpit, then sat sideways in the second observer's seat, just as a young male voice cut through the overhead speakers: "ScotAir Fifty, I say again, ScotAir Fifty, this is the USS *Eisenhower*. Do you copy, over?" The voice was tinged with urgency.

Doc looked down at the UHF radio before looking back up at Scott with raised eyebrows. "He's on UHF guard, the emergency frequency. I just turned that on a minute ago!"

"I wonder how long he's been calling?" Scott asked.

Doc gestured to the left, where the two F-15's could still be seen holding in formation. "Scott, I asked our friends out there to help us find a ship to ditch beside. Maybe they did."

Scott put the microphone to his mouth to reply, then stopped and looked at the copilot.

"What did you say? What do you mean, 'ditch,' Doc?"

"We don't have a choice, Scott."

"Why? Of course we do!" Scott sounded frantic. "We can't ditch! Hell, we don't have life rafts, we've got a hole in the side the size of Cleveland, we've . . ."

"Scott!" Doc arched a thumb over his shoulder in the general direction of the left wing. "We've got a problem we didn't expect. We don't have enough fuel now to make it back." Scott's eyes were wide with alarm as Doc filled in the details of the leak in the number one tank caused by the cargo jettisoning process.

"I don't know which one got us. I never felt an impact."

Scott dropped his eyes and shook his head. "I guess I remember feeling that impact, but I was pretty busy at the time." He looked back at Doc, his voice constrained. "You know, we'll never survive a ditching."

Doc could see Scott breathing hard as his eyes focused again on the forward gauges. Suddenly he whirled to the right to study the fuel readouts on the engineer's panel and do some mental math. Finally he sat back with a long sigh and looked over at Doc again with a haunted expression.

"I . . . see what you mean. Not enough fuel, however we cut it."

"We can't get closer than fifty miles from the coast, and that's optimistic."

The voice from the *Eisenhower* returned, causing Scott to jump slightly.

"ScotAir Fifty, I say again, ScotAir Fifty, this is the USS *Eisenhower*. Do you copy, over?"

Scott hurriedly selected his microphone panel to the UHF radio and looked back at Doc. "You recognize the name?"

Doc Hazzard shook his head no.

"My old home. That's a flattop, Doc. That's the nuclear aircraft carrier I served on until last year. She's got rescue equipment, helicopters, and even a hospital aboard."

Scott keyed the microphone. "USS *Eisenhower,* this is ScotAir Fifty on 343.0. I hear you five-by."

"Yeah, but where *is* she?" Doc asked.

"That's exactly what we're going to find out," Scott said as he held the microphone and waited.

The voice came back tinged with excitement. "Roger, ScotAir, we have you five-by as well! We have an urgent message for you. Go immediately to the Medusa Weapon, enter the number '1' on your keyboard, and punch 'enter'. That should deactivate the weapon. Then report back to us on what happens. It is critical that you do this immediately. Message is from the Pentagon. We'll stand by."

Doc saw Scott's face go chalky white as he looked at the right seat and then straight ahead.

"What's that about, Scott?" Doc prompted.

Scott was shaking his head very slowly. His eyes snapped around to Doc's. "I was thinking of that, Doc. A minute before we dumped it. We could have just turned it off. But I didn't know the code."

"ScotAir, did you copy the instructions?" the Navy operator asked.

"The weapon is gone," Scott told the operator. "We dumped it almost ten minutes ago."

The voice of the F-15 lead pilot came on the frequency.

"Ah, ScotAir, that was the message we were sent to deliver, but you jettisoned before I could talk to you. We're monitoring the *Eisenhower,* by the way."

There was a long delay before the frequency came alive again.

"ScotAir, this is the *Eisenhower.* We understand the weapon is gone. Can we be of any assistance?"

Scott snorted, glanced at Doc, and rolled his eyes as he punched the button.

"You bet you can! Tell me precisely where you are, *Eisenhower,* in terms of latitude and longitude. We may need to put this aircraft in the water alongside you if you're close enough, and if we do that, we're going to need your rescue help."

Another voice—undoubtedly one of the watch officers, Scott concluded—came on the frequency.

"ScotAir? *Eisenhower* here. Say again."

Scott repeated the request.

There was another short delay.

"Ah, ScotAir, why don't you transmit your coordinates first, along with your speed, altitude, and heading."

Doc shook his head in anger, but Scott raised his right hand to silence the protest as he looked closely at the global positioning satellite navigation readout and keyed the transmitter. "We're currently showing thirty-three degrees, forty-five-point-eight-five minutes north, seventy-three degrees, forty-one-point-five-zero minutes west. We're at twelve thousand feet, heading two-six-zero degrees magnetic, at a speed of two hundred ten knots. Now. How do we find you guys?"

Scott let up on the transmit button and glanced at Doc. "They'll need the captain's clearance to pass their position. They may just give us vectors."

"Security thing?" Doc asked.

Scott nodded.

There was silence for nearly thirty seconds before the *Eisenhower* came back.

"Okay, ScotAir, fly heading one-eight-five degrees and maintain your altitude."

Scott dialed in the new course and nodded at Doc's immediate turn to the south, then punched the transmit button again. "Okay, relay to the airboss I intend to ditch alongside the ship, and we'll need immediate rescue assistance. We have five souls on board, and one is badly injured—orthopedic injuries—another needs cardiac attention and monitoring."

"ScotAir, we're bucking seventy-knot winds down here and thirty-foot seas. Airboss is asleep. The flight deck's closed. Nothing's flying off this deck, including our helos."

Scott closed his eyes and thought a few seconds before replying.

"Okay, *Eisenhower,* here's the deal. Is this the watch officer?"

"Affirmative."

"We're crippled. We've got a cargo door missing and damage to our tail, and one engine physically off the airplane. We have a total of zero life rafts. Did you get that? Zero. We do have life jackets for all five of us, but one is injured too badly to swim, even with the jacket. If the seas are running thirty feet, we don't stand a very good chance of hitting the water without digging a wing and cartwheeling, and with this huge opening in the side, the bird will sink instantly, even if she doesn't break up. We're a Boeing 727 as you probably know. Translation? Without helos to pick us up quickly, we're dead. Would you please pass all that to the captain?"

"Roger, ScotAir."

"Is the captain still the same one as a year ago?"

"Affirmative."

"Then tell him Lieutenant Commander Scott McKay is urgently requesting his help."

There was a long pause. "You're Navy, Commander?"

"Recently deactivated. VF-142. Tigger was my call sign."

"Roger, Tigger. I'll relay."

Doc's expression was one of arched eyebrows and mock surprise, and Scott turned to meet it.

"What?"

"Tigger?" Doc asked, chuckling. *"Tigger?"*

"Yeah, Tigger. I tended to bounce a lot of landings in pilot training. They named me Tigger, you know, spring in my tail? You have a problem with that?" Scott asked. He tried to fake a scowl, but his heart wasn't in it.

"No!" Doc replied, holding his hands up to dismiss the idea while trying to keep from laughing. "Not at all."

There was silence between them for a few seconds.

"But?" Scott asked.

"But what?"

"You were going to add a 'but.' "

"No, not really. Just something about understanding your landing techniques better now."

Scott shook his head and smiled thinly before retreating into silence and his own thoughts. Doc watched him out of the corner of his eye as he fussed with the course and the engine instruments and tried to suppress the growing fear that was gnawing at him.

A brief hint of wet hair brushed the back of Scott's neck as Linda's voice found his ear. She was still clearing her throat, the trauma of exposure weighing heavily on her.

"Can we survive a ditching at sea, Scott?" she asked softly.

He turned and tried to smile. "We . . . have a chance. If we could land straight-ahead in the water, our biggest problem would be to get out of the belts and out of the airplane before it sinks."

"But it could cartwheel?" she asked.

Scott searched her eyes for a few seconds, then looked down and nodded his head without answering. Linda put her hand on his shoulder.

"It's too bad . . ." She paused to cough and clear her throat again. "It's too bad we can't just land on the carrier itself."

Scott shook his head vigorously. "Our wingspan's far too great for a carrier. We'd take out the ship's superstructure—the island—with our right wing if we tried it, even if they could clear the flight deck aft of the island in time. We'd end up whirling off the deck in flames."

The voice of the duty officer cut through the cockpit noise again.

"ScotAir, this is the *Eisenhower*. The captain says to tell you he's going to turn the ship downwind to enable a helo launch. We're working out a splashdown plan for you right now, Tigger. We recommend you go ahead and descend now to five thousand feet, present heading."

"Roger. Thanks a million! We're out of twelve thousand for five thousand feet."

Doc began the descent as he peered at the radarscope and brought their course to the left a bit to avoid another red splotch of vicious weather.

Vivian Henry had been following the exchange. She leaned forward now and tapped Scott on the side of his arm. "Scott?"

"Yes?" He leaned to the right to hear her.

"How much time is left on the countdown?"

"Ah, Doc's been keeping that."

Doc glanced at his watch. "Just under two minutes, Vivian, if that thing's still intact."

Linda motioned toward the copilot's window. "Are we . . . far enough away?"

Doc shrugged. "I don't know. We're close to sixty miles distant by now. But it's quite possible it just fragmented on impact with the water."

Linda could see Vivian quietly shaking her head.

"You disagree, then?" Linda asked.

"Rogers didn't expect this prototype to be dropped from an airplane, but the original design was supposed to be hardened enough to survive almost anything. If he built it to those standards, it's still intact."

Doc sighed. "I don't know, Vivian. I figure it would have hit the water with a terminal velocity somewhere above three hundred fifty miles per hour."

"The only question I have, Doc," Vivian continued, "is whether you fellows can fly this jet without electronics."

31

• • • •

The captain of the USS *Eisenhower* entered the Combat Decision Center at flank speed, moving with familiar ease through the multiple rows of computer displays, blinking lights, and electronic wizardry. The act of tossing his gold-braided cap on one of the consoles was a gamble, since his eyes hadn't adjusted to the low light level, but the hat slid to a perfect halt in front of the Tactical Action Officer—TAO—before anyone could announce the captain was on deck. He put a beefy right hand on the shoulder of the ship's TAO and gestured toward one of the radarscopes.

"Show me his current position and where you think he dumped the damned bomb."

The TAO nodded and pointed out the two coordinates, as well as the radar targets now moving south toward the position of the carrier. "The Boeing and the Air Force F-15's are right here, about seventy miles north. The bomb site is approximately one hundred forty miles north. The ship will be on a downwind heading in three minutes, sir. Over the deck wind speed can be stabilized at about forty knots. We'll have two helos turning up top in five minutes."

The TAO studied the captain's face for a few seconds. "Are they still expecting a detonation?"

The captain shrugged. "Nobody really knows. Personally, I suspect the damn thing was a hoax. We've never been briefed on anything like a Medusa Weapon, and I don't buy the idea that a single nutty scientist could build such a thing at home."

"But the official word is it's real?"

The captain nodded. "The Pentagon is convinced it's a live nuke. At least if it does detonate, it should be a thousand feet or more underwater by now, and that should shield the continent, in case this Medusa Wave threat turns out to be valid. But if I'm wrong, we're going to find out how well we've hardened these ships against electromagnetic pulses."

There was silence between the two of them for a few seconds before the TAO cleared his throat and spoke again.

"I understand you know the pilot of that aircraft, sir?"

The Navy captain chuckled. "Mr. McKay?" He nodded. "Good kid, good officer, even for a pilot—and a dangerous handball player. That's how I knew him. Normally I don't get to know the Tomcat jocks. But he was the only character on the ship I could never seem to beat."

The TAO smiled as the captain reached for his hat at the precise second a strange power fluctuation pulsed through the CDC, momentarily dimming the already subdued lights. It was a flicker at first, followed by the sound of cooling fans slowing down.

"What's that?" the TAO asked in alarm.

The captain looked around quickly as wild bursts of visual static exploded across various radar screens and computer displays and the projected wall map dissolved momentarily into shards of random images.

"Oh shit," the captain muttered.

"What?"

The TAO's eyes were darting back and forth, his mind rebelling at the sights and sounds of electronics gone berserk.

"Oh *shit*," he repeated.

It was real, after all!

ABOARD SCOTAIR 50—8:01 P.M. EDT

The high-pitched squeal of tortured electrons could be heard all too clearly through the overhead speakers in the cockpit as Doc and Scott looked at each other in instant alarm, chills running up and down their backs.

There was an odd flash of light outside that could have been lightning, followed by a brief intense flare on the radarscope before it went dark. As Scott looked, the global positioning satellite display also flared and died.

Doc noticed his digital watch was blank at the same moment the remaining two electrical generators tripped off-line, leaving them with only battery power.

"Loss of all generators," Scott announced. "Keep flying her, Doc. I'll get Jerry's panel."

Scott threw off his seat belt and squeezed between Linda and the center console in a fluid leap to the engineer's position.

Jerry had opened his eyes and was trying to make sense of things from the floor as Scott tackled the number two generator and tried to get it back on-line.

"Battery power's failing, too, Scott. It's fluctuating all over the place!" Doc yelled.

"Hang on," Scott replied.

A series of weird light pulses in the battery-powered emergency lights caused an unreal flickering in the cockpit as Scott activated the appropriate switch and restored one of the two engine-driven electrical generators.

Light flooded the forward panel.

"I've got number two back," he announced.

His fingers labored to bring the number three generator to life and parallel it with number two in powering the airplane.

It refused to connect.

The thought that something else might be closing on them from behind gripped his middle, and he tried to suppress it.

The Medusa Weapon was thermonuclear. If it had caused this, was there a shock wave, too? Was there a wave of radioactivity?

The field switch for the number three generator finally closed, and Scott made the appropriate adjustments before closing the remaining two switches to repower all the circuits.

"It's holding, Doc," he said.

Scott returned to his seat as Doc assessed the situation. "Radar's out, autopilot's out, radios are probably out, but I haven't tried them."

Scott looked over at the two F-15's, still off their left wing. He could see both pilots working, heads down, in their cockpits. Scott checked that the UHF radio was still selected to his microphone.

"Wolf flight, you fellows still hear us? Did you experience any electronic problems just then?"

The helmet of the lead pilot came up, and he saw him look over before replying.

"Affirmative, ScotAir." Static almost blocked his voice, then diminished. "Jesus Christ, I think your bomb just went off. I've lost my computer over here."

"Scott . . ." Doc began, his eyes examining the instrument panel in front of him.

"Yeah?" Scott jerked his head to the right and followed Doc's finger to the center panel.

"This isn't tracking right. The computer's feeding it garbage."

Scott checked the navigational computer on the center console, as well as the inertial reference systems. They were both spitting out endless streams of useless numbers in their displays.

"Don't try to connect the autopilot to the computer," Scott said sternly.

"No problem," Doc replied. "The autopilot isn't working, either."

"Keep on steering one-eight-zero until we get the *Eisenhower* back on-line. At least we've got basic flight instruments, airspeed, attitude, and altimeter."

They both stared into space for a few seconds, feeling stunned.

"My God," Scott said quietly. "It was real all along. All this time we were carrying a real hydrogen bomb just fifty feet behind us."

Doc was shaking his head slowly. "I didn't really believe it, either." He looked over at Scott with an ashen expression. "You gonna call them?"

Scott jerked his head in Doc's direction, thoroughly distracted. "What?"

"The ship. You gonna call the ship?"

"Oh. Yeah." Scott checked the UHF frequency again and held the microphone just short of his mouth as he glanced up at Doc. He raised the microphone and punched the button to call the *Eisenhower*.

There was no reply.

He tried again.

Same result.

Scott dialed the emergency frequency into one of the standard aviation radios, but it was completely dead.

"Doc, the VHF's aren't even working."

"But the UHF is?"

"Yeah. Why is that?"

"Isn't that UHF Air Force surplus?"

Scott nodded. "You're right. I'd forgotten that. It's probably shielded."

"I doubt anything else in here with an electronic board is working, including the flight computers and navigation radios."

"How can we find that ship without navigation?" Scott asked Doc.

"I don't know. It's a big ocean. Radar's out, too, or we could probably spot them on the surface."

"Scott, why don't we ask our shadows out there for help?"

Scott nodded and mashed the transmit button.

"Wolf lead, our radar's out. Is yours still working?"

"Not yet, ScotAir. We're working on it."

"Are you in contact with your command?" Scott asked.

"Not now," was the reply.

"We were wondering if you could help us locate the *Eisenhower* if we can't talk to them anymore?"

Scott heard the microphone trigger in the F-15 and could hear the lead pilot take a breath before speaking. "I was thinking of asking you the same question regarding our tanker."

How on earth could we help him with that? Scott wondered.

"That was a lame joke, ScotAir," the F-15 lead added quickly. "We're going to be in rather critical need of finding an airborne gas station in about thirty minutes."

COMBAT DECISION CENTER, USS *EISENHOWER—*
8:03 P.M. EDT

Slowly, the glowing displays in the electronic nerve center of the nuclear-powered aircraft carrier came back on-line.

"Status, Chief?" the captain asked.

"Coming back to normal, sir, on most equipment. We've got a couple of antennas not responding up top and one radar out. But satellite links are back. Flash traffic indicates an orbital confirmation of the explosion."

"Mr. Wilson?" the captain addressed one of the watch officers.

"Sir?"

"Time to tell our commanders. Flash CINCNAV our status and any damages. Preparing to assist in recovery of crew of the civilian airliner . . . provided they're still out there." He turned back to the chief of the watch.

"Are the radios back up, Chief? Can we talk to the aircraft?"

"Yes, sir." He gestured to one of the consoles, and the captain picked up the microphone and looked at the chief of the watch. "That was ScotAir Fifty, right?"

"Yes, sir."

He punched the mike button. "ScotAir Fifty, this is the *Eisenhower*. How copy?"

The voice of Scott McKay responded almost immediately.

"Loud and clear, *Eisenhower,* thank goodness."

"Commander McKay? This is the skipper."

"Hello, Captain. Thanks for helping us out."

"Your little package apparently blew up, Scott. Any effects up there?"

Scott quickly summarized the strange anomalies.

"Okay," the *Eisenhower*'s captain continued, "I'm going to pass you over to the airboss in a moment. He'll get you vectored in and coordinate with you how we're going to handle this. We've got to keep the ship downwind while you're ditching so we can get the helos off the deck. We're almost at maximum permissible wind speed for launch."

"Understood, sir."

"Good luck."

The captain replaced the handset and looked at the officer who had just joined them, the commander of the F-14 squadron.

"Well, Bill, what do you make of his chances?"

The Navy commander looked at his feet for a few seconds before engaging the captain's eyes.

"Tigger's a good pilot, sir, but it'll be a miracle if we get even one of those people out of there alive. We're running thirty-foot crests out there."

"Prospects of landing intact are that bad?"

"If they don't break up on impact, I'll be astounded. He'd have to land on the crest of a wave so precisely it would be unprecedented, and even then with a cargo door open, he'll sink like a rock."

"You're saying it's hopeless?"

The commander shook his head no.

"Not hopeless, but close to it. Their chances of surviving are very remote."

ABOARD AIR FORCE ONE—8:08 P.M. EDT

For more than two minutes the satellite links were transmitting gibberish instead of the highly scrambled and secure data stream that normally connected the President's airborne teleconferencing suite to its counterpart Starsuites in the Situation Room and Pentagon. Slowly, however—coaxed by a team of technicians digitally massaging the satellite transponders back into linked operation—connections were reestablished.

In the Pentagon's Starsuite the President's image finally coalesced into a wide-eyed and obviously upset Commander in Chief waiting on the other side of the airborne table.

"Okay, what's your status there?" the President asked. "I've received confirmation that we've had a detonation."

General Kinney stepped closer to his side of the conference table and briefed the President on the growing evidence that the explosion had caused some very strange effects.

"I need the bottom line, General. Are all our command and control networks and systems still operational?" the President said.

"Yes, sir."

"So no apparent damage to military channels, right?"

"We have no idea how much dropped off-line, sir. All sorts of connections were affected, including this one. But we're operational worldwide."

The President nodded. "Okay."

"And everything seems to be coming back on-line. We have no assessment of civilian impact. Frankly, we're having a lot of trouble getting through the civilian communications lines, and that's worrisome."

The President sat down and studied the general for a second.

"This thing was under thousands of feet of seawater, General. How could it have boggled our hardened communications links?"

The general raised both hands, palms up. "I don't know, Mr. President. It's too soon to tell. But I'll bet we're going to find this was no ordinary nuclear event. And if it *was* the Medusa Wave, all the evidence of how it was built just vaporized."

The President frowned. "And if you'd succeeded in tinkering with it at Seymour-Johnson, Goldsboro right now would be another Hiroshima, with all the attendant horrors."

The general chose not to reply.

"What's the status of those people on the 727?"

The general filled him in on the impending ditching alongside the *Eisenhower*.

"The *Eisenhower* was inbound to Norfolk and trying to skirt the south side of the hurricane. He's the only one close enough for a rescue."

"And the two F-15's didn't get there in time to deliver the code, right?"

"No, sir. They found the Boeing just as the bomb was being jettisoned."

The general knew much more, but details on the near miss and the dangling passenger could wait for later briefings.

The President studied some papers on the table before looking up again.

"I want you to notify me immediately when you have word on the ditching and rescue. Tell the captain of the *Eisenhower* from me personally to spare no effort to save those people."

"Yes, sir. I know, for one, the FBI is still dying to get their hands on the scientist's wife."

The President looked stunned and came forward in his chair. "Still? I thought that was a moot point."

"No, sir. Her husband may have built it, but she's still the shipper who put a thermonuclear weapon on board a civilian airliner and intended to take it to the Pentagon. I'd say she's about number one on the FBI's most wanted list at this moment."

ABOARD SCOTAIR 50—8:08 P.M. EDT

Trying not to move him any more than necessary, Vivian Henry worked as rapidly as she could to put a life vest around Jerry Christian as he lay on the floor. With Doc flying and Scott rifling through the flight manuals for last-minute tips on ditching a Boeing 727, Linda, still shaking with trauma, began pulling the small orange life vest packages from behind each seat and unsealing them. Fumbling with the straps, she slowly helped each of them put on their inflatable vests.

"Okay, we need all of us concentrating on this plan," Scott said, motioning Vivian and Linda forward.

Doc glanced over. "Go ahead, Scott. I'm listening."

"Our problem," Scott began, "is going to be getting out in time and trying to stay together until they can get all of us in the helicopters. If this was a calm, smooth surface ahead, I'd say our biggest worry would be scooping up too much water through the cargo door and sinking. But we've got huge waves down there, and my strategy is going to be to land crosswind along the top of one of the crests and parallel to it. If I succeed, the tail will dig in first, then the wings, as the wave subsides beneath us. Whether we come to a halt straight-ahead and intact or get spun around and break up is pure guesswork. We've all got to be firmly strapped in, and we need to make sure we've secured Jerry's strap down there."

Linda cleared her throat. "Ah . . . there's a chance, I take it, that we could be knocked out, right?"

Scott nodded. "I'll be brutally honest with you, Linda. There's a chance we'll all be knocked unconscious for too long to recover. If only one or two of us are still conscious and able to react when we stop, whoever's conscious will have only a few seconds to pull the rest of us out of the seat belts, pull the inflation lanyards, and try to kick us toward the door."

"Scott, we've got safety cords on each of these vests," Doc added. "Shouldn't we tie all of us together right now?"

Scott thought back to his water survival training and shrugged. "That's probably a good idea, as long as we don't get tangled up trying to get out of the cockpit."

"What about Jerry?" Vivian asked.

Scott sighed loudly. Jerry was worrying him deeply. The odds of getting the injured and anesthetized flight engineer out the door and into a rescue basket without massive additional damage to his crushed legs and pelvis were grim.

But it wasn't something he could say aloud.

"Well," Scott began, "we'll just have to nurse him out and get him in the baskets first."

"Baskets?" Linda asked.

"Billy Pugh nets, or whatever they have waiting for us." He

described some of the types of water rescue devices the Navy used. "If it's the one I expect, just roll yourself into it and go limp. The helo crew will do the rest."

Linda was looking through the door toward the back of the cargo cabin, and Scott followed her gaze to the small mound of Antarctic research materials they had labored so hard to relocate and tie down at the back of the aircraft.

"I'm sorry about your equipment and research, Linda," he said gently. "I wish there was another way."

"It's okay."

"Can you recover? Professionally, I mean?" he asked.

She nodded. "But first I've got to survive this swim, don't I?"

Vivian leaned forward. "Scott?" she said. "What is this going to feel like when we hit the water? Honestly."

He shrugged. "I'm guessing. I've never ditched a plane. But we'll get the flaps out and gear down and go as slowly as we can, and if I do it right and we're lucky, it'll be like a very hard landing, with a waterfall coming through the door immediately afterward. The winds are sixty knots, but I can't land directly into the wind, so I'm estimating that we'll have the equivalent of a forty-knot headwind, and if I can slow us to a hundred knots, that'll mean we'll touch down at sixty knots, or about seventy miles per hour. That's surviv-able."

Doc looked over. "You say you want to go in with gear *down*?"

Scott nodded. "I know what the book says, Doc, but with the gear digging in, we'll slow faster before we actually get the fuselage in the water."

"Could cause us to cartwheel, too."

"It could." Scott nodded. "But it makes more sense to me. You disagree?"

"Never ditched one," Doc said. "Neither has Boeing. I think we're all guessing."

"There are no life rafts, you said?" Vivian asked.

Scott nodded and sighed. "I . . . didn't expect any overwater flights when we started this company. Life rafts are expensive and quite heavy . . ." His voice trailed off in embarrassment.

"The FAA doesn't require them, Vivian, even for crew members," Doc added, "unless you're doing extended overwater flying, which we weren't planning on doing."

"Until I came along," Vivian added with a grim expression.

Doc turned toward her quickly. "I didn't mean it that way, Vivian. You're as much a victim in this as we are."

Linda reached out a hand and took Vivian's. "That's the truth, Vivian. We all heard it back there."

"We did, and we all feel the same, Vivian," Scott added. "You shouldn't feel guilty."

Vivian nodded, her eyes fixed on Jerry, who had lapsed back into an anesthetized sleep.

There was silence among them for a few seconds before Scott spoke again.

"Okay, if the plane begins to sink, swim out of this cockpit and toward the cargo door. Even if it's below the waves, you've got a good chance of getting clear and getting to the surface. Don't give up! That's the main thing."

"The water down there," Doc added, "may be influenced by the Gulf Stream, and if so, it may be in the sixty- to seventy-degree range, in terms of temperature, and reasonably, well, warm. But it won't feel warm. It will be one hell of a shock to your system, but at least, thank God, it's not the North Atlantic."

The voice of the controller aboard the *Eisenhower* cut into their thoughts.

"ScotAir Fifty, descend now to one thousand feet, come left, heading one-four-zero. We're going to bring you below the prevailing ceiling, which is three thousand six hundred, and alongside the ship. Call the ship when we're in sight."

"How far, *Eisenhower*?"

"Twenty-one miles. When you call the ship in sight, we'll transfer you to the airboss for a briefing on what we've worked out for the splashdown zone."

"Roger, *Eisenhower*."

BRIDGE, USS *EISENHOWER* — 8:08 P.M. EDT

From the depths of the hangar bays below, the forward elevator had raised two SH-60F Seahawk helicopters to the flight deck. With the ship now steaming at greater than thirty knots and the wind coming from the stern, the wind speed over the flight deck was down to forty knots—with occasional gusts to forty-five.

A small cadre of deck crew spotted and prepped the helos and adjusted the chocks and chains as the pilots and aircrewman strapped in. With a final signal from the airboss, both crews started their engines and began bringing their rotors up to speed as the ship pitched and rolled through the gigantic waves kicked up by Hurricane Sigrid.

On the bridge, several senior officers were huddled with the skipper over a large piece of paper containing a diagram of the ship.

"We need to keep sailing downwind, but if we have him aim to touch down just ahead of us, moving from our left to our right—like this—along the wave crests, with any luck he'll come to rest no more than a thousand yards off our starboard side."

"So," the captain repeated, "he'll be about forty-five degrees into the wind?"

"We're steering zero-one-zero degrees right now. The wind is directly behind us, coming from one-nine-zero degrees. The prevailing wave crests and troughs are running roughly west-northwest to east-southeast. So if he makes his final approach on a heading of, say, one-zero-zero degrees . . ."

"Roughly east-southeast, in other words?" the captain asked.

"Correct. That will align him with the wave crests and yet put him mostly into the wind. If he keeps us in his right windscreen and uses a touchdown aim point just beyond our bow, that will get him in as close as we dare."

The captain studied the hastily scribbled lines and straightened up.

"Agreed. But make damn sure he understands not to land short. We don't want any risk of the ship running him over in the water. That's a nightmare we don't need."

The officers turned to go as the captain caught one by the shoulder.

"One . . . more thing."

"Yes, sir?"

"Get the television cameras all rolling and call up the guys from our TV studio. I want every Navy TV camera on board trying to capture this. I can't recall a 727 ever ditching before, and this could prove valuable for safety purposes, however it turns out."

"You want a camera on board the lead helo, sir?"

The captain nodded. "Have them record whatever they can, regardless."

"Aye, sir."

The Officer of the Deck—the OOD—appeared at the captain's side. "Captain?"

"Yeah?"

"Sir, there's a secure call for you from Air Force One."

ABOARD SCOTAIR 50—8:10 P.M. EDT

Doc stabilized the 727 at a thousand feet and worked to adjust the throttles on the two remaining engines as Scott, Linda, and Vivian scanned the dark gray waterscape ahead for signs of the aircraft carrier. With daylight savings time, it was still light, though the setting sun remained hidden by the overcast.

"Scott, can I make a suggestion?" Doc asked, his eyes on the instruments.

"Sure," Scott replied, as he watched the horizon.

"Yeah, well, I'd like for you to fly this landing."

Scott glanced over at the big copilot in surprise. Doc looked agonized.

"Why, Doc?"

"Neither of us has ever ditched. Either of us can do it, but from the left seat it takes you longer to operate the flaps and gear and things. I should be playing my normal copilot role. It's more efficient."

"You've got far more experience . . ."

"I know I do." Doc cut him off. "I know I've got a hell of a lot of time in these birds, but I'm telling you, we need to work like a normally configured team now. Your place is flying, mine is supporting your aeronautical orders as rapidly as humanly possible."

"Which would you really *rather* do, Doc?"

Doc looked at him with a scowl. "Dammit, I'd rather fly! You know that. But that's not the best way to handle this."

"Look, Doc . . ." Scott began.

"No, *you* look! I appreciate the continuous vote of confidence. I appreciate the fact that you're a careful team player sensitive to utilizing your resources correctly. But listen, dammit. If we have to make some last-second adjustment in here, we're not going to have time for you to search out the right lever. Simple fact is, I'm far faster from the right on flaps and gear and radios and all than you are from the left, and you know I'm right. Okay?"

Scott searched Doc's eyes for any indication that the argument was some sort of subterfuge.

It wasn't.

"Okay, Doc. I'll take over now," Scott said, taking the control yoke.

32
•••••

The huge carrier that had been his professional home for so long loomed into view as the onboard controller vectored them across the bow of the *Eisenhower* at a distance of a half mile.

They had already explained the ditching plan.

Scott dropped the 727 down to five hundred feet to study the wave pattern as Doc worked the radios. The winds were howling from the south at a steady sixty-two knots, but the ship was steaming at top speed to the north to keep the deck winds reasonable for the helicopter launch.

"How fast *can* she go?" Doc asked.

"That's classified, but it's above forty knots," Scott replied.

Doc turned back to his right and strained to check the fuel readings.

"We're down to two thousand three hundred pounds, Scott."

Scott acknowledged the information as he turned to Linda and Vivian. "Check Jerry one last time, please. Vivian, check to make sure the cockpit door is securely tied open, and both of you fasten all your seat and shoulder belts, including the crotch belt."

Another radio transmission from the ship came through the overhead speakers, but he missed the words.

"They want to know if you're ready, Scott," Doc said, holding the microphone.

Scott licked his lips and checked the altitude, then nodded. "I'm going to circle the ship clockwise and get the gear and flaps out. We'll get into position ahead of them as planned and do it then."

"Two minutes? Five minutes?"

"Tell him four to five minutes."

Doc passed the word and the controller acknowledged.

The overhead speakers came alive again with the voice of the F-15 leader.

"ScotAir, you have a visual on the ship now, affirmative?"

"Affirmative," Doc replied.

"Roger, we're bingo fuel. We've got enough navigation equipment back on-line to find our tanker, but not enough gas to stay with you."

"No problem, guys. We appreciate the escort."

The two F-15's pulled up and away and headed west. Within seconds they had disappeared into the overcast.

"Okay, Doc, flaps two," Scott ordered.

"Roger, flaps two." Doc's left hand moved the flap handle to the first indented position and monitored the gauge as the leading edge flaps and slats came out, followed by slight rearward movement of the large extendable surfaces on the rear of each wing.

"Flaps are at two," he reported.

"Flaps five, please," Scott added.

Doc repeated the command and moved the lever to the next gate. The flap gauge indicator needles began moving again, stopping at the appointed position.

"Gear down. Landing checklist."

Doc's hand reached for the handle, then hesitated. "Ah, Scott, I'm really uncomfortable with using the gear."

Scott glanced at him with a puzzled expression.

"I thought you didn't care one way or another."

Doc nodded. "So did I, but I've been thinking about it, and I reread the ditching section of the emergency pages and figured out why they don't want it used."

"Tell me," Scott said.

"Two reasons. First, it exposes some pretty weak floor beams in the gear well and gives the water a chance to breach the floor and cascade in, sinking us faster."

"That does make sense," Scott responded.

"And since the gear is behind our center of gravity, it could rotate us nose-first into the waves. Scott, they say we can expect to go no more than six hundred fifty feet once we hit the water anyway, and that's without the gear."

"That's three to five G's deceleration, right?"

"Right."

Scott was nodding. "Okay, forget the gear. I agree."

"Thanks."

"But we're going to need to pull the landing gear warning horn circuit breaker or we'll be listening to that instead of each other."

Doc had already thrown off his seat belt and threaded his way past Jerry. He leaned behind Jerry's flight engineer panel to locate the right breaker, which he pulled. He then adjusted several switches on the flight engineer's panel and turned toward Scott.

"I'm going to secure things in the cabin. Hold her steady."

"Roger," Scott said.

In two minutes Doc was back and fastening himself in his seat. "Done."

"Anything we've forgotten? You're reading the checklist, aren't you?"

"We've got it all done, Scott. I shut down the air-conditioning and closed the outflow valves on the panel, set up the fuel and opened the crossfeeds, then I went back and double-checked the aft entry door closed, and made sure the cargo net around Linda's stuff was still secure, and replaced the emergency exit hatch. With everything closed, even though the cargo door is gone, there's a chance she might even float a few minutes, if . . . ah . . ."

"If we don't break up on impact," Scott finished.

Doc nodded slowly. "True," he said simply, diverting his eyes out to the right. He could see the *Eisenhower* steaming north as Scott turned from west to north, keeping the carrier on the right. There would be a few more minutes of maneuvering, Doc reminded himself, then they would point their nose to the east-southeast just ahead of the carrier and descend until they were barely skimming the waves and had passed the carrier's intended course. There would be a moment of decision, then, as Scott looked for the right spot.

Why am I so calm? Doc asked himself. The prospect of surviving a crash landing in high seas and then swimming for his life was hardly calming. He'd always been a terrible swimmer and very suspicious of the sea.

He glanced at Scott, then back at Vivian. A few hours ago they had been just a nonscheduled aircrew with a couple of strangers aboard. Now they seemed like family.

Of course, he reminded himself, Scott had seemed like family since he met him—like a son—though he was always careful not to let on he felt that way.

His thoughts turned to Vivian and what she'd endured—how she'd been made the victim and the scapegoat at the same time. He was feeling very protective of her, and the feeling was growing. Whatever happened, he was determined that she survive.

Doc took a deep breath and rubbed his head as he tried to focus on the steps he was supposed to take after the aircraft came to rest in the water.

Start switches off, pull the fire switches, initiate the evacuation.
Hopefully it would be that easy.

On the bridge of the *Eisenhower,* several sets of field glasses were tracking ScotAir 50 as the 727 maneuvered to the northwest and prepared to turn on what would be its final approach. The two SH-60F Seahawk helicopters were up to speed and standing by, rotors turning furiously on the angle flight deck. A few additional deck crew had emerged to watch, and several television cameras were trained on the commercial jet. The sheets of rain that had pelted the carrier earlier had subsided, and nothing but high winds and angry gray skies covered the ship as it plowed repeatedly through giant waves.

"Okay, *Eisenhower,* we're turning in for the ditching run," Doc told them.

"Understand, ScotAir. The helos will reach you within a minute of splashdown."

"Ready?" Scott asked as he glanced behind him at Linda and Vivian.

Linda's hand had been on his shoulder for some time. He wanted to tell her to put it on the back of the seat and brace, but the reassurance from her touch was a continuous flow of energy, and he decided to wait until the last few seconds.

"We're ready," Linda said.

"Let's do it," Doc added.

"Okay. Prayers will definitely be in order. Doc? Flaps twenty-five. Set speed."

"Flaps twenty-five."

The whine of the hydraulic motors driving the flaps into position could be heard in the distance again as the aircraft slowed and the roar of the slipstream outside the open cargo door diminished.

"Flaps thirty, then flaps forty. Set target speed at one-zero-eight knots."

Doc's hand moved the flap lever to the final position and his eyes followed the flap gauge needles as they moved obediently to the full-extended position. He reached up to his airspeed indicator and set the speed at one hundred and eight knots.

"I'm starting final descent," Scott stated as he tweaked the throttles for the two remaining engines back a tiny bit and lowered the nose slightly. The altitude had remained at five hundred feet, but now the size of the wave fronts below began to take on startling dimensions as the 727 settled through three hundred and two hundred feet above the water, rocking and bucking through the turbulent air, their speed over the water less than seventy knots due to the howling crosswind.

Scott held the 727's nose twenty degrees to the right of the flight path he wanted to follow as the aircraft crabbed into the wind to stay aligned with the waves.

The *Eisenhower* was coming abeam them on the right.

"Doc, tell me when we've passed his centerline."

"Roger. We're very close."

"Linda? Vivian? Secure your hands on the seats in front of you and bury your faces against the back of your hands and brace."

He felt Linda's hand pat him twice as she withdrew it from his shoulder.

"We're past the centerline of the carrier, Scott," Doc confirmed.

Scott dropped them carefully through a radio altimeter reading of one hundred feet as Doc began calling off the remaining distance. The waves looked gigantic, the huge swells moving from their right to their left as they flew almost parallel to them, trying to stay somewhat into the wind. His left hand was moving the control column constantly, making continuous corrections as the wildly gusting wind threatened to destabilize their flight attitude every few seconds. It felt as if the Boeing was almost hovering over the water.

"Fifty feet, Scott. That's an average. It keeps changing."

• • •

From the perspective of the *Eisenhower*'s bridge the 727 was all but in the water, and the various crew members watching held their breaths and waited for the plume of spray indicating contact.

But the Boeing kept skimming just over the waves.

"Scott, we're moving away from the carrier! We need to put her down!" Doc shouted.

Scott felt himself overrule an immediate response. He was too busy trying to compute a flight path along an undulating landscape in constant motion in fifty directions at once. Every time he picked a monstrous swell and eased the 727 over to set down on the back side of it, the swell seemed to disappear in another monstrous mound of water that threatened to engulf them head-on.

The winds were brutal, howling from the right, the huge waves rolling from right to left as well. If he touched down ahead of a wave, instead of just behind it, they would break up. But to pick the right spot he had to cross-control the aircraft, and the aim point was constantly shifting.

Scott could see the carrier slipping away in his peripheral vision to his right. He could feel the tension in the muscles of his neck. He tried to position the 727 above yet another huge crest, but banked too sharply to the left to catch it and found himself on the forward side of the wave. With rudder and a small burst of power, he came up and slipped to the right, leaping the Boeing to the right enough to position them on the back side of the crest, then kicking the left rudder to align them.

At last, this one was working.

"This is it!" Scott cried out.

It was a long swell, maybe forty feet from trough to crest, which seemed to extend forever ahead of them—a mountain of water with a clearly defined top and a broad back side, foam streaming off the top of it close enough to touch. He worked the rudder and aileron with great care and constant motion and felt the 727 moving into the correct position, the wings aligned with the wave and not the horizon.

Almost perfect!

Time stretched to slow motion again as he let the bird down the final few feet, holding the power, feeling with the tailpipe of number two engine for what would start out as a gentle impact.

The sudden force that began with a gentle rolling motion to the left built in a heartbeat to a massive gust determined to pick up the right wing and roll them to the left in an impossible and violent motion that caught him completely unprepared.

One second they had been in perfect position, the next they were pointed too far to the left, accelerating over the top of the crest, the left wing slicing toward the *front* of the wave.

"NO!" Scott's voice was a constrained yelp as he yanked the control column and threw the yoke to the right, jamming the throttles all the way to the firewall.

The 727 responded instantly, the nose popping up and the aircraft rolling right wing down as he sensed too late that the right roll was going to go too far. Scott reversed the throw on the yoke, but the right wing tip was still descending toward the top of the swell, now positioned just to their right and rising.

The pitch of the Boeing increased with a strange lurching motion, a tug at the back of their seats, and Scott realized the number two engine exhaust cone was dipping into the water and sucking them in like an anchor. At the same moment the right wing tip dug into the waves by mere inches, kicking up a plume of salt spray and yawing the 727 violently to the right.

He was losing it.

The two remaining engines had taken several seconds to reach full power, but suddenly they were kicking the 727 in the rear end with over thirty-five thousand pounds of thrust as the crest passed beneath them.

And they were flying again, leaping free of the surface and clawing for altitude.

Scott could feel Doc groping for words as he leveled the aircraft at two hundred feet.

"Jesus, Scott!"

"It wasn't right. I almost lost it."

"We'll have to log a touch-and-go. Christ!"

"Are we too far out now?"

Doc looked to the right and began nodding energetically. "Yep."

"Which way should we circle, do you think?"

Doc strained to see the carrier out of the right side. His voice echoed off the window. "Bring her left, Scott. The wind will take us far enough to the north of him and you can realign and try it again."

Scott rolled the Boeing into a thirty-degree left bank and gained more altitude.

"I'll keep us at five hundred."

"What do you want me to tell them?"

"Tell them we're coming back around to try it again."

"Okay. Okay, you want to stay at flaps forty?" Doc asked, his eyes flaring and his voice alarmed.

"Yeah. I'm just going to do a wide circle."

Doc relayed the information to the *Eisenhower* and watched the ship disappear to the right. The turn seemed to take forever, the howling wind bumping and bouncing them around as the compasses slowly clicked off the turn through north and west toward south.

The *Eisenhower* appeared again in their windscreen, perhaps three miles to the south, as the 727 flew to the west of the carrier's intended path and then stabilized on a southeasterly heading and once again crossed to the east of the ship's course.

There was a massive sigh from the left seat as Scott readjusted his hands on the yoke and throttles.

"Okay. Here we go." He repeated the final warnings and inched the aircraft down to fifty feet again to look for the right wave.

"The problem, Doc, is the cross-controlling," he explained. "I had it perfect until we caught that gust. I wasn't anticipating that. I will this time."

"Just keep it calm and steady, Scott," Doc said.

Scott nodded.

Once again the angles seemed to be impossibly complex as he maneuvered over the first wave, then another one, barely hanging over the water.

Doc found himself worrying whether Scott could actually do it. Would he run them out of gas trying? Or would he suddenly force himself to dump it in, choosing the wrong moment?

Perhaps I should take it, after all, Doc thought, immediately killing the idea. This was Scott's show. Scott's duty. And he had to trust his airmanship.

"This is nuts, Doc!" Scott's voice cut through his thoughts. "If I could land into the damn wind, we'd be far slower over the . . ."

Scott stopped in midsentence, his eyebrows flaring, the controls held steady as they skimmed less than twenty feet over the top of another massive crest.

"Oh my Lord!" Scott said.

Suddenly his right hand shoved the throttles forward again, this time short of the firewall, and as Doc watched in alarm, Scott pulled the 727 away from the water and began climbing.

"Max power. Flaps fifteen."

"Flaps *fifteen*?" Doc asked.

"Yes, dammit! Flaps fifteen."

"We're going around?" Doc asked.

"Maybe. Maybe something else," Scott said.

Doc had already positioned the flap handle. He instinctively checked the power setting as he tried to figure out what on earth Scott meant.

"What are you doing? What should I tell the ship?"

There was no answer at first as Doc watched Scott flying and calculating something at the same time.

"Scott?"

Instantly Scott turned to the copilot. "Take the airplane, Doc. Get us to a thousand feet and orbit the ship at a reasonable distance. Clean up the flaps. Conserve the fuel. I'll take the radio."

"Scott, *what are you doing*? We don't have that much fuel to play with."

"Just . . . just listen," Scott said as he confirmed that Doc's hands had closed around the yoke.

"You've got it?"

"Yes, I've got it! But why?"

Scott pulled a piece of paper from his pocket and with shaking hands started scribbling figures. Just as quickly he stuffed the pen and paper back in his pocket and keyed the radio.

"*Eisenhower,* this is ScotAir."

"Go ahead, ScotAir. Are you coming back around?"

"Ah, what are the winds out there now, not over the deck but ambient?"

There was a pause from below before the voice returned.

"We're showing a steady-state wind of seventy-one knots from one-seven-zero degrees, ScotAir."

"Okay, is the captain on the channel?"

Another pause, and then another voice, but not that of the captain.

"What do you need, ScotAir? This is Airboss."

"Okay, please listen. I know how long it takes at flank speed to turn the ship one hundred and eighty degrees. Please do that now. Please bring yourself around to a heading of one-seven-zero degrees."

The response took several seconds.

"Are you nuts out there? The only way we've prepared these rescue helos for you is by running *with* the wind. At this speed, if we turn the ship around, we'll be pumping a hundred and five knots of wind over the deck, for Chrissakes!"

Doc watched, astounded, as Scott smiled, nodded, and raised the microphone to his lips. He keyed the transmitter in almost leisurely fashion and waited a few seconds. When he spoke, it was a carefully pronounced four-word phrase that left Doc stunned.

"That's precisely the point."

There was no response from the ship.

"Scott, what in hell are you thinking?" Doc asked.

Scott waved him off as he keyed the transmitter again.

"*Eisenhower,* the approach speed for our aircraft at our current weight is one hundred and eight knots. If you turn into the wind and run at flank speed, you'll be giving me a wind over the deck of over one hundred and five knots. I'm aware that you've already cleared the new flight deck. If you'll just rig the forward net, I can put this mother down on the deck like a helicopter."

"Holy Mother of God, Scott! You want to land on the *carrier*?" Doc almost shouted.

Scott glanced at him with a vaguely maniacal smile. "You'd prefer to get wet?"

"No! No, but I mean, you said . . . you said we couldn't land on the carrier because we're far too big. We'd take out the island and flip off the deck in flames, remember?"

"I remember, and that's true, Doc, at normal speed. Doc, don't you see? I wasn't thinking combined winds! I was figuring normal landing speeds and maybe thirty knots to forty knots of wind over the deck. That *is* too fast. But with a hundred knots of wind, good grief, we're a vertical landing craft!"

"In theory, maybe."

"No, in fact. Think about it."

Another voice cut through the cockpit from below.

"Scott McKay? This is the captain. We're wasting time. I can't turn this ship until I park my helos, and if I do that, your rescue is gone. There's no way I can approve the idea of a civilian airliner approaching this flight deck under any conditions. You know that. The 727 is not approved for carrier operations, and I've got a billion-dollar warship to protect."

Scott closed his eyes and sighed before replying, focusing all his concentration on the argument and his memories of the skipper.

"Captain, we're not going to make it out of this aircraft if we ditch. That's the reality. The waves out there . . . they're unbelievable. We've got five lives aboard and some very valuable government scientific research equipment which we'll lose if we ditch."

"Scott, I cannot imperil this ship."

"Come on, Captain, a hundred-thousand-pound aluminum bird has a chance of sinking an eleven-hundred-foot steel ship? I lived there, remember?"

"Then you know the rules and the perils, Scott. One mistake and we've got burning wreckage all over this ship, a fire to fight, deck lives that may be lost, and a critical warship out of service for months."

"Captain, please listen to me! You're the guy who once lectured me that there were times we had to make it up as we went along. So that's what I'm doing."

"Bottom line? No way in hell, McKay, are you bringing that civilian bucket of bolts on my ship."

"Captain, please. Open your mind to this. My speed over the edge relative to the ship will be less than ten knots. TEN KNOTS! You and I can run that fast, for crying out loud. I don't need the wires or a tailhook. The net can catch a fully loaded Tomcat at a hundred knots. We weigh right now about a hundred thousand pounds, and my brakes are working fine. I'll bet you a year's pay we won't even get close to the net. I guarantee the wings will never get close to the island. It's a piece of cake."

"It's suicidal, McKay," the captain responded, but Scott heard the transmitter click off, which meant he was thinking about it.

Scott knew the layout of the bridge. He could imagine several senior officers all frozen in place, and a couple of them beginning to converge on the captain to tell him every possible reason why it couldn't and shouldn't be done.

Scott pressed the button again. "Sir, before you listen to those other guys who're right this second beginning to babble that this idea is nuts, do you realize that a few years back Boeing ran tests designed to land the 737 on our carriers, and the tests were successful and showed it could be done?"

Another long pause before the captain replied.

"I didn't realize there was a successful conclusion to those tests, Scott," the captain responded.

"Yes! Yes, there was. Trust me. It *can* be done, and that was with a 737 at one hundred thirty knots, the ship at forty, and a fifteen-knot breeze. In other words, a hundred-thirty-thousand-pound craft at a closing rate of seventy-five knots. I'll be going less than ten. Ten damn knots! I know we're a 727, but for all practical purposes it's the same."

Scott shook his head in frustration as he glanced at Doc. "The XO, OOD, airboss, all of them will be frantically throwing his own words back in his ear about now. 'This is a United States warship,' they'll say. 'You can't do it, sir.'"

Scott pressed the transmit button again.

"Sir, we're running out of time. Please! We . . . we dumped that bomb in time with no help whatsoever from the U.S. military. It's time I got some help."

"That's a cheap shot at me, McKay, considering the helos and everything else we're trying to do for you."

"But it will all be for naught if we hit the water. This way we've got a chance."

"Tell him," Doc interjected urgently, "tell him there's little chance of fire, since our tanks are almost dry."

Scott relayed Doc's words.

Another interminable period of silence passed as Doc continued to circle the ship and turn back to a northerly heading.

"I'll need authority to do this, Scott," the captain said suddenly.

Scott hit the transmit button instantly.

"You've already got the authority, Captain. We both know that. But by the time you dump this on the Pentagon and they figure it out, we'll already be out of gas and in the water."

Doc was shaking his head. "I'm not believing any of this."

"Doc, quick. Check the fuel."

Doc began to unstrap to comply, but Linda reached out a hand and stopped him.

"I've been watching, Doc. The number one tank has zero. Number two has seven hundred pounds, and the number three tank has about a thousand pounds. There's nothing in the other tanks labeled 'Aux.' "

"Thanks, Linda." Doc turned to the left seat. "Scott, that's seventeen hundred pounds. That's vapor!"

Scott nodded as he realized what he was seeing through Doc's window. The wake behind the *Eisenhower* was changing, angling off suddenly to the right, which meant the captain had ordered a turn.

For nearly thirty seconds more there was radio silence. Then the *Eisenhower*'s transmitter was keyed, and Scott could hear other voices murmuring in the background before a long sigh came over the speakers.

"Okay, Scott. Okay. This is probably going to cost me my command, but for some stupid reason, you're making sense." There was a pause while the captain's hand moved against the surface of the microphone, the scratching sounds coming through clearly. "Now here's the deal, as that jug-eared billionaire from Dallas says. I'm going to launch my helos while we reverse course and rig the forward net. We'll get you a landing signal officer in position, but get this clearly. You make a mess of my flight deck, McKay, and I'll personally drown you. Understood?"

Scott nodded, a broad smile covering his face. Linda could see his clenched right hand past the edge of the seat as he lightly pounded the side of the yoke, then triggered the transmitter again.

"Yes, sir! There will be no mess, Skipper. Thank you, sir!"

"I'm turning you over to a thoroughly stunned airboss now, son. You two work out the details of the approach and be fast about it. The helos can stay up for thirty minutes and it's going to take us five minutes to reverse course. That means we've got only a twenty-minute window to bring you aboard."

"Not a problem, sir. At best, we've only got about ten minutes of fuel left."

33
• • • •

Amidst a flurry of wide-eyed bridge activity more intense than anything he could remember in peacetime, the captain of the *Eisenhower* sat in his command chair and shook his head in wonder. The solution had been there all along, but no one—not even the ex-F-14 jockey stuck in a crippled 727 whose life was on the line—had thought of it until the last minute.

There were, he knew, myriad problems. This was no piece of cake. For one thing, as the officer serving as airboss had pointed out, it would be far too dangerous for McKay to use minimum approach speed over the edge of the deck, in case there was a sudden lessening of wind speed. McKay should carry at least an extra ten or fifteen knots.

But even then the figures added up. If the deck winds stayed at one hundred and five knots and McKay used one hundred twenty-five for an approach speed, the 727 would float over the edge at twenty knots.

Matching the aircraft's flight path with the wildly pitching deck would be the biggest challenge. He'd ordered a quick review of squadron records to make sure his memory of McKay's excellent flight history was accurate.

It was. McKay—Tigger, he corrected himself—had been a superlative pilot, well disciplined, well liked, and very professional. If anyone could master the challenge, he could.

And if not, well, he had almost forgotten the relay from the Commander in Chief to do everything possible to save those lives. The message was a flash in writing, and he ordered an extra copy made and put in the bridge safe. If the USS *Eisenhower* ended up host to a damaging tragedy, he had been following presidential orders to the letter.

The captain looked out over the approach end of the flight deck, where the deck crew was finishing the rigging of the aircraft-catching net. He was worried about someone being blown off the ship in the process, but they seemed to be managing. Normally the flight deck was shut down with winds over fifty knots. The upper lip of the net was high enough to catch the nose of a 727, and as long as it did, the right wing should never get close to the multistory superstructure on the right side of the flight deck known as the island.

The radio discussion between Scott McKay and airboss had subsided now. The ship was coming steady on a course of one-seven-zero, and the few deck crewmen assigned to stay outside were lashing themselves down against the hundred-knot winds now howling over the deck, rattling even the windows on the bridge.

"Steady on course, Captain," the OOD reported.

"Very well, all engines ahead flank, indicate nine nine nine."

"Uh, nine nine nine, Captain?"

"All she has, mister. If we're going to create a hurricane within a hurricane, let's do it right."

"Aye, sir. All engines ahead flank, indicate nine nine nine."

The sound of an engine telegraph ringing and being answered reached his ears as he picked up the field glasses and trained them on the 727 now almost hovering less than a half mile to the north, off the stern, at five hundred feet.

The captain picked up the interphone to the airboss.

"Up to speed, and you're cleared for recovery operations."

"Yes, sir."

"And keep those cameras rolling. This will be one for the books, however it turns out."

ABOARD SCOTAIR 50—8:28 P.M. EDT

"Scott, we've got to do it now. We're literally down to fumes."

Scott nodded. "Okay. If we misjudge it and flame out before the main wheels are over the edge of the deck, I'll bank left and put her down in the wake of the ship."

Doc nodded.

"Tell him we're commencing approach, Doc."

Doc relayed the word as Scott nudged up the throttles slightly to fly them up to the appropriate glide slope, indicated by a light system called the meatball.

"Gear down. Landing check," Scott ordered.

Doc ran through the checklist items as the gear lowered into place with the same indication problem on the right main.

"Ignore it. It held at Seymour-Johnson."

"Ignored."

"I'm coming up on the glide slope, Doc. Call my altitude in fifty-foot increments. The radio altimeter will read about a hundred twenty feet as we come over the deck."

"Understood. We're showing five hundred fifty now."

"Okay, slowing to one hundred twenty knots indicated."

Doc nodded.

"No reversers, Doc. Don't let me forget I can not use the thrust reversers. We'd back right off the ship into the water with this wind."

"I'll keep you from retarding the throttles, too, remember?"

Scott nodded, breathing hard. "Right. Thanks, I might have forgotten. We'll keep the thrust at the same levels until they have us tied down. Once we touch, full-forward yoke, raise the flaps, speed brakes out."

"Speed brakes?"

"That's wrong?"

"We won't need more drag, Scott, just less lift."

"Oh. Right. No speed brakes, then."

"We're four hundred feet."

The great ship loomed before them, its deck pitching and rolling in the heavy seas as the nuclear-fired engines thrust its thousand-foot length forward at top speed. The turbulence from the wind whipping around and eddying off the island was a danger, Scott knew, and he was favoring the left side of the glide path as he nursed the 727 forward and down, feeling totally disoriented by the strange mix of speeds: one hundred twenty through the air, fifty over the water, and less than twenty knots in relation to the flight deck. He could feel his heart pounding hard, each beat echoing like a bass drum in his ears.

Again the deck pitched up markedly, drastically changing his aim point. Scott pulled the yoke slightly to readjust his approach angle and adjusted the throttles forward a hair.

"Three hundred fifty feet, Scott."

The altitude was an absolute measurement of the distance from the bottom of the aircraft to the surface of the ocean, more than a hundred feet below the lip of the flight deck.

A sudden zone of heavy turbulence engulfed them, forcing Scott to move the yoke rapidly in several directions to keep aligned. He could imagine how scary the gyrations must look from the perspective of the carrier, especially that of the LSO—the landing safety officer—operating the signal equipment.

The right wing tip entered the wake turbulence of the island, rolling the 727 slightly to the right as Scott fought to bring it back to centerline without losing the glide slope.

"Three hundred feet," Doc called out.

That's two hundred off the deck, Scott reminded himself.

He could see several deck crewmen hunkered down around the landing zone, and the net blowing concave toward him in the amazing gale the ship was creating. He flexed the yoke forward slightly to get back down to glide slope, then had to adjust just as rapidly to keep from sinking too fast.

The deck was dropping sharply as the ship's bow pitched up, but Scott rode it out, holding his approach angle and waiting for the stern to come back up. Chasing every movement could prove disastrous. He had to follow the meatball and keep the center of the ship in his peripheral vision as well.

Yoke forward, brakes full, as soon as we touch, he mentally reviewed. *No reversers, no speed brakes.*

"Two hundred fifty feet above. Speed is marker plus fifteen," Doc called out.

Once, years ago, he had handled the controls on a Sea King helicopter approaching the deck, and it had felt much the same.

Scott shook his head slightly to expunge the memory. It was dangerous. These controls were different. This was a 727 requiring forward thrust and glide path control. He wasn't landing, he was flying it to a touchdown.

"Two hundred feet."

The stern appeared to rise before him, shudder, then drop suddenly, changing his aim point too far down the deck. It would come back up, he reminded himself, and he was moving so slowly with respect to the deck, he could wait it out.

"One hundred fifty feet—almost there," Doc called.

The stern was still dropping and the aim point creeping forward toward the net. He didn't want to touch that far down the deck, but he had to wait for the upthrust of the stern.

But the temptation to adjust the Boeing's flight path downward was too great, and unconsciously Scott relaxed a bit of back pressure on the yoke and changed the glide path—just as the ship's bow found a massive wave trough and pitched forward.

With a speed he hadn't anticipated, the deck was roaring up from below. They were still a few yards shy of having the nosewheel pass over the lip of the deck, and that edge was now rising in Scott's perspective, threatening to become a barrier to hit rather than a threshold to cross.

He goosed the power and pulled back too sharply, causing the Boeing to leap back up nearly fifty feet, far above the intended glide path, but close in enough to continue.

The stern reached its apex and began dropping again as the cockpit and nose gear moved slowly forward past the rear edge of the flight deck, and he felt the aircraft drifting right.

No, the ship was *moving* left.

The turbulence from the island caught them full on the right wing, rolling the 727 sharply right as Scott overcontrolled trying to roll it back to the left.

The deck rose to meet him at a frightening rate.

Scott shoved the throttles forward and hauled back on the yoke to abort the approach as the LSO ordered a waveoff at the same moment. The nose of the Boeing was coming up, but not fast enough toprevent the main wheels from impacting the carrier's deck with thunderous force, the left one first, then the right one.

The uneven impacts propelled the 727 back in the air at a dangerous angle as Scott yanked harder on the yoke and banked sharply left to get up and away from the deck.

"Scott. We don't have fuel for a go-around!" Doc yelled.

"I'm just going . . . off here . . . to the side . . . to regroup," Scott struggled to say.

"We're repositioning," Doc snapped into the microphone. "We're not going to break off the approach."

"Wave off, ScotAir. Go around and reinitiate."

"No!" Doc replied. "There's no time. We're almost out of gas."

Scott stabilized the aircraft several hundred feet in the air, just to the left of the ship, and throttled back until the airspeed was hanging just below one hundred and eight knots. The carrier was essentially stationary in the cockpit windows to the right, the rear lip of the flight deck roughly aligned with the main gear of the Boeing. Scott brought the yoke forward slightly and dropped until the 727 was a mere fifty feet above deck level, watching as the stern of the carrier fell again and anticipating its next rise.

"I'm going to time the top of this rise and just move over and set down from the left," Scott said.

"Roger, but make it fast, Scott! I'd be afraid to look at the fuel gauges."

The voice of the LSO crackled through the speakers amidst the roar of the wind being transmitted by his mike.

"ScotAir, you can't approach from that position. Wave off. I say again, wave off and go around."

Doc punched the mike button.

"This will be a helo approach from the left quarter of the deck, guys. Get used to the idea, and get ready. We're out of time."

The stern was almost to the apex of its rise now, and Scott moved the yoke enough to slide them smoothly to the right, keeping the 727 a mere fifty feet over the side of the deck as they crossed with a relative forward speed of essentially zero.

They were virtually hovering now, some forty feet over the flight deck, the relative speed of ship and aircraft a perfect zero in an amazing sight Scott almost wanted to hold on to and examine.

But it was a dangerous place to be, and he prepared to move the yoke forward to descend at the exact moment number three engine reached the end of its fuel supply and flamed out with a *pop*.

The carrier had been stationary in their perspective, but now it began to recede ahead of them, very slowly at first, the rear main landing gear of the 727 moving backward over the remaining flight deck.

Scott and Doc realized what was happening simultaneously.

"Flameout!" Doc saw Scott's hand flash forward, jamming all three throttles forward to the firewall. Any more rearward movement and the main wheels would be over the water, off the back of the ship. They had to land now!

Scott moved the yoke forward smartly, dropping the Boeing toward the pitching deck some forty feet below the main wheels.

• • •

From the perspective of the LSO, the 727 had hovered over his head like a blimp, and he could think of nothing of any use to say to the pilot as the huge airliner floated into position over his flight deck and just . . . *stayed* there.

Suddenly the jetliner began moving backward as it hovered over the landing spot—slowly at first, then at an alarming rate. He poised his finger over the transmit button to order more power, but the nose was pitching down, the Boeing descending, the main wheels impacting the flight deck with a resounding metallic *boom* he could hear clearly above the roar of the wind.

They were down. The main gear was a mere ten feet forward of the rear lip of the deck, but they were down. The LSO glanced toward his deck crew, ready to order the 727 tied down, but something was happening in front of him as the ship reached the apex of another wave and began to subside.

The 727 was rolling backward!

As soon as they made contact, Scott jammed the yoke full-forward to hold them on the deck and prevent the nose from bouncing up in the hundred-knot wind. He'd keep the remaining engine at full power to hold their position and carefully move the aircraft forward, away from the rear edge of the carrier, but as he pushed up the throttles, number two engine also *popped* and died.

Suddenly there was nothing pushing ScotAir 50 forward into the hundred-knot wind, and as the carrier's bow pitched up again, riding over another huge wave, Scott realized they were rolling toward oblivion.

"BRAKES!" Doc cried out.

Scott's feet were already full-forward on the brakes as Doc jammed his pedals full-down as well.

Still they were rolling backward.

"Pressure! Brake pressure . . ." Doc fumbled for the words and pointed toward a small gauge on his forward panel, and Scott understood instantly. The brake accumulator had failed. There was no hydraulic pressure left to stop them.

Scott's hand found the safety-wired emergency air brake handle and turned it before his conscious mind grasped what he was intending to do. There were men running toward them on the deck, waving their arms, and a voice on the radio was calling for them to put on their brakes. There couldn't be much room left behind the main wheels, and the ship's bow was still tilting up, dropping the stern, accelerating them backward.

Scott jammed the handle full to the right, to the stops, remembering the warning that the air pressure did not act immediately. Seconds would tick by, and they didn't have many more.

From the point of view of the LSO, the 727 was going to go off the ship backward. It was too late now, he realized. For some reason the crew couldn't use the brakes, and his deck crew had no way to throw a chain around the gear or raise a barrier in time.

The four wheels of the main landing gear were only a few feet from the edge, but there was a chance the plane would stop as the mains rolled off the edge and the belly smashed onto the deck.

There was a greater chance, he knew, that the nose would simply pitch up and the 727 would slide backward into the sea.

Deep within the plumbing system of the 727's brakes, the air pressure released seconds before from the emergency bottle finally overrode the various valves and pistons and compressed the hydraulic fluid to the necessary pressure, instantly stopping the rotation of the main wheels.

There was a flurry of activity outside, and through a sheet of rain that suddenly lashed the deck, Scott could see several members of the deck crew converging beneath his plane with wheel chocks and lines at the same moment he felt a forward deceleration and realized the captain had probably ordered all engines stopped. He could feel chains being wrapped around the nose gear to hold the 727 in place as a voice came through the cockpit speakers.

"ScotAir, do not release your brakes, and do not lower your rear stairs. Your tail section's hanging over the water."

"Roger that," Doc acknowledged.

Bright searchlights had snapped on all over the flight deck, illuminating the pelting rain that was blowing horizontally beneath the dark, gray skies overhead, still visible in the post-sunset twilight. To

Scott, the scene was at once familiar and surreal, as though he had never left the ship.

But here he was in the same spot, this time in an airliner.

From nowhere two helmeted Navy crewmen wearing rain gear appeared in the cockpit door and took a quick measure of the situation. Orders were barked into a handheld radio as one of them knelt down to begin unstrapping Jerry.

Scott sat in shock for what seemed like an eternity until he realized Linda's hand was massaging his shoulder. He patted her hand and heard her seat belt snap open as he released his. Scott turned around in the seat, unprepared for the feminine wave that engulfed him as she wrapped her arms around him, her cheek pressed tightly against his, her body quaking slightly as she tried to catch her breath.

"You did it!" she whispered. "You did it, you did it, you did it! That was amazing!"

Scott's arms slowly moved around her as Doc moved his seat back and sighed, then leaned over and clasped Vivian's outstretched hand.

Another crewman appeared in the cockpit door as the two other crewmen gently moved Jerry out on a stretcher.

"Come on, all of you. NOW! We've got to get you out."

The crewmen wrapped large coats around Vivian and Linda and handed two more to Scott and Doc as the two pilots followed through the forward entry door down a metal ladder held steady by several deck crewmen. The wind was incredible, its strength threatening to blow them over, but it was slowing somewhat below eighty as the *Eisenhower*'s speed diminished.

Several crewmen had scooped up Linda and Vivian and were rushing them toward the island, but another grabbed both Scott and Doc and turned them roughly to look where he was pointing.

"WHAT?" Scott yelled.

"THE CAPTAIN WANTS TO MAKE SURE YOU SEE THIS, SIR!" the crewman yelled back, shaking his finger toward the rear of the 727.

The nose gear of the Boeing had already been lashed to the deck with chains until one of the flight deck's yellow gear—a small tractor—could hook up to move it forward.

But the crewman was pointing to the main landing gear, and

Scott followed his gaze, standing transfixed at what at first seemed an optical illusion: The main wheels seemed to be resting on the absolute edge of the rear lip of the *Eisenhower*'s deck.

But it was no illusion.

There was less than a foot of deck space left.

EPILOGUE
• • • •

The President entered the Air Force One Starsuite and nodded to the assembled military brass in the Pentagon.

"Gentlemen, while we sat it out here at Wright-Patterson, you've obviously had one hell of a night there in D.C., but I'm relieved to hear all your homes and families came through the hurricane intact."

The Chairman of the Joint Chiefs glanced at the other officers in the Pentagon Starsuite before looking the President in the eye. "With a few minor exceptions, sir, yes. Many of us had property damage . . . as you did, for that matter."

The President nodded. "I'm told the West Wing will take some time to dry out, but other than broken windows and some wet carpets, I don't believe we've lost anything of historic value."

He paused and surveyed the grim faces on the other side of the table. "I've been in a meeting for the last hour with the Situation Room on the hurricane damage, but this gathering is about Medusa. So with that, are we ready to brief, John?"

The Chairman inclined his head toward the commander of the Air Combat Command. "Yes, sir, but since General Kinney carried the brunt of the battle yesterday afternoon, I've asked him to fill you in."

Ralph Kinney took a deep breath and rose to his feet as he ran a hand through his dark hair and glanced at his notes. He was acutely aware of the President's fury at the senior Air Force leadership just eighteen hours before, and equally aware of the crushing fatigue bearing down on him from thirty hours on his feet.

He purposely refrained from looking at the empty chair where the Air Force Chief of Staff was supposed to be sitting. The four-star general had been summarily fired around midnight.

"Mr. President, as you well know, the core of the bomb we encountered yesterday was, in fact, what the designer claimed: a twenty-megaton thermonuclear weapon. The key question is: Was this bomb some exotic, electromagnetic pulse weapon as well?"

"And the answer?" the President asked.

"In a phrase, we're not sure. Some very odd things occurred when that bomb exploded, and we simply don't understand what they were, or what they mean."

The President sat forward. "Tell me, General."

"Well, sir, if you detonate a standard warhead within a few feet of sea level at that exact distance from the coast, you'd expect an electromagnetic pulse, and you'd expect it to cause problems to nonhardened electronics. That is precisely what we experienced along the East Coast, and in the air, and at sea. Nothing exotic, just anticipatable destruction of exposed electronics in airborne aircraft, ships in the area, and coastal cities from New York to Charleston. There was massive damage to telephone and telecommunications, and computers of all sorts have been knocked out or at least knocked off-line. The list is already very long, but since Sigrid was battering the coast at the same time and a lot of electrical power was out, we probably won't know the full extent of the damage until offices and banks and municipalities try to boot up their computers. I won't try to catalog everything right now, but you should know that the precautions you took in shutting down transportation certainly worked. We had only one airborne incident, an Air France Airbus 340 inbound to Kennedy that lost all four engines but managed to get them restarted. Everyone else was safely parked when the bomb went off. Same for rail. Switches and signals went nuts, but since nothing was moving, there were no accidents."

"That's good to hear," the President said. "But let me get this straight. While the bomb produced a standard EMP, which caused some damage, it did not produce a so-called Medusa Wave. Is that what you're saying?"

General Kinney shook his head. "I wish it was, sir, but no. There's more. We didn't get the monstrous electronic catastrophe we feared, but we got something unexplained that may be a new phenomenon. Immediately after the explosion and for nearly thirty seconds, there was a sustained and unprecedented ripple in the electromagnetic spectrum that knocked computers off-line as far west as St. Louis and caused disruptions and power surges all the way to California and Washington State. There is no known way that could have happened, but it did."

The President looked puzzled. "So it *did* produce a so-called Medusa Wave, just a weak one?"

Ralph Kinney glanced at the two scientists sitting beside him before replying.

"Sir, whatever it was, it should not have occurred with a standard nuclear detonation. There is no way, I'm told, that an EMP should have been detectable on the West Coast or anywhere in the Midwest. I've got two nuclear experts here from the Nuclear Regulatory Commission, sir, who can fill in some details for you."

"Wait . . . wait a minute, General. You said the bomb exploded at or near sea level. But the damn thing was dumped out of the 727, what, fifteen minutes before? Why didn't it sink?"

One of the two scientists spoke up, explaining that the stainless steel bomb casing must have stayed intact and remained watertight.

"Is that *possible,* gentlemen?" the President asked incredulously. "Could it really have fallen thousands of feet, stayed intact, and then *floated*? It had to have been lead-lined. How could it float?"

The second nuclear scientist stood and offered an answer that was even more vague.

Finally Ralph Kinney got to his feet again, motioning the two NRC men to sit. "Mr. President, let me summarize what these fellows are saying. They can't explain all the reasons why it floated, but the fact is, there's virtually no other reasonable explanation. You see, if the bomb had sunk as much as three or four hundred feet, the water would have absorbed the majority of the EMP, and none of these coastal effects would have occurred. In fact, if it had gone down as much as eight hundred feet, it would have been shielded from us by the wall of the continental shelf. Mr. President, I'm told there is no nuclear device known to man powerful enough to project an electromagnetic pulse from deep beneath the ocean's surface. Therefore, given what this weapon did when it exploded, it had to have been on the surface."

"Or," the President continued, "if it *did* have such an effect from hundreds of feet underwater, it would mean that the Medusa is a valid theory and a weapon of unprecedented destructive power."

An Army colonel was introduced and began running down a requested damage assessment and describing the process of unsnarling the transportation system. The President sat back in thought, only half-listening.

"Mr. President, the airlines are in a massive state of confusion, with aircraft and crews in the wrong places nationwide. They estimate three days before the situation approaches normal. Amtrak reports they'll need at least three or four days to get back to normal. Communications, except for the Eastern coastline, should be essentially normal within twenty-four hours."

There was a small commotion in the back of the Starsuite and the Army colonel paused and looked around before continuing.

"The Navy reports all our subs—and those of other nations we'd been tracking in the Atlantic—have all reported in without damage."

Once again the colonel stopped and glanced around, aware that someone new had come into the Starsuite: a man in civilian clothes, who was whispering urgently in General Kinney's ear. The Army colonel scowled slightly, then continued.

"Finally, Mr. President, you requested a briefing on both the effect to the economy, and separately on marine life and the ecosystem near the epicenter of the explosion, and we're working on both. We expect there will be some radiation damage, but . . ."

General Kinney stood up suddenly and moved to the colonel's side, motioning him to be seated. "Ah, excuse me, Mr. President."

"Go ahead, General."

"Sir, we . . . have a gentleman here from the U.S. Geological Survey, a Dr. Pierson, with information . . . you need to hear immediately."

The President came forward slowly in his chair. "Go on."

The USGS representative stepped forward to the edge of the table and consulted a sheet of paper in his hand before speaking. He turned to General Kinney, who nodded and gestured to the screen, then turned to look at the President.

"Ah, sir, I have a refined assessment of the position of the weapon yesterday evening when it exploded."

"You mean, the distance from the coast?" the President asked. "The latitude and longitude?"

"No, sir. The depth."

The President cocked his head slightly as his eyebrows inched up. "I thought it was at sea level, Dr. Pierson."

"No, sir. We triangulated using worldwide seismic data. It was considerably below the surface when it detonated."

The President stared at the USGS scientist.

"How far down was it?"

There was a long pause as Dr. Pierson swallowed, glanced at the general again for reassurance, then back at the President.

"A depth of two thousand four hundred feet."

WASHINGTON, D.C.—APRIL 23—
SEVEN MONTHS LATER

Doc Hazzard unfolded himself from the backseat of the unmarked Lincoln and stood in the front driveway of the White House, looking at the sky. It was an unseasonably cool spring morning, with fast-moving cumulus clouds shooting by in the teeth of a fresh westerly breeze against a dazzling blue sky.

"Captain Hazzard? If you're ready, sir, please follow me."

The rapid walk through the hallways of the White House ended in the Cabinet Room, where Charles Fortner, the Chief of Staff, was waiting.

"Well, Doc, you're looking hale and hearty."

"Senator Fortner, I appreciate your seeing me, not to mention sending the car to National Airport."

"The least I could do. The President was quite sincere when he told all three of you fellows to call us if you needed anything." He motioned Doc to a seat at the ornate Cabinet table. "So, Doc, what can I do for you?"

Doc shook his head. "Not for me, sir. It's for Vivian Henry."

"Is she doing all right? I'm told she's moved to Colorado and joined ScotAir as your operations manager."

Doc smiled and studied the table for a few seconds. "Yes, sir. It's an exciting time for us. Thanks to your and the President's intervention, we got our contract back, and business has been booming.

Scott's even out searching for another 727 to lease. That'll make three."

"And Vivian?"

Doc looked the Chief of Staff in the eye. "Senator, are you aware of what started that whole sequence of her flying the bomb to Washington?"

"Doc, just call me Charlie. I haven't been a senator for a long time."

"Yes, sir . . . ah . . . Charlie."

"Yes, I'm aware her ex-husband's will wouldn't pay her the remaining insurance funds unless she did so. Correct?"

"Essentially, yes. And those were finally paid over, even though the estate lawyer wanted to deny them for several weeks because she didn't actually deliver the bomb and wipe out Washington."

"You're kidding!"

Doc laughed and shook his head in amazement. "No, so help me. It took a district judge down there to change the lawyer's mind."

"So what remains, Doc?"

"Her pension. You knew the OPM denied it, fought her all the way to the U.S. Court of Appeals, and she lost there. The court order had been poorly drawn, and for that she lost everything."

Fortner nodded slowly. "And you want to know if we can do anything about it?"

"I've looked into this, sir. I don't know what can be done, if anything, but this just isn't right. It's legal pettifogging, stealing an annuity she more than earned because someone over whom she had little control didn't use the right magic words. For a woman as wonderful and loving and as abused and battered as she was to be treated this way by her government . . ."

Charles Fortner cocked his head slightly and smiled as he studied Doc's face, which was showing a tinge of embarrassment.

"Why, Captain Hazzard, I do believe you have a special feeling for this lady!"

Doc couldn't suppress a smile in return. "You're damned right I care for her, sir. I'd marry her in a second if she'd consider it."

"And you're wearing her down, I hope?"

"Trying. Trying hard."

Fortner looked at a folder of documents Doc had slid across the table, then glanced up as someone came into the room behind Doc.

"Doc, I've read about Vivian's victimization by the OPM. Now, I'm not sure what we can do . . ."

A familiar voice from behind caught Doc by surprise.

"But we'll look into it immediately and fix it if we can. I hate bureaucracy, too!"

Doc looked around to see the President behind him and jumped to his feet.

"Mr. President!"

"Sit, Doc. You too, Charlie." The President shook Doc's hand and sat down in the chair next to his. "I want you to fill me in on all this in a minute and join us for lunch, but I also want to tie up a loose end."

"Sir?"

"When we had all five of you here for the appreciation ceremony in the Oval Office, I had only the preliminary results of the internal investigation I'd ordered into the FBI's conduct during the crisis. Their attempt to arrest Vivian Henry aboard the *Eisenhower* after your landing was embarrassingly stupid, and that's why I got involved personally before you reached Norfolk. But what we could never seem to understand was what had convinced the FBI that afternoon that Vivian wanted to blow her government away. Do you know what it was?"

"No, sir. She assumed—we all did—that it was her background as a nuclear engineer."

"That contributed, but no, she was screwed again by the OPM." He related the story of the OPM clerk and her mistaken identification of Vivian Henry as a woman who'd threatened to blow up their building. "The clerk discovered her mistake, but decided not to tell anyone, and the FBI went berserk."

"That clerk, by the way," Charles Fortner interjected, "is history."

"I appreciate knowing that. I'll tell Vivian."

"By the way, Doc," the President said, "how's your flight engineer doing? Jerry Christian, was it? I was glad he could make the ceremony, even in a wheelchair, but the man was in pain."

Doc smiled slightly. "Thanks for asking, sir. Jerry will appreciate that. There . . . was a question of his walking again, but he's surprised all of us. Last week he discarded his cane, and we think he'll be back on flying status in another month."

"Great news," the President said as Charles Fortner nodded in agreement. "Give him my best, and Scott, too."

"I will, Mr. President."

"Oh, and how is Dr. Linda McCoy?"

Doc's smile broadened. "That, sir, is becoming an interesting story."

SNOWMASS, COLORADO—MAY 18

The off-season around Aspen was an annual financial strain for resort owners, but a window of opportunity for low-cost government-hosted conventions in the rarified air of the Rockies. With global warming a validated worldwide threat, two hundred world-class scientists and their support staffs had gathered in the mountains for an emergency conference on the latest findings.

Linda McCoy had spent three days listening to a dizzying variety of findings and viewpoints and wrangling with her colleagues in discussions that spilled from conference hall to the parking lot and continued into the night before numerous fireplaces in the condominium-style accommodations. Consensus was growing, but the process, as she'd put it the day before, was messy.

Linda, feeling weary, looked at her watch and read six o'clock. There was another evening meeting discussion she'd promised to attend, but her ears were full of words and her mind was numb—which explained the momentary lack of recognition of the young man leaning against the wall in the foyer.

He had obviously been waiting for her, and for a split second, Linda assumed it was another print reporter looking for a hallway interview.

" 'Scuse me, ma'am. You wouldn't know where a feller could find a little companionship around here, would you? Maybe a young lady who'd like to have dinner with a poor hardworking jet jockey?"

"Scott!"

He grinned at her and nodded. It had been three months since their last meeting, an uncomfortable lunch in Boulder when he had made a sophomoric attempt to kiss her on the way to the car. He'd kindled a hurricane of disturbing feelings then that had been diverting her attention ever since, but she regretted pulling away. Perhaps it was all the publicity and the kidding of her colleagues about the prospect of getting together with the young pilot who'd so selflessly saved the country from a nuclear holocaust, but the attention had irritated her into maintaining a cool distance from Scott. They had shared something in that airplane which demanded friendship, but anything more felt too rushed—yet she had wished almost every night since the Boulder meeting for another chance.

And now . . .

Without a word Linda walked to him with a smile and pulled Scott into her arms, kissing him deeply. His arms tightened around her, his right hand gently ruffling her hair as they lost themselves in each other for a tiny eternity. When Scott slowly pulled away, a small retinue of scientists in the foyer began clapping, a gesture that would normally have irritated and embarrassed Linda.

Instead, she turned with a broad smile and nodded in their direction. "You shall be meeting without me this evening, gentlemen," she said.

"Why's that?" Scott asked with feigned innocence.

"Because we have a lot to talk about and because I've got a wood-burning fireplace I can't wait to try out."

SANTA FE, NEW MEXICO—MAY 21

Dr. Louis Benedict placed his morning coffee on the side table and sat carefully in his recliner as he picked up the remote to surf through the morning shows. His seventy-third birthday was past by three days, but the retired administrative chief of the Los Alamos facility had hardly noticed. He was determined not to be depressed, even though he was alone, a widower of ten years' duration from a childless marriage.

He flicked past a familiar image, then returned. It was Pete Cooke, *The Wall Street Journal* reporter, on *Good Morning America,* talking about his new book. Louis smiled to himself. He was mentioned in the book, a bestseller called *Waltzing Medusa,* which was about Rogers Henry and his barely foiled plot to remove Washington from the map and kill Vivian in the process. Pete had sent him a warm thank-you after interviewing him in Santa Fe, and

Louis had rushed out to buy the book as soon as it was published. He had quickly found his name inside and was relieved to see that he'd been correctly quoted and portrayed in a way that made him feel good.

Dr. Benedict's attention returned to the television screen in time to hear Charles Gibson asking Pete about the five people on the ScotAir 727, and how they were doing.

"Jerry, the flight engineer, is divorced now and living near the company headquarters in Colorado. His recovery has been slow. There was extensive damage to his right leg, in particular, but there is hope that he'll be back flying very soon." Pete continued with a short discussion on the current activities and whereabouts of the other four who'd been aboard the 727.

"And how about that operations manager in Miami," Gibson was asking, "who, according to you, purposefully misled Scott McKay into thinking that he and his flight crew were responsible for misloading the cargo that contained the bomb, leaving behind the cargo they were supposed to take?"

"He was fired after he lied to a congressional committee about it," Pete said, "and he's now been indicted for that lie."

"What's the bottom line of this story, Pete? We barely escaped, as you put it in the title of your book *Waltzing Medusa,* and the technology is still unknown. We know it was developed by this lone nuclear scientist, but there's no known record of how he did it."

"None," Pete Cooke replied, "and anyone with a modicum of intelligence would never want it to be built, much less used, again. But, predictably, our government is now gearing up to try to discover how to make this very weapon they originally abandoned, with the lame excuse that we must develop it, just in case someone else develops the technology first."

The interview ended with a handshake and wishes for success, but Louis Benedict was lost in thought.

He put down his coffee and got to his feet, padding out to the garage, where his file boxes were stored, remembering something in the package Rogers Henry had sent him a long time ago, the one that contained the drawings of the instantaneous nuclear trigger. There had been a computer disk as well, an old eight-inch floppy. It supposedly contained the same plans, and he'd confirmed that at one time, but he realized that he'd never actually read everything on the disk.

Eight-inch drives had all but disappeared in the late eighties, but he still had an old Radio Shack Model II, and he turned it on now and inserted the disk.

As expected, the files contained the same details about the trigger, and he paged through them dutifully before preparing to take the disk out.

But there was something odd. The disk was indicating full, but the files he had seen were less than a third of the capacity. That meant there were machine files—hidden files—not showing up in the main directory.

Louis searched his memory for the right codes, finally remembering enough to call up information not normally displayed, and a huge file popped into view.

He opened it and found page after page of computer codes. The conversion program was buried in another old file box, and it was 11 A.M. before he found it and sat down before the old screen again to key in the appropriate commands.

Suddenly the screen was filled with drawings and diagrams, formulas and figures—and a narrative addressed to him!

"Congratulations, Louis, you've cracked the none-too-obscure code. What follows is top secret and known only to me. I have succeeded in principle in finding the theoretical basis for Medusa, and all my notes follow for safekeeping. Please do not copy or print this, but store it carefully. If anything happens to me, you will be the only one who holds the key. Use it wisely, but don't forget what we went through to get it."

Louis Benedict exited the program immediately and snapped off the computer, his heart pounding. A major government program had been launched to find precisely what he had in front of him, and if they succeeded, the world would once again be facing a new means of inflicting misery. His hands were shaking as he replaced the disk in its cover and slipped it back in the folder.

The afternoon passed with a leaden pace as he roamed his living room and den, trying to decide what to do. Should he call Pete Cooke? Should he call the Pentagon? Who should know, and when, and how?

By 8 P.M., his normal bedtime, he was still in a quandary, and with a fire burning in his fireplace at midnight, the options finally coalesced into one.

Louis Benedict returned to the darkened garage and retrieved the folder with the disk in it. He moved back to the living room and stood for a second in thought before reaching down to pull back the fireplace screen. With one fluid motion, he tossed the folder into the fire. It landed just short of the nearest flame.

The edges of the folder began to turn brown as Dr. Benedict watched, remembering the years of frustration he'd gone through in trying to keep the Medusa Project alive and give Rogers Henry enough time to find the key. The key was now beginning to smolder before his eyes.

And suddenly that was intolerable.

He quickly reached in and yanked the folder to safety, opening it to verify that the disk had not been damaged. It hadn't.

Dr. Louis Benedict quietly returned to the garage and placed the folder back into its file box, satisfied with the knowledge that it would stay safe—and unused.